Mark Bastable grew up in South London and, after an abortive sojourn in publishing, discovered computer languages. A freelance career as a peripatetic nerd followed. Amsterdam, Boston, Barcelona and Stockholm are just some of the cities in the gutters of which Mark has woken up.

Back in Tooting now, Mark is the Director of a Management Consultancy, a contributor to *Esquire* magazine and also writes comedy for TV. He has a nine-year-old son, Conor, who goes into bookshops and arranges his father's novels face-out all the way along the 'Contemporary Fiction' section, as you may have already noticed.

If you would like to comment on MISCHIEF or ICEBOX by Mark Bastable, you can e-mail the author at: mischief_postbox@hotmail.com.

Also by Mark Bastable

Icebox

Mischief

Mark Bastable

review

First published in 2001
by HEADLINE BOOK PUBLISHING

First published in paperback in 2002
by HEADLINE BOOK PUBLISHING

A REVIEW paperback

10 9 8 7 6 5 4 3 2 1

ISBN 07472 7197 6

Typeset by Palimpsest Book Production Limited,
Polmont, Stirlingshire

Printed and bound in Great Britain by
Mackays of Chatham plc, Chatham, Kent

HEADLINE BOOK PUBLISHING
A division of Hodder Headline
338 Euston Road
LONDON NW1 3BH
www.headline.co.uk
www.hodderheadline.com

For Conor, eventually

Beareth all things, believeth all things,
hopeth all things, endureth all things.

Charity never faileth.

St Paul

You have to be cynical. You can't *not* be
cynical. The more people that I have encouraged
to be cynical, the better job I've done.

Frank Zappa

I am too much of a sceptic to deny
the possibility of anything.

Aldous Huxley

CHAPTER ZERO

It began one late-spring evening in a splash of blood-red, when Charles Hardie Rollins was shot getting out of his limo.

Rollins, better known to his public as 'TV funny-man Chuckie Rolls', had paused to acknowledge the fans, when his face and chest erupted in a spray of scarlet that clashed terribly with the red carpet beneath his feet. The crowd screamed, and a sticky, crimson glob splattered across the smile of a little girl stepping forward with a bouquet of tulips.

Chuckie's spectacular arrival at the Café Royal undeniably overshadowed the glamour of the Lord Biffley Annual Show-Business Awards Dinner – which was a pity, for Chuckie was to have been the guest of honour. And it was particularly poignant that the nation's favourite comedian should have his evening cut short in this way because, a mere fortnight before, Chuckie had said (in intimate conversation with Roy Waxforth and eight million viewers) that despite his recent illness, he could *guarantee* that he would be at the Café Royal to pick up a Biffo 'for services to comedy'. It seems that he had consulted Madame Jessie, the showbiz clairvoyant – and she had foreseen him mounting the steps to the stage and accepting the award from his admiring peers and adoring public.

Confident in Madame Jessie's pronouncement, Chuckie had been looking forward to his big night out, and 'nothing short of a blunderbuss', to use his unfortunate phrase, was going to stop him showing up. But as Chuckie was slammed back against the door of the car, as he slid to the ground with slow and perfect comic timing, as his astonished breath bubbled crimson froth all down his several chins, it certainly looked as though the Joking Geordie wasn't going to be there to collect his Biffo after all . . .

CHAPTER ONE

Mason was at home and he was panicking. He'd looked in every drawer of the sideboard and he hadn't found a box of matches. He'd scoured the kitchen, lifting grubby tea towels and scrabbling amongst prehistoric pots of herbs, and hadn't found any matches there either. He'd excavated various ethnic bowls full of souvenir holiday pebbles, and come up with four poker dice, two ticket stubs to a play he'd never seen and a couple of Walkman batteries of undetermined vivacity, but still no matches.

Standing in the middle of the living room, biting hard on his little finger, he cast his eye around, and it seemed that everywhere he looked he saw the pack of Marlboro Lights – but no bloody matches. He wondered whether there might be a forgotten box in the pocket of a jacket in the bedroom wardrobe, and he was just heading there when the phone rang. He jigged to and fro in the doorway, calculating whether he could make it to the bedroom, frisk his clothes and get back before the phone stopped chirruping. He was making no progress at all.

'Shit, all right,' he groaned, and picked it up. 'Yeah?'

'Well, dear, that's not a very polite way to answer the phone. What if I'd been someone about a job?'

It was Dear Dot, agony aunt to readers of *Women's Work* magazine. It was also Frankly Freda, 'your sexual sounding-board' from *Feminine Pulse*. Moreover, it was Ingrid, 'the Swedish Stunna who'll put you straight!' from *The Lad*. It was several other people too, but primarily, it was Mason's mum.

When he was a teenager, all Mason's friends seemed to be constantly at war with their parents, and he was faintly embarrassed that he got on so well with his mother – who was the only parent around. In an attempt to compete with his contemporaries' stories of three-month groundings and the confiscation of skateboards, he used to try and work up the occasional little spat into some sort of huge familial schism, but it was never very convincing. It didn't help that his mates all congregated in his mother's kitchen to play thrash-metal records and wolf corned-beef sandwiches. They thought his mum was the pussycat's PJs – and as she wasn't much past thirty when they were fifteen, Mason suspected that she was the focus of more than a few of their nocturnal fantasies, somewhat to his disgust.

'If you'd been someone offering me a job, you wouldn't have been phoning at twenty to eight on a Saturday evening,' he told her. 'How's you?'

'Oh, I'm fine. Busy – working too hard. No chance of that happening to you, I suppose?'

Mason was in the process of feeling around down the back of the sofa with one hand, whilst lifting all the cushions with the other. The phone was trapped under his chin, which didn't aid clarity of speech.

'Errgh . . . sunnin'll turn up,' he reassured her, indistinctly.

'Well, yes, of course it will. In the meantime, how are you off for money?'

Mason pulled his hand out of the back of the sofa. No matches – just a curtain hook and some loose change. 'Uh . . . I'm twenty-two pee better off than I thought I was,' he said, counting the coins, 'but I'll try not to let it change my lifestyle. No, I'm okay. Don't worry about me.'

'I don't, generally, but even you have to eat. I'll send you some money. You've gone all muffled. What are you doing?'

The phone was nipped between ear and shoulder again, as he attempted to lift one end of the sofa and look underneath it.

'I mookin fera match,' he said, through trapped jaws. He dropped the sofa, and collapsed on to it. 'Phew, sorry. I'm looking for a match.'

'Oh, Mason, I do wish you'd give up smoking. Now that really *does* make me worry about you. If I send you money, I don't want you to go spending it on cigarettes. It's a filthy habit, and so anti-social. Anyway, have you heard from Chris? Is she well?'

This was not a subject Mason wished to pursue – not with a posse. 'I dunno. Fine, I guess. I haven't heard different.'

'Any sign of romantic interest?'

'What – in my life or Chris's?'

'Either.'

This, Mason thought, is the trouble with mothers. They phone you up out of the blue on the, frankly, pretty slim pretext of offering you largish amounts of money – and then it all turns out to be a callous ploy to get you to talk to them.

'I don't know!' The failure to find a match was beginning to make him tetchy. 'I'll phone you next week with any available hot gossip, after I've seen her.'

'I'm not asking for gossip's sake, dear. I'm simply interested in you both. Anyway, I'll let you get on with watching the telly, or whatever you do all evening. Call me soon.'

'Yeah. Thanks for the money, by the way. I'll see you.'

He put down the phone and zapped the TV on, hoping it would take his mind off both Chris and the lack of a match. He turned up the volume as a voice-over announced that now, live from the Prince Rupert Theatre in the heart of London's Theatreland, it was time for *The Grand Illusion*, starring Pe-e-e-eter Pinkus!

Mason slid down to a comfortable slouch. He couldn't resist Peter Pinkus. The bloke was so transfixingly awful that he kind of froze one's finger as it hovered above the channel control.

Pinkus introduced his show with a couple of standard dove-producing tricks – but he overlaid them with his own particular gimmick. He had the bawdy, music-hall touch. He was the Saucy Sorcerer, the Wicked Wizard. Where another magician might produce a run-of-the-mill dove, Pinkus would say the magic words – *Who Wants Stuffing!* – and a frozen chicken would emerge from the ruffle of silk handkerchiefs. Pinkus would look appalled at this unexpected turn of events. Performing the trick in which a regular illusionist might strew the stage with Flags of Many Nations from the breastpocket of his jacket, Pinkus would declaim the potent spell *Keep Your Hand on Your Ha'penny!* and a parade of women's knickers would spew forth. Pinkus's open-mouthed astonishment conveyed to the audience that this was as much a surprise to him as it was to them.

After a nonentity cabaret singer had knocked out a pedestrian version of 'That Old Black Magic', Pinkus, all smirks and winks, set about performing the trick that would end his career.

'I was at a cocktail bar last night, ladies and gentleman,' he told the audience, archly. 'Had a Slow Comfortable Screw. No! No! Listen!'

The crowd roared with glee, and Mason winced. Why did people laugh at stuff like that? Couldn't they see it coming? You just knew he was about to follow it up with a gag about having a knee trembler.

'Then the barmaid suggested a Knee Trembler – and after that I had another drink,' Pinkus hammed. The camera swept the front row of the audience, all of whom were dabbing away the tears of laughter with the backs of their hands.

'Jesus,' Mason groaned, shaking his head.

Pinkus pressed on. 'And I thought to myself, "Self," I thought, "why don't you create a magic cocktail?" So that's what we're going to do here tonight, ladies and gentlemen, with your help. Can I have a volunteer, please?'

A little old lady with owlish glasses was pulled from the audience.

'And what's your name, love? Dottie? Big hand for Dottie, ladies and gentlemen. First time on the telly, Dottie?'

Dottie turned out to be a natural. She nodded vigorously. 'If I'der known, I'der put me best teeth in!' she vouchsafed.

Pinkus mugged elastically at the camera. 'Oo, we got a right one here! Now – Dottie – we're going to mix my magic cocktail. It's called Peter's Purple Pleaser. Fancy a mouthful of my Purple Pleaser, Dottie?'

'Don't mind if I do!' Dottie declared.

'Are you sure?'

'Yes! Yes!' Dottie insisted. 'I'm atserlutely positive!' The audience, racked with hysteria, were sliding off their seats onto the floor by now.

The magician held up a glitter-covered cylinder, about the size of a wastepaper basket. He had Dottie check that it was hollow, and then he held it up to the camera, peering through it from one end. He put it down on his velvet-draped table, and shepherded Dottie into position next to it. A vacuously glamorous assistant wheeled on a cocktail cabinet, and, with much pose-throwing and bottle-spinning, Pinkus began passing the alcohol to Dottie, who was instructed to pour the contents into the cylinder.

'Little splash of gin, Dottie. Bit more – that's it. Glug or two of brandy. Oh, no – don't drink from the bottle, dear, it's rude.'

Mason had seen this trick before. After all the folderol, and some flash and smoke to accompany the incantation, Pinkus would snatch away the cylinder to reveal a vulgar little cherub-statue, which would piddle an arc of purple water into the audience. At this masterly *coup de théatre*, the punters would screech and clap like hyperactive toddlers.

'. . . some Cointreau, Dottie, to taste . . .'

'Ooh, are you trying to get me tiddly?' Dottie asked girlishly, giving a bashful little flutter of her lashes.

'God – that is *really* unpleasant,' Mason observed, grimacing. 'Bring on the peeing cherub, Pete.'

Pinkus asked Dottie to stand back, as he moved to the climax of the illusion.

'Now, ladies and gentlemen – I apply a sprinkling of magic dust . . .' With a camp little back-kick of the foot, he tossed some powder across the table, and there was a flash of violet. As a billow of smoke rose into the air, the Saucy Sorcerer grasped the cylinder's rim and turned with a flourish to the camera. 'I say the magic words – *Who's a Pretty Boy, Then?* And here it is, ladies and gentlemen – Peter's Purple Pleaser!'

And he whisked away the cylinder to reveal a perfect and erect twelve-inch phallus, rooted in a nest of thick pubic hair.

The audience gasped and was silent. Dottie tottered back a few paces and nearly swallowed her second-best teeth.

Pinkus, facing the auditorium, realised that the reaction was not as expected and whirled round to check his props. He froze for a moment, appalled, and then dived to grab the ghastly member. He was met by Dottie's swinging handbag coming the other way, and it caught him across the bridge of his nose, flooring him.

'You wait your turn, sonny,' the old lady advised the whimpering conjuror, as he knelt clutching his face.

The picture faded on a shot of Dottie striding purposefully towards the magic table.

'*I'll* handle this,' she hiccuped.

CHAPTER TWO

This is Mischief. This is Trouble. This is Chaos. This is the Tiger's Smile – alone, in a room lit only by the kaleidoscope flicker of the television screen.

Mischief extends a leg, to turn off the VCR with an agile toe – and then leans to one side, flipping the switch on the table lamp with a delicate finger.

These are Mischief's hands, reaching for the truncated deck of cards, fanning it on the coffee table. Here are the deft digits of the Trickster, walking crabwise, like a piano exercise, along the spread, down the scale of the numbers – stopping at the leftmost card, and tapping it. Beside the fidgeting hand, the bubbles in a glass of champagne refract light, rise and expire, as Mischief ponders, as Mischief plans, as Mischief grins – and then, casually, flicks the card with a fingernail from the table. It spins out, neat and true, across the carpet, and into the cold fireplace.

Mischief lips a cigarette. It hangs there, lodged in the corner of a lopsided smile, as the Joker stands, fizzes a match, touches it to the tip of the cig and inhales. Then, bending with the match between finger and thumb, Calamity's Choreographer sets light to the corner of the card in the hearth. The card buckles, blackens, withers, giving up a ghost of grey smoke that's sucked into the chimney, and becomes nothing.

'One,' says Newton's Child, and turns to pick up the champagne. The glass is drained, slowly, with contented relish.

'Fly away, Peter . . . One.'

A week later Mason had a nasty, though not unpredictable, moment. He was in the Grapes and Grizzly Bear on Berwick Street – a woody, cluttered pub, all roll-your-own Woodbines and sepia photographs of First World War flying aces. He picked up a copy of the *Clarion* from

7

a pile of tabloids on the bar, and his lunch lurched in his stomach as he scanned the front page.

CLIFF HANGER!
Moonquest Stars in 300ft Crane Ordeal.

The story was an exclusive by Christina Bell.

At the sight of the name, he bit his lip. He folded the paper widthwise, so he couldn't see the pencil sketch of Chris that accompanied her by-line, and made a mental note to congratulate her, next time they met, on a front-page story.

'Good morrow, Mason. Can you I treat you to a small libation?'

Mason looked up from his paper. 'Hiya, Bart. Yeah, pint of lager, please.'

Bartholomew Devereux Molyneux Scott lowered one buttock onto a barstool and waved a slim hand at the barmaid, who shimmied across as if hypnotised. This was a talent of his friend's that Mason had never entirely got used to. Practically every woman that encountered Bart fell instantly into an adoring trance, under the influence of which, as many had confided to Mason over the years, they were not responsible for their actions. This barmaid, for instance, was standing in wait of Bart's next utterance as if her brain had been turned off.

As Bart said good evening, all her lights came back on.

'Good evening,' she purred, and twitched her eyebrows up and down.

'A pint of the cooking lager, if you please,' Bart asked, 'and a Guinness. Take your time with the Guinness – make it a perfect exemplar of the pint-puller's art. Stint not, neither cut corners in the pouring thereof.'

Bart and Mason had been friends since childhood. They'd met because Mason's mother used to supplement the income she earned from freelance writing by tending the gardens of posh families in the pink-gin belt of Surrey. Often, she'd drag her son along to these places, and he'd mooch around resignedly on the vast lawns, and fetch the occasional watering can.

One day, when Mason was ten years old, he was wandering in the grounds of a huge Weybridge mansion when he happened upon a potting-shed. The door was ajar, and the sound of some power-tool could be heard. He pushed the door open a little, and saw a tall, slender boy of about sixteen, with straight black hair falling across his eyes, bent over a sheet of two-ply, drilling a hole. The older boy looked up, and noticed his visitor.

'Hello, small urchin,' he said, pleasantly.

Mason tended to distrust Big Kids. It came from being bullied so much at school. He was always being dragged around the playground in a headlock by some crewcut thug, whilst other kids aimed Doc-Martened punts at his arse. They picked on him, as far as he could tell, because he was bright and because he didn't have a dad. His mother always used to tell him that the nuclear family was a thing of the past, and that home lives such as their own, far from being the exception, were practically in the majority these days. Roger Smith's gang at St Michael's Primary, if they were aware of this demographic shift, shared the eighties Tory view that single-mother families were the source of all society's ills, and they were conducting their own little campaign for a return to Victorian values.

'Hello,' Mason said, hovering at the door of the potting shed, ready to run.

'Come in, come in,' the sixteen-year-old invited, flicking his hair back with a toss of the head. He put down the drill and opened a cupboard under the workbench. 'Tizer? Or some wine, perhaps? I'm Bart – who are you?'

Warily, Mason introduced himself, and accepted a chipped mug of Tizer. 'What you doing?' he asked, nodding at the bench.

Bart hefted the sheet of wood to the vertical. A poster of Buck's Fizz was pasted to it. Bart lifted up Cheryl Baker's skirt, which had been carefully cut out to form a hinged flap, and there was a half-inch hole drilled through the board beneath it.

'Ask me what it's for,' Bart suggested.

Mason was intrigued. He pondered a moment, and then said, 'What's it for?'

Bart grinned. 'As you ask –' he twitched his eyebrows – 'it's for wanking.'

Mason was a pretty well-informed ten-year-old. His mum worked occasionally for *Cosmopolitan*, and copies of the magazine were strewn all around the flat. He immediately saw a flaw in the design of Bart's device. He pointed at the drilled hole.

'I don't think you'll get your willy in there,' he opined, sagely.

Bart roared with laughter. 'No, no! Bless your tousled little head. This will be hung in my bedroom. I'll drill a corresponding hole through the wall, which will allow me to see into the au pair's room. Though I haven't yet decided what I'll do about disguising the opening on her side. Any suggestions?'

Mason couldn't think of any. 'Do you like Buck's Fizz?' he enquired, frowning. Even on a brief acquaintance, it didn't seem likely that this posh kid was a fan.

Bart looked momentarily perplexed. 'God – no. Total waste of good champagne. Why do you ask?'

Mason nodded at the poster. 'That group. They're called Buck's Fizz.'

Bart glanced at the picture again. 'Are they? I wouldn't know – I just bought the first poster I saw in the shop.' He reached for a packet of cigarettes from the bench, and lipped one, furrowing his brow. 'Do you think it matters?'

Mason explained that they weren't a boys' group, and told Bart that his own mother would start asking gently offhand questions about his sexual orientation, if he were to put *them* on the bedroom wall.

Bart flipped Cheryl's skirt back down, and picked up a lighter. 'I'm not sure that the aged em and pee even know where my room is,' he shrugged, lighting his smoke. Then he grinned suddenly. 'Though I suspect that the latter knows precisely where the *au pair's* room is. Which could be intriguing.'

Over the next few years, the two of them became intermittent friends. Bart was away at boarding school most of the time, but their parents had got chummy, and so they sometimes crossed paths in the holidays. Even as a teenager, Mason could never quite understand why someone so assured, so rich and, more to the point, six years his senior, chose to be nice to him. But it became apparent that Bart took the flattering default view that everyone in the world was worthy of his full attention and charm. He also assumed that everyone would like him – which meant, of course, that everyone usually did. And if they didn't, he remained blissfully unconcerned, continuing to treat his detractors with graceful courtesy. It was rare to see Bart express anger or hurt. Any negative feelings he had towards his fellow human beings were expressed in gentle, wry teasing, or ambivalent faint praise. Bart was opinionated, certainly, and he expressed disapproval – but he was never less than polite in the presence of those with whom he had a difference. Mason had used to think that was a sort of hypocrisy – but he'd come to understand that it was breeding.

By the time Mason was in his late teens, the age gap between him and Bart seemed to have narrowed. They shared a flat when Mason got his first job in the West End – or, to be more precise, Mason took a room in Bart's Kensington apartment, for a nominal rent and a commitment to do all the cleaning. It was Bart who had introduced him to Chris, for which he was deeply grateful at the time.

So, seventeen years after that first meeting, Bart pulled an ashtray across the bar towards him, pushed his hair out of his eyes and said, 'Coffin nail?'

'Uh, no, thanks. But have you got a match? I've given up fags, but I'm okay as long as I've got a match to chew.'

'And what would our friend Sigmund have to say about that, we ask ourselves? Ah, my Guinness . . .'

Bart sipped his drink and then wiped off the foam moustache with the back of his hand.

'Anyway, Mason, what's going on with you?'

'Not a whole lot. The humiliation of Peter Pinkus has been the highlight, depressingly. Did you hear about that?'

'Yes, I saw the papers. Banal and predictable outrage, as ever. Did Chris do a piece on it?'

'I don't know. I don't generally read her rag.' Mason shrugged. This was true – but he didn't avoid it merely because it was a crappy tabloid. He picked up the *Clarion* from the bar. 'She's got a front page today – look.'

'Ah, another showbiz mishap,' remarked Bart, and read the piece out loud.

CLIFF HANGER!
Moonquest Stars in 300ft Crane Ordeal.

Film fans watched in horror today as hunky star Cliff Benching and actress-wife Dawn Mabbutt were stranded in a tiny window-cleaners' cradle 300ft above London's West End.

Heart-throb Cliff and former Bond-girl Dawn, 34, were filming a scene for Moonquest II: The Legend of Grendor. *But a mechanical failure left the sexy screen duo hanging around in a downpour for three hours, while engineers looked for the fault.*

FEAR

Close friends of the controversial couple, whose black magic sex secrets shocked moviegoers worldwide, revealed that buxom Dawn has a FEAR OF HEIGHTS.

When they were finally brought to earth, Dawn was weeping uncontrollably and Cliff, who is thought to have demanded £3million to recreate the role of the Emperor of Zingroth, looked shaken by his ordeal.

TERROR

Speculation grows in showbiz circles that Dawn's terror of high-rise stunts may ironically be just the contract-loophole that Moonquest *producers need to drop the curvy cabby's daughter from the lucrative Empress Tringka role.*

But one insider told the Clarion, *'There is no question of Dawn being axed. She won the part on her own merits.'*

Bart put the paper down on the bar, and gazed at Chris's by-line for a few moments.

'One is ever mindful, is one not, that Christina is, in conversation, lucid, witty and original; one holds firm to the conviction that she commands the love and respect not only of oneself, but of one's peers. Valid thus far, Mason?'

'One guesses so, yeah,' Mason obliged.

'Then one must assume, for it is the only possible explanation, that she writes this crock of shit as some kind of joke, hm?'

'Actually, I think she writes this crock of shit as some kind of living,' Mason said, trying to break it to him gently.

'Ah, yes,' sighed Bart and shook his head sorrowfully. 'This living-earning thing. I tend to forget people have to do that.'

'Can I have another match?'

Bart pushed the matchbox along the bar. 'Help yourself. You know, I do like to see disasters occurring to celebrity nincompoops,' he mused, indicating the newspaper. 'Whether it be an unfortunate balls-up like this one, or a set-piece such as the Pinkus thing, or, indeed, what happened to that airhead Thingummybob – there is something in such events that allows one to feel that there are benign forces afoot in the universe, some sort of natural justice at work.'

'Plus, it's a hoot,' Mason pointed out.

'That too,' admitted Bart. 'Er . . . who do I mean, by the way, when I say "that airhead Thingummybob"?'

'Chuckie Rolls.'

'What? No, I don't mean Chuckie Rolls. Most definitely I don't. Wrong gender.' Bart frowned. 'Why on earth would you think I meant Chuckie Rolls?'

'Because someone shot him with a paintball at a posh dinner.'

Bart looked incredulous. 'What – at the dinner table?'

'No, not at the actual table. He was getting out of the car, waving to the fans and all that, when suddenly – *kerpow* – he got hit by one of those paintballs they use in war games. Head to foot in red paint, all over his tux.'

Bart roared with laughter. 'Oh, wonderful. I don't know why people get despondent these days. Life just keeps on getting better and better.' He slapped the bar, giggling. 'But, to get back to my original point, I was thinking about that woman who does PE in a cerise leotard. God – what's she called? Hang on . . .'

He beckoned the barmaid, who hurried over, willing to perform any small service that would make Bart happy.

'What is the name of that woman who used to be an Olympic egg-and-spoon racer or something, and now tells you what shape you're supposed to be if you were born under the sign of the crab? Dresses up like an Egyptian goddess – for which she is peculiarly gifted, as she has the face of a jackal.'

The barmaid frowned for a moment and then her face brightened with understanding. '*Oh-ohh* – Melody Peters – the Pink Priestess!' she announced.

Bart spread his hands wide. 'Of course! Thank you, dearheart.'

'Any time,' the barmaid replied, but managed to make it sound like an invitation rather than an acknowledgement.

'So,' Mason said eagerly, 'what happened to Mystic Mel?'

'Well, my old mucker, I suggest that I relate this sorry tale of punctured pomposity over supper.'

'Ah, no, sorry. I'm meeting my mum for dinner at Raphael's in half an hour.'

'Yes, you told me. Still, I shall come along. Your mother will be overjoyed. We haven't seen each other for months. It will make her evening.'

'Yeah, but . . .'

'She will tell me how I've grown. She'll compliment me on my table manners. Listen – we'll have another one here and then get a cab. We'll be a bit late, but I'll say it was my fault.'

'But—'

'Can I interest you in another match?'

CHAPTER THREE

Chris turned off her computer, picked up her lukewarm coffee and sat back. That day's *Clarion* was lying on the desk beside the mouse-mat, and she glanced at it, and grinned. Even after four years in the job, she still got a little thrill from seeing her name at the top of a story. And she was secretly and slightly guiltily pleased that the paper had introduced line drawings of the hacks to accompany their by-lines. 'We want the punters to identify with you,' Ray had said at a staff meeting. 'We want them to trust your face.'

They'd got in a police-artist, for God's sake – someone whose usual task was to draw suspects and to reconstruct the decomposed faces of corpses found in shallow graves. But Chris had to admit that he'd caught her precisely – loopy hair, somewhat hard pale eyes, wide mouth crammed with teeth. She'd asked him to draw a cigarette hanging from her lip – she was after that casually sexy Lauren Bacall thing – but he refused. After a bit of coy flirting, she talked him into suggesting a coil of smoke around her cheek. No one would notice it but her – and that was enough.

She knocked back the last of the coffee and stood up. It was still light out – the clocks had just gone forward – and she was anticipating the walk to the tube in the late sunshine, looking at the daffodils in the Embankment Gardens.

As she headed for the lifts, pulling on her coat, Ray Churchill's head appeared around the door of his office.

'Got a sec, Chris?'

She sighed. 'Well, I was about to . . . Yeah, okay.'

Ray gestured at a chair as she walked into his room. He went to the drinks cabinet. 'That time of day, yeah? What can I get you?'

Chris accepted a beer, and schlipped it open as Ray poured himself a scotch and sat down.

'Nice piece on Cliff and Dawn. Cheered up a quiet day.' He sipped his drink. 'Suggest anything to you?'

Chris swigged from the can, and swallowed. She hated it when her editor did this. He had an idea, and now he was going to make her try to guess what it was. She wouldn't be able to, of course, but her admission of it would allow him to parade his brilliance as an inventive and inspired newsman.

She shrugged. 'Not really. What do you mean?'

Ray leaned forward. 'Come on. You're a smart cookie. Think.' He paused, looking at her. 'No?'

Chris ran her eyes around the room, taking in the huge TV, the piles of magazines and rival newspapers, the pinboard covered with black-and-white glossies of car-wrecks and cheesecake bimbos and celebrities swinging punches at the camera. She pursed her lips, and looked back at him.

'Nope. Sorry. Call me stupid.'

Ray chuckled. 'Nah – you're not stupid. Just haven't been in the game long as me, love.' He got up and poured another scotch, then turned and leaned back on the windowsill. 'Think about it – Cliff and Dawn. Peter Pinkus. Chuckie Rolls . . . See?' He wagged a finger. 'Some joker's out to fuck around with celebs.'

Knowing the game, Chris put on an expression of wide-eyed astonishment. 'God! Do you think so?'

Ray nodded smugly. 'Sure of it. Take my word. And I want you to find out who it is. I want the *Clarion* to own this one, before the *Voice* twigs.' He reached forward and picked up that day's copy of the *Daily Voice*. 'Look at their lead today. Fucking coup in Africa somewhere. I ask you.'

Chris nodded. 'And there's Morris, too.'

A week before, Morris Keen, retired Formula One driver, had found a crop circle depressed into a wheatfield on his farm. He'd mused in the press that this might be a message from an alien civilization, cryptically attempting to announce their presence using a cereal medium. Three days later, another pattern had appeared in the same field. The aliens had evidently dispensed with the enigmatic – the pattern was quite clearly a huge human hand, giving the two-fingered fuck-off sign. The heroic race-ace had become a laughing-stock.

Ray chuckled and pushed himself forward off the sill. 'Exactly! I was hoping you'd see that.'

Chris beamed obligingly, knowing that that meant he'd missed it.

'I want a chummy, gigglesome angle on this,' Ray was saying. '*Who is this mischievous tinker playing tricks on our favourite personalities?* That sort of shit. Yeah?'

'Absolutely,' Chris agreed. 'I'll start on it tomorrow.'

As she left the building, she smiled. This was going to be fun.

Bart had been correct about Maria Dixon's reaction to seeing him unexpectedly. She was delighted.

'Bartholomew!' she yelped, when her son and his friend turned up three-quarters-of-an-hour late at Raphael's. 'How lovely to see you! It must be almost a year.'

'Ten months and seventeen days,' Bart confirmed, switching it on like a promiscuous lighthouse. 'I have counted each weary sunset, Maria. How are you?'

'Well, up until this moment, I was extremely annoyed.' She turned to her son. 'I've been sitting here for nearly an hour, Mason.'

'How lovely to see you, Mason,' he said, drily. 'It must be almost a fortnight.'

Once they were settled at the table and had ordered a bottle of wine that cost, Mason noted, more than an entire week's dole money, Bart said, 'Maria, would it bother you terribly if I were to smoke?'

She put a reassuring hand on his. 'Bartholomew, you are a responsible adult. If you wish to poison your system and shorten your life, that's entirely up to you.'

Mason saw an opening here to score a point. 'I've given up, Mum. Haven't had a fag for a week.'

'Really?' Maria said. 'Jolly good. It's a disgusting habit.' She turned back to Bart. 'So, dear, what have you been doing with yourself?'

'Oh, nothing of great moment. The same dreary round of careless dissipation. Though I do have some scandal for you.'

Mason sighed and poured himself two days' worth of Social Security as Bart embarked on an unlikely tale of what the upper crust are wont to do with three feet of rubber pipe and a gallon of 7-Up. There were waiters milling about taking orders, re-filling wineglasses and changing the ashtray each time Bart tipped his cigarette. Mason felt a half-forgotten dread coagulate in his stomach, and a footprint of sweat bloomed between his shoulder blades.

As a teenager, he'd had a fear of restaurants. Just one look at a menu, and he'd sweat and tremble; his appetite would desert him and he'd be overcome with the desire to flee to a small room done out in white tiles and porcelain, where he could press his forehead against a nice cool mirror. He'd cured himself by working up from high street Wimpys, progressing slowly to unthreatening wine bars – and eventually he became a more-or-less functioning diner-out. But he still had points of vulnerability. For instance, his chest tended to thump if the food was presented as exquisitely beautiful, rather than merely edible. The tricolor pâté he ordered at Raphael's resembled a collaboration between Mondrian and a haiku painter. His ears were buzzing. He wanted to press his head against a mirror.

'Mason, you're not eating a thing,' his mother observed.

'Yeah, well, one of the advantages of being a grown-up,' he replied queasily, 'is that your mum can't make you eat your dinner.'

The thought of having to eat made him feel ill – but the thought of incurring the disapproval of the staff was even worse. He had to take his mind off it.

'What was it you were going to tell me about Melody Peters?' he asked Bart, desperately.

'Oh, good. Is this more scandal?' Maria said.

'Not precisely,' Bart told her. 'This was on national television – but I got the inside track from a friend at DayBreakTV. Apparently they had Melody Peters on there one morning to promote her new video of exploitative trash for the fat and foolish. It is entitled, if memory serves, *Astrobics: The Starsign System to a Slimmer, Sexier You.*'

'Or *Fate, Fitness and Fucking,* as Chris referred to it recently,' Mason added.

'The idea *was*,' Bart insisted. He didn't like to be interrupted once he'd launched into a story. 'The idea was that the Pink Priestess, as her publicity refers to her, would be interviewed by that human sugarcube who presents the breakfast show – Sally Fairfax. They were to do the interview whilst performing some of Melody's exercises.

'Run-of-the-mill tacky thus far. But it soon becomes apparent that

18

Melody has been overtaken by the most *terrible* attack of flatulence. She's backfiring like a New Delhi moped.

'"And this one," she says, lying flat on her back, "is very good for the abdomen, which is ruled by Pluto," and she hugs a knee to her chest and she lets go with a trump that registers five on the Richter Scale.

'Sally looks at her sidelong and grins weakly.

'Dear Mel appears unperturbed. Trouper that she indubitably is, she gets onto her hands and knees to demonstrate the Leo Push-up – and she launches yet another knicker-bloater.

'Still, you have to give her credit. Despite the glint of panic in her eye, she informs Sally and the viewing millions that the Gemini Stretch is an exercise for two people, and suggests that Sally might like to assist her.

'"This one is good for the upper thighs," Mel explains. "If you sit opposite me, and then you put your left foot against the inside of my right knee. That's right. And I put *my* left foot against the inside of *your* right knee, like that. And we push gently against each other so that—"

'*Brrthlrrrupupphrrrfffthbububbperupppbrubble-bup-hupbiphiphippft!*

'And she lets rip with a snort that dislodges tiles from the roof of DayBreak House. It's a belter. You can't fault it for style, content or star-quality.

'Sally Fairfax is covered in confusion, but evidently relieved to be covered only in that. "Thanks, Melody," she says, flustered and slightly green. She glances at her teleprompt, and faces the camera to tell us that her co-presenter will now introduce the regular pop music slot.

'"And now," she announces cheerfully, regaining her bright composure, "it's back to Horn for Shitline . . ."'

CHAPTER FOUR

Mason had got through three glasses of port and the remaining wine before the end of the meal. By the time they'd all had coffee and were winding up the evening, he was fairly drunk and absolutely starving. Maria and Bart had ordered a taxi to take them to Chelsea and Kensington respectively, and yet another waiter, whose job it was to inform customers that their cabs had arrived, informed them that their cab had arrived. They offered to detour via Camden to drop Mason off, but he felt like a stroll. He accepted his denim jacket from a waiter who was holding it at arm's length like an old fish, and wandered out to the street, where Maria and Bart were getting into the car.

'You know, perhaps all the victims have something in common,' he murmured, as Bart wound the window down. 'Maybe they're all Capricorns or something.'

'Or they're all just nincompoops.' Bart shrugged. 'See you next week.'

Mason sauntered across Oxford Street to Wardour Street. A trip to Soho always reminded him of a custard tart – something he was convinced he enjoyed, despite never having had a really good one. He had a rather romantic vision of the area, as if it were a snakes' nest of sex and peril, peopled by mavericks and outcasts, alive with strange philosophies and covert cliques.

When he'd first come to Soho, at the age of fifteen, the district had seemed like Babylon on Cup Final day. On street after street, he strolled past secretive little pubs, cellar-bars full of music and gaudy neon signs announcing GIRLSGIRLSGIRLS and STRIPTEASE! – or, more usually IRLS IR SGIRL and S RIPT SE!. He used to dream of wading chest deep into those murky waters, where he would be carried away by the undertow of sleaze and washed up on the shores of depravity. If time had not been against him, he might have taken that plunge – and damn the risks. Unfortunately, his exams were coming up, and he had to be home by nine-thirty.

Still musing on the connection between the practical jokes, he turned along Old Compton Street, glancing sidelong at the leather-clad mannequins in the sex shops. It was beginning to drizzle. The red lights in the upper windows looked cosy and welcoming – not that he'd ever have the nerve – and the neon of the amusement arcades reflected in gutter puddles. It was a sterling attempt at cinematic atmosphere, but Mason couldn't see that Soho had anything more dangerous to offer than a nasty case of Sega-wrist. He ducked into a late-night coffee shop on the corner of Frith Street, and ordered a latte and a custard tart, taking them to a window seat, where he picked up a discarded *Guardian*. He lit and extinguished a match, and started chewing.

The cappuccino machine gurgled greetings as a tall, lean, fiftyish man walked in. He was wearing a three-piece suit of mid-seventies cut – all wide lapels and slight flares – and a crumpled green shirt with a button-down collar, which held in place a thin red leather tie. He was utterly bald and humming 'The Ride of the Valkyries', in a very public sort of way. He was, in Mason's immediate estimation, a loony of the first rank.

'Strong tea, Mario,' he said brightly to the moustachioed Italian at the counter, 'and a macaroon.'

'No macaroon,' replied the Italian crossly. 'Why you always ask for macaroon? You *know* we never got macaroon.'

The man ran his bent fingers across the smooth dome of his head as if he were pushing back a mane of thick, undisciplined hair. He tut-tutted perplexedly. 'No macaroons, Mario? But you know I only come here for the macaroons – and you've never *got* any.'

'No! You right! We never got macaroons! You crazy man.' He dumped a cup of tea on the counter. 'Eighty pence.'

'Well, in that case, I'll take a filter coffee and an apricot Danish, please.'

'You don juan tea?'

'Not without—'

'Not without macaroon – yeah, yeah, I know.'

Mason watched all this from behind the newspaper, ready to duck back into the sports section at the first sign of an attempt to drag the general public into it. As the transaction was concluded, and the loony turned to find a seat, he offered up a silent prayer for invisibility.

Inevitably, the weirdo sat down at Mason's table, placing his coffee and Danish carefully in front of him. 'Well, here we are then,' he said, out of the blue. 'What do you think of garlic, playmate?'

Mason lifted the *Guardian* in front of his face, as the question was repeated. He couldn't understand why he always attracted nutters.

Suddenly, three long fingers appeared over the top of Mason's paper. Slowly and gently, it was pulled down to reveal the smooth crown, the thin eyebrows and finally the bright green eyes of . . .

'Elvis Presley. How do you do?' One foot was lifted to the level of the tabletop. 'Blue suede shoes, eh? Attention to detail. Can't beat it. And you are . . . ?'

Mason groaned, and gave up, just hoping that the loony wouldn't turn out to be violent. He introduced himself, in a mumble.

'Now to get back to your original question,' the loony continued, 'you asked my opinion of garlic.'

'No, I didn't.'

'And am I glad you did, because if there's one subject on which we vampires have strongly-held opinions, it's garlic. What do you do for a living, young Mason?'

'I'm a vampire-hunter,' Mason said, tersely.

The loony looked startled. 'Well, you're very good at it, aren't you? There you are, simply sitting there, and I just stroll over to you like a lamb to the slaughter.'

Mason growled. The only way to get rid of these people was to be blunt. 'Look, mate, I just want to sit here in peace and drink my coffee and read my paper, all right? I mean, no offence and all that, but could you give it a rest?'

The loony frowned. 'That's a fib, Mason. It's *not* your newspaper, is it? You found it.' He took the open paper from Mason's hands and turned it round, pointing to a scrawl above the front-page banner. 'Look – "256". Most likely the number of a hotel room – and I think you're a Londoner, not a tourist. So – this isn't your newspaper. Attention to detail, as I said.'

Despite himself, Mason grinned. 'It's a fair cop,' he admitted. He was beginning to suspect that the bloke wasn't a loony at all. He tried to think of him as an eccentric – an *amusing* loony.

Suddenly, the eccentric cupped a hand to his ear. 'Listen! Hear that?'

Mason cocked his head. 'What?'

'The plaintive bleat of a pint calling your name. Can't you hear it?' He stood and walked to the door, pulling it open. 'Coming?'

Even at twenty-seven, Mason couldn't help conjuring all those childhood injunctions about not going off anywhere with strange men.

'You're not really a vampire, are you?' he asked, in a tone of mock-timidity that was nothing like mock enough.

'Well, of course – but I drink only the good stuff and you're just cheap plonk.'

Mason paused, and tutted at himself. It seemed just the kind of adventure he had been waiting for. After fifteen-odd years, a real Soho character was inviting him to go for a drink at some after-hours dive, and here he was – the self-styled Denizen of the Neon Night – thinking perhaps it was time to potter home and give it zeds. Pitiful.

'All right,' he said, picking up his matches and making for the door. 'Why not?'

Following out onto the street, Elvis paused and turned back to the counter.

'Goodbye, Mario,' he waved. 'Thank you.'

'Hey, you crazy-man, you stop call me Mario!' the Italian yelled as the door swung shut. 'My name is Giorgio!'

Fifteen minutes later, Elvis and Mason were seated at a table in a basement bar somewhere in London – this being the finest level of geographical exactitude to which Mason would be prepared to commit himself. He thought he knew the West End pretty well, but Elvis's ducking and weaving had disorientated him completely.

They'd cut down unlit backstreets and dog-legged across gloomy courtyards; and then, as they were striding past a darkened betting shop, Elvis had suddenly veered into an alley and down some metal stairs. Mason trotted to keep up with him as he stopped in front of a door marked Fire Exit, and kicked it sharply, causing it to spring open towards him. Mason followed Elvis down a short matt-black corridor and through a beaded curtain which emerged onto the serving side of a bar. The barman, with his back to them, didn't realise he had company until Elvis stepped up behind him and, at the top of his voice, yelled, 'EVENING, MARIO!' The unfortunate man was still in the air as Mason scurried around the bar, following Elvis, already rehearsing apologies. The barman clambered down from the glass-rack, one hand clutched to his chest and breathing heavily.

'Fuckin' Jesus, John-Paul,' he growled at Elvis. 'Why can't you use the front fuckin' door like any other fucker? And don't call me Mario, you wanker.'

'Two lagers, please, Mario,' Elvis said, unperturbed. 'And allow me to introduce you to my friend Mr Dixon. Mason – this is Mr Wainwright, but all his friends call him Mario.'

Mario Wainwright was a large hairy man who, but for the lack of an eyepatch, reminded Mason irresistibly of the baddie out of *Captain Pugwash*.

'Pleased ta meetcha. The only fucker who calls me Mario, by the way, is this berk.' He glanced at Elvis. 'And any friend of Mr Getty's is probably a pain in the arse. But I'll give you the benefit of the doubt.'

'Stick the beers on the tab, Mario.' Elvis grinned. 'I'm just going to use the potty.'

Mason took the drinks to a table, sat down and looked around the club. It was low-ceilinged and low-lit, done out in black and red. The music was scratchy r'n'b, sufficiently subdued to talk over. The clientele was almost exclusively male, and not particularly vampiric, though one was wearing a cape.

Mason knew that for the recovering nicotine addict, this was absolutely the worst bit – unfamiliar place, unfamiliar company, late at night, glass of something screaming to be accompanied by the punctuating drag. To take his mind off it, he concentrated on the practical jokes. Rubbing his eyes and going over it again, he didn't notice Elvis return.

'Headache?' Elvis asked. 'You need new Jar-o-Beer, now available in this handy pint-sized dose.' He sat down. 'What's on your mind?'

Mason took a sip of beer. 'Oh, probably nothing. It's just something I got interested in. There's been this series of pranks, and ... Are you sure you want to hear about this?'

'I have never yet heard of anything I *didn't* want to hear about,' Elvis remarked, shrugging. 'Fire away.'

Over the course of a couple of pints, Mason related the whole thing. Elvis listened, nodding, asking for the occasional clarification. Finally he leaned back, and clasped his hands in his lap, frowning.

'I think you're right,' he said. 'There is a connection.'

There was a short silence, as Elvis stared into space, pinching his nose and thinking. Then he got to his feet, and belched loudly.

'Oops. Pardon. That comedian who got Pollocked . . .'

'Chuckie Rolls,' Mason said. 'Hit number one.'

'Yeah, him. I don't think he *was* number one.'

Mason raised his eyebrows. 'You know of one before that?'

'No, I'm pretty sure he was the first. Also, either you've missed a couple, or your perpetrator is allowing himself some licence.'

And he wandered off towards the toilets. Twenty minutes later, Mason was still sitting alone, an empty glass in front of him. He went to check the loos, but Elvis wasn't there. In fact, as Mason soon discovered, he wasn't anywhere.

Elvis had just left the building.

CHAPTER FIVE

When Chris got to work the following morning, there was a yellow-sticky on her screen.

My office. Now. RC

She'd been expecting it. On the way in she had picked up a copy of the *Voice*. They were running a front-page that read, *Who is the Joker? Only* The Voice *brings you the laughs as they happen!*

'Fuckers!' Ray yelled, throwing a copy of the rival paper across the room as Chris entered. 'Bastards!'

Chris closed the door behind her and sat down. 'Mind if I have a cigarette?' The building had a no-smoking policy, but it was accepted that the editor's office was exempt.

'Sure,' Ray said, stubbing out a Benson's and lipping another. He slumped in his chair and pushed back his thinning hair. 'Bastards,' he muttered, chin on chest.

Chris waved out her match and dropped it in the ashtray. 'I think we're still all right, actually,' she said, exhaling jets of smoke from her nostrils. 'I was thinking about it on the tube.'

Ray looked up, hopefully. 'Yeah? What you reckon?'

Chris paused. She wanted this assignment. It might have legs. Might have profile too. She was professional and ambitious, and she could see that the story would put her line-drawn face on a lot of front pages.

She took another drag and flicked ash. 'Different angle,' she suggested. 'Not the what-a-laugh one. How about *Who is this sicko tormenting our beloved celebs?* We get indignant. We ask what the police are going to do about it. We demand action from ... I dunno ... the Government, whoever.'

Ray bought it. In fact, he told Chris that he'd been thinking much the same thing himself. Tell the truth, he was delighted she'd got there on her own. She was coming on, getting the feel for the business. For him, he said, that was the joy of being an editor. The mentoring of promising staff. He had his eye on her, and she was doing just fine.

Back at her desk, Chris picked up the phone, and called Scotland Yard.

Inspector David Jennings – sixteen years in the job, flawless record, handful of tricky cases wrapped up – was beginning to doubt that he was a copper at all. In the last year, he'd not so much as seen a criminal, let alone arrested one. He'd been sent on courses, been overloaded with paperwork and had finally wound up at the Yard, becalmed in OS12 – the section reserved for those officers awaiting transfer. He'd watched colleagues come – played brag with them, winced at their racist jokes, good-humouredly borne their teasing about his reading *The Mill on the Floss* at lunchtimes – and he'd watched them go – to jobs in Ealing CID, or Traffic in Mitcham.

But he'd been passed over, given the go-by. Jennings's seven-year-old son, Jake, had a book about a teddy bear in a toyshop who was never bought. As he read his boy that story at bedtimes, David Jennings knew exactly how the teddy felt.

He was just past forty – and not unteddyish, with his thinning sandy hair, friendly brown eyes and his slight tummy. He knew he didn't look the part of the steely, case-hardened copper. But he also knew that wasn't the reason he was docked in this backwater. It wasn't his face that didn't fit – it was his personality. The Met had no niche for gentle, curious officers whose philosophies owed more to Kierkegaard than Kojak.

Jennings was playing patience on the computer when the phone rang, and he was summoned to the office of DCI Jagger. He pulled on his tweed jacket, tucked in his errant shirt-tails and ambled along the corridor.

'Mornin', Mary Poppins,' grinned a fellow copper who passed him in the corridor.

Jennings gave no reaction but an amiable smile, and knocked on the door of the DCI's office.

Jagger was sitting at his desk, all spidery eyebrows and prominent Adam's apple. He indicated that Jennings should sit, which he did, hands on his knees.

'Got a job for you, at last,' the DCI announced, with evident relief. 'Get you out of my hair, anyway.'

A phone call had come in that morning from the newspapers. They were making a fuss about some joker who was targeting celebrities. The powers that be wanted to be seen to be taking it seriously. Jagger tossed a copy of the *Voice* across the desk.

'Not your usual reading, I don't suppose,' he muttered. 'More a *Watchtower* man, aren't you?'

As Jennings scanned the front page and the supporting pieces inside the paper, Jagger explained that the Special Crime departments wouldn't touch it. In fact, it was difficult to see under whose auspices the damn thing fell.

'Don't have a department for the investigation of Playing Silly Buggers with Malice Aforethought, do we?' he pointed out.

Jennings looked up. 'Um, perhaps that's because it's not a crime,' he suggested, simply.

Jagger beetled. 'Are you taking the piss? Listen, cocker – I've had enough of you sitting around here on your arse humming fucking 'Jerusalem'. I want you doing something – however bloody useless. A journalist from the *Clarion*'s coming in at noon. You can start by being self-righteous in print.'

He turned to his computer screen. 'Pick a tag-along rookie from the pool downstairs to help you. Now bugger off, Moses.'

Jennings padded back down the corridor, pensive and annoyed. He'd been given a silly, frivolous little assignment, just to get keep him out of the way. He knew that he should be used to it by now – his entire career had been a series of idiotic or unglamorous jobs, interspersed with periods of 'proper coppering', as they called it in the canteen, only when his bosses could absolutely not avoid involving him. His promotions had been given grudgingly, not because the hierarchy delightedly recognised his potential but, he suspected, because the Met's lawyers had looked at his spotless record and started fretting about employment tribunals and court cases.

He sat down in his chair and picked up a biro to chew. He stared out of the window, the copy of the *Voice* on his lap. It was depressing, being told to deal with this nonsense, but he'd do it, and do it well. Despite everything, Jennings still believed in a cosmic system of just rewards, and also that there was dignity in all labour. He'd get this case sorted out. Efficiently and by the book. And, more to the point, he had no intention of giving his superiors and colleagues the satisfaction of seeing him fail. He'd show them.

Though those superiors and colleagues would have scoffed at the idea, the truth was that David Jennings was naturally bloody-minded.

Chris arrived at Scotland Yard just before noon. She was asked to take a seat and wait. She was looking forward to grilling this copper. It would be a challenge, given that she really didn't have much to accuse him of, to put him on the defensive and get him to admit that the police weren't taking these practical jokes seriously. She was ready with all the usual implicit threats of bad coverage in the press and damage to image.

She was checking the batteries on her tape recorder when a voice said, 'Ms Bell?' She looked up to see a slightly tubby, dishevelled man of forty or so, smiling at her like a vicar. He introduced himself as Inspector David Jennings – and chucklingly spelled it for her – and then he gestured towards the door.

'Fancy a bit of lunch? I have a craving for pizza. We can have a glass of wine and a chat.'

'I was hoping for more of an interview than a chat,' Chris said, standing. 'This is a serious matter, Inspector, and—'

'Oh, do call me David,' Jennings insisted. 'And believe me, I can be very serious over a Napoletana.'

They headed for a pizza-chain place on Victoria Street. At the junction, the traffic lights were in favour of cars, but there were none approaching so Chris stepped off the kerb to hurry across. Jennings put his hand on her arm.

'Much safer to wait for the green man,' he smiled, nodding at the pedestrian signal opposite them.

Chris bridled momentarily at being treated as if she were six years old, but as she turned to give Jennings a mouthful, he tipped his head to one side and said, 'Sorry. I *am* a policeman, you know.'

In the restaurant, as Jennings ordered a bottle of Frascati, Chris put her tape recorder and cigarettes on the table and opened her notebook. She hit *Record* and taped herself and Jennings ordering pizzas, which she then played back.

Jennings chuckled as he heard his voice coming from the little speaker.

'Will I appear in your newspaper as "Italian fast-food lover Jennings, 41"?' he asked. 'Or perhaps "portly pizza-eating plod"?'

'"Dough-boy detective"?' Chris suggested quickly, hoping to needle him. But Jennings chortled roundly, and nodded.

'Very good. Very fast.'

'Sorry,' Chris smiled thinly. 'I *am* a journalist, you know.'

She was rather disconcerted by Jennings. She had not expected a Scotland Yard copper to be so, well, *pleasant*. She knew it was possible that his bonhomie was just a front intended to encourage her to go easy on him – but she generally trusted her instincts on these things and her instincts were telling her that he was exactly what he appeared – a nice bloke. Not that she would let that stop her doing her job.

'So,' he said, as their food arrived, 'what do you think this whole thing is about then?'

'That's what I'm supposed to ask you,' Chris pointed out, cutting her pizza.

Jennings nodded, chomping, and then swallowed. 'True. But I have absolutely no idea. I mean, why should the police take it seriously at all, actually?'

Chris smiled inwardly, and glanced at the revolving tape. She knew what that sentence would look like on the page. Sipping her wine, she suggested that the series of tricks played on celebrities was part of a nasty little campaign by some weirdo or stalker. It could get out of hand. Who knew what kind of warped mind was behind it, and where it might ultimately lead? As they ate, she extemporised all sorts of ghastly and lurid outcomes.

'No one's been hurt yet, certainly,' she admitted. 'But what if someone were to be injured, or even killed?'

Jennings grinned, and patted his mouth with a napkin. 'You sound like my granny. "It's all good fun now, but don't coming running to me when you break your neck."' He leaned forward on his elbows and clasped his hands under his chin. 'Do you really think it's some sort of jovial psychopath? It could all just be a coincidence, couldn't it? I mean, should the police put time and resources into this, frankly? I'm not sure we give a hoot.'

Chris's eyes flickered to the recorder again. Then she shook her head and tapped out a cigarette. 'No. There's something here. I can feel it.'

30

Jennings picked up her matches and struck one, holding the flame towards her, cupping it with one hand. 'And of course, it would be a much better story if that were the case.' He paused. 'The thing is, newspapers need a unique angle, don't they, in the best of all possible worlds? And it looks to me as though your competitor, the *Daily Voice*, has stolen a march on you with this one.' He blew out the match and rolled it between finger and thumb, watching it revolve. Then he raised his eyes to Chris's face. 'So what will be the *Clarion*'s angle?'

Chris held his eyes for a moment, and then shrugged. 'Don't know yet.' She looked away and picked up her wineglass.

Jennings put the match on the rim of the ashtray, then leaned down to the tape recorder. 'The Metropolitan police have put an expert team on the case,' he said slowly and clearly, 'and we are using all the methods at our disposal to track down this sick individual. We welcome the *Clarion*'s support in our efforts to keep this country safe from . . .' He looked up at Chris, and grinned '. . . the Trickster.'

He sat up again, and turned the recorder off. 'Will that do?' he asked, innocently.

Chris nodded.

'Jolly good,' Jennings replied. He reached for the bill. 'Let the Met get this. It's the least we can do for our friends from the press.'

That afternoon, Mischief walked into a random telephone box on Tottenham Court Road. The walls and windows of the booth were covered with the advertising cards of prostitutes – cheaply reproduced pictures of impossibly beautiful women selling illusion and doomed hope.

Mischief tutted. All lies – it was all lies. The services these cards offered were no different to those of clairvoyants and astrologers, politicians and faith-healers. Half-an-hour of individual attention for the gullible and needy, billed by the minute, each second charged with cold-eyed contempt.

And later, after the sexual release or the laying-on of hands or the promises of inevitable happiness written in the constellations – after the trick had been fleeced – nothing would have changed. The same unhappy desperation would well up again in the sucker's heart, and bubble and overflow, until the inevitable trip was made once more up the stairs of some clip-joint in Soho, Harley Street or Camden Town, where it could all be siphoned off like before, for cash on the nail.

Mischief piled a little stack of fifty-pence coins on the shelf of the booth, unfolded a piece of paper and dialled.

'McKinnon's Skip Hire? Yeah – I wanted to order a skip to be delivered tomorrow, to Bloomsbury . . .'

Five or six similar phone-calls followed, and then Mischief reached into the briefcase on the floor of the booth, and took out one of a hundred small cards, and a pack of Blu-Tak. The card was an eye-catching dayglo green, and very noticeable when it had been stuck to the wall of the booth, amongst the promises of exotic eroticism.

Mischief visited several dozen phone booths in the West End that afternoon, and as many tourist hotels, where handbills were discreetly left on foyer tables and in brochure racks.

As the offices emptied and the pubs filled, the last task of the day was to drop an envelope through the door of a smart house on Venton Street. The envelope also contained a card – a larger one, carrying an arcane design and a number.

'Eleven,' Mischief grinned, and headed towards a bar near the British Museum.

A key turned in the front door as David Jennings was coming back down the stairs of the terraced Tooting house, having checked on Jake for the third time that evening.

He smiled as Sue came in, and he trotted down the last few steps to kiss her and take her coat.

'How was your class?' he asked, hanging the coat on a hook. He'd barely seen her earlier. She'd shot out of the door as soon as he'd come in from work, calling, 'Microwave a casserole! See you later!' She was a punctual woman and didn't want to miss a minute of her aromatherapy course.

'It was all right,' she said. 'I'm dying for a cuppa.'

She headed for the kitchen, and Jennings trotted after her, entranced, as he always was, by the way her deep brown hair with its silver tracings moved in waves on her shoulders.

'You smell nice,' he told her. 'What was this week's aroma?'

'Bergamot,' she said, filling the kettle. 'Do you want tea?'

He took the kettle from her as she turned from the sink. 'Here, let me do it. You go and sit down.'

Five minutes later, he took the tea through to the front room and put hers on the little table beside the armchair in which she was sitting. He lowered himself onto the sofa, and looked across at her as she polished her glasses on her blouse. He'd rather hoped she'd be sitting on the sofa, to be honest.

'I've got an assignment,' he told her happily.

She lifted her glasses to the light and peered at them. 'About time. You're wasted, generally. Did you give Jagger a piece of your mind, like I said?'

'No – he called me, actually.'

Sue glanced at him, as if that hadn't been the plan at all, so no credit was due. 'What's the case?'

David Jennings hesitated. He couldn't think quite how to phrase it. Sue would not immediately perceive that it was the fact he had a case at all that was important, not the case itself. There was a danger she'd think he'd been fobbed off. She often felt he was fobbed off, and was never overly charitable about it. One couldn't blame her, really – only a copper could know how the system worked in the Met.

'It's a manhunt, I suppose,' he ventured, still apparently cheerful. 'Proper detective work.'

Sue picked up her tea. 'Jake all right tonight? No fuss about going to bed?'

Jennings shrugged. 'Well, a little. But it's half term and . . .'

'Oh, David,' Sue sighed irritatedly. 'We agreed – half-past eight. How can I be expected to get him to do as he's told if you cave in like that?'

Jennings gave her a sheepish look from under his eyebrows. 'Yes. Sorry.' There was a pause as they both sipped their tea. Then Jennings said casually, 'Well, shall we take our tea up, then? Moderately early night?'

Sue set her mug down on the table and reached down to the floor for her bag. 'You go up. I want to do some reading.'

Jennings nodded. 'Oh. Okay. Will you be long?'

'A couple of chapters,' Sue told him, opening her book. She looked up. 'It's half term. You don't begrudge me a lie-in, do you?'

Jennings got to his feet, stretching. 'No. No, of course not. You deserve it, darling.' He picked up his tea. 'Well. Anyway. I'll be off then. Night-night.'

'Night.'

On the way to the bedroom, he looked in once more on Jake, whom he adored, and who adored him.

CHAPTER SIX

The following day, Mason woke up at the unusually early hour of eight-thirty. He rolled over and looked across the vast expanse of his bed stretching away to the horizon – like the Gobi Desert, but not as lively. He groaned. There was something he had to do today, and it tinged his mood with foreboding. He detected the flavour of excitement there, too. He slooshed the feeling around his mental palate – a dash of fear, a jigger of resentment, a soupçon of regret and, perhaps, a subtle mélange of tenderness and lust.

He got it. He was having lunch with Chris.

They had split up about four years previously, after a three-year relationship, at Mason's insistence. After several months he realised that he had made a terrible mistake. It took him a year to convince her to have him back, and when she did, it didn't work. In retrospect he saw that he had irritated her by creeping around apologetically all the time, trying to make amends. Nine months into the second attempt, she dumped him. A year later, they both agreed to finish a ten-week fling that they'd drifted into – and they parted on the solemn understanding that that was definitively and incontrovertibly it. In fact, they were so sure that there was no longer any chance of them becoming romantically involved, that they would go out together for dinner every couple of weeks to say so. Mason felt that they had become very close friends, but neither of them hankered any more for that mystical moment when something would click softly deep inside their hearts and make everything as perfect and simple as once it had been.

'It's all sorted and cool now,' Chris had said recently. 'No issues left to resolve.'

'And I'm Pope Pius XI,' Mason had muttered, under his breath.

He dragged himself out of bed, and showered. He dug out the T-shirt Chris had bought him in Milan, just because he felt like wearing it, and he cut his toenails, because they needed cutting and he might as well. He cleaned his teeth twice, and gave serious consideration to polishing his shoes. He was ready to leave the house by ten o'clock.

Mason liked to be punctual, but he'd left himself two-and-a-half hours to travel eight stops on the tube which, he had to admit, was a little over-cautious, even given the inefficiencies of London Transport. So he wandered into the kitchen and made a cup of tea and some toast, even though that would mean another ten minutes of teeth-cleaning.

Sitting at the kitchen table, he fingered through the letter-rack. There was an unopened bank statement postmarked three months earlier, and he made a mental note that it would be ripe soon. And there was also a fat, windowed letter addressed not quite to him, but to someone very similar. The envelope suggested, in dayglo pink, that the recipient *may already have won £250,000!!!!* He opened it and pulled out a wodge of paper, of which the first sheet was a covering letter. *Dear MR DIXOB,* it began:

Have you ever dreamed of a World Cruise?? Have you ever longed for a second home?? What would you do with £250,000 (A QUARTER OF A MILLION POUNDS!!!) in cash???

Yes MR MYSON DOXOM, all this could be yours!!!

You are one of only a handful of carefully-selected individuals residing in MUSCOVY-$(TREET to receive this ONCE-IN-A-LIFETIME-OPPORTUNITY from Literature International Ltd!!!

Please let me stress MISS MYS&%^ DOXY, that this is an entirely free draw, and you are under no obligation to join the Literature International Book-Direct Club. However, may I take this opportunity to point out to you some of the wonderful advantages of—

'No, you mayn't,' he told it. He turned to the page offering him a choice of free gifts. Freda, his cat, hopped up on the table to check it out too.

'Shall we go for the device for trimming the hair in one's nostril's, Freda?' he asked her, scratching behind her ears. 'Or the Regency-style travel alarm clock with built-in radio? Oh – look – here's just the thing. A feline hysterectomy reversal kit.'

Freda mewed interest, and he picked her up and took her over to the fridge. 'Nah. Just kidding. You really ought to learn to read, then I couldn't play these unnecessarily cruel tricks on you.' He poured some milk into her bowl, and stood there watching as she dived in. 'You shouldn't touch that stuff, you know,' he told her. 'It's crammed full of lactose or something. If I can give up fags, you can kick this terrible milk habit.'

He sat back at the table and flicked through the catalogue from Literature International Ltd.

'Hey, Freda, listen up – it's the three-name page.'

Mason would have been the first to admit he knew bugger-all about literature, but he knew what prejudices he liked – and one was that anything written by someone with three names was unreadable dross. He recited the list to the cat. 'Mario Vargas Llosa. Alice Thomas Ellis. Gabriel Garcia Marquez. Piers Paul Read . . . What a forbidding bunch.'

Freda gave him a pitying look, and wandered off to the front room to see if the telly was on.

'Typical!' he yelled after her. 'That's the problem with young cats today! They just goggle at the TV hour after hour! No application!'

As he stopped shouting, Mason realised how very quiet the place was. It was slightly worrying. The only thing ever to break the silence in the flat was his own voice. He'd noticed recently that he'd fallen into the habit of talking aloud, not only to the cat and to himself, but to inanimate objects. He'd berate the kettle for its slowness, and ask the iron whether it was hot yet. He guessed it must be because he spent so much time alone.

This solitude sprang partly from financial necessity. As his mother had often pointed out, 'There's no *shame* in poverty, dear – it's just very, very boring.' But, on top of that, he'd simply lost interest in going out much. Faced with the choice of either an inexpensive night with some mates down the pub or an evening at home desultorily watching the telly, he'd consider all the effort the former required – having a shower, pressing a shirt, walking to the boozer, talking – and decide that the payback wasn't worth it. Slumped comfortably on the sofa, with the channel-zap at his fingertips and a coffee on the occasional table, he was totally in control. No one could persuade him to play pool, or engage in futile drunken conversation, or go for an Indian he didn't really want.

Mason went back to the three-name section. 'Hello, this is a new one.

Hendrick Balfour Mooney. Blimey, it's got to be kosher – no one'd make it up. Hendrick Balfour Mooney. *The Sky-Clad Priest.* "A semi-fictional history of Druidism and the Occult in the British Isles."' He chuckled. 'Tales of moonlit sex and bullshit hex, no doubt. Ancient spooky goings-on in what we now call Basingstoke. Recommended altar-side reading for the likes of Cliff and—'

He stopped dead, realising what he'd been about to say.

'For the likes of Cliff and Dawn,' he finished, quietly.

He recalled a phrase from Chrissie's front-page story about Cliff Benching and Dawn Mabbutt getting stuck on the crane. It was something like *Cliff and Dawn, whose black magic sex secrets shocked the world.* The reference was to an interview some five or six weeks earlier. They were both Druids, and they had, as it were, come out. Reading between the lines of the piece, one couldn't help concluding that Druidism was just a dreary *al fresco* Rotary Club. Still, the hack who'd ghosted the article had managed to twist and wring accounts of the ancient rituals so that a meagre chaliceful of juicy prurience had dripped out.

But – Mason felt a thrill as he thought it – Cliff and Dawn were Druids. Melody Peters was an astrology nut. Morris Keen, the crop circle guy, appeared to believe in aliens.

He laughed. *That was the connection!*

As he grinned, pleased with himself, the phone in the front room rang.

He pushed his chair back and ran down the hall, to beat the answering machine clicking in. Diving over the arm of the sofa, he grabbed the phone.

'Yeah? Hello?'

'Hello, Mason. It's me – Chris. You're all out of breath.'

'Yeah, sorry. I didn't hear the phone. I was in the bedroom . . .'

. . . having disgusting sex with a blonde who can't keep her hands off me – so there, he wanted to add.

'I thought you'd already left. I was afraid I'd missed you.'

'Why? Is there a problem? . . .'

. . . like you're going to cancel because you got a better offer, you cow?

'A bit, yeah. Can we change the venue? Can we make it the Lion House, in Bloomsbury? It's on Venton Street.'

'Er, yeah, of course.'

. . . I'll do whatever I'm told, jerk-off that I am.

'Same time, though, all right? One o'clock.'

'Yeah, fine. Why the change?'

. . . Afraid your snooty colleagues might see me if we go to the pasta place near your office?

'I'll tell you over lunch. See you soon.'

'Oh, right. Bye . . .'

. . . love.

David Jennings lounged back in his chair with his feet propped up on an open drawer, tapping a cheap biro against his bottom teeth. He had three problems.

The first was knowing where to start. He was faced with the task of tracking down someone who had done nothing wrong, unless one counted the minor and arguable offence of criminal damage with a paint-ball gun. He had no leads, no suspect, no motive and no idea what charges he would bring if he actually found someone to pin all this nothingness on. He also had no real support from his bosses, except the shrugging offer of a rookie from what was known at the Yard as the Leper Colony.

And there was his second problem. The Leper Colony was comprised of those enthusiastic recruits whom no one wanted – posh kids, idealistic youngsters from the ethnic minorities, young women who were seen as bolshy or feeble or merely plain. Jennings had a lot of sympathy for them. After all, he was in a similar colony himself – a sort of quarantine pen for the middle ranks. He'd looked through the résumés of all the available lepers – the PC George Ngilas and the WPC Fiona Bartlett-Clarks – and most of them looked to him like bright and promising coppers. He could have picked almost any one of them, but he couldn't bring himself to do it. These kids were going to have a hard enough time in the job, without an association with David 'Holy Joe' Jennings appearing on their records. They needed to get out to the city's nicks to be sneered at and ignored, to have the mickey taken mercilessly and to endure the terrible, wearing, endless practical jokes. They needed either to toughen up and survive, or to be driven out, humiliated and disillusioned.

What they certainly didn't need was to come under the wing of an inspector who was, even now, faced with problem number three, which blared from the front page of that morning's *Clarion.*

Jennings sucked his biro and leaned over to pick up the paper.

TRICKSTER LATEST: COPS 'DON'T GIVE A HOOT'!!!

Over a leisurely lunch in a West End restaurant yesterday, the senior officer in charge of the Trickster case admitted, 'I'm not sure we give a hoot.' Sipping wine bought with taxpayer's money, Inspector David Jennings asked our reporter, 'Why should the police bother?' This shock revelation—

The phone rang, and Jennings picked it up. He winced, listening, and nodded, tapping the biro on his knee. 'Yes, sir. Yes ... No. I ... No. No, I'm aware of that. Yes, sir. Twelve o'clock. Yes. I'll be there, sir.'

He replaced the phone calmly and lodged the pen in the corner of his mouth. Then he picked up the newspaper again and stared at the headline. And he smiled, a secretive and satisfied smile.

Mason switched the TV over to the snooker for Freda, put out some lunch for her, and quit the flat.

He'd left himself time enough to stroll from Camden to Bloomsbury, and he had James Brown on the Walkman, explaining that he was a sex machine. The very thought of suggesting such a thing to a woman made Mason's stomach hurt.

As he walked, he tried to put together a profile of the practical joker.

One: obviously it was someone with a sense of humour, albeit a rather childish one. Two: if the paranormal connection was right, then it was someone with great contempt for all alternative beliefs and pseudo-sciences. Three: it had to be someone with money to sink into the project, because there must have been bribes involved in setting up the Pinkus gag, and perhaps hired help on the Morris Keen scam. Four: the perpetrator would need quite a bit of time, too, and a certain freedom of movement.

Mason turned into Venton Street with minutes to spare. Just before he reached the restaurant, he stopped briefly to look at a group of people on the other side of the road. There was a small knot of women, each attached to a little girl of seven or eight, and they were all clustered about the closed front door of a Georgian townhouse. All the little girls were dressed in raggedy dresses, and they seemed to be singing to themselves. Looking up the road, he noticed two or three more pairs of women and raggedy little girls hurrying along towards the main group.

'Hiya,' came a voice beside him. It was Chris.

'Oh, hi,' he replied turning towards her and attempting to stifle the delighted grin that painted itself across his face every time they met. They cheek-kissed.

'What's all that about, do you think?' Mason asked, nodding to the little crowd across the street.

'I'm not entirely sure,' she replied, 'but I suspect it's why we're here. Let's get in to the restaurant and I'll tell you about it.'

The Lion House was a few doors down, almost opposite the action. It was a blackboard-and-cheap-wine bistro, and well within Mason's restaurant tolerance. They sat opposite each other at a window table, Chris insisting on the seat that faced up towards the milling congregation outside the Georgian terrace.

'I think I'm in luck here,' she said, checking that she had a good view. 'If that's my target, this is the perfect place to be.'

'What the fuck is going on?' Mason asked.

'We got a tip-off at the office. Dead mysterious. Someone phoned up and said, "Make sure you've got a reporter in Venton Street this afternoon." End of message.'

'So who are that lot?' Mason said, looking back over his shoulder at the women and little girls.

'I went and asked them. They're prospective Little Orphan Annies and their pushy mothers. Apparently they're all responding to an ad in *The Stage*. Auditions are being held at that house, 56 Venton Street, at one-thirty. Strange place to have auditions, but I can't see a story in it.' She picked up a copy of the hand-written wine list. 'What do you want to drink?'

As Chris studied the wine list, Mason surreptitiously studied Chris. Her henna-red hair was growing out at the roots. She'd put on a little weight since they'd been going out together. Her mouth was definitely too wide for her face and you had to admit that she had no tits at all, to speak of. She was, in short, utterly beautiful.

Mason knew her so well that he couldn't even tell if he fancied her any more – and there was his dilemma. He found it terribly difficult to be witty around her, because she knew all his jokes. He couldn't be flirtatious with her, because she knew all his ploys. And he would have failed miserably had he tried to be cool and aloof, because she knew when he was pretending. It was a loop, really. Precisely because she knew him better than anyone in the world, he couldn't be natural when he was with her.

'Red?' she said.

She ordered a bottle of house red, which arrived immediately. Mason poured two glasses.

'Cheers,' he said. 'It's lovely to see you.' It was too. He was always apprehensive before meeting her, and yet so pleased to be with her after the first thirty seconds.

'You too.'

'I saw you got a front page a few days ago – the Benching Drenching.'

She laughed. 'You should write headlines.'

'I've got a theory about the Cliff and Dawn thing,' he said, hoping to surprise her.

'You think there's some sort of connection between the victims, right?'

'Uh, yeah,' Mason admitted, a little crestfallen.

'Oh, dear,' she said, sympathetically. 'You look crushed. Sorry. It's just that we've been talking about it in the office. Personally, I'm not even sure it's all the same person. Could be just a lot of copycat capers.'

'*Copycat capers?* Did you actually *say* that? You've got to get off that fucking tabloid, sweetheart, before it's too late.'

'Actually, it's really difficult to write good tabloidese,' she remarked, defensively.

'So what? It's really difficult to get a dill pickle into a matchbox,' Mason told her, 'but that doesn't make it worthwhile.'

She was looking out of the window again. Whilst they'd been talking, the little crowd of orphans and their mothers had been joined by some tourists in Hawaiian shirts and Hasselblads. Another knot of American-looking types passed the bistro as they peered out. Some of them were holding yellow handbills and checking door numbers, evidently searching for an address.

'Order me a tuna salad,' Chris said, getting to her feet. 'I'll be back in a minute.' She took her notebook, and strolled out to the street.

Mason ordered Chris's salad and a burger for himself. He craned around to watch her talking to a couple who had fetched up outside number 56. She had her 'really interested' face on.

He wondered who else would recognise that face – the professional, open one that she never wore except when she was working. Who else could know her so well as to be able to distinguish that public expression – the slight raising of the eyebrows, the nodding tilt of the head – from its private equivalent? Who in the world would invest as much time as he had, in getting to know the difference?

In the back of his mind, Mason tended a little menagerie of highly dangerous ideas, as if he were one of those weirdos who keep snakes in the basement, poking them with sticks and saying with shuddering glee, '. . . and this one's lethal. One bite from this baby and you'd die in excruciating agony within two minutes.' Now, gazing at Chris through the window, he began toying with the most poisonous snake in his mental cellar. It was an evil, green-eyed little specimen that usually came out at night. It lived on speculation and throwaway reference; implications and rumours. It was called She-met-someone. He had learned how to handle it safely, but one day it was bound to bite. Every time he arranged to see Chris, he dreaded that this would be the occasion when she would seem a bit subdued, a bit sad, and would say, 'Mason, there's something I want to tell you. I'd rather you heard it from me than, you know, just gossip or something. You see, *I've met someone . . .*'

He wondered how he'd react. Obviously, he'd like to think he'd say, 'Listen – we both agreed that it couldn't work between us. I've got . . . you know . . . obviously I've got mixed feelings, but you're a lovely woman and you deserve all the joy in the world. I really hope you'll be very, very happy.'

In reality, he knew that he'd probably rush from the room with his hands clamped over his ears, screaming, 'I DON'T WANT TO HEAR IT! YOU CAN'T MAKE ME LISTEN, YOU SLUT!' He was pretty mature like that.

Chris came back into the restaurant, and Mason put the snake away.

'What is it?' he asked.

'They're tourists – mainly Yanks – and they're expecting to have tea with Mary Poppins.' She passed him a yellow handbill. 'They've all got these – they picked them up out of the brochure rack in the foyers of their various hotels.'

Mason read the flyer. It was done in a pseudo-Victorian typeface, and had a border made of little umbrellas.

Due to Public Demand

MARY POPPINS' TOWNHOUSE
56 Venton Street WC1
Will be Open to Visitors
For an Extra After Noon,
Being May 15th Year of Our Lord 2001

Ladies and Gentlemen of Breeding
Are Invited to Take Tea
with Miss Poppins Commencing at
Thirty Minutes After the Hour of One O'Clock
(Post Meridian).

Guests May Wish to Visit the Poppins Museum,
the Gifte Shoppe and Divers Exhibits of Peculiar Interest

Children Must Be Accompanied. Ladies Should Wear Hats.

'This is absurd,' Mason said, wrinkling his nose. 'I mean, Mary Poppins is a fictional character.'

'So's Sherlock Holmes, but thousands of people turn up at two-hundred-and-whatever-it-is Baker Street every year,' shrugged Chris.

The waitress came over with the food. She was continental-scruffy and had that just-slept-in look. Mason tried not to stare.

'Am-bearrr-guh, please?' she said, in a French accent so moistly sexy that Mason was afraid that his side of the tabletop might lift a couple of inches. Chris glanced at him and gave a little frown. And it occurred to Mason, for the first time, that maybe his ex had snakes of her own.

'Ah, hamburger,' Chris said, directing a sweet smile at the waitress. 'That'll be for my friend Mason here – the famous homosexual.'

'And toona salade fourrr you?' the waitress deduced.

'Thanks,' Chris replied, and then, turning to Mason, continued in a matter-of-fact voice that the waitress could not fail to overhear, 'So *how* many of the Brigade of Guards did you suck off at this party?'

The waitress gave a quizzical look and retreated to the kitchen. Chris watched her until she was out of earshot.

'You've still got your fetish for accents and untidy hair, I notice,' she observed offhandedly, spearing a tomato segment.

'It still matters to you, I notice,' Mason parried, ketchupping fries.

'Not at all,' she shrugged. 'I just don't want you to make a fool of yourself by stepping on your own panting tongue, or something.'

Mason felt that there was always the horrible possibility that this last remark might be the simple truth. He didn't like what it implied. 'Anyway,' he resumed, brightly, 'back to my theory about the joke thing . . .'

'Now, *they* don't look like tourists,' Chris interjected. She was looking out across the street again. 'And they *certainly* don't look like Little Orphan Annies.'

The throng outside 56 Venton Street had been swelled by the arrival of two cabloads of women in various styles of dress that Maria Dixon would have described as *obvious*. One of them appeared to be checking the number on the house door against a small card in her hand.

'I'll just be a couple of minutes,' Chris said, getting to her feet. 'Sorry, but it *is* my job . . .'

She snatched up her notebook and scooted out of the bistro again. With a resigned shrug, Mason set about the burger. Then a thought occurred to him. He called the waitress over.

'Excuse me,' he said. 'This is a bit of a strange question, but do you know who lives in that house over there? The one with all the people outside?'

The waitress gave the kind of French shrug that, in Mason's experience, tended to necessitate a trip to the launderette. '*Non*, but I ask ze manageuresse,' she rolled, and went to consult a woman who was sitting at another table, apparently doing the accounts. After an exchange which involved much pointing into the street, and peering round the curtain, she came back.

'Oo lives zair is a man colled Enri Westlake – 'e is a loyer, yes?'

Mason grinned weakly She *had* to be putting that accent on. It was perfect. Not that he could ask her out or anything – not in the middle of a lunch with Chris.

'Henry Westlake,' he confirmed. He knew the name. Westlake was a leading QC with a reputation for irascibility. He was also a reincarnationist, and in a recent well-publicised book had used his belief in the eternal indestructibility of the soul in support of an argument for the return to capital punishment.

'A loyer, *ouai*. Yes.'

'Henry Westlake, a lawyer. Right. Thanks.'

'Okay.' The waitress made to go, and then hesitated. She turned back to Mason and said, 'Now, I ask you a kestyon, yes?'

Mason smiled. Obviously it was one of those days when, for reasons you can't imagine, you've just got it.

'Fire away,' he murmured, seductively.

'I am verry new in Lon-Don,' the waitress began. 'I am all a-lone 'ere and I know not many peoples. Zo, I sink I ask you – do you know where are ze nightclubs fourr young women oo like ze sex only?'

Though smitten, Mason was shocked. 'Umm . . .' he replied, knowledgeably.

'You know, I ask you be-koz I 'ear what your friend say and I sink you unnerstan what I want.'

'Well, yeah.'

'I want find ze place where I go for meet wiz . . . uh, *qu'est-ce que c'est* . . . uzzer lesbiennes.'

'Ah,' Mason gulped. 'Oh. Right. Aha . . .'

With a faint gurgle, he wilted, as only a man can wilt.

CHAPTER SEVEN

David Jennings went to the gents on the way to his noon meeting with DCI Jagger. He slipped into one of the stalls, faintly embarrassed, even at forty-one years old, that he couldn't use the urinals. He was okay as long as he was on his own, but if anybody came in, everything just seized up.

He stood at the bowl, scanning the obscene graffiti, when he heard footsteps and voices outside.

'All right, Pete?'

'Yeah, not bad, as it goes. Here, you seen that new little Paki girl they got down in the colony? Something Sheikh?'

Throaty laughter.

'Worth a shake, is she?'

'Yeah – not bad, actually. Y'know – for an off-night. Get a curry thrown in too, I shouldn't wonder.'

Jennings grimaced. When the papers talked about institutional racism in the police, they made it sound too formal and treatable. The real problem was the mind-set that gave rise to this sort of charmless banter.

'Hey – heard this? What do you say to a Paki in uniform?'

A deep chuckle. 'Dunno. Go on.'

'"Coupla pintsa lager and the set menu for two."'

The guffawing was accompanied by the whoosh of the hand-drier.

'All right – what do you get if you cross a coon with a Paki?'

'Tell us.'

'A car-thief who can't fuckin' drive!'

The door slammed shut and David Jenning was left in the silence. He flushed the toilet, washed his hands at the basin and looked up at the mirror. His cheeks were spotted red with anger and frustration.

Not for the first time it occurred to him that he didn't belong here, in the job. It was arrogant and foolhardy of him still to believe, after sixteen years, that he could change things, and be a success on the back of those changes. But he was damned if he was going to be driven out. He'd joined because he really did believe in justice – and that conviction hadn't crumbled. He didn't necessarily believe in the Law, because the statutes were so often flawed, but he had absolute faith in a higher abstract principle of rightness. And the police force, imperfect as it was, offered the best medium in which to act on that principle for the good of his fellow human beings.

David Jennings ran this argument past himself almost as a litany. It comforted him and gave him strength.

He pushed back his thinning, sandy hair, and straightened his flowered tie. Then he turned and walked out of the lavatory towards DCI Jagger's office.

The interview that followed was not pleasant. Jagger waved about a copy of the *Clarion* and raged at Jenning's clodhopping, ham-fisted handling of the press. Hadn't he been on the damn media course only last month? Jesus! What the bloody hell did he think he was playing at?

Jennings listened calmly, tapping the tips of his fingers on his knees.

'Perhaps, sir,' he suggested, when Jagger paused to catch his breath, 'you ought to hand the case over to someone with a better feel for these things.'

Jagger shook his head firmly. 'Oh, no, son. Do you think I was born fucking yesterday? You're stuck with this one, Moses, and it's your head on the block if the axe falls. Gottit?'

Jennings nodded. 'Completely, sir.'

Having been dismissed, Jennings decided to go out and buy a kebab, and then walk in St James's Park to think. He pulled a folded copy of the *Clarion* from his inside pocket as he got into the lift, and scanned the front page once again. Still reading as he got out on the ground floor, he bumped into a short, slight Asian officer in uniform, just catching her arm with his elbow as they passed each other. She yelped as her plastic carton of salad spun from her grip and burst open on the floor.

'Sorry! Sorry! Sorry!' she exclaimed hurriedly, as he turned to help her pick up the scattered slices of tomato.

'Why are you apologising?' he asked, bending down. 'It was my fault, wasn't it?'

She looked at him sidelong, appraisingly, a leaf of lettuce in her palm as she crouched. She seemed to be weighing up her options.

'Yeah,' she said finally. 'Yeah – it was.'

Jennings grinned, squatting beside her. He shook vinaigrette from his fingers and held out his hand. 'Detective Inspector David Jennings. How do you do?'

She offered her hand warily. 'WPC Zerkah Sheikh, sir,' she said.

Jennings dropped the last of the spoiled salad back into the plastic carton, and stood up. Zerkah Sheikh stood up too.

'Sorry about your lunch,' Jennings said. 'Can I buy you a pizza? I have a hankering for a Marinara.'

Her eyes narrowed. 'No thank you, sir.'

Jennings nodded. 'Ah, I see. No fraternising with the upper ranks. Don't blame you.'

He paused, and tipped his head to one side. He licked salad dressing from each thumb, and then steepled his fingers against the tip of his nose, thinking.

'Tell you what,' he suggested, interlacing his fingers and pointing at her, 'how would it be if I were going to offer you a job?'

By the time Chris came back into the restaurant, Mason had talked his way out of the conversation with the waitress. He'd invented a few gay clubs and said they were all in Plaistow. Served her right.

Chris sat down, looking amused.

'It's another gag from the prankster, isn't it?' he asked.

'Looking that way, yeah.'

'You know who lives there, don't you?' he threw away, smugly.

'Henry Westlake, the barrister,' Chris replied, offhandedly, as she scanned her notes.

'Henry Westl— How do you know that?'

'I asked a traffic warden. Westlake has a resident's parking permit,' she replied, simply. She looked out of the window. 'I think this may soon get interesting. When it all gets going, I might have to dash. Sorry.' She sighed wearily and picked up the bottle of wine, peering at the level. 'Have you left any of this for me?'

'Yeah, 'course. But, listen, we can sit here for the time being, can't we? I mean, we're supposed to be having a nice time together. And you can see what's going on from here.'

'Oh, yeah, sure. I'm really sorry, though, Mase. This is not quite the lunch I'd planned.'

Mason immediately felt guilty. Chris had a career to run, after all.

'It's okay. So who are the women?'

Chris poured herself some plonk, and took a deep gulp of it.

'They're . . .' She paused. 'Umm, actually I'm not sure what the ideologically correct word for it is, these days. They're prostitutes. Ladies of the night. "Hookers" is probably the word I'll use in the write-up.'

Mason looked out at the street. Another cabload of women had just arrived. There were thirty or so now. 'You'll need a collective noun, I reckon,' he said. 'What's the collective noun for whores? A spread?'

'A rubber of whores?' Chris suggested. 'A living?'

They both sniggered, which buoyed the atmosphere again.

'So what are they doing here?' Mason asked, taking a bite of his burger.

Chris handed over a card. 'Apparently these have appeared in all the phone boxes around King's Cross and Soho and Victoria and so on, alongside all those cards that say "New Young Blonde" and "Watersports".'

It was a bright green card with orange type. You had to admit that it caught the eye.

WOMEN!

Sick of police harassment?
Crippled by regular fines?
Screwed by the law, in their cars and in their courts?

Together we can change the system!

Join
Working Women Against Needless Convictions
First meeting 56 Venton Street, WC1 1:30 March 15th
WWANC – an honest buck for an honest fuck.

'Sounds like a good idea to me,' Mason shrugged.

'They think so too.'

'So how's this being taken by Henry Westlake? Is he home?'

'I dunno. Apparently they've stopped answering the door to Orphan Annies, Poppins groupies and hookers alike. But that's not the point, is it? That lot out there are holding up traffic – and that's news.'

She gazed out at the throng, which was now spilling halfway across the street. A second crowd was gathering to watch the first, and voices were being raised. Chris laughed.

'Actually, it's pretty funny.' she said.

'Eat your salad. You'll waste away.'

'Zif,' she grinned ruefully, and Mason grinned back.

'Zif,' he said – as he always did

Chris had been completely accurate earlier when she'd mentioned Mason's fetish for accents. And it wasn't just exotic ones, either. He got turned on by practically any accent that wasn't his own. When he'd first met Chris, she'd had a broad Midlands accent, and employed a whole host of endearing expressions that he'd never heard before. 'As if' – or 'Zif', as she said it – was one such. As she said it now, his heart skipped – or at least broke step momentarily. He realised that he was getting a tad misty and looked around for the waitress, to order some mineral water.

'So,' Chris mumbled through a mouthful of beanshoots, 'what have you been doing with yourself?'

'Well,' Mason said, 'I met a weird bloke who calls himself Elvis Presley. In fact, he reckons he's got this prankster thing taped.'

'Yeah? What's his theory?'

'Ah, well, he went to the loo and never came back, so I didn't find out. But I think that all the victims have something in common—'

Chris held up a hand and looked out along the street. 'Wait a minute. Here comes the artillery.'

A huge truck was advancing on number 56 carrying a skip. Chris fumbled in her bag and took out a twenty-pound note, which she gave to Mason.

'Lunch is on me – or rather, it's on the *Clarion*. Can you keep the receipt for me? Sorry. Listen, call me in the week – okay?' She was collecting her things together, keeping her eye on the action outside.

'We'll have a proper lunch soon, yeah?' She leaned over and kissed his cheek. 'See you.' And, with a quick smile, she was out of the door.

Mason sat in silence for a minute. Then, picking up the ketchup bottle, he said to it, 'What they have in common, right, is some kind of interest in the paranormal. See?'

The ketchup bottle seemed about as fascinated as Chris had been. He put it back on the table, and sighed.

The truck carrying the skip turned out to be the first of a convoy. Twenty skips had been ordered from around London, all directed towards number 56. As they made their various ways through Bloomsbury towards their destination, they boxed in several cabs full of hookers who, fuelled with righteous zeal, were in no mood to be made late for the WWANC meeting. Decanting themselves from the cabs, having decided it would be quicker to walk, many of the girls tarried a while to explain to the truck-drivers that London, a bustling city built along medieval lines, did not lend itself to the easy passage of large lorries, particularly in the middle of a busy working day.

Mischief, leaning against the railings of 56 Venton Street, was pleased to note that the crowd of hookers, ambitious mothers and American tourists was being swelled by delighted representatives of the press, and even a camera crew.

It was Mischief, in fact, who suggested offhandedly to one of the impatient matrons that the *Annie* auditions had been cancelled because the part had already gone to a pushy mother's orphan who had turned up early to beat the crowds. The mothers on the street, pushy though they were, conducted themselves according to a tacit code of pushiness. It was their conviction that turning up early was pushing pushiness further than it should be pushed. They began to bang on the door of 56 – and if there's one thing at which your average pushy mother excels, it's banging on doors.

Meanwhile, a certain tension was building up between the tourists and the working girls. Some members of the latter contingent, standing around on the street as they were, had adopted an entrepreneurial, free-market approach to the situation, and were now applying themselves to securing a slice of the lucrative tourist trade. Circumstances were further complicated when a Mrs Vera Stanwick of Crewe, noticing that her Little Orphan Hayley was wandering off down the street, called 'Come over here, baby' – words that attracted the attention of a Mr Joe Schlitz (of Hoboken, NJ) whose wife had decided to dash off to Heal's on Tottenham Court Road. Mr Schlitz, believing that Mrs Stanwick was addressing him, walked over and remarked that, if her place was nearby, he had about twenty minutes to spare, and how much for a blow-job?

Mrs Stanwick surprised both herself and Mr Schlitz by decking him with a powerful straight right.

A Ms Shirley Enfield (of Balham High Road), also known as Sindy, labouring under the same misapprehension as Mr Schlitz in regard to Mrs Stanwick's occupation, opined, in a clear, carrying voice, that this unsympathetic response to a potential client typified the kind of behaviour that got prossies a bad name. Ms Enfield went on to suggest that if Mrs Stanwick (or 'you stuck-up cow', as Ms Enfield referred to her, not having been formally introduced) couldn't hack it on the streets, then perhaps she should leave the tricks to those industrious girls who weren't quite so picky about what was required of them.

Mrs Stanwick asked Ms Enfield what she meant by that.

Ms Enfield replied that if she (meaning Mrs Stanwick) didn't know, then she (Ms Enfield) wasn't going to tell her (Mrs Stanwick).

Mrs Stanwick, interested to discover whether she possessed a left uppercut to complement her fearsome right jab, experimented on Ms Enfield, but it must be said that Mrs Stanwick turned out to be a one-handed fighter. The left rocked Ms Enfield on her stiletto heels, but by no means laid her out.

A Ms Babs Roxburgh (of Monterey, CA) and a Ms Carol Spink (ibid.) sought to intercede in the affray, but were hampered by a Mrs Doreen 'Ingrid' Parsons (of Crouch End, N6). Ms Spink smote Mrs Parsons with a cardboard tube containing a poster of the royal family, recently purchased outside Victoria Station. Things hotted up.

It was at this point that Henry Westlake, the lawyer and reincarnationist, emerged from the front door of number 56. His lunch had been disturbed and, as one might have guessed from his circumference, he regarded lunch as a serious ceremony that required undistracted concentration. From the top step of the porch, he demanded to know what the bloody hell was going on out here. The tone he used was one that had cowed juries and had made mass murderers blanch, but it had little effect on the increasingly fractious mob on Venton Street, except to make them aware of his presence. The hookers, mothers and tourists turned in one coordinated movement, like a school of fish, and streamed up the steps.

Alarmed, Henry Westlake took a pace back, and swung at the advancing torrent of indignant visitors with the only weapon at his disposal – which was a turkey-drumstick that he had not, until that moment, realised he was still holding. He got in a couple of good thwacks with the poultry leg before he was overrun.

Mischief looked along the street. Two police cars had parked at the corner, unable to get any closer, and the coppers were now charging towards the house. Mischief withdrew to a doorway across the road, and watched, grinning, as Henry Westlake was hauled away with various other randomly arrested participants in what was by now a most unseemly free-for-all.

'Rough justice,' murmured Michief, murmured the Trickster, murmured Newton's Child.

CHAPTER EIGHT

Zerkah Sheikh was waiting outside the office of Inspector Watts, the Yard's office administrator. Her new boss, Inspector Jennings, had given her the task of finding an operations room for what he had decided to call Operation Loki.

Zerkah was astonished to find herself employed on a real case. It wouldn't be entirely true to say that she couldn't believe her luck, because that would imply that she believed in luck at all. She didn't. She believed in work. You got a break, and then you worked like crazy.

Jennings, she knew, had given her such a break, though she couldn't quite see why. Over a pizza, he'd explained about the case and told her he needed an assistant. He also warned her, quite candidly, that if she were to take the job, she could be making a career move that would blight her for years to come.

'I just want to work,' she told him. 'I'll take it.'

She looked up and down the corridor as she waited for Inspector Watts to make time for her. She'd been there half an hour already. She might simply have e-mailed him, but it was her experience of the Met that e-mails were generally ignored, and e-mails from sheikhza@metpolice.gov were ignored with almost enthusiastic promptness. So she was prepared to stand there and wait for as long as it took.

She wondered why Jennings had picked her. She couldn't believe it was just because he had knocked her salad all over the floor. All through their lunch, she had waited for him to let slip some off-colour hint that he was planning to get into her knickers, but none came. And there had been no casual racist remarks or – what would have been worse – hearty and hamfisted attempts to convince her he was totally unprejudiced, as long as she could do the job. He wasn't even very bossy, as bosses go. He talked to her like an equal, though a young and inexperienced one. He'd winced, once, when she called him 'sir' within the waitress's hearing.

Still, whatever his motive, Jennings wanted her on the case. And Zerkah intended to make the most of it. She peered into the office again, and saw Inspector Watts bent over the desk reading a magazine. She bit her lip. Earlier, when she'd first knocked, he'd been on the telephone, and he'd covered the mouthpiece to tell her to wait in the corridor. Now he wasn't even *pretending* to be busy.

She knocked on the glass, and opened the door again, sticking her head around and smiling.

'You free now, sir?'

Watts looked up from *Motorcycle Mechanics*, frowning.

'I thought I told you to wait outside?'

'Yes, sir,' Zerkah agreed, politely, 'but I thought you might have forgotten me.'

Watts tutted. 'Well, I haven't. Wait outside.' And he lowered his head again, and went back to his magazine.

'Yes, sir,' Zerkah muttered, withdrawing.

It was twenty past three.

At ten to five, Watts folded up his magazine, turned off his computer and, as he left the office to go home, he told Zerkah that he could see her tomorrow morning at eight thirty sharp.

'What,' Mischief wondered, gazing at the dental hygiene section of the local Market Harvest hypermart, 'is a *Sports Toothbrush*? Is cleaning your teeth an Olympic event now? Is there a Modern Pentadentathlon? Flossing, brushing, slooshing, gobbing and the downhill gargle?'

Replacing the new streamlined brushing device for today's fast-moving world, the Trickster progressed to Frozen Foods.

'High in polyunsaturates; high in fibre. Low in saturated fats, which are associated with raised blood cholesterol levels and increased coronary risk . . .' A young man in an Aran sweater was reading to his girlfriend from the notes on the back of a beef korma that he had picked out of the freezer cabinet.

'Yuh, that'll do, James,' the ash-blonde replied. 'In fact, get a couple and we'll put them in the fridge.'

Mischief moved in, wearing a smile of inoffensive reasonableness.

'Excuse me. I couldn't help overhearing you there. I wonder if you can tell me – what actually *is* a polyunsaturate?'

'I'm sorry?' the Aran sweater replied, glancing worriedly at his girl-friend.

'These polyunsaturates that carry less association with raised blood cholesterol levels and increased coronary risk,' Mischief insisted. 'Why are they better for you than saturated fats?'

'Well ... er,' the Aran sweater began, 'you see, they don't, you know, give you heart attacks as much ...'

'They reduce coronary risk by not giving you heart attacks?'

'Umm ... exactly ...'

The ash-blonde sighed impatiently. 'Polyunsaturates are just healthier, obviously. Look, are you doing some kind of survey?' she demanded.

'Oh, I'm sorry,' Mischief said, 'I didn't explain. Yes, I'm involved in research concerning consumer-awareness of the latest developments in dietary science. Have you read in the newspapers recently any articles indicating that a diet high in tostanmarmites may have a pelotherapeutic effect on certain types of phoren lesions?'

'Umm, I think we did see something about that, didn't we, Helen?'

'Maybe in the *Independent*,' ash-blonde suggested.

'Yuh, that'll be it,' Aran sweater declared. 'Amazing stuff. But then, it's just common sense, I suppose.'

'Well, I can see that you both take a very responsible attitude to health and diet,' the Trickster congratulated them. 'As a representative of the food retail industry, may I say how gratifying it is to know that there are customers who appreciate our efforts to keep the consumer informed. I'd give the Madras a miss, if I were you. It's been shown that cardamom can cause penile withering in donkeys.'

People believe such *shit*, thought Mischief, wandering towards the bakery. You just overload them with jargon and theory. You tell them that they should leap at financial opportunities because Jupiter is in Scorpio this week – and they blow their wages on porkbelly futures. You insist that their wedding ring gives off vibes of an imminent illness in the family – and they're scoffing down the antibiotics like there's no tomorrow. You get some actor in a white coat to suggest that butter will make their hearts explode – and they start spreading axle grease on their sliced white as if their lives depended on it.

But tell them to name five planets. Get them to explain the workings of the space-time continuum. Ask them what a hardened artery is.

'Mummy, can I have a cream cake? Mummy? Mummy, can I have a cream cake? Mu-um? MUM? Can I have . . .' A four-year-old was being trolleyed past a display of cakes and buns.

'Nah, Shelley. They're not real,' lied Mummy, offhandedly. 'They're just toy ones.'

Jesus, kid, get used to it. You're going to spend the rest of your life having people tell you lies – just to shut you up, or take your money, or feed your insecurities. But it worked, Shelley. You just shut up and believed it; people do. They believe that their paraplegia can be cured by some American millionaire touching their brow. They believe that their tomorrows are drawn in the patterns of tea-leaves. And at least one of them, apparently, believes that for every drop of rain that falls a flower grows.

Life's too short, Shell. Life's too short.

Mischief passed the deli counter and turned up the canned goods aisle. The tinned tomatoes section was always a high spot of the supermarket trip. On every visit, there was a new kind of tinned tomatoes on offer. It had started when ordinary tinned tomatoes had been joined on the shelf by tinned chopped tomatoes. Then, a year or so later, the consumer had been introduced to the convenient delights of Tinned Chopped Tomatoes with Italian Herbs (*Ideal For Sauces, Pizzas and Casseroles*). The floodgates were open. In a very short time, the tinned tomatoes section had expanded to include Tinned Chopped Tomatoes with Indian Spices (*Ideal For Curries*) and Tinned Chopped Tomatoes with Chilli and Red Beans (*Ideal For Chilli Con Carne*).

Pausing only to re-package the original tinned chopped tomatoes as The Original Tinned Chopped Tomatoes (*Ideal For Recipes Requiring Tinned Chopped Tomatoes*), the dedicated men and women of Tinned Chopped Tomatoes Inc. had formed a huddle and set to work on something really special. And now the fruit of their labour was available to a breathless general public. Ladies and gentlemen, let's hear it for Tinned Chopped Tomatoes With Added Pips (*Ideal For Authentic-Style Home-Cooked Meals*).

The punters couldn't fling them into their trolleys fast enough.

CHAPTER NINE

To his horror, the Reverend Michael Cutforth was making headlines.

Clapham Cleric Slams Docs was one such. *Paradise Closed to Pill-Pushers, Claims Holy Joe* was another.

All this commotion had been generated by a piece that Cutforth had written for his parish magazine. To quote him:

> *If we believe, as Christians, that Our Lord cured the blind, the lame, even lepers, simply by touching them, then we have, in principle, allowed the possibility of what is now called faith-healing.*

The Reverend Cutforth later realised that, had he left it there, his little essay would have had no effect beyond the confusion felt by his less theologically inquisitive parishioners. But he had concluded the piece as follows:

> *. . . and so I believe that all Christians, and most especially Christian physicians, must think hard before dismissing the adherents of faith-healing as cranks or charlatans. In fact, I will go further: I contend that a good Christian must allow that faith-healing is a modern reality. Or else, what is faith?*

As soon as the xeroxed copies of the *Clapham Parish Voice* hit the streets, the inexorably ravenous media fell upon it. Cutforth's article was picked up by a quality national, in which it ran as part of a series on alternative medicine. One of the tabloids, in the middle of a quiet week, promoted the issue to the level of a controversy, and ran a phone-in vote under the banner: *Potty Priest or Crusading Cleric?* YOU'RE *the Jury an our Clarion-Call lines!*

Now it was Sunday morning, and the Reverend Cutforth, nervously munching toast and marmite, was contemplating the sermon he was about to give. Preoccupied, he turned on the television, which he tended to regard as a meditative tool. Usually he would just let his eyes rest on the flickering screen, while his mind drifted off and pottered about. Today, however, this was not possible. As the cranky old set went through its sluggish routine of putting a picture together, the Reverend Cutforth recognised his own face flipping lazily through the rising frames of the incontinent horizontal hold. Cutforth paused, a slice of toast gripped between his teeth,

The television picture changed to a shot of a middle-aged woman standing outside the church. For a moment Cutforth couldn't place her, but then realised that she was the lady from the flowershop.

'Oh, he's a strong-willed young man, the pastor,' she said, with an approving frown. 'He'll not kowtow to the Establishment – not him. He's the sort who'd rather stick to his principles, even if it means losing his job.'

Cutforth groaned. He wondered if the Bishop was watching.

The presenter's face appeared. 'So, as feelings run high here in South London, the controversial cleric is in this house behind me, doubtless seeking spiritual guidance as to what—'

The controversial cleric turned off the TV and sought spiritual guidance. He poured himself a brandy.

'I hope you'll let me off this one, Lord,' he said out loud. 'Er . . . have one yourself.'

A mile away in Balham, at precisely the moment that the Reverend Michael Cutforth was asking God to waive the licensing laws, an inconspicuous figure was walking up the path of a well-tended garden at the furthest limit of the parish.

Mischief stopped at the green front door. It was a cared-for door. The paint was recent and streakless. The stained-glass sunrise window was scrupulously clean. The brass letterbox had been polished weekly.

Having screwed the top off a tube of superglue, Mischief squeezed the contents into the tiny gap between the door and doorjamb along the top edge. Another two tubes filled the crack along the vertical. Just to be sure, another tube was spent between the bottom of the door and the crazy-paved doorstep. With casual stealth, Mischief crept around to the dahlia-clad back garden, where another four tubes of instant cement sealed the back door. It would trap the occupants for maybe forty minutes. Even thirty minutes would be enough.

A little surprise nestled deep in the pipes at the high end of the church organ. One arpeggio, and that would be number five in the bag.

A little later, Cutforth was peering from behind a pillar at the first full house he'd ever played to. The place was packed. Every pew was crammed, and the aisles were full of jostling camera crews. The pastor glanced at his watch. Mr Sumner, the organist, was uncharacteristically late, but Cutforth didn't feel he could delay any longer. After a quick word with one of his regulars in the front pew, he climbed the five stairs to the pulpit. The hubbub of conversation faded, and Cutforth began.

'Good morning.'

As he spoke all the television lights came on. They were blinding, and in their blue-white glare Cutforth lost sight of the congregation completely. He blinked a few times, but he couldn't see a thing.

'Oh, dear . . . good gracious. Now I know how Saul felt on the road to Damascus,' he said. There were a few titters from the audience. 'Er, yes, anyway, good morning. And how nice to see so many gathered for this act of worship – not that I *can* see you, now,' he quipped, rubbing his eyes. This time there was a definite ripple. Cutforth allowed himself to relax a little. They were friendly, at least. 'Umm, due to the lack of an organist, I have asked Mrs Piper to lead us in the first hymn, *Praise my Soul the King of Heaven*, which is number 325 in your hymn books.'

Mrs Piper's strong, confident, atonal contralto burst forth with the opening lines of the hymn, and the rest of the congregation, having given her a sporting head-start, set off in shambolic pursuit a few bars behind. Thanks to an early spurt, she kept her pursuers at bay for most of the first verse. Just as they were gaining ground, the male members of the following pack realised that crafty old Mrs Piper had chosen a key in which only use of the most uninhibited falsetto might allow them to keep pace on the corners. By the time they'd changed down an octave, she'd opened up an unassailable lead of three lines, which she held to the tape. She sat back in her pew, smirking, whilst the rest of the congregation were still breathlessly encouraging each other to praise with them the God of Grace.

Cutforth was waiting for the last few stragglers to cross the line when Mr Sumner, the organist, pushed his way through the crowd at the back, and walked purposefully up the aisle. He nodded to Cutforth, mouthed 'not my fault', and took his place on the organ seat.

At the back of the church, in the final pew, Mischief smiled.

'Ahem. The subject of my sermon today,' said Cutforth, 'is the miracles of Our Lord and of his Apostles. I just felt,' he continued, 'that it was a topic I should touch on. I don't know why.'

There were a few titters from the congregation, and knowing laughter from the TV crews.

'If we look at the story in today's reading, I expect most of us believe that it was miraculous for Our Lord to have cured a chap of the palsy. But was it miraculous simply because it was Jesus Christ Who did it? Would it have been a miracle if He had cured a man afflicted with, for instance, athlete's foot?'

'No!' chorused a handful of people, cheerfully. This, they reckoned, was good stuff. Worth getting out of bed for.

The young pastor was surprised but delighted by the response. He pressed his point home with a fist banged on the lectern. 'Right! Now, the Apostles, they performed miracles too. So, how did they know how? Did Jesus tell them? Did He leave them a little book: *Miracles for Beginners – Impress Your Friends, Break the Ice at Temples?*'

'No!' offered the delighted congregation, who were happy to do this kind of thing all afternoon.

'No! They could do it because they were filled with the Holy Spirit! They had been born again in the church of Jesus Christ!'

'All right! All right!' agreed the congregation.

Cutforth's heart was pumping; the heat of the lights was making him sweat. He was giving them a sermon that would keep them talking right through till the pubs shut.

'Miracles *can* still happen – the power of God is still amongst us! That's the wonder of the power of God! I can feel it here today! Can you feel it here today?'

'YEAH! YESSIR!'

The congregation were on their feet. Cutforth's hair was wild, and his eyes were flashing. He felt like Little Richard. He wished he'd kept up his piano lessons.

'All right! Now, we're going to sing a hymn, and I want to hear the power and the love of God in every note! Hit it, Mr Sumner!'

Mr Sumner slammed into the first chord of 'Jerusalem', and inside the organ pipes that corresponded to the octave above middle C, four hundred pingpong balls stirred and bobbled, as they waited impatiently for their particular keys to be depressed. The congregation threw themselves lustily into the first line as the Reverend Michael Cutforth egged them on, slapping his hand on the pulpit and trying to inject a little bluesy gospel into the notion of Those Feet walking upon England's mountains green. Mr Sumner hit the B above middle C. In the corresponding pipe there was a single pingpong ball, which was launched on a rush of air, out into the vaulted roof of the church.

It described a silent arc above the seething congregation, bounced on a beam and dropped from thirty feet onto the bald head of the Bishop of Wandsworth. It ricocheted off his shiny pate, and shot straight into the gaping mouth of the lady from the flowershop.

At that moment, Mr Sumner played a big rich chord in the loaded octave, and several columns of pingpong balls were whooshed into the upper atmosphere of St Will's. Suddenly the air was full of pingpong balls, which rained down on the congregation like a plague of eyes. They pinged from pew to pew; they ponged off Sunday hats; they pinballed from this nose to that forehead; they caromed along the aisles and shot up into the creases of Mrs Piper's bloomers. They got under the feet of roving cameramen, who skidded to the floor still filming; they settled in the laps of scribbling journos; they were bright meteors on the front-page shots of a dozen snappers.

The dismayed and confused Michael Cutforth surveyed the scene from his pulpit. He cringed as the Bishop stepped on a pingpong ball and fell flat on his Very Reverend bottom. In an instant of epiphany, Cutforth saw that the most sublime moment of his preaching career was really terribly, terribly ridiculous. He felt less like Little Richard than Little Bo Peep.

At the back of the church, Mischief sat quite still, viewing the mayhem with calm satisfaction. It could hardly have gone better.

'Let us therefore cast off the works of darkness, and let us put on the armour of light,' murmured the Trickster. 'Romans, chapter 13, verse 12.'

CHAPTER TEN

Mason woke up crying. He'd dreamed of Chris, yet again, and she had screamed at him, pulling away as he tried to kiss her, spitting, hissing, 'I don't *love* you, Mason! I just don't *love* you any more!' He'd turned to his mother, who'd shrugged, and smiled. 'No one does, dear. Obviously.' Chris was alight with lust – she had that flush and that lip-chewing grin that he remembered so keenly – but still she pushed him away. She wouldn't touch him, not even for a quick fuck. 'I just don't love you. Are you *stupid*?'

'*Am* I stupid?' he wondered. He thumped the back of his head repeatedly into the pillow, staring at the ceiling. It was mid-morning. The sun was high and bright and Chris would be at work, concentrating on her writing, talking to her colleagues, drinking coffee, not thinking of him. Maybe she was looking forward to a date that evening, had put on daring underwear, knowing it would be appreciated. She might be taking time out to make a promised phone call, lighting a cigarette and talking dirty in a low voice, right there in the office, as she had once to him . . .

'Christ, *please*,' Mason begged silently. 'Please, please.' Three years and still these dreams, these terrible, self-flaying visions. When was it going to stop? 'She *can't* not love me. She loved me *before*. She loved me to death. How can she not love me?'

He got up, dragged on a pair of jeans and went to the kitchen. He made a cup of tea, and took it through to the sitting room, where he sat on the floor and picked up the phone. He dialled Bart's number.

'Good morning, Mason – how's life?' came Bart's unfailingly cheerful voice.

'Crap,' Mason told him. 'I'm having a major Chris attack. Do you fancy a drink at lunchtime?'

Bart sighed. 'Can't, I'm afraid. I have a visitor, and she appears to be staying all day. Not that I mind – on the contrary. Look, old love, I think it's time for some harsh truths.'

Mason sighed. 'What, again?' He looked at himself in the long mirror beside the window, naked to the waist, cross-legged, hunched and defeated. It wasn't that pretty. His hair was getting too long, falling over his red-rimmed, grey-ringed eyes. His three-day stubble was dark against the pale, sunless skin of his face, and his lips were dry from sleep and alcohol. He glanced at the two empty Muscadet bottles beside the sofa, and the bowl of congealed tomato soup that he hadn't got around to eating the previous night. A litter of chewed matches surrounded the ashtray, and he leaned over to pick up the box, shaking it. It was empty.

'You haven't moved an inch,' Bart was saying. 'And I understand that. But it's time now. Get away for a while. Pootle off to France or the States or something. *Live*, Mason.'

Mason lobbed the empty matchbox towards the wastepaper basket, and it bounced off the wall onto the floor. 'Oh, yeah – I'm sure the Social would pony up for a fortnight at Disneyland, if I were to put it to them,' he snapped. 'Be fucking serious.'

He could hear Bart lighting a cigarette, and exhaling. 'You know that I'd give you the money, Mase. As much as you need.'

Mason gulped and tutted at himself. 'Yeah, sorry – I know you would. But it wouldn't help to run away, would it?' He dipped his index finger in the cold soup and licked it.

'A problem in London is not necessarily a problem in New York, old thing. Anyway – the offer's there. Listen, give me a call tomorrow and we'll sort out a roister – yes?'

'Yeah, let's. Who's the woman, by the way? Anyone I know?'

Bart chuckled. 'You *don't* know any women, Mason – that's half your trouble. But I'll work on it. I shall add it to my list of entertaining projects.' He took a drag on his cigarette. 'Anyway, I must dash. I can hear the poppet coming upstairs carrying my breakfast and the newspapers. And, with my usual exquisite timing, I feel yet another erection coming on.'

'Oh, thanks,' Mason said. 'Rub it in.'

'I plan to,' Bart admitted.

Bart was thoughtful as he put down the phone. Thoughtful and a little cross. He loved Mason dearly, and wanted to help. But he was also irritated that his friend was still, after all this time, in the grip of a lovelorn depression. To Bart, who rode the waves of life's troubles with the balance and confidence of a surfer, any prolonged unhappiness smacked of self-indulgence.

Over the last year or two, on any evening out, Mason's conversation had threatened to skid at any moment into sticky, sorrowful self-analysis. Sometimes it was difficult for Bart not to lean across and shake the kid by the shoulders and tell him to snap out of it.

Bart smiled, mocking himself. 'The kid'. But he recognised the appropriateness of the terminology. He did feel like Mason's big brother. It had always been like that. When he had been at home during the summers in his teens, and Maria had hauled Mason around to visit, Bart had not in the least resented having to amuse him. The kid was bright and funny, and strangely unimpressible. Bart was unused to having people not be impressed by him, and he rather enjoyed the challenge.

Nobody had been happier than Bart when Mason and Chris hooked up. Chris's cynicism – brittle and crystalline – was slowly dissolved by Mason's clear, constant affection, like rock-salt in spring water. But since it had all gone wrong between them, that ability of Mason's to be just who he was, to put his feelings out on show and to believe in their value, had become – well – a drag. It was sad and a little sorry, like seeing an aging actress forever rerunning her once-acclaimed Juliet, oblivious to the balcony creaking, the backdrop fading, the audience wincing because Romeo is half her age.

And, as he lit another cigarette, Bart had to admit that he felt guilty too. Not because he was responsible for Chris and Mason meeting in the first place, but because there was something afoot that he was keeping from his best friend – and Bart was not naturally deceptive, even by omission. He would have felt better about it if Mason were involved in a proper life of his own – a job, a woman, a goal. Anything.

What Mason needed, Bart decided, was not so much a diversion, as a disruption, to break the cycle of longing and hope and disappointment. Something would have to be arranged.

Bart looked up as his lover came into the bedroom carrying a breakfast tray. She put it down on the bedside table and shucked her dressing-gown.

'Who was that on the phone?' she asked, clambering onto the huge bed, and leaning over to kiss him.

'It was Mason,' Bart said, sighing.

She stopped, halfway to his lips, and her shoulders sagged.

'Oh,' she nodded.

Bart put his hand to her face. 'Yes. I know. Intrudes on the moment somewhat, doesn't it?'

That evening, Mischief poured another glass of champagne, lit a cigarette and finished pasting newspaper reports of Michael Cutforth's humiliation into an increasingly thick scrapbook.

On the facing page were glued clippings of the Venton Street Jam. It had been the lead piece in two tabloids, and all the other rags used it inside. *Vice Girls Brawl on Lawyer's Doorstep*. And Westlake had got arrested too – disturbing the peace. Quite a result.

The newspapers, from the rags to the qualities, had adopted Mischief's campaign like a family adopts a puppy. They were cooing over it, giving it the run of the place, feeding it constantly and even delighting in telling it off when it misbehaved. It had become the centre of their attention, and each day they waited eagerly, watched closely, to see what engaging and noteworthy new naughtiness it might get up to next. Even the TV stations were taking an interest, popping in each evening like a next-door neighbour to hear what the little scamp had got its nose into today. It was vital to Mischief's plans that the media should pump up the campaign. The idea was to undermine the credibility of these charlatans and spooks, making them risible in the eyes of a public who, it seemed, habitually gave them inexplicable respect.

Mischief smiled, sipped champagne, and spread the cards on the coffee table. There were fewer now, but still a way to go. The card that carried the number nine was missing, having been posted overseas some time ago. It had been addressed to a Mr A.G. Sparkes.

And if the word on the wire was correct, the A.G. Sparkes hit was working out beautifully.

In 1981, the name Arnie Sparkes was familiar only to that cultish band of science-fantasy readers whose every summer was enlivened by the publication of the latest novel in the *Dreamland* series. That year, in fact, was a sad one for those readers, because it was then that Arnie finally tired of living on the meagre income generated by his tales of sub-hippy sorcery and sado-masochistic sex. He announced that he would work no longer in the woodnymph-and-nookie genre. He quit California, moved East and disappeared.

Four years later, a book called *Metaperception: The Dreaming Road to Success and Happiness* hit the stands. It was written by one A.G. Sparkes, and it laid out a method by which anyone could achieve their most cherished aspirations by interpreting their dreams.

Metaperception was one of America's first half-baked self-help books, and it sold in numbers beyond even its author's wildest directed-dreams. Arnie had hit on a good thing. In the 1988 follow-up, *Rousing the Colossus: Harness the Power of Metaperception*, A.G. Sparkes revealed that the 'You' you are when practising Sparkesian sleep – the controlling, happy, confident You – is actually a higher form of life. Arnie, for instance, was so much higher a form that, as he revealed two years later in *Metaperception: The Path to Nirvana*, he was now like unto a god.

To his credit, Arnie wasn't snobbish about his deification. All of us, he said, have the potential to become gods – and the secret was available to anyone who cared to study for a week at the Universal Church of Human Divinity in Woodstock, New York ($2500 per seeker-after-truth – local State taxes may apply). By the mid-eighties, Arnie's congregation had evolved into a byzantine hierarchy that made the Catholic Church look like a local scout group. Oiled by a constant influx of tax-deductible contributions, the machinery of the Church rolled smoothly and unstoppably onward. This was just as well, because no one in the Church had actually set eyes on the Divine Arnie since early '91.

He still lived in his modest clapboard house in Cape Cod, protected by video cameras and a 24-hour security team. In all weathers, day in and day out, a uniformed guard would be posted at the front gate, moving on the occasional gawper and discouraging Jehovah's Witnesses. Arnie could be seen from the street, wandering from room to shadowy room, like a figment of his own imagination. He would occasionally bark orders through the intercom to his personal Cerberus – but no one was allowed into the house itself. No one, that is, except a succession of blonde and lissom live-in *au pairs*, each of whom was replaced at the end of her three-month contract.

Over the years many blonde, lissom ex-Arnie *au pairs* had been approached by journalists wanting the inside story on life with a god – but not a single one of them had agreed to be interviewed. As one disgruntled New York hack had remarked, 'I bet they get paid more for keeping their mouths shut once they've left the house than they did for keeping them open when they were in there.'

The truth about A.G. Sparkes, had any former pillow-plumper decided to tell it, was less exciting than popular speculation. Arnie simply hàted the human race. He just *loathed* people. He despised everything about them, from their dumb and futile triumphs to their pointless little tragedies. He didn't want the stupid, bleating, grinning, squalling creatures around him – and he could afford to indulge his aversion.

Arnie, essentially, was a miserable old bastard.

Mischief had no way of knowing the depth of Arnie's contempt for his fellow human beings, but it was a fair bet that anyone who shut themselves away from the world for two decades was no Pollyanna. Working from a terminal at an internet café, Mischief had contacted *Hot Poop*, the American gossip magazine, and planted a story that purported to be the first ever interview with a former Arnie housekeeper.

The subject of the interview was one Lindy-May Corn, who revealed that Arnie was a deeply lonely and withdrawn man. Sure, he liked to fool around, but you could tell that his heart wasn't in it. As Mischief had Lindy-May point out, a woman can tell, right? It was like something was missing from his life. Kinda funny, huh? Here was this old guy – still good-looking an'all, but, even with all his money and his, like, fabulous wealth, he was real sad, y'know? Lindy-May guessed it was true what they say – money can't buy you happiness, right?

You know, one time, over breakfast, A.G. had looked at her and said, 'Lindy-child, I've been successful, and I've been rich, and I've helped a few folk along life's Interstate, but you know what I miss? I miss having someone make me laugh. Sometimes,' A.G. said to Lindy-May that bright New England morning, 'sometimes I feel like I'd give a million dollars for a real, good, honest-to-God, big-hearted laugh. Yup – *one million dollars for a real good laugh.*'

Without a word of a lie, Lindy-May just reckoned that was about the most sorriest thing any human being could ever say.

Multitudes around the world agreed with her. Touched by Arnie's sorrow, and wishing to offer something in return for all he had done for humanity, magazine readers across the globe set aside the article, sniffed back a tear and turned their minds to the selfless task of giving Arnie a giggle. With no thought of reward, and certainly without any expectation of receiving a cool mill in folding bills, these altruistic chuckle-makers resolved to brighten A.G. Sparkes's final days.

The morning after the Lindy-May article appeared in *Hot Poop*, Arnie was woken at five o'clock by the sound of a voice coming through a bullhorn outside. Some guy seemed to be denying that he would say his wife was fat. Peering out from behind the curtains, Arnie saw a man in a loud-check suit addressing the house from the sidewalk.

'... BUT THE COASTGUARD ASKED HER TO MOVE SO THAT THE TIDE COULD COME IN!!!' the man shouted, in tones of nerve-grinding jollity. 'SHE WENT TOPLESS IN KEY WEST AND CAUSED AN ECLIPSE IN MIAMI!!! I WOULDN'T SAY SHE HAD A BODY-HAIR PROBLEM, BUT SHE HAS DANDRUFF IN HER PANTYHOSE!!! AND WHAT ABOUT KIDS TODAY?? MY KID CAME HOME FROM SCHOOL ...'

Arnie, disgusted and uncomprehending, told the security guy to move the jerk away. But even as Cerberus was accompanying said jerk to the end of the street ('... AND THE KID SAYS, "CUZ THAT'S WHAT DADDY SAID HE WAS GONNA DO TO THE BABYSITTER!!!" HEY, BUD, KEEP YOUR HANDS OFF THE SUIT, OKAY? OUCH!!! UGH!!! ...'), a quartet of circus clowns drew up outside the house in an exploding automobile. The fenders popped off the car in a cloud of smoke, and the soft-top concertinaed up and down of its own accord. The clowns, all size twenty-four boots and revolving bow-ties, flollopped onto the sidewalk and began kicking each other in the seats of their generous pants. As they tumbled and tripped and threw buckets of water, Cerberus came pounding back up the street, hollering at them to get away from Mr Sparkes's front gate. He ran open-mouthed into a custard pie, which undermined his authority somewhat, and he felt ill-equipped to deal either with the clowns or with the gag-telling jerk, who returned to resume his bullhorn patter whilst holding a handkerchief to his bloodied nose.

'OKAY, SO DERE'S DIS GUY WHO'S GODDA PEDIS SHAPED LIKE A TEDDIS RACKET ...'

A cab pulled up and disgorged a drag queen with a ghetto-blaster.

She flicked the tape to 'play' and proceeded to give her mime of Barbra Streisand performing 'The Way We Were' on a small boat in heavy seas. It was a gutsy performance, which she continued even when accidentally clouted about the head by the next arrivals – a duo who recreated the timeless Laurel and Hardy routine that involves a bucket of whitewash and a ten-foot plank.

Arnie retreated towards the back of the house. He couldn't understand it. Why were these weirdos invading his nice quiet life? Seething with detestation for his fellow man, woman and drag queen, he went through to the kitchen. In the back yard, a man with a beer-gut was doing the trick in which a condom is pulled over the head as far as the top lip and then inflated by blowing like mad through the nose. Catching sight of Arnie, indistinctly, through his lubricated rubber mask, the man gave a cheery little wave.

'Hi there, Mr Sparkes,' his mouth said.

Shocked and a little scared, Arnie yanked down the blind and slumped back against the refrigerator. He closed his eyes, took a deep breath and screamed, 'FUCK OFF! JUST FUCK THE FUCK OFF!!'

But, as Arnie was to discover over the ensuing weeks, months and years, there was no chance that these delegates of drollery, these messengers of mirth, would ever fuck off. Indeed, they were mere envoys from the Land of Laughter, which was about to develop a new tittering tourist trade with cranky old Cape Cod – or, come to that, with anywhere else Arnie Sparkes might decide to hole up. The whole world had decided to make Arnie laugh.

'. . . AND THE FARMER SAYS, "SUIT YOURSELF, MISTER – THE COWS ARE OUT IN THE BARN!!!" HAHAHAHAHA!!! HEY, MR SPARKES, I KNOW IT'S AN OLD GAG, BUT I ALWAYS SAY A GAG'S ONLY AN OLD GAG IF YOU'VE HEARD IT BEFORE – AM I RIGHT, MR SPARKES, HUH?? AM I RIGHT????'

CHAPTER ELEVEN

One morning a few days later, Bart hoiked himself up on to one elbow on the bed, pushed his hair back with the other hand, and said, 'I want to talk about Mason.'

Chris looked over her shoulder at him. Her legs were astride a small stool, and she was bent forward with her hands flat on a dressing table.

'What – this instant?'

Bart swung his feet onto the floor, and stood up. 'As soon as we're finished here. Tell me, are you, on the whole, pro- or anti-cane?'

'In the bedroom – anti. I prefer something with a bit more weight.'

'Pity. I rather like this.' Bart indicated a canework easy-chair.

'Can I be of assistance?' asked a passing salesperson.

Chris straightened up, letting go of the price tag that hung from the mirror of the dresser.

'No – I'm just looking, thanks.'

'Story of my life,' Bart remarked.

They strolled out of the furniture department of Harrods and made for a restaurant down the road towards Chelsea. Chris apologised for having insisted on the detour to look at dressers, but went out of her way to assure Bart that his opinion on such matters was always welcome. And it was true that, as long as she had known him, she had deferred to Bart on matters of taste. They had met when she was a rookie on a giveaway girlie magazine and had been researching London's Most Eligible Bachelors. Some editorial Tamsin or Tara had suggested Bart as a candidate, and she had tracked him to a basement drinking club on Greek Street, where he was being lovingly assaulted by a peripheral member of the royal family. She'd sidled up to him on the blindside of the panting acolyte, and said, 'Hello. Can I talk to you?'

He'd turned towards her, clasped her hand and yelled, 'Melanie! How's Auntie Sara?' Then he'd explained to the third-rank Windsor that his cousin had turned up and that, much as it grieved him, he really must give her some attention.

Chris had known instantly that she couldn't help getting on with a man who could lie with such fluent gallantry.

When they arrived at the restaurant down the street from Harrods, there was a brief but unseemly squabble amongst the waitresses over the delivery of menus. The winner smirked as she whooshed a napkin fondly into Bart's lap, and then tossed another carelessly at Chris's midriff. Chris bit her lip against a welling chuckle.

'Jesus, Bart,' she said, as the waitress reluctantly retreated, 'doesn't it get boring?'

'Does what get boring, dearheart?' Bart asked, tapping out a cigarette.

His question, Chris knew, was disingenuous, but indicative of Bart's perception of the world. He'd talked once about being tall – he was six foot five – and he'd said that, to him, everyone else was the same height. They were 'down there'. He supposed, he said, that average-size people were always aware of how tall other people were, because they had to adjust their viewing angle. But if you were to ask him what height someone was, he'd have no idea – and, what's more, he couldn't imagine what it must be like to *have* an idea.

And it was the same, Chris suspected, with his effect on the opposite sex. As far as Bart knew, all men went through life as he did, being flirted with, propositioned, bothered by women. It was like the hum of the fridge – too constant to be noticeable.

'So,' Chris said as the wine was poured, 'what about Mason?'

Bart nodded. 'Hm. Yes. He's not a happy boy, you know.'

'And?'

It was too defensive a retort, and Chris knew it. She reached across and picked up Bart's cigarette packet. She looked at him, and he looked back, tilting his head.

'Something's still there, then,' he observed, with a slight pursing of the lips.

'Of course.' She lit a Sobranie. 'You know that.'

There was a silence, interrupted by the waitress asking, somewhat breathily, if they were ready to order. Bart asked for the special, whatever it was, and Chris said she'd have the same. She picked up her wine and sipped it, looking at Bart.

'I want to send him away,' Bart said, eventually. 'Give him some money, if he'll take it, and just get him out of the rut he's in. Send him to the States, or Japan. Anywhere.' He stubbed out his cigarette. 'What do you think?'

Chris put down her glass and tried to think what she thought. Something lupine moved inside her, something fierce and lonely, something framed against a horizon. She had loved Mason so much – once.

She thought of Christmas. As a child, there had been a huge thrill in Christmas, an unabridgeable rush of excitement and belief – a completeness of faith in it. When you're grown-up, you do the washing-up before the presents are opened. You sort out the drinks, and organise rubbish bags to put the wrapping paper in. Much as you love it, you're not transported by it any more. It's just a day with hours and minutes. It needs organising, because it's an event. It has a tomorrow.

God, if it could be childlike again. If only, with all you knew as a grown-up, you could still get that rush. That would be so much better even than it had been, because you'd understand it, and savour it. You'd know how precious that was. But that's the paradox – you can't ever feel like you felt before, because having felt it before makes it feel different if you feel it again.

Chris looked up at Bart. 'Do you think he'd go?' she asked.

Bart shrugged. 'I hope so. He needs to get away.'

'And you want to get him away from me.'

On other tables, glasses chinked. Smoke drifted in the air. A champagne cork popped to hooted approval.

'Yes,' Bart said. He put his hand across the table, and touched Chris's fingers. 'I think it's for the best, my sweet.'

Chris nodded.

'Whose?'

Bart looked to the side. He pushed his hair back, and scanned the table. 'Have you got the lighter?' he said, reaching for his cigarettes.

'Two specials!' announced the waitress, and slid the plates onto the table. 'Black pepper?'

Over the meal they talked about journalism and wine and politics. Bart's take on all of them was self-deprecatingly solipsistic. His throwaway refrain was that he didn't think about anything much outside of its effect on his day-to-day life. Chris knew this was a facetious conversational pose, though a defensive one. Bart was kinder and more thoughtful than he pretended. It was one of the things that made him lovable. And so, if he thought that Mason should go away, then she had to accept it was true. Except . . .

Except, there was something else there. There was an advantage to Bart in Mason's going. She knew him well enough to know that.

'Well, my love,' Bart said, patting his mouth with a napkin, 'no prospect entrances me more than trailing you around the shops for the rest of the afternoon and ending up at dusk in some discreet eaterie to while away the twilight hours in idle intimacy.' He was back to his public self. He was Bart-in-spades again. 'But there is a little matter I must attend to this evening, and there's no getting away from it.'

Chris folded her knife and fork. 'Okay. I'm distraught, obviously.'

'You'll get over it,' Bart assured her. 'A digestif, before we peck each other's cheeks and part?'

'Rude not to, eh?' Chris grinned. 'Brandy?'

'Very,' Bart nodded. 'Oh, sorry. Did I mishear you?'

Standing by the kerb on Sloane Street, looking for a cab, Bart took out his mobile phone and left a brief message on Mason's answering machine. He felt a bit guilty about it, to be honest, but it couldn't be helped. He had somewhere to go, and he was going there.

CHAPTER TWELVE

Mason's dreams were getting worse. That morning, he'd woken up from a real sweat-sodden one about his father.

A dream of his father. He hadn't had one of those in ages.

In this dream, Mason is doing what he does for a living. He's putting together a page layout – except that he's eight years old in the dream, and working on the kitchen table at home. He's clumsy and he's knocking over cups of tea and jars of flowers and – for God's sake – urns full of ashes. It seems that every time he moves, something else spills or breaks or shatters. And his father's going, 'Oh, you clumsy oaf. Pay attention, you idiotic little shit.' But he's doing his best. He's really trying. And he's whining, 'Sorry, sorry, sorry.' And, to make it worse, he's crying, which his father hates. He's crying, and trying *not* to cry, and knocking stuff over, and his dad's getting crosser and crosser . . .

It really screwed up Mason's morning, that dream. It made him think about things he didn't want to think about.

When Mason's mother, Maria, was sixteen, she attended a posh drama school. She hoped to become a West End actress, and, as a step in the right direction, she played Lady Macbeth in a low-rent room above a pub in Islington. One night she was chatted up by Marty Puxley. He was a cartoonist. Did stuff for *Private Eye* and the Sunday supplements. And he was funny. He really was very, very funny.

Ever since he could remember, Mason had been told how funny his dad was, and by the time he reached adulthood he didn't even know any more whether that was something he remembered himself, or just something he'd been convinced of. But he was certain that his dad made him laugh when he was little. He was pretty sure he remembered that.

He certainly recalled, in a black-and-white-movie sort of way, his father telling him bedtime stories when he was really small. He used to illustrate them, on a big drawing pad – sketching caricatures and landscapes as he went along. And Mason was always the star of these improvised yarns. 'Mason and the Amazing Tricycle'. 'Mason's Seaside Adventure'. Even all these years later, the smell of a Magic Marker made Mason grin happily.

Having gone to college and done graphics himself, Mason understood how economical and scathingly apposite his father's published cartoons were. The old fella had a thin-sliced, zizzing gift for satire. He'd been quite famous in the seventies for sketching mordant portraits of Thatcher and Pinochet and Reagan. There had been an exhibition of satirical art at the Tate a few years back, and two of Marty Puxley's originals were in there, as examples of political lampoon.

But here's the thing that stayed with Mason, that he hid like an ill-advised tattoo. Marie and Marty had split up when their son was six, and it was all Mason's fault. He knew it was his fault, because as an adult, what he mainly remembered of his father was this . . .

'For Christ's sake, watch that paint, you little bastard. Nine out of ten? What happened to the other one? Sod off, I'm busy. What? What do you want? Jesus – call that a dog? How many legs is that? Doesn't look like a dog to me. Yes, yes, very impressive, I'm sure. Now bugger off and let me work.'

Mason didn't find that memory quite so funny. They broke up, his mum and dad, because his dad hated him. Mason was convinced of that. The old man just couldn't stand being around him. Mason couldn't blame him, really. He knew that he would never be as good an artist as his father and he could see how it must have irritated him to have a mediocre child. After all, Marty Puxley was an extremely gifted man.

After the split, Mason used to go and see his dad on weekends. He lived in Camden, which is how Mason had got to know the place. But then Marty started making trips to America, and the weekends got postponed and, eventually, he just stopped turning up at all. He lived in San Francisco or somewhere now. Worked for *Rolling Stone* and magazines like that. Mason hadn't seen him since he was thirteen.

But he caught his dad's cartoons from time to time in newspapers. And though he loved his father's work, it still caused a little hiccup when he saw the scrawled signature in the corner of the frame – 'Puck'.

Actually, what with his dad and Chris, it was amazing that Mason ever opened a periodical at all.

* * *

'Excuse me,' said a six-foot purple duck, indistinctly, 'are you with the Kidderminster Massed Drums?'

Mischief turned, slowly. One has little choice but to turn slowly when one is dressed as a portly kangaroo.

'Because I've lost my sticks, and I was hoping you had a spare pair,' the duck explained, his beak bobbing forlornly.

Mischief's kangaroo head waggled from side to side. 'No, sorry.'

The TV studio was milling with perplexed but excited people in bizarre costumes. It was the night of the Annual Charity Telethon, a live event that had presented to Mischief an irresistible opportunity for a hit. Preparation had all been somewhat hurried, as the announcement of featured celebrities had been made only the previous day. Mischief's plan required a wheel-oiling bribe, and the tight timescales meant that the bribe would have to be personally delivered. The problem, then, was to deliver it without being seen face-to-face. Hence the kangaroo outfit.

Peering out through the slit in the kangaroo's neck, Mischief waddled to the canteen, looking for a man whose e-mail had promised that he would be wearing a yellow Rug Rats T-shirt. Spotting him sitting on his own in the corner nursing a cup of tea, Mischief flollopped over. The guy looked up, as the large kangaroo bumped into his table. He noticed an envelope sticking out of the kangaroo's pouch.

'That it?' he asked, under his breath.

Mischief nodded the kangaroo head, and the man took the envelope.

'Same again after I do it?'

Again, the kangaroo nodded.

'Done deal,' the man said, and he got up and walked out of the canteen.

Mischief turned around inelegantly, made for the toilets on the far side of the canteen, and went into the first stall. It was not easy taking the suit off in such a confined space. As the kangaroo collapsed to the floor, it got stuck on one sneakered foot.

'What on earth do I think I'm doing?' Mischief muttered, grinning.

There were voices outside by the basins, and much opening and shutting of the main door. Mischief sat down on the closed toilet seat, lit a cigarette and waited. It seemed that everyone in the studio had decided to take a leak just then. The kangaroo's head lolled on the low-level cistern, its eyes staring blankly at the toilet-roll holder.

Eventually, there was a lull in the activity, and Mischief got up, opened the door of the stall, and slipped back out into the canteen, envisaging some unsuspecting punter going into the loos later and finding a dead marsupial draped over the bowl in trap one.

Striding down the corridor towards the exit, Mischief turned a corner and walked slap bang into Maria Dixon. There was a brief moment's unspecific apologising before recognition kicked in and Maria exclaimed, 'My God! What are *you* doing here! What a lovely surprise!'

Mischief hesitated for a second before hugging Maria, and kissing her cheek.

'Maria! How are you? I was just dropping something off for a friend. What are *you* doing here?'

'Well, I'm trotting out my party piece for the Telethon,' Maria explained. 'Look – do call. Please do. I must dash, actually. Super to see you!'

Amidst promises to phone soon and arrange dinner, Mischief backed away towards the main door, heart racing. That had been a very awkward moment.

Outside, roped off from the entrance, a gaggle of fans were awaiting the arrival of Damon Chiswick, movie star. His car drew up just as Mischief stepped out into the night, and the gaggle of mousse-haired teenage girls shrieked and waved at him. Damon winked at them as he and his minder trotted up the steps to the studio. As he passed Mischief, he said in an aside to the hired help, 'The blonde in the red jacket . . .'

Mischief tutted. Damon really deserved what was coming.

CHAPTER THIRTEEN

The following morning, as Mason was sitting on his bed tying up his shoelace, the phone rang.

'Damn,' he muttered. He hobbled through to the front room, one shoe off and one shoe on, and picked up the phone. It was his mother.

'There's something I think I ought to tell you,' she said, after an exchange of hellos. 'Your dad's back in the country.'

Mason blinked, and sat down heavily on the sofa.

'God. Is he?' He reached for the box of matches on the small table. 'So ... er ... Well – Jesus,' he murmured, lighting and extinguishing a match. 'Have you seen him? Does he want to see me?'

Maria sighed. 'I don't know, dear. He didn't say.'

'Oh. Did he even mention me?' He stood up, phone held to his ear, and paced lopsidedly up and down the room, shaking the matchbox idly in his loose fist. 'I mean, surely if he wanted to see me, he'd let me know, wouldn't he? It's been nearly fifteen years. You'd think he'd be curious, at the very least of it.'

'Yes,' his mother said, after a short silence. 'You'd think so.'

'How long has he been back?'

'Well, apparently he came back for some millennium event, and he just stayed on.'

Mason paused by the window, rested his forehead on the pane, and groaned.

'Five *months*? He's been here *five months*? Bloody hell.' He turned and sat on the window-ledge. Then he stood up and started to pace again. He couldn't stay still. 'How long have you known he was here?'

Again, Maria sighed. 'A few weeks. I didn't say anything, because I was hoping he'd get in touch with you direct. But I saw him recently and ... I felt you should know.'

'Five months. So he was here for my birthday ...'

'Oh, Mason, I'm sorry. Perhaps I shouldn't have told you.'

'Not even a fucking card. Though why break the habit of a lifetime?'

'What will you do?'

Mason stopped pacing and looked at himself in the mirror. He was wearing his one and only suit and a blue nylon tie. He was fresh-shaven and he noticed that he had a few specks of blood on his collar. But it was his last clean shirt, so sod it.

'I've got a job interview in an hour. I'm going to go to that.' He took a comb from the inside pocket of his jacket and ran it through his hair. 'Apart from that – nothing.'

'I see,' Maria said. 'All right.'

'Listen – if you talk to him, don't you go persuading him to come and see me, okay? If he decides to do it off his own bat, then fine. But—'

'I know,' Maria said quickly. 'I wouldn't. I know.'

'Right,' Mason nodded. 'I've got to run. I'll be late.'

'All right, darling. Good luck.'

Mason said goodbye and hung up. As he went through to the kitchen to lock the back door, Freda slipped in through the catflap. Mason bent and picked her up, and she clawed affectionately at the lapels of his suit.

'You know what's going to happen, don't you?' Mason asked her. 'I'm going to bump into him on the tube. Life's like that. Eight million people in this town, and I'm bound to sit next to my dad on the Northern Line.' He put Freda down and poured some milk into her bowl. 'Not that the old bastard would recognise me, of course. Not until after I'd punched his lights out.'

He picked up his keys from the table, and left the flat, closing the door behind him. As he reached the gate, he stopped and looked down.

'You've only got one shoe on, you idiot,' he said aloud. And as he said it, he could hear his father saying it, and tutting in that disappointed, dismissive way he used to have. And probably still had.

DI David Jennings and WPC Zerkah Sheikh were taking elevenses with the unfortunate Reverend Cutforth. They weren't getting much out of it.

Neither of them was surprised. They'd visited David Daemon, Chuckie Rolls and Henry Westlake, and they hadn't got much out of them, either. During the drive to South London, Jennings had observed that they were a week into the investigation and still clueless.

'And I use the word with the full authority of DCI Jagger,' he grinned ruefully, 'because it's the adjective he employed when talking about us in this morning's briefing.'

Sitting in the kitchen of the vicarage, the Reverend Cutforth did his best to be helpful as Jennings asked the planned questions, and Zerkah scribbled notes.

Had he noticed anyone suspicious or unusual at the service?

Well, yes. *Everyone* was unusual – but not suspicious, really.

Had he been contacted by anyone in the days leading up to the plague of pingpong balls?

Gosh, yes. The newspapers, the television, a whole string of either supportive or critical phone-callers – and the Bishop, of course.

Could he think of anyone whom he might have upset or offended?

'Apart from the entire membership of the BMA?' Zerkah suggested, licking her pencil.

Jennings shot her a warning look.

Cutforth winced. 'I seem to have offended everyone, don't I?' he murmured sadly.

Jennings drew the interview to a close, thanking the vicar for his time. As they stood in the hallway, and Jennings asked Cutforth to call if anything – anything at all – came to mind, Zerkah looked at the painting over the hall table. It was Millais's *The Light of the World* – a Muslim prophet done up like a girlie, all fey little smile and long white dress. Though she didn't practise the religion into which she'd been born, Zerkah still felt a jolt of cultural disapproval at this appropriation of part of her heritage by the Christians.

She glanced down at the table, running her eye over the copies of the parish magazine, the bicycle clips, the takeaway menu from a local Indian restaurant. There was a card on the table too, half-hidden beneath a flyer from a window-cleaning company. She slid it out.

'Anyway,' Jennings was saying, as he opened the front door, 'thanks again. We'd better be off.'

Zerkah turned, smiled at the Reverend Cutforth, and nodded to her boss as he stood aside to let her go first.

'Well, that was a bit of a dead loss, wasn't it?' Jennings remarked as he got into the car.

Zerkah started the engine. 'Sir – what's a hierophant?' she said.

82

Jennings raised one eyebrow. 'Er . . . it's a sort of priest. One with insights to the mysteries of faith. Why do you ask?'

Zerkah was looking in the wing-mirror, and pulling out. 'He had a weird card on his hall table that had that word on it.'

Jennings froze for a moment, and then slapped his hand on the dashboard. 'Stop!' he yelled. He sat back in his seat, and looked at his shocked assistant as she stamped on the brake. He grinned. 'Sorry. Desperately melodramatic. I do apologise. Just reverse back in to the kerb, would you?'

Zerkah did so, watching Jennings out of the corner of her eye. He had cupped his hands over his mouth and was staring at the glove compartment sightlessly. She waited.

'Hmm,' he mumured eventually. He wiggled one index finger in his ear, as if to bring himself out of his trance, then he turned to her. 'That house. Absolutely standard-issue vicarage. Lots of ill-matched mugs in the kitchen. Devotional tracts on the bookshelves. Religious painting in the hall – as you noticed, I noticed.'

Zerkah blinked. She was pretty sure that Jennings had had his back to her when she was looking at the picture.

'So,' he went on, 'here is a fundamental principle of detective work. To wit, anything out of place is interesting. Not an original principle, admittedly, but valid nevertheless.'

Zerkah nodded. 'Is that out of place then? I mean, he's a priest, and he's got a card with a priest on it.'

Jennings smiled. 'Not a priest. A hierophant. And I bet the card had a number on it too.'

Again Zerkah blinked. 'Yes. Number—'

'Five,' Jennings interrupted.

Zerkah grinned. Impressed as she was, she couldn't resist the slight rebellion. 'Vee, actually. Roman numeral.'

'Yes, okay. Picky, picky,' Jennings nodded, tutting good-humouredly. 'But believe me, that card is not a Christian artefact. So what is it doing on his hall table?'

'I don't know, sir,' Zerkah admitted, 'but I have a feeling you're about to tell me.'

Jennings opened the car door. 'Nope. No idea. Could be nothing at all. Back in a tick.'

And he shambled up the garden path of the vicarage, his shirt-tail flapping out from under the back of his tweed jacket.

Walking back from the job interview at a graphic design company in Dean Street, Mason decided to pop into the Coin and Cup for a swift drink. He sat at the bar, loosened his tie and ordered a half of lager and a ham roll.

He took a mouthful of beer – which made him gag, as the first sip of the day always did – and lit up a match. He spent a few searching moments thinking about the job interview, which he'd blown by being sulky and uncommunicative, and then he reached into his pocket for the Trickster list. He'd taken to carrying it around, obsessively, and pondering it at idle moments, adding new pieces of information as he came across them. For one, he had discovered that Peter Pinkus, the magician, was a crystal freak who believed that a fragment of quartz hung around the neck would act as a 'focus for spiritual power', whereas a similar piece of turquoise would protect against headaches, or some such tosh.

Mason had also scribbled in Henry Westlake and the Reverend Michael Cutforth, for whom the paranormal links had been a cinch.

The pub was deserted – even the barman wandered away to some backroom. Mason peeked into the bread roll to confirm that there was some ham in there, and flattened the list on the bar.

Who	How	What	Why??
Chuckie Rolls	Paintball	Comedian	
David Daemon	Trick Prick	Illusionist	Crystals
Cliff'n'Dawn	Stuck in Air	Actors	Druids
Morris Keen	Crop V-Sign	Racing Driver	Aliens
Henry Westlake	House Party	Barrister	Possession
Rev. Cutforth	Pingpong	Clergyman	Healing

Taking a bite from the roll, he gazed, head tipped sideways, at the piece of paper. He still couldn't see where Chuckie Rolls fitted in. He chewed contemplatively, brushing crumbs from his lap.

'Got it yet?' said a voice in his ear.

It was Elvis Presley, the neighbourhood vampire.

'Oh, hi,' Mason said, swallowing the last of his lunch. 'What a coincidence.'

'There's no such thing as a coincidence.' Elvis shrugged, his eyes scanning the length of the bar. 'This is my territory.' He frowned. 'Why don't pubs supply enough stools any more? Or staff, come to that?'

He strolled round the bar and helped himself to a vodka. He dropped some ice into his drink and wandered back to lean against the polished wood.

'It's pixies. Pixies stealing the barstools,' he suggested. He indicated the sheet in Mason's hand. 'The perpetrator appears to be some kind of radical rationalist. Let's have a look.'

Mason handed over the list, which Elvis studied through narrowed green eyes, nodding.

'A.G. Sparkes,' he said, handing the paper back. 'Add him to the bottom.'

'What – the Metaperception loon? Why?'

A week after the planted interview broke, the real Lindy-May Corn had come forward and exposed the hoax. It was too late. The news that Arnie had no desire to be told a side-splitting gag received nothing like the coverage of the original set-up. The idea had already entered the public consciousness and its consequences were unstoppable.

'The recluse, yeah,' Elvis confirmed, sipping his vodka.

'What makes you think it's part of the same thing?' Mason frowned. 'I mean, it happened in America, for a start – and all the others have been this side of the water.'

'One of the victims had to be a recluse; it was time for one,' Elvis said, simply. 'And the only alternative-beliefs recluse whose life has been messed with recently is A.G. Sparkes. Also, the *modus operandi* feels right.'

Mason screwed up his nose and looked around the pub, confused. 'I'm not with you. One of the victims *had* to be a recluse? Why?'

'I'm giving you a clue, Mason. You wouldn't want me to spoil your fun by handing it all to you on a plate, would you?'

Sagging back against the bar, Mason sighed, and struck a match. 'You're a great bloody help, you are,' he said. 'Anyway, do you fancy meeting up later in the week?'

'All right. Saturday. The Orange Pub in Covent Garden. Noon. Okay?' Elvis suggested.

'Sure. You'll turn up, will you?'

'Silver bullets permitting,' Elvis said, knocking back his vodka and heading for the door. 'I'll see you.'

'Silver bullets are for werewolves, not vampires,' Mason called after him, but he was gone.

Mason stared at the closed door for a moment, and then turned back to the bar. *Why* did one of the victims have to be a recluse? He looked at the descriptions of the others. A comedian, an illusionist, a couple of actors. No pattern that he could see.

He tried synonyms. *Comedian* – comic? humorist? clown? *Illusionist* – magician? prestidigitator? conjuror? *Actor* – thespian? player? star? He felt that it probably wasn't as straightforward as that. After all, 'recluse' wasn't A.G. Sparkes's *occupation*, exactly. *Recluse* – hermit, loner, ascetic?

Sipping his beer, Mason considered the various convictions of the victims.

Arnie's Metaperception thing, one had to admit, looked like a total con – a charlatan's pitch. It was different to the other victims' loopy beliefs, which at least had some pedigree. The notion that there are aliens out there was so widespread as to be almost respectable. And the idea that crystals had healing powers was just a twist on ancient fetishism. If, as Elvis had suggested, the Trickster was a radical rationalist, Mason couldn't see that he was being that rational. After all, for millions of years human beings had put their faith in unprovable interpretations of the world – and so what? It wasn't going to stop just because a few nutcases were humiliated in primetime. Mason didn't suppose that a single crystal freak had watched the prank played on Peter Pinkus and then ripped the lump of balsite from the leather thong around their neck and flung it in the bin, resolving to up their vitamin C intake instead.

Mason shrugged, and took another swig. Obviously the Trickster had a bit of a chip about alternative faiths and worldviews, but Mason couldn't give a monkey's what people believed in – any more than he cared about their sexuality or their dietary habits. He may well think that their faith was daft, but he expected they'd think the same about his own.

He chuckled. 'Well, they might, if I had any,' he told himself.

He ran his eye down the list one more time. There *was* a pattern, over and above the alternate-beliefs thread – he was sure of it. He tutted, drained his pint and got to his feet.

'A much better question, of course,' he muttered, 'is why I care.'

He stopped, recognising the validity of the question. He *did* care. He cared very much. That needed thinking through.

He sat down again, and ordered a further pint from the suddenly attentive barman. He lit and extinguished another match, and drew a pentangle in the froth on the top of his beer with the tip of it. Then he lodged it in the corner of his mouth.

Why was he so interested in this? Well – there were the obvious reasons, of course. He was unemployed, single, more or less miserable and had nothing better to do with his time. After all, he pointed out to himself, there's only so many hours a day that can be passed in desultory masturbation.

He sipped his beer. Then he sipped it again. Then he knocked back a good half-pint of it.

Yeah – the Trickster thing filled his useless time. There was another reason, though, that he had become so determined to solve the mystery.

'It's the rock-climbing thing all over again,' he murmured, flicking the matchstick from one corner of his mouth to the other.

During one of the just-barely-friends periods with Chris, he'd had dinner with her, and she'd mentioned interviewing a rock climber. She was very impressed by him – banged on about his singlemindedness, his seriousness, his physique. Mason had nodded and joined in the admiration, all the time wanting to lunge across the table, scattering condiments and wineglasses, to grab her by the shoulders and scream, 'Did you *sleep* with him? *Did you?*'

The following day, he'd signed up for a course in rock climbing. He was going to learn how to do it, get good at it, and then just drop it into the conversation one day. 'Yeah – it was after you mentioned it that time. I just thought, y'know, might be fun. So I've been doing it most weekends for the last six months. I'm scaling a sheer five-hundred-footer in Wales next Sunday. Wanna come?'

In fact, he'd slipped off the wall-bars in the gym during the very first lesson and broken his wrist. He told Chris he'd done it playing five-a-side.

But the principle was still sound. Because, as things stood, he was just too familiar an element of Chris's life – little more than a snapshot, stood on the mantelpiece, framed and dusty, unregistered except as part of the out-of-focus background detail. She needed to be given some new and fascinating angle on him, so that she could see him in 3-D again.

And now she was the *Clarion*'s Trickster correspondent. She was professionally tied up with the whole affair. So if he were to come up with the perpetrator, how could she fail to be impressed, delighted, grateful? She'd interview him – The Man who Unmasked the Trickster – and she'd have to think about him as someone who achieved things; things that were relevant and useful in her life.

That would be all he needed. He could take it from there.

Mason grinned and finished his drink.

Maybe it *was* a bit like the rock-climbing disaster, but it was much more workable. All it needed was a lot of application and a modicum of luck. He was going to make this one work. He was going to put some serious time and effort into it. He was going to become irresistible.

He put his hand in his pocket and pulled out some change. He counted it, then called the barman over and ordered another pint.

As the barman took a clean glass down from the rack, Mason stopped him.

'No – hang on,' he said. 'Make it a half. I've got work to do.'

CHAPTER FOURTEEN

David Jennings ran a finger along the tops of the books on what Sue referred to as her 'esoteric shelf'. Most of the volumes there were crumbly, foxed hardbacks, the gold-leaf letters on the spines faded, the titles close to illegible. A few were newer paperbacks, usually with pictures of clouds or rising suns on the covers, and shoutlines promising that 'revelations', 'insights' and 'hidden knowledge' awaited within.

It would be fair to say that Mr and Mrs Jennings were divided on the matter of faith. When they'd married, Sue had been fashionably agnostic, and David had accepted it, because he thought he perceived in her if not a theological hunger then at least a sort of spiritual peckishness. He'd never been an evangelist for his own beliefs – he considered aggressive proselytising rather rude – but he had hoped that his wife's snackish curiosity would gradually draw her towards the tenets that supported his own life; tenets that, in the end, made him loveable.

And he was right, in a way. About two years into their marriage, Sue had made concerted efforts to explore the mysteries of her husband's faith – just after her flirtation with Buddhism and before her intense study of druidic lore. At the time, David had been disappointed that his wife's restless and inquisitive soul hadn't decided to settle long-term within the compass of the spire's shadow, but he accepted that the path to a solid oak front door is often serpentine. He knew that Sue was a woman of many chafing contradictions.

David and Sue's friends – or, to be more accurate, David's friends and Sue's friends – often wondered aloud amongst themselves about the Jennings's marriage. His friends in the church thought her too sharp, too undemonstrative, too uncharitable for him. And her friends in the Groups thought him too unchallenging, too uninquisitive, too narrow for her.

In David's eyes at least, the marriage made perfect emotional sense.

Certainly his wife could be difficult, spiky, wounding. But he recognised that for what it was – a defence. Human beings, he knew, are not naturally briar-clad or shuttered-up. Some simply learn to be that way in order to protect themselves. If he could gradually prune away the thorns, coax open the windows, his wife would be freed, at last, with a kiss. Through the tangled branches, through the gaps in the nailed boards, he could see the simple beauty, asleep – drugged, anaesthetised. Occasionally – in the quiet of the night, unexpectedly, just often enough to sustain his vision – she would stir, and hold out a hand towards him. And he knew then that he was right to persevere, however scratched his cheeks by the flaying tendrils of her tangled indifference; however bloodied his nose as the cold wind whipped the shutters suddenly open and just as suddenly closed.

The liberation of Sue, in fact, was David Jennings's life's work.

He found the volume he was looking for, and pulled it out. He sat in the chair by the fire, and carefully opened the book at the contents page. He ran his finger down it, and then leafed through, careful of the delicate, ochre pages, to the section he wanted.

He smiled, reading the list that headed the chapter. He wrinkled his nose and looked up, thinking.

'Where's the hermit?' he asked himself, aloud.

There was a shriek of irritation from upstairs. Jennings tensed, and laid the book aside. He got up and went into the hall.

'Everything all right?' he called.

He could hear the patter of footsteps along the landing. He climbed the stairs, and went into the bathroom, where Sue, sleeve rolled up, was pulling the plug out of the bath.

'What's up?' Jennings asked.

Sue yanked the plug from the hole by its truncated chain. 'What is *wrong* with that child?' she demanded, straightening up. 'I told him not to get water on the floor, and a minute later he slooshed a great bloody wave over the edge. He just doesn't *listen*.'

'He's only a little boy, love,' Jennings suggested.

'Christ! Why do you *always* take his side?' Sue demanded, flinging the plug against the tiles. 'Go and settle him. Tell him what an awful mother I am.'

She pushed past her husband and descended the stairs.

Jennings breathed in through his nose, biting his bottom lip. Then he turned, and walked along the landing to Jake's bedroom. He pushed open the door, and heard the tinkle of the windchimes – the charming, delicate, madly expensive crystal windchimes that Sue had bought as a surprise for their son at some craft fair. He poked his head around the door, and looked in, beaming.

'Hello, bumface,' he said, happily. And he was rewarded with a gulping, reluctant giggle.

When Mason got home from Soho in the early evening, he discovered that Freda the cat was deeply pissed off. He had left that morning without feeding her, and she had expressed her displeasure by knocking a houseplant off the living-room windowsill. The pot had smashed, scattering soil and ivy right across the carpet.

'Freda, you cow!' he yelled as he walked into the room and saw the mess. 'Where are you, you clumsy pain-in-the-arse?'

Freda strolled into the room and surveyed the damage. It looked fine to her, apparently – except, perhaps, the soil should extend a little further towards the sideboard. She began scraping the dirt in that direction.

'Stop that, beast!' Mason admonished, and, picking her up, carried her into the kitchen, where he threw her to the floor. 'I was in a hurry this morning, okay?' he explained as he opened a tin of chicken-flavour Paws. 'My mind was on the interview,' he pleaded as he put the bowl on the floor. 'I'm sorry – it won't happen again,' he apologised, watching her wolf down her lunch.

Back in the living room, on his hands and knees with a dustpan, he noticed the video recorder blinking, letting him know that it had recorded something. For a minute he couldn't remember what he'd taped, and then he recalled last night's phone message from his mother.

'Is it recording? Hello, it's Mum. Mason, I'm going to be on the Channel Six Telethon tonight a little before midnight. I'm doing this spoof where I solve celebrities' problems. Now, can you record it for me? I never seem to record the right thing when I set my video wotsit. I'll call you tomorrow. Bye.'

The message had been followed by an uncharacteristically terse one from Bart, cancelling a meeting they'd arranged. At the time, knowing that he had an interview to go to the following morning, Mason had thought it just as well that he'd been stood up. He'd set the video recorder and hit the sack early, amused by his mother's faith in him as a VCR operator. Many's the time he'd taped a documentary on open-cast mining when he'd intended to vid *Seinfeld*.

Having cleared away the dirt and flora, Mason rewound the video tape and sat down to check that he'd caught Maria's performance. Running from the top, he fast-forwarded through a parade of corporate businessmen in execrable suits presenting cheques the size of coffee tables to the third-rate comic who was linking the charity show. Then there was a brief interview with a shower-capped twerp sitting in a bath full of baked beans. As Freda hopped up onto his lap, Mason took his finger off the fast-forward in time to hear the twerp announce that this stunt had raised fifty-seven pounds thirty-eight for famine relief.

'For Christ's sake,' Mason asked Freda, 'why didn't the egotistical jerk-off just send the poor starving bastards the baked beans?'

'And now,' said the link-man, with a cheery twinkle, 'we're going to raise the tone a little, with a scene from the classics, performed for you tonight by Damon Chiswick, of the Royal Shakespeare Company, and Belinda Bartlett from *Money-Go-Round*. Ladies and gentlemen, the Channel Six Telethon presentation of *Antony and Cleopatra* . . .'

The camera panned to a set that was the quintessence of variety show Egyptiana – backdrop of pyramids, plastic palm tree, Edwardian chaise longue – and in the foreground stood Damon Chiswick, all tanned biceps and steely peepers.

Damon had just returned from Hollywood, where he had been applying his RADA-honed talents and pumped pectorals to the role of Samson in Fezzerini's Biblical epic *Delilah's Power*. It was his first break into bigtime movies, and he'd given it the works. All over LA, producers were talking of his commanding lens-presence, his production-enhancing British accent and his inexhaustible energy. This energy had been in evidence not only on the sound-stages, but also in Damon's willingness to take the time and trouble to coax performances out of the lowliest cast member. To ensure that everyone gave of their best, he'd spent a lot of his free evenings in the private coaching of two-line concubines and ewer-bearing slave girls – and even Fezzerini had to admit that the care Damon had lavished on these minor performers really came through on the rushes. Those starlets looked honestly petrified of Damon's musclebound, mercurial Samson.

And now, for the Channel Six Telethon and for no fee whatsoever,

Hollywood's latest heart-throb adopted a Graeco-Roman pose, gripping the hilt of his stubby sword and raising a hand towards the wings. As the camera reached his face, he mugged like crazy, just to let everyone know that it was all in fun and actually comedy was really quite difficult and he was available for Cary Grant roles.

'Hark,' he projected, 'here cometh the Queen of all Egypt, the Jewel of the Nile, the beauteous Cleopatra, whom I fancieth something chronic.'

He waited for the laugh.

He gave up waiting.

'Marry,' he continued, 'her eyes are as twin stars in the firmament. Her lips are as twin fires at dusk. Her hands are as twin doves on the west wind. And she has a fine pair of hooters on her, to boot, withal.'

Off-mike, the show's linkman gave an encouraging cackle, but it was really no help.

Then, to enthusiastic whooping, Belinda entered stage right, done up in a straight black wig and heavy eye make-up. She had been shoehorned into a Cleopatra outfit that might have been a good fit on an overweight Barbie doll, but was struggling to contain the present occupier. She teetered to centre stage. There was a brief hiatus whilst she checked the floor for her mark, and then she scanned the horizon for her idiot-board. Belinda's regular job was as a decorative supernumerary on the game show *Money-Go-Round*. She operated a multi-coloured contraption called the Wheel of Fortune – which task involved her spinning a large wheel, simpering whilst it revolved and then twittering delightedly, 'Ooh! That's gween, Bob! Histowy and Geogwaphy!!'

It was generally agreed that this feat, performed weekly with consummate panache, taxed Ms Bartlett to the very limits of her ability, but the viewing public was entranced by Belinda's evident enthusiasm, her stunning baby-blues and her vertiginous, unfathomable cleavage. Apart from the incongruity of having Belinda perform with one of the leading classical actors of the day, the joke tonight was that Ms Bartlett was a firm believer in reincarnation. According to interviews she had given to the gossip mags, she had once been a handmaiden to Queen Nefertiti. She had also attended at the court of Marie-Antoinette, chatted with Nell Gwynn on her nights off and held Boadicea's coat during the occasional impromptu brawl. One might have thought that spinning the Wheel of Fortune on a game show was a bit of a come-down after all that, but as Belinda herself was wont to say, 'That's weincarnation for you. It's a way of life.'

'Hail, good Antony,' she squeaked, her eyes running across her cue-card as it was held up out of shot. 'Is that a sword in your umm ... sca ... scabbard or are you just pleased?' She smirked at Damon, as if awaiting congratulation, but he only stared back at her expectantly, his eyebrows raised.

'Oh, wight,' Belinda said, checking the idiot-board again. 'Er ... or are you just pleased to see me? Sowwy,' she added, under her breath.

'I come hotfoot from Rome, where an army gathers to march on Alexandria,' Damon declaimed, 'and she's not too pleased about it, let me tell you!'

'Oh, Christ,' Mason sighed. 'This is dire.'

The studio audience weren't prepared to commit themselves even that far. The gap where the laughter should have been was tangible. Belinda read through her next line, her lips moving silently. Once she'd got it straight in her mind, she turned to Damon.

'Er ... I didn't know those little Rwoman skirts had flies,' she said, surreally.

'What?' Mason frowned, sitting up and paying attention. 'That's not right, is it?'

Damon grimaced accusingly. 'Alas and alack!' he spat. 'I am undone.'

'Aha!' Mason shouted at the TV. '*That's* when you do the flies gag, you bimbo – *after* he says he's undone. Bloody hell.'

Belinda floundered. She had a feeling that this wasn't how it had gone in rehearsal.

'Umm ... pardon?' she murmured, weakly, leaning towards Damon.

Damon refused to quit. He was a real pro.

'We must wage war against the forces of Rome, my Queen,' Damon growled. 'We need an army. Can you raise one?'

Belinda chewed her bottom lip. What she could see on the next card didn't look right, but she didn't see that she had any choice.

'Or would you prefer a bite of my asp?' she said, weakly.

Mason shrieked with laughter. 'No, no! There's got to be a "raising armies" gag there! Oh, for God's sake, this is embarrassing.'

Damon couldn't have agreed more. Shaking his head, he decided to give the feed-line another shot. Slowly and carefully, he said, 'We-need-an-army. Can-you-raise-one?'

Belinda was biting the knuckle of her first finger. She read her next line in a tone of tentative inquiry. 'Umm . . . it's harder than you sphinx?'

'Jesus!' Damon hissed, disgustedly.

'I'm *sowwy*,' wailed Belinda. 'All the cards are in the wong order!' She burst into tears.

Damon was accustomed to having actresses weep uncontrollably in his presence and he knew that the best thing was to ignore it. Usually, this meant getting a firm grip on the headboard and pumping away regardless – but he was pretty sure the principle applied on stage too.

'Then we must flee on horseback, my queen,' he delivered stolidly. 'Are you prepared to ride all night?'

Belinda sniffed and gulped, and glanced unhappily at her cue card. 'I don't know about waise one,' she snivelled, 'but I could certainly engage their intewest.'

'That's it!' Mason yelled. 'That's the gag that follows the "army" feedline! Well done, Belinda!'

The studio audience, who had remained silent throughout, gave Belinda a faint ironic cheer at this point. She looked up and smiled wanly.

'The cards are in the wong order,' she explained to them, wiping her nose on her wig. 'It's not my fault.'

'No chance of you learning the fucking script, I suppose,' Damon muttered, perfectly audibly. 'Or would that be a little too much like hard work?'

The audience howled disapproval at this slur on their beloved bimbo. And the bimbo herself was stung.

'It's all wight for you,' she yelled, striking Damon with her rubber viper. 'You're *used* to learning stuff. Anyway, *you're* not so clever. A girl in the canteen told me you don't even know the wight place to put your wil—'

The TV picture cut back to the linkman.

'Well, hahaha, that's live TV for you!' he chortled. 'Brilliant, hahaha! Thanks, Belinda and Damon. Weren't they great, folks? And now, let's go over to Agony Corner, where Maria Dixon is sorting out the problems of a few familiar faces . . .'

Maria's piece was a paragon of polished professionalism compared to the previous sketch. Mason kept half an eye on it, whilst he retrieved the Trickster list from his jacket. He suspected that the humiliation of Belinda Bartlett was the latest hit, and the reincarnation connection seemed to clinch it. Or maybe Damon Chiswick was the target – he hadn't come out of it too well.

He mused again about the perpetrator. Either someone had been bribed to mess up the cue cards, or the Trickster had some kind of access to the studio floor. If it had been a bribe, then it confirmed that the Trickster had funds to plough into the campaign. Mason made a quick mental résumé of the suspect. Opportunity and access. Sense of fun. Time to spare. Contempt for woolly paranormal stuff. Money.

'And now, before we check on our grand total so far,' the linkman was saying, 'let's go out to the car-park and see how the sponsored volleyball is going.'

The picture cut to a woman in big yellow glasses and dangly red earrings.

'Well,' she enthused, 'the boys and girls are doing dead great. They've kept the ball in the air for nearly two hours now, which is dead fantastic. Only another three hours to go, and they'll be in the *Guinness Book of Records*! Brill! Let's watch them in action . . .'

There was a shot of a bunch of adolescents playing volleyball exhaustedly. They looked profoundly disillusioned with the entire charitable business.

Mason shook his head, and reached for his matches. The trouble was that thousands of people *might* fit the suspect profile. He needed more to go on.

The camera panned away from the volleyball players, across the car-park and back to the earring woman. As it did so, Mason caught a glimpse of a figure in the middle distance, striding hurriedly toward the street. Startled, Mason sat bolt upright and rewound the tape. He ran it again from the volleyballers, and froze the frame as the walking figure centred in the shot.

'Jesus,' he gaped. 'I don't believe it. Freda, look.'

There was no mistake. The frame was clear as air, and the figure's face was turned three-quarters into the camera, glancing at the volleyball players. He was tall and lean, with a thin, pointed nose, and full, feminine mouth. He was dressed in a dark, narrow-trousered suit and plum-coloured shirt, open at the neck. He was flicking his straight black hair out of his eyes with sharp twitch of the head.

It was Bartholomew Molyneux Devereux Scott.

CHAPTER FIFTEEN

Mischief took out the cards again, and spread them on the table. It had been a good night, last night. Two in one.

Belinda Bartlett had been easy. In fact, if you wanted to make a fool of *her*, all you had to do was let her keep breathing. But getting the smug, self-serving Damon Chiswick had been a real bonus. He qualified as a target because of his frequent boasting about being highly superstitious – he'd practically made it a trademark, a tenet of faith for the talented thespian. In interview after interview he reeled off the litany of his superstitious rituals.

He believed rigidly in the standard theatrical hogwash, of course – never mentioning *Macbeth*; not wishing fellow performers good luck. But then there were all his personal obsessive tics: he always wore crimson to first rehearsals; he had to have a poster from his repertory debut in the dressing room; he always purchased seat G9 for matinees, because he had to know it was empty.

The Trickster's campaign was really having an effect now. It was common knowledge that a famous TV personality had refused to talk to one of the hag-rags about her interest in cartomancy; and one tabloid astrologer had hired a bodyguard, just in case.

Mischief consulted the list. Next up – Number Twelve. No – Number Twelve was not quite due. So ... Number Thirteen.

Mason ran the tape again.

'It makes sense, of course,' he told Freda. 'Bart has all the necessary attributes to be the Trickster.'

Freezing the frame, he went into the kitchen to make a cup of tea, and Freda trotted after him. As the kettle hissed, he tried to look at this new theory objectively. The cat jumped up onto the table, and he tickled her thoughtfully between the ears.

'Here I am, making a sort of obsessive hobby of looking for the Trickster, and it turns out to be my best friend. What would be the probability of that, Freda, eh?'

The kettle boiled and he immersed a teabag, and then beat it up with a fork-handle. 'Take that! And that! And that!' he told it, kicking it around the cup. He bent to get the milk carton out of the fridge and Freda mewed a feline hint. Mason poured milk into the cup and put the carton back in the fridge.

'Whoever the Trickster is, he's bound to have friends,' he mused, flicking the teabag into the bin. He grabbed a couple of Rich Tea biscuits from the packet on top of the fridge, and wandered back into the sitting room. Freda followed him, bleating disgruntledly.

On the TV screen, shimmering in the freeze-frame, Bart looked pretty goddam shifty, if you wanted Mason's opinion.

He sat down on the sofa, and Freda, who was not a cat to bear a grudge, hopped up onto his knee. He dunked his biscuit and picked up the remote, rolling his finger to and fro across the fast-forward and rewind, making Bart dance left and right, hair tick-tocking in front of one eye.

'You crafty sod,' Mason grinned. ' "Entertaining projects", indeed. Oh, shit . . .'

His biscuit had split itself into soggy and non-soggy halves, and the soggy portion had plopped back into the teacup, sinking without trace.

'Shift arse, Freda,' Mason tutted, lifting her off his lap. 'God, I hate it when that happens.'

He went back to the kitchen and put the kettle on again. He tipped the sludgy tea down the sink, pulled a fresh mug from the shelf, and drowned another teabag. Freda sprang up onto the table again, and as soon as Mason opened the fridge, she started lobbying.

'Yes, yes. Wait a minute, furball,' Mason said, tipping the carton. 'Ah, damn. You're wasting your time, anyway. We're out of milk. I'll go over to the shop. Keep an eye out for burglars.'

He left the flat. (*Money, keys, fags,* said a Pavlovian voice inside his head as he opened the front door. *I am a non-smoker,* he replied firmly.)

The man in the corner shop smiled as Mason walked in. 'Lovely day, Mase,' he said. 'Twenty Marlboros?'

'Don't give me grief, Barry,' Mason replied.

In his first flush of fervour after quitting smoking, he had told Barry

Wright never, ever to sell him cigarettes, however he might plead and beg. Barry thought this highly amusing, and now took great delight in tempting Mason every time he set foot in the place.

Mason took a carton of milk out of the chill cabinet and, as was his habit, stood there in the middle of the shop, hoping that he'd be inspired to buy whatever it was that he'd only remember once he got back to the flat. As he gazed around the store, he noticed the front page of the *Clarion.*

There was a little symbol of a Joker on a playing card, and the line, *Joker latest: OUR £10,000 REWARD! See Pages 6, 7, 8.*

'I'll just take the milk and the *Clarion*, thanks,' he said.

Chuckling, Barry handed over the change. 'Well, any time you feel like a drag,' he called as Mason left the shop, 'I've got a wide selection of smoking materials. I'll be happy for you to browse through my stock.'

'I'll bear it in mind,' Mason promised.

Back at the flat, he discovered that he'd left the teabag in the mug and the tea was now the colour of sin. He poured the thick gunk down the sink, put the mug in the washing-up bowl and took the penultimate clean cup from the shelf. While he waited for the kettle to boil, he opened the *Clarion* at page six, and scanned the Joker piece.

Who's Spoofing the Spooks? the headline demanded. And there was the line drawing of Chris, looking simultaneously sultry and serious. As well as puffing up the reward on offer, her article filled in the missing link to Chuckie Rolls.

'Clairvoyance,' Mason explained to Freda. 'Yeah, that'll do.'

He made yet another cup of tea, submitted to the cat's pleas for milk, and went back to the front room, where he picked up the scribble pad.

Bloody everyone would be a Trickster sleuth now, he realised. The chances of the Trickster being known to a sleuth was one hundred percent, which meant that it was no coincidence at all that he was friends with the culprit.

'I was *bound* to be,' he chuckled. 'That's probability for you.'

The phone rang just as he was dunking another biscuit, and he picked it up.

'Good day, ol' pal-o-mine,' said Bart's voice. 'And what a wonderful day it is. I'll bop upon the nose anyone who says different.'

'What's so wonderful about it?' Mason asked keenly.

'Oh, you know – the sun has got his hat on. That sort of thing.'

'So why'd you stand me up last night?'

'Oh – a little something I had to do.'

'How'd it go?'

'Er . . . it went very well, actually.'

'Pretty much according to expectations?'

'Umm, yes, pretty much.'

Mason nodded. Bart was definitely hiding something. He was being far too deferential.

'You were on the telly,' Mason dropped in.

'What? When? What telly?' Bart asked, suddenly flustered.

Mason smiled, pleased that his friend was shaken by news of his fleeting appearance on the box. It was not often that Bart was ruffled.

'I got you on tape, crossing a studio car-park. What on earth were you doing there?'

'Er . . . well, I was just sauntering past on my way to, umm, where I was going, and I popped in to see what was going on. I can never resist a spectacle.'

'Oh, right. So what was this little thing you were doing, by the way?'

At last Bart showed a hint of irritation. 'Mason, this dogged inquisition is most unlike you. I am afraid I am not at liberty to disclose the nature of my activities at the present time.'

'Well, that's me told.'

'It is.'

There was a brief silence.

'By the way,' Mason said, '*à propos* of nothing whatsoever, does the name A.G. Sparkes mean anything to you?'

'Yes. He's the American conman who's currently being waylaid on every continent by people telling him that their dog's got no nose. And serves the swindling bastard right, if you want my opinion.'

'Oh, right. I knew the name rang a bell, I just couldn't place it.'

'Well, if you need any more bells identifying, I'm in the book. In the meantime, I feel I should buy you a square meal as an apology for having stood you up last night. Name a date, a venue and a style of conversation, and I'll fulfil the obligations of my conscience.'

'Uh, Friday night for the time. Wendy's Diner for the place. And the conversational style should be drunken. How's that?'

'Fine. That's the style we do best. Then again, let's be fair to ourselves – we've put in the long, hard hours of practice. I'll see you Friday around eight.'

'Great. See you then. Bye.'

Mason put the phone down and grinned broadly.

Elusive. Bart was definitely being elusive. Mason could see that this was not going to stand up at the Bailey, but it was enough to convince him that Bart was the Trickster.

'Ladies and gentlemen of the jury,' he said to the mirror, 'let's look at the evidence. The accused has the resources: compared to Bart, Croesus was barely scraping by. The accused has the opportunity: there are no demands on his days apart from the time-consuming task of booking restaurants. The accused has the charm: he could sell condoms to a nunnery, so talking his way into a TV studio, for instance, would be a breeze. The accused has the humour: he would think the Trickster project a tremendous hoot. The accused has the contempt: he despises frauds and dupers and those who he feels play on people's weaknesses.

'It's him all right,' Mason concluded. And his biscuit broke in two and plopped into his tea.

CHAPTER SIXTEEN

Zerkah got into work at seven forty-five, and was not surprised to see Jennings already there, gnawing at a biro and staring out of the window, his feet up on the radiator. As she opened the door of their little operations room, he looked over his shoulder and said, 'Morning, Zerkah. Fancy a brew?'

He went over to the filing cabinet, on top of which stood the electric kettle that he'd brought in especially, and he made tea as Zerkah took off her coat and sat down.

The room was tiny. The two desks were butted up against each other, and the phone had a lead that didn't quite reach either desk, so it was marooned on the floor between the filing cabinet and the door. It was ancient – jet-black bakelite – and it had a dial rather than a keypad. Jennings was delighted with it.

The afternoon that they'd moved in, Jennings had pinned up evidently ancient examples of his son's artwork on the back wall. There was a picture of a rocket, or possibly a tree, on fire, or possibly in bloom. And there was a portrait of Jennings himself, or possibly a blue football, standing beside a house that might have been a goalmouth.

On Jennings's desk, there was a photo of the artist, sitting on a tree-stump in the snow and grinning – all gappy teeth and grandma-knitted scarf. Zerkah had noticed Jennings gazing at the photo when he was thinking. At three-thirty every afternoon, if they were in the office, he called home to talk to Jake about his day at school.

As she thanked him for her cuppa, Zerkah noticed an addition to the décor of the room. Three rows of cards had been pinned up on the back of the door, and across some of them a large dayglo-pink tick had been drawn.

'I called both Damon Chiswick and Belinda Bartlett last night, sir,' Zerkah said, nodding towards the cards.

'Ah!' Jennings exclaimed, picking up the highlighter pen. 'And?' He walked over to the door and stood by the array of cards.

'They both received cards that evening. In good-luck bouquets.'

Jennings took the top off the pen and pointed to one of the cards. 'I'm assuming Damon got this one?' he asked.

Zerkah nodded. 'Yes – but I don't see why.'

'Think about it. What's his latest film?' Jennings said, as he drew a tick across the picture on the card.

Sipping tea, Zerkah furrowed her brow. She swallowed as she put the cup down, and tutted at herself. 'Oh, right. Samson.'

'Well done. And Belinda?' Jennings asked, his pen hovering.

'You don't have to tease me on that one, sir. I've worked it out all on my little own.'

Jennings raised his eyebrows. 'Have you? *I* haven't.'

Zerkah opened her mouth to speak, but Jennings held up a hand. 'No – wait. Don't tell me.'

He tapped the marker against his teeth, and looked at his feet. 'I don't know much about her. She's on the telly, isn't she? I don't really watch the telly. Well, except the Cartoon Network. Jake and I love the Cartoon Network.'

'Sir—' Zerkah interrupted.

'No, no – I'll get it. Hold on.' He was holding the pen between his fingers and sucking the end of it, his eyes flicking around the office as he pondered. 'She does some sort of quiz show, doesn't she?'

'Sir . . .' Zerkah began again.

At that moment the door opened, catching Jennings in the small of the back. He stumbled forward as DCI Jagger came in.

'Bloody stupid place to stand, Moses,' Jagger remarked, as Jennings turned, rubbing the base of his spine. 'Well? What progress?'

Zerkah was embarrassed by the change that came over her boss in the presence of the DCI. Just a second ago he'd been relaxed and smiling, looking intelligent and keen-minded. Now, all of a sudden, he was twisting his fingers around each other and acting sheepish. It was a pitiful transformation.

Jennings backed up against the filing cabinet. 'Er . . . none, really, sir,' he said. 'Bit of a dead end, to be honest. But we'll keep plugging away.'

Jagger glowered. 'The papers are having a fucking field day with this, you realise. They're making you look a right prat. Not that that's too difficult.'

'Er, I'm working on it, sir,' Jennings nodded. 'I think we can bring that under control.'

'Believe it when I see it,' Jagger remarked. 'Got any leads? Any clues? Any fucking idea at all?'

Jennings glanced at Zerkah, who tilted her head towards the cards on the back of the door, signalling with her eyebrows. He looked back at Jagger.

'Umm, well, not really, no.' He scratched his head, his hair sticking up in thin wisps. 'I've been thinking, sir. Perhaps this isn't the right assignment for me. Perhaps another officer could—'

'Don't start that again, Moses,' Jagger snapped. 'I told you – you're stuck with this one. It's just you and Doris Patel here.'

'Doris Sheikh, sir,' Zerkah put in, stiffly.

Jagger jerked his head around to look at her, and he pointed a thick, hairy finger. 'You be very, very careful, love,' he said, quietly, 'or you'll find yourself on the next boat home.'

Jennings coughed. 'Er . . . anyway – we're hopeful of an imminent breakthrough,' he suggested, with a weak smile.

'I won't hold my breath,' Jagger remarked. 'In the meantime, some of us have got proper coppering to do.'

Jennings hurried forward and opened the door for the DCI before he could turn to do it himself. As he stalked out, Jagger peered at Jennings's face.

'And clean yourself up, man,' he snorted. 'You look like a tart.'

Nodding, Jennings closed the door and turned to lean against it, letting out a long slow breath.

Then he frowned. 'Clean myself up?' he asked Zerkah.

She looked at him, her fists clenched on the desk in front of her. She was seething with anger on her own behalf, and she was deeply disappointed in her boss. She liked Jennings; he was decent and clever and she enjoyed working for him. But she couldn't bear to see him being so craven and bumbling in the presence of the brass. She had thought he'd have had more self-respect. And he was trying to wriggle out of the assignment too. Where would that leave her – back on the bench, ignored and useless?

'He'll never let you off this case, sir,' she said tightly, as Jennings sat back down at his desk and picked up the pink highlighter.

He put his feet up on the radiator. 'Well, he *might* have done ten minutes ago, actually. But he certainly won't now, no.' He grinned. 'Not in a million years.' He sucked the end of the pen.

Zerkah frowned. 'Huh?'

'Look,' Jennings said. He picked up a copy of the *Clarion* that was on top of a large pile of newspapers on his desk. He showed her the front page, with its splash about the reward for the Joker, and its promise of a three-page feature inside. 'What do you think are the chances of you and I ever getting hold of a high-profile case like this again? If they thought there was any possibility of it being a success, we'd *both* be on the next boat home.'

'Oh, I get it,' Zerkah nodded, breaking into a smile.

'So,' Jennings continued, 'it's probably best if we keep pleading with Brer Jagger not to throw us into the briar patch, don't you think?'

'Yes, sir,' Zerkah agreed.

'Good. Now – what was all that about cleaning myself up?'

Zerkah reached for her handbag and pulled out a make-up mirror. She walked across to Jennings and held it in front of him.

'I did try to tell you, sir. Your pen's leaking.'

Jennings looked at himself. His teeth and lips were bright dayglo-pink.

'Oh, dear. I see the DCI's point,' he admitted. 'My skintone just cries out for something closer to crimson.'

When Chris arrived at the pizza joint on Victoria Street, David Jennings was already there. He waved her over, and poured her a glass of wine.

'I'm getting this one myself,' he said, wryly, 'so as not to place a burden on the beleaguered tax-payer.'

Chris winced slightly. 'Sorry. It's—'

'your job. Yes, I know.'

As they ordered, Chris took out her tape recorder and turned it on.

'So – what's new with the Trickster?' she asked.

Jennings pursed his lips, and steepled his fingers. 'You need this story to run for a while yet, don't you?' he asked.

Chris nodded.

'And I need to solve the case,' Jennings continued. 'So – we both need something out of it.'

Again, Chris nodded. 'In a way, I suppose, yes.' She lit a cigarette. 'Where's this going?'

'We have a lead. You can help me,' Jennings said. He laced his fingers and tapped his thumbs together. 'But to get your help, I'll have to give you more than I want you to use. So – the question I have to ask myself is, can I trust you?'

'A lead?' Chris asked. She blew out a long stream of smoke. 'What sort of lead?'

Jennings grinned. 'Umm ... when I say that I have to ask myself whether I can trust you, you're supposed to leap in with all sorts of forceful reassurances that I can,' he said. 'Still – there's always the nice man from the *Voice* who's always ringing me.' He stopped a passing waitress. 'Can you box my order, please, and bring me the bill?'

'No – hang on,' Chris said hurriedly. 'Okay – you can trust me. If it helps the story, you can trust me.'

'You want the pizza to take out, or not?' the waitress asked irritatedly.

Jennings apologised for the confusion, and said he'd eat in. Then, as the waitress walked away, he switched off the tape recorder. He reached into his pocket and took out a clear plastic envelope with a card inside it, and held it up between finger and thumb.

'Do you know what this is?' he asked Chris.

She peered at it and nodded. 'Yes.'

'I mean, do you know *exactly* what it is? What its use is? What it represents?'

'Yes. What's the point?'

Jennings put the envelope down on the table. 'The unfortunate Reverend Cutforth got this in the post a day or so before his memorable sermon,' he explained. 'We've done some checking. All the other victims received one too – each an ... umm ... apposite card from the set.'

Chris bent forward to look at the card more closely. 'Have you got hold of the others?'

'Unfortunately not. They were all thrown away or tossed lightly aside. They can't have appeared to have had any significance. The kind of people we're talking about get all sorts of weird things in their letterboxes.'

The pizzas arrived, and Jennings set about his. Chris ignored hers, and took another drag on her cigarette.

'Yeah, I suppose so,' she nodded. 'So – why show it to me if I can't use it?' She topped up Jennings's wine. 'And I can see *why* I can't, of course.'

'Thank you,' the policeman smiled, picking up his glass. 'So why can't you?'

'Because if we run it in the paper, the Trickster might stop sending them.'

'No, I don't think so,' Jennings said. He cupped the wineglass in his hands. 'The Trickster is an obsessive. He wants to go right through the cards. You don't set up a racket like this, with all the planning and thought and invention it must take, and then change the rules of your own game halfway through. I think that he'll play it out, if he can.'

Chris nodded again. 'Yeah, that rings true.' She was more and more impressed by Jennings. He might look like a corpulent country curate, but his mind was lean and streetwise. 'So?' she pondered. 'Ah. The Simon Says effect.'

Jennings laughed. 'Is that what they call it in journalism?' He sipped his wine. 'But, yes. If we make it known, every celebrity in the country will be deluged with cards like this. People'll start sending them simply to confuse the issue, or to put the willies up the latest soap-baddie, or just for a giggle.' He folded a piece of pizza and pronged it. 'That'll be no good to anyone but the post office.'

He crammed the pizza into his mouth, and waved his fork in a rolling-along gesture.

'But on the other hand,' he went on, through a mouthful of American Hot, 'I want to let it be known that anyone who receives one of these should get in touch, so that we can be there when the Trickster makes his move.' He took a gulp of wine to wash his pizza down. 'So, Scoop, how do we do that?'

'By oblique reference,' Chris said, shrugging. 'I can phrase it so that it gives no details away, but anyone who gets a card will see what I was referring to. And I can work up the whole mysterious secrecy of it too, to keep the readers happy.' She shared out the last of the Lambrusco. 'But – I need something from you in return.'

'Aren't you going to eat your pizza?' Jennings asked.

She glanced at it. 'No. I'm not that hungry. Do you want it?'

'Yes, please.'

'First,' Chris said, lifting her plate, 'I want you to keep me informed. If you do get any cards reported, I want to know.' She reached across and picked up Jennings's empty plate. 'Second, I want to be there when you nab the Trickster. It's as much my career as yours on the line here. Okay?'

She was holding both plates in mid-air, and Jennings eyed the one with the Veneziana on it.

'Do I get the pizza too?' he asked.

Chris grinned. 'God, you're cheap, aren't you? Well?'

'I give you my word I'll do my best – that's all I can say.'

'You know,' Chris said, placing the empty plate on her side of the table, 'I suspect your word is pretty good, Inspector Jennings.'

As she reached across to put the Veneziana in front of the policeman, the edge of the plate caught the rim of his glass. It tipped towards him, and his hand shot out, scooping it upright. The pizza began to veer off the plate, and as Chris tried to flip it back, it slid over the edge. Jennings's other hand came up underneath it, fingers wide, and he caught it in mid-air.

'Whoops! Only the thought of wasted food could make me move so fast,' he chuckled, lowering the pizza onto the tablecloth. 'That and the fact that my wife would go bananas if I came home with mozzarella all over my corduroys.'

As Chris apologised, he coaxed the plate back under the pizza, and took another sip of wine.

'I must wash my hands,' he said, standing up. 'Don't eat anything. I'll be back.'

While he was gone, Chris paid the bill. She felt it was the least she could do – she was going to get a lot more out of their arrangement than Jennings was. She picked up the envelope, and looked at its contents. The light above the table was reflecting on the plastic, obscuring the detail, so she slipped the card out and scrutinised it. She turned it over in her hands, studying the ancient design. She wasn't sure what she was looking for, but she wanted to see the card close up, in case there might be some clue there – but there was none visible.

She shrugged and slipped it back into the envelope.

On the pavement outside, as they parted, Jennings asked her to call him when she'd written the piece about the cards, so that he could check that it didn't give too much away. Chris nodded, and then said, 'You know, I'm going to have to sell my editor a change of tack on this. Up to now, we've been saying the police are hopeless.'

Jennings wrinkled his nose. 'That can be very useful sometimes. But I'm hopeful that this might come off. So – tell you what – can't you make me hopefully hopeless?'

Chris laughed. 'Do you want to write the bloody piece yourself?'

'No,' Jennings said, shaking his head. 'I'm a copper. That's all I've ever wanted to be.'

CHAPTER SEVENTEEN

When Mason arrived at the Heart of Oak, Chris was already standing at the bar, talking to a tall, Nordic blond guy in a five-hundred-quid suit. Mason walked across, forcing back little thrills of jealousy. Was this Viking *the One*?

'Hiya, beautiful,' he said cheerily to Chris, with carefully measured intimacy.

'Hi, Mason. This is Pieter – he's our African Affairs guru.'

'Nice to meet you,' said Pieter. 'I've heard a lot about you.'

What – I featured as part of the usual post-coital gossip about former lovers, did I, you smug, good-looking creep? Mason didn't say.

'All good, I hope,' he said. 'Would you like a drink?'

'No, no. I'm just going to finish this one, then I'm off – but let me get you one.'

Don't try and ingratiate yourself with me, fuckface, Mason managed not to sneer.

'Oh, well, yeah, thanks. I'll have a lager,' he said.

'And anything for you, Christine?' Pieter asked.

You won't get anywhere with her by calling her Christine, you klutz. She hates being called Christine. Her name's Christina.

'Yeah, I'll have another dry white wine, Piet, thanks.'

See? See? She doesn't even fancy you – you make her uptight, otherwise she'd be drinking pints. Ha. Tough luck, shit-wit.

Some day, Mason scolded himself, I'm going to forget myself and actually say one of these terrible things out loud.

They chatted politely for fifteen minutes or so. Mason made real efforts not to despise Pieter, but he couldn't resist the occasional sidelong dig.

'Nice guy,' he commented, as Pieter left.

'I could tell you liked him,' Chris said, straight-faced. 'Shall we see if we can find a table outside?'

They took a table in the concrete garden. The sun was dipping beyond the low wall, and it shone through Chris's deep red hair.

'You've done your roots,' Mason commented.

'Certainly not. My hair is just naturally a particular shade of red that most people associate with henna.'

'Zif,' he grinned.

'Zif. So, what's all the fuss about?'

Mason had called Chris that afternoon, saying that he had some incredible news to tell her. He'd almost giggled with glee. Even now he was beaming with pent-up anticipation.

'Yeah, okay,' Chris said, smiling. 'Take that bloody stupid expression off your face. I admit I'm intrigued, all right? So?'

Mason took a deep, calming breath. 'The Trickster – it's Bart,' he announced, as if it were a commonplace.

Chris's eyes widened and her mouth hung open. She was lost for words.

Mason leaned forward across the table. 'Yeah, I know!' he said, excitedly. 'Incredible, isn't it? Bart is the Joker!'

Chris shrieked and put a hand over her mouth. 'Bart?' she cackled. 'You're nuts, Mase! *Bart?* You're completely loopy!'

This was not quite the reaction that Mason had anticipated. Chris was supposed to be surprised, then fascinated and then impressed. She wasn't supposed to snigger.

She straightened her face. 'Sorry,' she said. 'Okay – I'm paying attention.'

Mason went through the profile he'd built – opportunity, money, attitude – and tied it into Bart, element by element. Chris nodded occasionally, looking grave, but he could see a badly suppressed grin tugging at her pursed lips. He felt he was being humoured.

'Well, all that proves,' she said, when he'd finished, 'is that Bart *could* do it. It doesn't mean he *is* doing it. There must be thousands of people who *could* do it.'

'Yeah, okay, agreed,' Mason nodded. 'But I haven't told you about the video. I was taping that telethon thing last night—'

'What? What on earth for?'

'Because my mum was on it.'

'Oh, yeah. Of course.'

He explained about the video, and his subsequent conversation with the uncharacteristically cagey Bart. 'Pretty conclusive, huh?' he concluded. 'Can I have a match?'

Chris lit a Silk Cut and sucked in a long drag. She held it a second, as she passed the matchbox across.

'Well,' she said, blowing smoke in two streams down her nose, 'the case for the defence. For a start, the circumstances on which your theory rests – namely that Bart has money and time – apply to a lot of people. I mean, you wouldn't necessarily need *loads* of money. No more, perhaps, than another person might spend on following a football team or collecting antique thimbles. *That* kind of money. Secondly, you wouldn't need that much time, either. All you'd need is a job that allowed you some freedom of movement. A motorbike courier could do it, for example. In fact, if you had a few spare coppers, *you* could do it, Mason.'

'I haven't got a few spare coppers,' Mason pointed out.

'Don't be obtuse. Now, as to the psychological profile – that's a right load of bollocks. Okay, Bart's incredulous about the paranormal. So what? That's just the way it is with the paranormal: you're either, on the one hand, all for it; or, on the other hand, you are an intelligent and rational human being. It's coming to something when a person can't reject all that quackery without being denounced.'

'Oh, come on,.' Mason interrupted. 'That's not what I said.'

'Yes, you bloody did,' Chris shot back. 'You said that Bart's attitude to the pseudo-sciences put him in the frame. But *every* half-intelligent person shares Bart's views. *Everybody* thinks that mediums and astrologers and reincarnationists are crap. I mean, *I* certainly do. In fact, whoever the Joker is, Bart or whoever, I think they're doing a great job. And so do *you*, surely?' she pointed out.

'No. I *don't* share Bart's views. That's the point,' Mason protested. 'I think the *jokes* are funny, but I don't get that heated about astrology and mediums and things.'

Chris snorted. 'You're not telling me you believe in all that shit?'

'All what shit? It's all *different* shit. I mean, there *might* be something in clairvoyance, for all I know, but I'm pretty sure that *astrology's* crap. The thing is, I don't think it matters. People can believe what the hell they like, as far as I'm concerned.'

'You think that's liberal,' Chris said, 'but it's just lazy and cowardly.'

'Why? If people want to describe themselves as "typical Librans" or believe that they used to be Oliver Cromwell or get ripped off by fortune-tellers or whatever, why shouldn't they? Who's it hurting?'

As soon as the words left his lips, Mason realised he'd made a mistake. Chris had stiffened and was looking at him with dead eyes.

'Oh, fuck. Sorry.' he said.

Chris sighed and slumped a little. 'No, it's okay. It's not your problem.' she shrugged.

Mason knew that this was typical of him at his most crassly and clumsily insensitive. It was an unenviable talent he had.

Chris had been the only child of a very close and demonstratively passionate relationship. Her father, Ray, was a film director and her mother, Jess, a scriptwriter. Chris's early childhood had been utterly happy. The Bell family had flitted around the world, making movies, taking holidays, being together. Chris had felt that she lived in a universe of three.

Ray Bell was killed in a road accident when Chris was thirteen. Jess Bell was distraught; she barely spoke to anyone, including Chris, for months.

And then Jess met a woman who claimed to be a medium, and she began to get interested in communicating with her dead husband. When she didn't find whatever it was that she needed through the first medium, she sought out another. When she was disappointed again, she moved on to another one. She hooked in to an international network. She would hear of some new and highly rated psychic in Barcelona, for example, and she would simply take off for Spain, leaving Chris with her grandparents. There was no financial necessity for Jess to work. Chris's father had left a large amount of money, so Jess devoted all her time to her quest. She spent a fortune – and she neglected Chris. After a fortnight or more in Salisbury or Seattle, she would return to the Derbyshire farm, occasionally elated or, more often, crumpled and hollow.

By the time Jess died, shortly after Chris graduated, their relationship had been a long time dying.

'Jesus Christ, Chrissie, I'm really sorry,' Mason pleaded. 'Fuck, I'm so stupid. Really . . .'

'Yeah, I know. As I say, it's my problem. It's okay.'

'Well . . . anyway . . .'

'Yeah. Anyway . . .'

He wanted nothing more than to give her a hug, but it might have made things even more awkward. He didn't feel he had permission any more to offer unsolicited physical affection. These days, if he so much as brushed her hand reaching for the mineral water in a restaurant, he'd apologise hotly, and agonise over whether she thought he was making a play. But he looked at her now, and she was a long way away, lost again in memory and rejection – and he wanted to pull her back.

When he had first met Chris, she had been suspicious and wary, unwilling to trust anyone who tried to get close, in case they later withdrew, as both her parents had in one way or another. He spent months coaxing her to open up, to trust him. And when she finally did, when she let him in and gave him the run of her soul, he heard something closing behind him. Having striven so long to gain access, he felt trapped in there. He began to pace the rooms of her personality, impatient and a bit panicky. He thumped on the walls, pushed against the doors. Chris tried to make it comfortable for him, rearranging the furniture of her heart and mind, fiddling incessantly with the décor, trying to get him to settle down. But he raged and spat and finally broke out, and ran. He proved her point, in other words.

Eventually, he regretted it, and crept back. She allowed him in again, but it wasn't the same. It was she who felt uncomfortable, biting back her irritation at the way he tiptoed apologetically around, cleaned up after himself, sheepishly asked if he could make some tea, or watch the telly. The tension between them was like a constant high-pitched whine from the central heating – and the only way to stop it was to switch off the warmth, and shiver on opposite sides of the bed, and fight over the duvet. One day, she told him to go.

So he was outside now, looking in, with no right to offer help at times like this.

He drummed his fingers on the pub table, watching her gazing silently across the garden, lips pursed, eyes watery. He couldn't bear it. He scooted his chair round the table and gave her a hug, pulling her head into his shoulder and squeezing her tight. She hugged him back. They stayed like that for a few minutes, and then let go of each other.

She sniffed and smiled damply. 'Listen, I've got to get going pretty soon,' she said. 'Let's finish these beers and then you can walk down to the tube with me.'

Outside the subway entrance, Chris said, 'Well, I'm picking up the Central Line. Which way are you going?'

'Oh, I think I'll just go for a bit of a wander. See you in the week?'

'Yeah, we'll talk sometime in the next couple of days, all right? And listen, I'm really sure you're wrong about it being Bart. You're going to have to get some hard evidence.'

'I suppose so,' he shrugged. 'Though God knows how.'

'And the other thing you're going to have to consider,' Chris continued, poking him gently in the chest with her forefinger, 'is what you're going to do if you're right. I mean, will it be the old Judas kiss? Will you shop him to the papers, or maybe the law? You wouldn't want to see your best mate banged up, would you?'

'No – you've got a point.'

'Okay. I've got to go. Give us a kiss.'

They kissed chastely and Chris disappeared down the steps into the station.

Mason waited a few seconds, as he always did after parting from Chris, as if something further might happen – and then he turned away up the street and headed towards Soho. As he walked, he bent his head from time to time and stroked his nose across the shoulder of his T-shirt, where she had left her perfume on him during their embrace.

Bart flicked through his address book and picked up the telephone. He tapped out the number and reached for a glass of champagne, sipping it as he waited for an answer.

'Wendy's Diner,' came a female voice.

'Hello,' Bart said. 'I'd like to book a table for two, for eight o'clock on Friday, please. The one by the window, preferably. Name of Scott.'

'Hey! Is that Bart? It's Tess!'

Bart grinned, 'Tess! How are you? I thought you'd be in Hollywood by now, fêted and adored.'

'No such luck. Not a bit fêted, and completely unadored. I could do with a bit of adoration, to be honest. Do you fancy the job?'

'I'm exercising my adoration muscles elsewhere, I'm afraid. Your recent beau is no longer in the picture, I take it?'

'No, the bastard. That finished weeks ago.'

Bart stood, and carried the phone over to the sofa. He picked his cigarettes up from the arm of it and tapped one out. 'So you're on the prowl again, are you?'

Tess tutted. 'There's no need to make it sound so feral. But, yes I suppose so.'

'I see,' Bart nodded. 'And if some likely prey were to cross your path, you'd pounce, like as not, hm?'

'Who do you have in mind?' Tess asked.

'Oh, no one in particular,' Bart shrugged, striking a match. 'But were you to wear a short skirt on Friday evening, who knows what sort of tip might come your way.'

CHAPTER EIGHTEEN

That week, summer came to London on a whim, like an ex-pat waking up one morning in Spain and deciding it was to time to go home.

The sun had fallen into the habit of getting up at dawn to take a turn around the park before breakfast. The ducks, still ruffled from sleep, waddled up the bank in the hope of croissants, and the early roses stirred in their beds and nodded welcome, scattering dew. Office workers got off the train a stop early, just to enjoy the walk – men with their jackets flung over a shoulder on one hooked finger, women feeling pounds lighter in cotton dresses, having left the lumpy overcoat in the wardrobe and the sweaters in the laundry basket, where they would lie forgotten until September proved treacherous.

During the morning, the sun lounged in the squares of the city, beaming happily as the Americans and Japanese bumped into each other, open-mouthed, heads tipped back to look at the columns and statues, their camera straps becoming entangled. The sun moved on. It slipped silently into galleries and museums, and reflected on the artefacts there. It played in the corridors and halls with the coachtripping schoolchildren, throwing up dust in games of illicit hide-and-seek conducted amongst the white bones of dinosaurs and around gleaming, silent locomotives and fire tenders.

Down to Soho for lunch, at a pavement café. And the sun, which had shimmered along sweeping foreign boulevards and spacious European avenues, flashed bright smiles at the passing girls, and fingered the silvered cruets on the little sidewalk tables, knowing that this was not natural to London at all, but a holiday memory recreated in narrow, clogged streets. Not that it mattered. The wine might be Spanish, the food Italian, and the whole idea French – but the white arms that the sun bathed, the pink faces that the sun burned and the pale thighs that the sun stroked were pure London.

In the afternoon, out in the Docklands, the sun looked at itself in the vast mirrors of the new buildings, tacked onto the back of the town like a covered swimming pool in the garden of an Elizabethan manor – impressive and expensive, but unconvincing and vain. As the sun circled Canary Wharf, the tower's shadow backed away around the other side, cowering like a bully discovered. And as the sun came down a little lower, peering around corners and peeking into windows, all the bully's friends deserted, scurrying for the trains, heading for home, not wanting to be caught there after dark.

The sun made for the suburbs to visit friends, red in the face after a long day in town. It lay full-length on a lounger in the back garden, and listened to the birds, breathed in the barbecue smoke from three doors down, let the breeze play with its hair like a curious toddler. After the children had gone to bed, there were a couple of drinks, a nibble at some tomatoes the sun had dried and brought in from Tuscany, a stroll down to the bottom of the garden with the host to see the fruit trees. The sun touched the hanging under-ripe plums and agreed that it would be a bumper crop this year.

And now the candles were being brought out onto the patio, and there were invitations to stay for dinner. But it was going to be another long day tomorrow, and at dawn the ducks had to be fed and the roses woken. Making polite excuses, the sun headed for the street, ducking under the privet arch, wanting to be back in town before dark.

Sitting around the candlelit table outside, still basking in the warmth that the departed guest seemed to bring to the place, everyone agreed how lovely it had been to see a bit of the sun today, and what a difference it made.

'Still,' said the family wit, biting into a peach, 'that's your lot. Typical London summer. One nice week, and it'll be pissing down again by Saturday.'

Mischief laid the *Clarion* aside on the bench, peeled open the front of the sandwich carton, and looked around, thinking.

It was midday, and the sun was bright, hot and high, blurring the far corners of Brompton Cemetery, making the distant headstones flutter like spectres. A few yards away, on the other side of the path, an old gentleman was laying a bouquet of marigolds on a new-white grave, and

Mischief wondered whether the mourned wife who lay there was indeed called Marigold. The old gentleman took his cap off and held it in both hands, gazing at the headstone.

Biting into the smoked salmon sandwich, Mischief thought about that morning's Joker feature in the *Clarion*, and the reference to the cards.

Chillingly, each of the victims had a spooky warning of the Trickster's intention. They all received a card – a macabre ancient symbol of what fate held in store. Police are anxious to hear from any celebrity who is sent one of these mysterious threats . . .

Having picked it over so long, Mischief knew the paragraph by heart. It had been inevitable that the connection would be made eventually – indeed, it was part of the plan. It provided another twist to keep the campaign at the focus of media interest: front page news.

But, of course, it increased the risk. Each card sent was a possible lead for the tubby inspector whose face appeared on page six, above the caption 'Trickster Sleuth David Jennings'. And the reward the paper was offering – which was topped almost daily by the *Voice*, and then raised again by the *Clarion* – encouraged the public to don deerstalkers, produce magnifying glasses and denounce each other on the letters page. Again, perfect for raising the profile, but eventually some amateur Sherlock out there might actually get a clue.

Mischief was feeling the pressure, and wondered whether it was time to quit. Perhaps the point had been made. The newsprint astrologers and primetime faith-healers were all blustering defensively in the features pages and on the chatshows. They were damning themselves out of their own mouths, and being sniggered at by cartoonists, commentators and columnists. Scepticism had become fashionable.

But Mischief couldn't be sure that it was any more than that – a fashion. Were people really thinking about the shit they were fed by these cold-eyed, patronising con-artists? Were they refusing to buy horseshoes for the front porch, lucky heather from pseudo-gypsies in the mall, Your Sun-Sign paperbacks for the Year Ahead?

The old gentleman across the way was muttering now, wagging his finger at the little plot. He was wearing a suit and tie and his shoes gleamed in the sunshine. He'd got himself all dressed up to come and see Marigold.

Mischief wondered what Marigold had believed. Had she read her horoscope every day, out loud over breakfast? 'Scorpio: a fine time to ring the changes. You know what has to be done, and now's the time to do it.' And then perhaps she'd looked over at the old gentleman, and said, 'Oh, yours isn't very good, Dan. "Gemini: don't take too much on today. Pluto's in your opposing sign and health problems loom." I don't like the sound of that. You give the allotment a miss this afternoon.'

Mischief remembered Robin, a friend who had managed to land the lucrative job of writing horoscopes for some local weekly in Oregon. He used to scribble them down on restaurant napkins, glugging wine and cursing.

'Fucking hell. Aquarius. Have I done a money one yet? Shit. "Avoid seafood on Thursday. Especially shrimp." That'll do. "Capricorn . . ."'

The old gentleman was walking back towards the path now, pulling his flat cap snugly over his bald head.

'Nice day,' he said, as he drew level with Mischief. 'Mind if I take a seat?'

'Not at all,' Mischief replied. 'Help yourself.'

The old gentleman sat down and unbuttoned his jacket. His face was thin and ruddy, and his fingers thick, with bitten nails. He gestured towards the grave with a tilt of the chin.

'Been to see the missis,' he said.

Mischief smiled amicably but said nothing, just gazed out across the graveyard.

'Passed away two months back. First of April. All Fools' Day.'

'I'm sorry,' Mischief offered, turning to look at him . . .

The old gentleman took out a tin of tobacco and some papers, and started to roll a cigarette. 'Well, no. Not really. It was for the best. Cancer. Riddled with it, she was. Lot of pain. It was best she went.'

'I see,' Mischief said.

'Couldn't bear to see her suffer.'

'No.'

A funeral cortège pulled in through the gates. First the hearse and then another sleek black limo for the chief mourners, followed by a line of incongruously cheery family cars in reds and yellows. The old gentleman licked the edge of the cigarette paper, and nodded towards the hearse.

'They've got a nice day for it. Nicer than the wife had.'

Mischief nodded noncommittally, not sure how to reply, as the old gentleman smoothed down the edge of the cigarette paper, and sniffed.

'We had our ups and downs, won't say we didn't. Forty-eight years, though.' He lifted the tobacco tin. 'Want one?'

'Yes – thanks.'

'Have this one. I'll roll another.' He plucked a Rizla from the pack. 'Wouldn't take no medication, see? Had a pal who made some sort of herb tea. Swore it'd make her better. I knew it wouldn't, but what can you do? Blackberry leaves or something – I dunno.'

'She wouldn't take morphine or anything?' Mischief asked, striking a match.

'Nah, nothing like that. Just this tea her pal made. Screaming she was, at the end. Terrible. I begged her to let the doctor give her something, but she wouldn't have it. Her pal reckoned the tea wouldn't work if she was on drugs, see.' He paused, looking towards his wife's grave. 'Begged her on my knees, I did. She wouldn't have it . . .' He turned away towards the gate, hiding his face. 'She wouldn't have it,' he whispered.

Mischief took a drag on the roll-up and waited.

'Still,' said the old gentleman, turning back to look at Mischief, his eyes pale and bright with tears, 'she's past suffering now, eh? She's at rest now.'

'I like the flowers,' Mischief said, nodding towards the gravestone. 'Was she fond of marigolds?'

The old gentleman smiled, his yellow teeth showing. 'Oh, she loved a marigold. She grew 'em in the garden. Oh, yes. Loved a nice marigold, did my Lily.'

The two of them sat on the bench, smoking in silence, looking out across the cemetery. Eventually the old gentleman pulled himself to his feet, saying he had to get back for a bit of lunch. Turning to go, he stopped and said, 'I don't believe in heaven, y'know. Can't be doing with all that. I know I'll never see her again. And that's hard. After forty-eight years, that's hard.'

'Did Lily believe in heaven?' Mischief asked.

The old gentleman shook his head. 'Nah. Blackberry leaves, that's what she believed in. I ask you. Bloody blackberry leaves. But what can you do?'

*   *   *

Zerkah Sheikh opened the door of the operations room, and walked in.

'Lunch, sir,' she announced, putting a small carrier bag on the desk.

Jennings was on the phone, and he held up a hand in a wait-a-sec gesture.

'Ah, how disappointing,' he was saying. 'Thank you. Yes. Bye.' He hung up, and sighed. 'What are we eating today?' he asked, reaching for the bag.

'I'm having a salad, and I got you a sandwich made of some innocent piglet that was taken from its mummy and brutally murdered to feed your bloodlust, sir,' Zerkah remarked. 'And if my family finds out I bought that, I'll be going the same way.'

Jennings winced. 'Look – you really mustn't do anything that offends your cultural sensibilities, Zerkah,' he said hurriedly. 'I mean—'

'I was joking, sir,' she said. She had discovered early on that her boss was hypersensitive to the possibility of offending against her background, and she rather enjoyed teasing him about it. 'Any joy with the bouquets?'

In the hope that it would lead to a credit card payment or recorded phone number, Jennings had been tracing the flowers that had been delivered to Damon Chiswick and Belinda Bartlett on the night of the Telethon.

'Not exactly. They were dropped off at reception by a kangaroo.' He unwrapped his sandwich. 'What have we got from forensic?'

Zerkah put down her disposable fork, and opened her handbag. She took out the plastic envelope that contained the Reverend Cutforth's card, and a folded sheet of paper.

'Actually, we got a match, sir,' she said. 'You'll like this.'

Jennings beamed. 'Really? Tell me, tell me.'

She unfolded the paper and read from it. '"Visual match to the fingerprints of WPC Zerkah Sheikh."'

'As expected,' Jennings nodded, chewing his sandwich.

'"Visual match to the fingerprints of the Reverend Michael Cutforth."'

'Likewise.'

'And here's the interesting one. "Computer match to file 2396/B7."'

'Someone with a record?' Jennings exclaimed, spraying bits of bread across the desk. 'Oops, sorry.' He brushed the damp crumbs onto the floor. 'You've looked it up, I take it?'

'Yep. 1994. £150 fine for the possession of cannabis. Horseferry Road Magistrates' Court.'

'Stop stringing it out,' Jennings grinned. 'Give me the name.'

Zerkah shrugged and glanced down at the paper in her hand. 'Christina Amy Bell,' she said, offhandedly. 'Occupation: journalist.' She looked up at Jennings. 'Er, could you close your mouth, please, sir? It's full of sandwich.'

Jennings swallowed. 'Sorry.' He frowned, thinking. And then he groaned and cupped his hand over his eyes. 'Oh, heavens. I know what's happened. I left the card on the table in the pizza place and ... Oh, you idiot, Jennings.'

'She must have taken it out of the envelope, sir,' Zerkah said. 'You'd think she'd know better.'

'No, not really,' Jennings sighed, subsiding in his chair. 'She's a journalist – naturally curious. It's my fault. I should never have left it there. Elementary error.' He pondered for a moment, and then grinned ruefully at his assistant. 'Elementary, my dear Zerkah.'

During that week, the challenge of proving Bart to be the Prankster became the main concern of Mason's life. He daydreamed all kinds of situations in which he caught his friend red-handed in the act of setting up a hit. He thought about finding an excuse to be alone at Bart's flat, to turn the joint over for evidence. He wondered where you got hold of those little tracking bugs they use in espionage movies.

One path of action he never seriously considered was simply to confront Bart with it. For a start, if Bart denied the accusation, it wouldn't mean anything. On top of that, Mason wanted to prove himself as clever as the Joker by trapping him. And he wanted to impress Chris too, of course. Mason was quite happy to admit to himself that it was a macho thing, with sibling-rivalry overtones.

And there was another reason for his obsession, of which he was also entirely aware. It was a displacement activity, intended to stop him thinking about the other major issue in his life. The human brain is reassuringly incapable of processing input from interminable daytime television whilst simultaneously pouring resources into agonising about estranged fathers.

And Marty Puxley was hanging around the back of Mason's mind now, like a flasher in the park. Going to the corner shop one lunchtime, Mason caught a glimpse of a bloke in a passing car who he was convinced was his father. And when the front doorbell rang unexpectedly one evening, Mason's first thought was, *Dad!* It turned out to be the local Tory candidate, who went on and on about the Child Support Agency, which Mason thought was pretty ironic.

Anyway, he needed to not think about it. So he focussed on stalking Bart.

But short of togging himself up in a mac and trilby and hanging around in darkened doorways, he was at a loss as to how to proceed. All he could do was keep an eye out for the next Trick. As it was central to the Prankster's scheme that all the hits should be public, Mason became an avid media-junkie. He bought eight newspapers a day, and sat through hours of television, channel-hopping at five-minute intervals. He acted as if he were institutionalised. He kept putting off washing his hair; he wore nothing but a tracksuit at all times; he mechanically shoved biscuits into his mouth without taking his eyes from the screen. He moved the electric kettle and teabags into the front room, and resented having to go to the kitchen for water. At about six-thirty on Friday evening, he realised that he had been watching TV for forty hours out of the preceding forty-eight.

'This is so dumb,' he told Freda, zapping the telly to mute. 'What possible advantage can there be in goggling at a rerun of *Little House on the Prairie*?'

Actually, Mason and Freda were barely on speaking terms by this stage. Her feeding schedule had been massively disrupted by his new habit of falling asleep in front of the box at six in the morning, and she was sick of it. She blinked at him without interest, and resumed gazing out of the window. She'd noticed that the cats across the street not only got fed at reasonable times, but they also had owners who buggered off to work and left them alone all day. Freda was considering moving in over there.

It was quite a relief for Mason to have some engagements looming – dinner with Bart that night, and a lunchtime drink with Elvis the following day. He had an hour or so to kill before meeting Bart at Wendy's Diner, and he had to formulate an approach. Would he drop some hint that he was hot on the Trickster's trail? Would he push the conversation that way and see how Bart reacted? As he climbed into a hot bath – his first in living memory – it occurred to him that talking about anything else would be a bit of a stretch. The Trickster was about all he had in his head.

'I think I'll just let Bart do the talking,' he told Freda, walking back into the front room wrapped in towels. 'Which will not be a radical departure.'

He flicked channels and zapped the sound on as the nation's favourite chatshow host galumphed down the steps of his glittering set to riotous applause. It was *The Waxforth Show*. Matey, chirpy and quirky, Roy Waxforth grinned bashfully at the camera as the studio audience whistled and whooped.

'Golly and jeepers,' Roy's smile seemed to say, 'all this fuss just for little old me?'

'Tonight,' he announced, 'my guest is a man who was once the *enfant terrible* of pop, and even now the very mention of his name raises the hackles of retired colonels the length and breadth of the Home Counties. Ladies and gentlemen, Mr Al Knox!'

To a sanitised orchestral arrangement of his first hit, Al Knox loped in from the wings. His gait was almost a nostalgia trip in itself – the slightly bobbing stride of the seventies rock star, which causes shoulder-length hair to bounce to best effect, and gives the impression that the act of walking has been re-thought from a new and challenging perspective that pisses off one's parents.

As the applause continued, Al shook Roy's hand and collapsed his gaunt marionette body into a chair. One had to admit that the years had been kind to the Knox physique. The tanned arms that hung loosely from his sleeveless T-shirt were wiry and strong. There was not the slightest hint of a stomach above the death's-head belt buckle that secured his jet-black Levis. The carefully ratty hair was still thick and tangled. He looked to be in better shape now than when he'd hit the headlines by saying 'shit' on *Nationwide* in 1974.

But if Time had taken a detour around Al's body, it was only in order to get a good run-up at his face. To describe it as lived-in would be an understatement. It was lived-in, partied-in, slept-in and caved-in. Lines and crevices criss-crossed Al's visage like the canals of Mars. This was a face that had launched a thousand trips.

Al Knox recounted a couple of louche anecdotes concerning his recent marriage, his detox, and his planned world tour, before mentioning, just in passing, his imminent record release.

'This is your new long-player *The Big Light*?' Roy cued. 'Tell us how that came about . . .'

'Well, I guess it really started last year,' Al began. 'I was travellin' back from a TV studio in Brighton to our 'ouse and I came off the road. Totalled an elm tree just outside Dorking. It was pretty heavy . . .'

The camera moved in close to Al's unironed face. The audience needed no prompting to fall completely silent. Even Roy had toned down his ocular twinkle a few notches.

'I remember lookin' down from a great 'ight, and watching these ambulance guys bendin' over me body. And then everythin' all got really weird on me. I was at one end of this long corridor, and at the other end there was this big light—'

'Hence the title of the LP, *The Big Light*,' Roy suggested, incisively.

'Yeah, right. So I was tryin' to go towards it, but there was something stoppin' me. And then I saw me grandad, standing at the other end of the corridor, and sorta smilin' at me. And 'e held 'is hand up and 'e shook 'is 'ead and 'e said, "Y'can't come across yet, Alex. Go back to the world. Give me love to yer Mum." Apparently, at that time, I was officially dead. No pulse, no heartbeat, nothin'. I kinda felt lost, like I 'ad nowhere to go. The big light'd faded – and there's *no* bleedin' chance of gettin' a cab in Dorking at that time of night, so I had to go back to me body . . .' Al shrugged, his story told. 'Thassit, really.'

'And your new record album is all about this experience. Would you consider performing one of those songs for us here tonight?' Roy enquired, as if the idea had just that moment occurred to him.

'What? 'Ere and now on the show?' Al replied, apparently flattered, but surprised to be asked.

When pressed, Al ambled over to the mike, slung the acoustic guitar around his neck and settled on a high stool. The applause died down and Al thrummed a chord. The guitar was perfectly in tune, but Al re-tuned a string anyway. The mike was at precisely the correct height, but Al fiddled with the stand and readjusted it to the same position.

He strummed through the first bluesy changes of *Big Light*, and the studio lights dimmed so that he was pooled in a single red-tinged spot.

As he came back to the top of the progression, Al opened his mouth and sang in the distinctive New Orleans croak that had made this Battersea boy famous.

> *It's just a step beyond the veil,*
> *Ooh, yeah, a step beyond the pale.*
> *And someone's there to take yoh hand,*
> *And take you to-ooh-ooh the Promised Land.*
> *You know, you don't have to take fright.*
> *It'll be all right,*
> *When y'reach the Bi-ig Light . . .*

Al's features, as he plucked a standard r'n'b rundown into the second verse, were fixed in an expression of distilled anguish. This wasn't one of the sit-on-my-face rockers that typified Mr Knox's earlier songs. This was the work of a mature, serious composer. Al rasped into the second verse.

> *An old man said to me one time,*
> *'Boy, you better toe the line . . .'*
> *But I just didn't understand.*
> *I guess that I had other plans . . .*

The pain and regret were palpable. He was taking his audience to the edge of the abyss.

> *But now I know-oh he was right.*
> *It's gonna come some night,*
> *When y'reach the Bi-ig Light.*

With a deft Chicago riff, Al switched keys and built up to the middle eight. A little flurry of licks signalled that this was to be the dramatic heart of the song.

'I'll lay you five-to-one that the next bit starts with either a *whoa-oh* or a *baby, baby*.' Mason told Freda. 'Trust me on this.'

Freda showed no inclination to take the bet at those kind of odds, and she wasn't a bad judge. What neither she nor Mason could have foreseen, though, was the note that Al came back in on.

'*Whoa-oh-oh, now, baby, baby, I wouldn't tell you no lie,*' sang Al, in the voice of a chipmunk on helium.

'*You know-oh-oh I won't ever say goodbye,*' he squeaked, sounding for all the world like Minnie Mouse having unnatural relations with a goat.

'*And now I see we'll never leave each other . . .*' Still projecting cosmic angst and tortured soulfulness, he appeared totally unaware of what was happening to his voice, which was now at the kind of sonic pitch used to drive termites out of buildings.

'Bloody hell,' Mason laughed. 'He can't hear it. He can't hear what's being broadcast.'

> '*Sister, mother, daughter, lover.*
> *Whoa-oh, yeah, now . . .*'

On the word 'now', Al hit a note that caused family pets all over the country to scamper, whimpering, from the fireside rug and seek sanctuary under the kitchen table. It was a note that would have made Chip'n'Dale's ears bleed.

Evidently, someone had inserted a pitch-controller somewhere in the chain that led from the mike to the master output in the studio control room. Al had sung only four lines in his new, electronically-enhanced voice – maybe twenty seconds of airtime – and it had taken the director and technicians at least half that to notice anything was wrong. They were too busy trying to be heard above the hubbub of *pan left four, kill the spot, roll tape, cue Ray* . . . But by the time Al sang the note that caused the director's dental plate to vibrate, all hell had broken loose up in the glass box. Everyone was shouting at once.

In the confusion, no one noticed that the guy in charge of mixing sound was omitting to check one of the many channels on the desk before him. He'd been paid a large sum of money not to spot that he had patched-in a harmoniser by mistake. He had also been persuaded that it would be worth his while to fail to realise that he was manipulating that channel every so often.

Al, meanwhile, oblivious of the chaos that reigned above him, was finger-picking through his favourite blues licks and bringing the song back to the verse.

'*So you don't have to ask me why,*' Al sang, '*I know this love will never die . . .*'

And as he emoted these words, his eyes brimful of real live tears, Al's vocals swooped back down from the ultrasonic and plummeted to a subterranean growl. A surreptitious twiddle had given Al a voice like something bubbling gloopily in the belly of the earth. The vowels stretched and sagged like pizza dough, and the consonants bloated, as if over-fed.

> *Bwut this li-iy-ffe, wwe gwotta chyange.*
> *This li-ife, wwe gwotta rwe-arrwange,*
> *Swo, baby, hwold mwee whoa-sswhoa tighttt,*
> *Wall thrrwooh the nighttt,*
> *Till whee rea-schh the Bwi-wig Lighttt . . .*

As the final chord faded, the studio audience, who had heard the straight version, went bananas. They cheered and clapped and screamed for more. Al Knox waved modestly, shrugging and nodding. He'd done a fucking top-drawer performance, and he knew it.

The reaction of the fans, however, was mild compared to that of the show's director, whose face was buried in his arms as he slumped forward on the console. Over the last six years, he'd sat dry-eyed through interviews with plucky ten-year-old leukaemia victims, alcoholic actresses and blind Olympic hurdlers – but Al Knox's performance was in a heartrending class of its own. The TV director, inconsolable, sobbed and sobbed.

CHAPTER NINETEEN

David Jennings was rather upset with himself for being so unprofessional as to have left evidence on a table in a restaurant. He really couldn't blame Chris Bell for inspecting it and perhaps destroying any fingerprints that might have been there; it wasn't her responsibility, after all. It was his.

He sat in the back garden with a glass of white wine, watching the bumblebees dip in and out of the camellias. He knew it was unlikely that there had been any prints, after both the Reverend Cutforth and Zerkah had handled the card – but what if there *had* been? It would at least have been a clue, and he was desperately short of those. He'd established a plot but he was short of a lead character. He had to admit that the planting of hints in the *Clarion* was a long shot – an indication of how little else he had to go on.

Through the kitchen window he could see Sue preparing dinner. It was Friday, so it would be shepherd's pie. Sue hated cooking, and she stuck to a rigid weekly rota of dishes in order to minimise the mental effort required. From time to time David would offer to prepare the meal himself, partly because he wanted to contribute, but mostly because escaping the chore improved his wife's mood.

He went back into the house, and walked up behind Sue, who was mashing potatoes. He kissed her on the back of the neck. She looked around and raised a quizzical eyebrow.

'How was your day?' she asked.

Jennings took a seat at the kitchen table. 'Not that wonderful,' he admitted. He told her about the forensic report, and what had led up to it.

'Well,' she said, spooning the mash out onto a baking dish of mince, 'there's no reason why anyone should find out, is there?'

'That's not really the point, love,' Jennings replied, unenthusiastically. His wife's response was typical of her. Not 'Well, I'm sure it won't matter in the long run,' or 'Never mind, we all make mistakes,' but something that managed to be simultaneously defensive and aggressive. It wasn't that she wasn't on his side – but even when she was pitching for him, she seemed to throw curve-balls.

'I'll tell you what, though,' she remarked, sliding the shepherd's pie into the oven, 'I'd make sure that that Zerkah girl doesn't go gossiping in the canteen, if I were you.'

'She wouldn't,' Jennings said, frowning. 'She's a good copper and a nice kid.' This wasn't the first comment that Sue had made along such lines. She seemed to have taken a suspicious dislike to Zerkah, despite never having met her.

'I sometimes wonder if you're not too trusting to be a policeman, you know,' Sue said, with a sidelong smile. 'There's a programme I want to watch. Could you pour me a glass of wine, please?'

The programme turned out to be Al Knox's appearance on *The Waxforth Show*. Sue had been a fan in her youth, and, as she told David at some length, there was still something dangerously fanciable about the man.

Jennings sipped his wine and watched Knox describe his near-death experience – the tunnel, the light, the encounter with his grandfather – and he furrowed his brow.

'I'm really not sure I can believe it works like that,' he murmured.

Sue glanced at him. 'I don't see why not. Who's to say? I mean, have you ever been that close to death?'

Jennings had to admit he hadn't.

'Well, there you are then.' Sue shrugged, turning back to the TV. 'Seems more believable than harps and pearly gates, anyway.'

'Oh, come on,' Jennings protested. 'I don't believe in that, either.'

'Don't you?' Sue asked facetiously, increasing the volume with the remote. 'The church just lets you choose which bits you want to believe, does it?'

There were so many potential replies to that that Jennings didn't know where to start. And if he had known, he wouldn't have started. It would lead to an entire evening of sniping and ducking.

'Mum!' came a call from upstairs. 'I'm out of the bath!'

'I'll go,' Jennings said, quickly, getting to his feet. On the television, Al Knox was ambling over to the microphone and picking up his guitar.

'Get his pyjamas on, and tell him he can have his dinner on a tray in front of the telly,' Sue said, eyes on the screen. 'But there'll be trouble if he spills anything on the sofa.'

'I'm sure he'll be careful,' Jennings said soothingly.

But as he bounded up the stairs, he prayed to God that Jake wouldn't spill anything on the sofa.

It was seven-fifteen when Al Knox finished his memorable rendition of *Big Light*. Mason was due to meet Bart at eight in Camden. The TV studios from which *The Waxforth Show* was transmitted were in Shepherd's Bush, so he reckoned that, with evening traffic, Bart would be hard-pressed to make it to the restaurant on time – if, indeed, he had actually been present at the Knox hit.

Mason fed Freda, and then strolled down past Camden Lock in the evening summer sunshine. At the restaurant, he asked for a table in the name of Scott, and the waitress grinned, and looked him up and down.

'Ah, you'll be Bart's friend, then,' she observed, pointing him towards the window table. 'Can I offer you a drink, or anything?'

As he drank a glass of wine and waited for Bart to show, Mason looked over the latest version of the List. There were ten hits – eleven victims, if you took Cliff'n'Dawn as individuals. Maybe twelve if Damon Chiswick, Belinda's leading man, counted.

But Mason still felt he was missing something. Elvis had implied as much, with all this stuff about there *having* to be a recluse. So – there was some kind of overarching pattern in all this; some kind of schema.

He wondered whether Chris was right about him, when she said that his relaxed attitude to alternative beliefs was lazy. Certainly, people were exploited by charlatans, but they were also exploited by advertising, orthodox religion, the pop industry, politicians – by every organisation that needed something from them, to be harsh about it.

Mason lit a match and started to chew it. Look at the tobacco manufacturers, he thought – there's exploitation for you. If you wanted to have a pop at someone who's doing real harm, the coffin-nail conglomerates presented a much more deserving target than some airheaded bimbo who thought she was Boadicea's sword-polisher in a previous life. As long as it gave people a bit of a lift, Mason couldn't see that it hurt. For instance, he suspected, though he would never have said it to Chris, that Jess Bell found it easier to cope with her husband's death once she latched on to the ouija network. Was that so awful, really?

At ten-past, as he scrunched the list into his jeans pocket, a taxi pulled up outside, and Bart unfolded himself from the back of it. He waved through the restaurant window, whilst paying the driver. The waitress, seeing him, rushed over and opened the door.

'Hello, Bart,' she winked, as he came in. 'Your friend's already here.'

'So I see,' Bart nodded, pecking her on the cheek. 'Come and be introduced. He's much more your type, I regret to say, than I shall ever be.'

Mason groaned inwardly. This was bound to be embarrassing. Bart sat down, and the waitress put two menus on the table, still smiling.

'Mason,' Bart announced, 'may I introduce Tess. Not only is she a talented burger-flinger and mixer of stomach-curdling Bloody Marys, but she also has a thespian talent of such awe-inspiring prodigiousness that the English theatre should hang its head in shame to admit that no major company has yet displayed sufficient perspicacity to entreat her to take a leading role.'

'In other words, I'm an out-of-work actress,' Tess added.

'Nice to meet you,' Mason nodded.

'And this crotch-moistening heartbreaker,' Bart began, pointing at Mason.

'Is a very old friend,' Mason interrupted. 'And I haven't broken any hearts recently. Or the other thing he suggested, either.'

'Well, it's early yet,' Tess said, and, still chortling, she turned and walked away.

Bart just sat there smirking. 'You've turned the colour of a Caribbean sunset, Mason,' he remarked. 'You really must not take these things so seriously.'

'Oh, sod off,' Mason muttered, embarrassed by his own embarrassment. 'And anyway, I'm not going to allow you to set me up with your cast-offs, just so you can get them out of your hair, you patronising berk.'

'She is not, as you so crudely put it, one of my cast-offs,' Bart said airily. 'Tess and I have never been intimate. I simply flirt because it is my way. I cannot help myself.'

'You make it sound like a congenital disorder.'

'Who can say, Mason?' Bart asked. 'Is it nature or nurture that has made me the shallow, frivolous gadabout that I so demonstrably am? It's a bitch, isn't it?'

'Must be terrible,' Mason agreed. 'What do you want to eat?'

They spent most of the meal talking about football. Bart was an avid, if untypical, follower of Crystal Palace. There had been many occasions on the terraces when Mason had cringed as Bart yelled to the flagging Eagles, 'Come on, me beauties! As the bard has it, "The game's afoot; follow your spirit, and upon this charge cry, 'We're on our way to Wembley! We're on our way to Wembley!'"'

Throughout the meal, each time Tess attended the table, Bart would break off from explaining precisely where Palace went wrong in the run-up to promotion, in order to point out another of Mason's apparently inexhaustible roster of good points.

'I have it on good authority from Masters and Johnson themselves,' he confided as she delivered a second bottle of wine, 'that Mason has caused the textbooks to be rewritten; he discovered a third type of female orgasm.'

Eventually, Mason steered the conversation to the Trickster. 'It's all about undermining people who promote beliefs out of the mainstream, isn't it?' he suggested, hoping to set Bart off on that track. 'It's an attack on other people's truths.'

Bart lit a cigarette and pushed back his hair. 'People don't believe things because they're true, Mason. They believe them because they fit.' He put both hands flat on the table, and leaned back. 'Look. Whenever anyone is telling the tale of their Damascene conversion – to Christianity, or Buddhism, or astrological insight – they always say, "Suddenly everything made sense, everything that had always felt true to me fell into place." In other words, up to that point, they had felt uncomfortable with the way the cosmos appeared to work. But, in an instant, that discomfort is replaced by a feeling that all is as it should be.'

Mason nodded. 'Yeah. What's wrong with that?'

Bart shrugged, and took a long drag. 'What's wrong with it, Mase, is that it doesn't make sense. All the systems of belief are different. People just pick the one that justifies what they already feel, as if it were some kind of absolute. But all that's happening is the formalisation of the insecurity that made them feel less than happy in the first place.'

Nibbling a chip, Mason mulled. He looked out of the window for a few moments, and then back at Bart. 'Still don't see what's wrong with it,' he said.

Bart clucked his tongue against his teeth, and pushed his plate to one side, hunching across the table. 'Very well. Try this. Let's say you have a sneaking suspicion that the moon is made of cheese. Despite all the scientific evidence ranged against you, this notion of a lunar Gruyère tugs at your mind every time you look up into the night sky. You start to think you might be mad. Then, one day, a man comes along and says that the moon is *indeed* made of cheese. Moreover, ancient civilisations based entire religions on that undeniable premise – a premise that *must* be undeniable, otherwise the ancients wouldn't have done it.'

Mason lifted a hand to interrupt, but Bart ignored it.

'Our missionary, the Grande Fromage, explains this revelation to you. Apparently, the truth of the cheesy nature of heavenly bodies has been repressed for centuries. And yet *you*, Mason, always felt it was so. What an insightful and special person you are! Tell you what, you seer, you really ought to buy this book, which explores the Cheddar essence of Neptune, and reveals the Limburg rings of Saturn. Also, by the way, the Church of the Orbiting Brie needs a new roof. We accept Visa.'

Mason chuckled, and reached across for the matchbox. 'Yeah, all right. What would you prefer?'

Bart tipped back on his chair and lifted his glass of wine, grinning lopsidedly. 'Well, I'd settle for you simply being sufficiently self-confident that you didn't need the structures of a formal rennet religion in order to support your lunacy. Better yet, I'd like to know what made you believe such tosh in the first place.'

'And what do *you* believe in, then?' Mason asked, flicking a match from corner to corner of his mouth with his tongue.

'Ouch,' Bart frowned, smiling. 'Now there's the problem, of course. You want to know? Seriously?'

'Yeah.'

There was a pause. Bart shifted in his seat and looked out of the window, at the cars accelerating along Camden High Street and the people bustling in the late-night launderette across the road. He turned back, flicking his hair out of his eyes with a toss of the head, and grinning bashfully.

'Love,' he said. 'As long as it lasts, and despite its vagaries.'

Mason pursed his lips, and looked at his friend for a few moments. 'Are you taking the piss?' he asked, eventually.

Bart snorted with laughter. 'No! Strangely, I'm quite sincere.' He pulled another cigarette from the pack. 'And you?'

'Well – not love,' Mason said, wrinkling his nose. 'Certainly not love. Sauvignon. Cheers.'

Around ten-thirty, Tess came over and said, 'I'm finishing here in about a quarter of an hour, and I'm going on to a party in Swiss Cottage. Would you two like to come?'

'Well, that sounds like a sound scheme. Why not, eh, Mason?'

Mason hesitated. 'Er . . . well, umm . . . I'm pretty tired, actually.'

'Oh, God's teeth, Mason,' Bart tutted. He turned to Tess. 'I imagine that my companion is overwhelmed by your beauty. Don't worry, I'll put him right.'

'I bet,' said Tess.

When she was gone, Bart said, 'What further proof do you need, Mason? The woman is smitten by you.'

'I'm not the heart-throb type.'

'In Tess's case, I suspect the throb occurs rather lower than her heart, old pal.'

Mason gave him an ironic 'haha' grimace. 'Look,' he said, 'even if she does fancy me, I've gotta say, in all fairness, I'm just not in any position to get involved with anyone right now. You know, what with Chris and everything.'

'You're not seeing Chris again?' Bart asked sharply. 'Is that what your recent attack was about?'

'Not *seeing* seeing, no. Just *seeing around* seeing.'

'Oh,' Bart said. 'Good.'

'Why? What difference does it make to you?'

Bart shook his head, shrugged. 'It's just that you both get so jumpy when you're going out together, that's all. It makes it difficult for a chap to enjoy a quiet drink with either of you.'

Mason bridled. 'Well, it may surprise you to learn that we don't run our lives simply to keep *you* happy, fuckface,' he said, loudly. He reached for Bart's cigarettes, and then drew his hand back – though it took a real effort.

'Whoa, boy!' Bart said, holding up both hands. 'Whoo, I touched a live one there, didn't I? Okay, I apologise. I tend to forget that you're still so ... umm ... involved. I kid myself that you're over all that.'

Mason unhunched his tensed shoulders, ashamed of himself now. 'Shit. I'm sorry. My fault. You're right. I should be over it. It still gets to me, occasionally ... But, yes, I *should* be over it. *She* certainly is, the cow.'

Bart smiled. 'Zif,' he said, simply.

Tess came back. 'I've nicked some wine from the bar – so are you guys coming to this party, or not?'

Bart raised his eyebrows, looking at Mason. Mason sighed, and handed him the bill.

It was a clear, fine night and they decided to walk. They stuck to the backstreets, and Bart kept up a constant patter, inventing spurious historical facts concerning each road they walked down.

Tess laughed and clapped at each new flight of fancy, turning to Mason at one point, and saying, 'Where does he get this stuff?'

Mason shrugged. 'I dunno. It's a gift. As is the ability not to belt him in the mouth, may I say.'

'This is it,' Tess said, as they reached a three-storey house, from the top flat of which music pumped out into the clear warm night. The street door was ajar, and they followed crayoned signs that pointed up the stairs. As they walked into the hall of the apartment, a punky blonde in a black latex minidress bounded out of the kitchen, waving an open can of Red Stripe.

'Tessa!' she screeched, slooshing lager all over the wallpaper. 'How are you, you tart?'

'Diana!' Tess squealed in reply. 'You're a fine one to talk about tarts, in that get-up.'

'I know,' the hostess confided, biting her bottom lip delightedly. 'But it does things for Rocco – and if it does things for him, it does things for me!'

'I feel so at home,' Bart murmured.

The three of them pushed into the sardined kitchen. Bart took the wine from Tess, and jangled it into the crowd of bottles on the formica worktop. He then slid through the middle of a group of braying guests, and opened the aged Frigidaire. He studied the contents of the fridge for a few moments and deftly lifted two bottles from inside. Closing the door, he straightened up in the midst of the clump of chatterers.

'Pardon me,' he said. 'Having dumped some undrinkable plonk on the table, I was just stealing the palatable stuff.' The guests laughed and stood aside to let him through.

'Amazing, isn't it?' he commented, having squeezed through the crowd back to Mason as Tess wandered off to mingle. 'If you're brazen enough about the truth, people think you're joking. Grab that corkscrew, and let's find somewhere to sit.'

Mason followed Bart, knowing already where they would end up. At every house-party there is a bedroom where people feel they're not supposed to go. Bart had an unerring nose for such bedrooms, and always went there. Eventually, inevitably, the party came to him. The two of them sat on the bed in an easy silence, passing the wine to and fro. Mason was gagging for a cigarette; the craving was worse than it had been for a month. He started to chew the skin of his knuckles.

Bart picked up a little plastic troll from the bedside shelf, and tossed it from hand to hand, his elbows on his knees and his head bent forward. He turned, peering out from under his fringe, and pursed his lips contemplatively. He looked at Mason for several seconds, idly swinging the troll by its hair.

'I'm sorry I touched a sore place talking about Chris,' he said, out of the blue.

'Sall right. Forget it.'

'You're going to have to move on, you know.'

'Yeah, I know.'

'Apart from anything else, she's got her own life to live.'

'Yup.'

'As do you, of course.'

'Of course.'

Mason swapped to the knuckles of the other hand, and chewed some more.

'I hate seeing either of you unhappy,' Bart mused, looking down at the troll again. 'But you most of all.'

Mason was at a loss as to what to say. 'Well . . . we go back a long way, as they say, you and I,' he finally managed.

'This is true,' Bart nodded. 'I value your friendship more than anything, I suppose.'

He paused, and put the troll back on the shelf, then reached into his jacket pocket for his fags. He flicked his hair back, and sighed, then sat up straight. 'I really do,' he said, lipping a cigarette. He lit the fag, and exhaled, and looked at Mason again, quickly. 'I hope it all turns out all right,' he murmured.

Mason could tell that something important was going on here, but he really couldn't imagine what it was. He felt in the pocket of his jacket and found a partially masticated matchstick. He began chewing, but all the snap and fibre had already been chomped from it.

'Here, can I have a match?' he said, brightly.

'What? Oh, absolutely,' Bart said, and suddenly the confusing gravity of the conversation was dispelled. He handed Mason the matchbox. 'Take the lot. I will not have it whispered abroad that Bartholomew Molyneux Devereux Scott is undergenerous in the lucifer department.'

'Cheers,' Mason said, as he took them. 'Incidentally, you come across very well on camera.' He had no idea why he'd brought it up. He supposed that the futile compliment was intended as some kind of trade for Bart's show of affection.

'Really? You must play me the tape sometime. And the bit with Maria on it.'

'How did you know about that?' Mason asked.

'Well, that's why you were recording it, wasn't it? To get Maria's sketch?'

'Yeah, of course. But how did you know?'

'I guess you must have told me.'

'I don't think so. I'm sure I didn't.'

'Well,' Bart shrugged, 'I suppose I worked it out all on my little own, then.'

The door slammed open and Tess burst in. 'Are you two anti-social gits still in here?' she exclaimed. 'Come and party, for God's sake.' She grabbed Mason's wrist and attempted to pull him from the bed. 'Come on, Mason. Come and dance. Come on—'

'No, er, no, thanks,' he flustered. 'I can't dance to crap music, and this is seriously crap music. I mean, if they play some Motown or Ike and Tina or something, then I might . . .'

At which moment, the opening riff of *Nutbush City Limits* faded up from the outro of the previous technopop dross.

'You two kids run along and have fun,' Bart suggested, grinning.

CHAPTER TWENTY

By the time Mason woke up the next day, Tess was gone.

There was a note in the kitchen (*Lovely night. Call me at the restaurant. Love Tess xxx*), and Freda had been fed. Mason leaned his forehead on the bathroom mirror and groaned.

His instinctive and completely idiotic impulse was to phone Chris, deny everything and then apologise. This, he realised as he glugged back a couple of paracetamol, would hardly be appropriate.

'Anyway,' he said to the mirror, 'sod the old cow. Sod the both of them . . .' And it was only at that moment, hearing his own dismissive anger, that he remembered the full horror of the previous evening.

The front room of the apartment in Greencroft Gardens was empty of furniture, and a red bulb had been put in. A handful of people were jigging about and mouthing the approximate words to *Nutbush City Limits*, as Tess dragged Mason into the room.

Tess turned out to be a head-and-crotch dancer. Her feet stayed more or less still as she flung her long dirty-blonde hair in loops and arcs, and swung her pelvis in wide, spine-cracking ellipses. Mason was a feet-and-hands dancer. All his dances were just variations on the Shadows walk. He snuck in Kali-esque movements of the arms from time to time, but essentially he was performing steps that were old-fashioned before he was born.

The big problem, Mason found, with dancing, was not knowing where to look. You couldn't gaze at your partner because the sustained eye contact made you look like some kind of potentially dangerous obsessive. On the other hand, you couldn't stare at your own feet because then you appeared the sort of person who might move their finger along under the words when reading. So Mason tended to close his eyes and pretend to be transported by the music. This was supposed to make him look deep

– though on one occasion, at a club in Greece, he'd opened his eyes after a long stretch to find that everyone had gone to the bar, and he was dancing with a middle-aged Cypriot taxi-driver called Demis.

He and Tess danced through three or four records, and then someone put on an obscure album track, explaining to his friend and the room in general, 'No, no, it's *brilliant* this. It's a really good dance record, believe me. Look, I'll just play this and then we'll go back to the chart stuff. This is *killer*, really . . .'

Needless to say, it emptied the place.

Mason and Tess walked through to the kitchen and secured a couple of beers. Punky Di and her friends were talking about the Prankster. Mason eavesdropped for a while and then sidled to the edge of the conversation.

'It's just like so really fascist,' Diana was saying to a group of assorted drunks. 'I mean, does this Joker guy have some sort of problem with people believing different things to him, or what? The message here is *conform or you'll be sorry*, right?'

'Yeah, you're right,' nodded a bloke in small round glasses. 'It's a really male-dominant thing, you know? It's a manifestation of imperialist dogma and missionary arrogance. It's all about cocks, right? You know what I'm saying? Like this guy is setting himself up as the big patriarch who knows best.'

'It's fucking funny, though,' Mason volunteered.

'Yeah, sure,' returned Little-Glasses, turning to squint at him, 'if you think that persecuting people for their beliefs is *funny*. I mean, that's how the Brown Shirts started out, right?'

Mason was certain that this argument was fallacious, but for a moment the cold logic eluded him. He addressed the point obliquely.

'Oh, fuck off, you four-eyed little twerp,' he suggested.

It could have got nasty at that point but, with a flinching sigh, Tess grabbed Mason's forearm and dragged him from the kitchen, as the enraged Little-Glasses was held back by his friends. Tess guided Mason into the now-empty front room. The muted stereo was playing *Give Peace Chance*. She made him sit on the sofa, and slumped down beside him.

'Are you drunk, Mason?' she asked. 'Or just naturally objectionable?'

He shrugged sheepishly. 'I'm probably naturally objectionable,' he said,

143

staring at his feet, 'but I think being drunk enhances my God-given talent. Sorry. It's totally out of character for me to be aggressive.'

This was a simple truth; Mason hated violence. Not violence as a concept, but violence as an immediate possibility that might involve *him*. He suspected that it went back to being bullied at school. As if to mitigate the impression she must have formed of him, he told Tess about terrible dreams he had, in which he was pursued by people intent on doing him harm – people who had no concept of the consequences to themselves of bashing his face in.

'Usually, in these dreams, I get cornered, and I try to talk my way out. I point out that if they kill me, they'll do years inside, and am I really worth that? But it doesn't help. They won't listen to reason, and my wussy pleading just infuriates them. They beat me to a paste,' he explained.

He slid down on the sofa, looking sidelong at her. 'But then again,' he muttered sulkily, 'fair play – the geezer was a prat.'

'He's just a bloke,' Tess said. 'Have some charity.'

'Jerks like that don't deserve charity. You've got to draw the line somewhere.'

'Why?' Tess asked. 'If he's a jerk, just let him alone to be a jerk. What's the problem?'

'Oh, God,' Mason murmured, smiling to himself, 'you sound like me, and I sound like—'

He had been about to say 'Chris'.

'—a bigot,' he substituted.

They sat silently for a while, tapping their feet to the record.

'So,' Tess said, 'is Bart gay, or what?'

Mason chuckled. 'No. He's just camp. Or, rather, he's theatrical – he's the personification of the notion that all the world's a stage. Why do you ask? Do you fancy him?'

Tess scratched the bridge of her nose and tipped her head to one side, thinking. 'I used to, sort of. But he's not someone to get involved with. All that badinage would get incredibly wearing after a while. I mean, you can't imagine yourself curling up in front of a roaring log fire with Bart, and just enjoying the silence.'

'There wouldn't be any,' Mason said, swigging his beer.

Lennon put the argument that instant karma was going to get them.

Mason crossed his legs, and then uncrossed them. He didn't know what to say. He was aware that, at this point, he should be grasping the opportunity to launch into some kind of airy chat-up, but he'd never been very good at it. It seemed such a false and pointless pavane – the pretended fascination, the insidious intimacy. It was like lying, and he was a terrible liar. He sipped his drink. He sipped it again. He tried to give the impression that he'd be talking a blue streak, were it not for the fact that his drink needed so much sipping.

'Has Bart got a girlfriend?' Tess asked.

'I'm not sure. He's really cagey about his girlfriends. You don't get to meet them, generally. It's like he considers girlfriends a different sphere of his life to regular friends. But I don't suppose he's going short. Why are you asking all these questions about Bart?'

Tess considered for a few moments. 'Diversionary tactics. It stops me asking questions about you.'

Mason gave her a quizzical look. 'So ask questions about me – I don't mind.'

'All right,' Tess said, sitting up, and bringing her legs onto the sofa so she was facing him. 'Question one: are you gay?'

'Uh . . . not as far as I can tell.'

'Question two: have you got a girlfriend, wife or significant semi-permanent life-partner?'

'Not so's you'd notice,' he replied promptly, still unable to see where this was leading.

'Question three: do you practise safe sex?'

'Ah.' He had caught up. 'Umm . . . to be honest, it's been so long that I can't remember.'

'I'll take that as a yes,' Tess said. 'Question four: do you want to sleep with me tonight?'

Mason felt a little shiver of apprehension zipped through him. 'Umm . . .'

Tess sighed. 'This is not a question you're supposed to have to think about,' she said. 'It's a simple yes-or-no.'

'Don't be so ingenuous,' he replied. 'Of course it's not.'

'You mean disingenuous,' she said.

'Look it up,' he advised her. 'I know what I mean.' He didn't. He was playing for time.

Tess stared thoughtfully into his eyes. He looked away, and scanned the room.

'I'm in danger of scaring you off, aren't I?' Tess said, at last.

'Perilously,' he admitted, looking back at her.

'All right. Let's go through the rituals,' she suggested, with a one-shouldered shrug. 'I'll put a record on.'

She went over to the record player and haunched down to flick through the CDs.

Nice arse, Mason thought. In fact, let's run the full sexist gamut on this one. Nice arse. Fair-sized tits with built-in bounce. Good face with terrific brown eyes. Incredible hair and lots of it. And, let's be honest, so much chutzpah that she just *has* to be wild in the sack.

So where's your problem? he asked himself. And he knew the answer. Her arse wasn't just that bit too broad. Her tits weren't that bit too small. Her face didn't have that quirky wide mouth. Her hair wasn't hennaed red, and she didn't have that take-it-or-leave-it tone that meant he'd have to work at it.

She wasn't Chris.

'You like ancient soul, yeah?' Tess asked over her shoulder. 'Marvin Gaye all right for you?'

'Sure.'

Tess pushed the disc in, and Mason stood up. The song, inevitably, was *Sexual Healing*. She walked over to him and dropped her arms around his neck. He linked his hands at the small of her back and shuffled in a little circle, as she swayed gently to the beat.

'Relax,' she smiled up at him.

There was still space between them. Mason could see the toes of his Doc Martens.

'In the immortal words of somebody or other,' Tess murmured, amusedly, 'Kiss Me, Stupid . . .'

Mason could see no polite way of delaying it. He dipped his face to hers, and their mouths met. Her tongue tasted of flesh, not cigarettes, as Chris's did. He'd forgotten that tongues could taste like that. It occurred to him that his own tongue must taste of flesh too, now he'd given up smoking. He ran a hand up and down her back, feeling the band of her bra, and the bump on the band where the bra fastened. Her breasts pressed just below his ribcage. Five feet eight or nine, he thought. About the same as Chris.

They broke the kiss and Tess rested her head against his shoulder. He put an unconvincing hand on the back of her neck, and they undulated together in silence. Mason felt like he was fourteen. He had genuinely forgotten how to do this stuff. He found himself worrying about close-dancing erections. This was a perennial no-win quandary, he reckoned, because if he got one, she'd feel it pressing against her, which would be embarrassing. On the other hand, if he *didn't* get one, she *wouldn't* feel it pressing against her, which would be embarrassing too.

Marvin Gaye gave way to Smokey Robinson, who had apparently heard that people considered him the life of the party, on account of him telling a joke or two. Mason wondered about Bart's furtiveness, and whether he'd overreacted in thinking it circumstantial evidence that he was the Joker. After all, as he'd so recently told Tess, Bart was equally cagey about his girlfriends. Maybe that's all it was – Bart had a new woman. The one who'd been there when he'd phoned up in crisis, and Bart had done the lecture about moving on, and giving up on Chris.

All that 'I value your friendship, I hope it all turns out right' stuff was odd, too. What was all that about? It definitely signified something. Something personal – it didn't seem to be a Trickster thing.

And while we're on the subject, Mason demanded as Tess nuzzled his neck, how did Bart know that I taped the show because my mum was on it? I certainly didn't tell him. The only person I told was—

Chris.

Something frozen burned along Mason's spine.

Oh fuck, he thought, closing his eyes against the sudden realisation.

Oh, Jesus fucking Christ. Oh, please God, no. Don't let that be it.

But it all fitted. Bart's questions about his attitude to Chris. His concern that their friendship should be re-affirmed. His evasiveness. His insistence on Mason forgetting Chris, finding another woman. Setting him up this evening with Tess. Even Chris's amused dismissal of the notion that Bart might be the Trickster. It all fitted perfectly.

Oh, Christ, Mason whispered silently, dropping his forehead onto Tess's shoulder.

Bart's going out with Chris.

Chris is going out with Bart.

It explained it all.

Bart and Chris are fucking each other.

147

He straightened, and gulped, looking up at the red bulb in the centre of the room.

Oh, Jesus. The bastards, the bastards, the bastards . . .

He wiped his palm across his mouth and stepped back from Tess. He put a finger under her chin and lifted her head.

'Hello,' she smiled.

'Let's go home,' he said.

CHAPTER TWENTY-ONE

Given that she had once been the most-snapped woman on the planet, it was perhaps understandable that Suzette scarcely even noticed photographs of herself. But the photo that was shoved under her nose as she sipped an orange juice at the bar of the Museum of Fashion was one that she had never seen before. It had been cut from an Italian magazine, and it must have been thirty years old if it was a day.

Suzette Winkworth (fifty-two, bestselling author and temporary corporeal residence of an eternal transcendent soul) found herself face-to-face with the image of Suzy the Wink (nineteen, kittenish clothes-horse, flat-chested flowerchild and temporary corporeal residence of any man who caught her fancy). The fifty-two-year-old eyed the teenager with all the dismissive contempt that measured maturity reserves for youthful excess.

'Could you sign it for me, Suzy?' slobbered the middle-aged man proffering the shot. 'It's always been my favourite of you. I've had it for years. And you haven't changed a bit, if I may say so.'

Suzette Winkworth looked up from the photo of what she had once been and into the face of what she had once made others become. The eager approval of how many mumbling, hope-stoned men had she tolerated in her life? How goddamn many? The eyes on this one were too dull and stupid to be worth even her thirty-second lecture on the vapidity of physical beauty. He was an unreclaimable drooler – she knew the type.

'I only autograph books, I'm afraid,' she said, and catwalked through the glass doors back to the table in the Sixties Room, where she was signing copies of her latest work.

She'd pulled a good crowd. Her British publicist, Madelaine, who was twittering as she marshalled the acolytes into a queue, had really pulled it out of the bag this time around. Suzette was impressed; and she was, by her own admission, not an easy woman to impress.

A podgy, rumpled lady stepped forward, clutching a copy of *Step Outside and Say That*, Suzette's new opus. She was typical of Suzette's readership – a readership that thrilled to the book's premise that the human body is merely a vessel to carry the soul, and no more important than the eggshell to the chick. What's more, the soul, if trained in the techniques that the book presented, could be trained to leave the body and fly, free and unencumbered, surfing the ether, swooping on the upcurrents of the lifeforce, before returning, refreshed, to the hovel of meat and bone that we so shallowly think of as our real self. It followed, then, that physical beauty was an irrelevance, a chimera, a sham. Suzette's book made that point repeatedly and at length.

To the podgy women who snapped up Suzette's books on the day of publication, this was a powerful notion; one that could be waved indignantly under the noses of disgruntled husbands and critical boyfriends. See? See? It doesn't matter what people look like! Don't take my word for it – this is Suzy Winkworth talking here! Suzy the Wink! The most beautiful woman in the world! Read chapter five! It's the beauty of the *soul* that's important!

All the podgy women had beautiful souls, just like Suzette's. And many of them had followed her to a further liberating conclusion arising from the irrelevancy of the physical being. Like their heroine, they had embraced celibacy. It made perfect sense – right there in chapter twelve. Having struggled with chapter five, the disgruntled husbands had even more trouble with chapter twelve.

The woman pushed her copy of *Step Outside and Say That* across the table for Suzette to sign.

'Could you make it "To Verity", please?' she simpered, dimpledly. 'You're looking gorgeous, by the way.'

Verity was right. Suzette looked great. She was slim; her hips were still narrow; her dark hair, kept long in unconscious rebellion against the Peter-Pan cuts of her heyday, was lit by the subtlest silver filigree. Her practised smile still gladdened the hearts of battle-weary paparazzi from Florence to Frisco. Of *course* she looked great. She *had* to look great. You couldn't go round the world telling people that beauty was unimportant if you looked like a hippo with toothache. People didn't buy it. And the podgy women *needed* Suzy to be beautiful – it was into that beauty that the noses of the disgruntled husbands were so self-righteously rubbed.

Suzette signed, handed the book back, signed another, handed it back, glanced at her watch. Madelaine was still chirping and fluttering at the waiting admirers, trying to keep them in line. She was a small, slender woman, like a stem of wheat. She was in severe danger of being milled.

From a seat on the other side of the room, half-hidden by a mannequin in a Mary Quant plastic minidress, Mischief watched as Suzette shrugged off her black-velvet jacket and hung it over the back of the chair, before accepting the next book from a glowing fan. The crowd was growing. More women were pushing forward, and the middle-aged men who had been hanging back, sheepish and open-mouthed as they gazed at Suzette from afar, seemed to be plucking up courage *en masse* to join the throng, each sucking in his stomach, and trying to look as if he had the evening free, should the subject crop up.

Holding an envelope in one leather-gloved hand, Mischief got up and strolled around the exhibits to the back of the crowd. A large, cross-looking woman in a patterned dress was saying to her neighbour, 'We'll never get to the front at this rate. They ought to organise it better.'

Mischief sidled in beside her, and tutted. 'Apparently she's got to go in ten minutes, you know.'

The large woman looked round. 'No! After we've waited all this time?'

Mischief nodded, and pointed at Madelaine. 'That lady organising said she's only signing five more – then she's off. It's a shambles, isn't it?'

'Well, I'm not having that!' the large woman declared, and started to elbow her way forward.

Mischief turned to another Suzy fan, whose beautiful soul was difficult to perceive behind her scowling eyes, as she watched the large woman charge through the throng.

'Weren't you in front of her?' Mischief asked. 'Some people! Honestly!'

The orderly queue disintegrated and the situation became confused. Madelaine was trampled like chaff. Press-fresh copies of Suzette's book flew through the air, and unkind words were exchanged.

In the tumult, Mischief slipped around to the back of the desk, slid the envelope into the pocket of Suzette Winkworth's jacket, and then, lighting a cigarette, walked out into the bright Saturday sunshine of the London weekend.

* * *

Mason binned Tess's note and went to take a shower. Afterwards, he lay on his bed, wrapped in towels, clasping a cup of tea and pondering.

When Bart had asked him in the diner what he believed in, he really hadn't known. But the answer, he supposed, if he'd given it some thought, would have been Friendship. And even that would have been a watered-down version of what he'd started out with, years ago. At fifteen or sixteen, fizzy with hormones and romantically unbruised, he'd believed in Love. But that had soon got knocked out of him, and he'd realised that the unshakeable constant in his life was affection not for lovers, but for friends. He and Bart had seen each other through some pretty murky stuff. And even he and Chris, although a disaster as a couple, had worked bloody hard at staying friends. He'd trusted them both. He felt an idiot.

Freda sauntered in and leapt up onto the bed. She rubbed her head against Mason's face, and then padded up to his chest. She clawed at the towel for a few moments, and then settled down, staring at him unblinkingly. Mason scratched her nose gently with one finger.

'I tell you what, Freda,' he said. 'One thing that aliens have going for them – they never let you down. And crystals are pretty reliable too. And if you put your faith in some Great Beyond, you'll *never* be disappointed, will you? Either you get to be proved right, and you can sit up there on your cloud gloating about it, or – bang – oblivion, and no one ever says "I told you so."'

Freda purred happily and pushed her head up under his hand.

'I'm giving you the inside track here, cat,' Mason told her. 'Friendship is a bloody shaky basis for a system of belief. In fact, if you come back as a human being and you're window-shopping for some solid tenet by which to lead a contented and fulfilling life, take my advice – any concept dependent on the constancy of other people is a total fucking no-no. I'd go for the lump of quartz, if I were you.'

Half an hour later, sullen and unhappy, Mason trudged down the hill towards the tube station. He was supposed to meet Elvis at noon, but he really didn't feel like it. Just to prove to himself how little anything mattered any more, he walked through the ticket barrier without paying, and stood on the left side of the escalator in defiance of the notices asking him to stand on the right. The indicator on the platform said that it would be eleven minutes until the next train. He slumped on to a bench, reached into his pocket for a match, and pulled out a sheet of paper. It was the hit list. He looked at it for a moment and gave a bitter little laugh. Then he folded it in half, tore it into strips, balled all the strips together and tossed the ball onto the tracks.

With a deep sigh, he rested his head back against the wall, closed his eyes and thought about sex with Tess. It didn't help. Whenever he tried to picture something he'd done to her, or she'd done to him, all he could see was Bart doing it to Chris, or Chris doing it to Bart. They appeared to be having more *fun* doing it, too.

The train was crowded, and he had to strap-hang. At Goodge Street, a lovey couple got on, all moist eyes and post-coital giggles. They stood next to him – though they could have been standing next to Godzilla for all the attention they paid to the world outside themselves. They simpered and pecked at each other, semaphoring their eyebrows and counting each other's fingers. Mason nearly retched.

As the train drew into Leicester Square, the boy said, 'What shall we do tonight? Do you fancy going out for some pasta?'

'Mmm,' the girl giggled. 'You've got to keep your strength up.'

The boy gave a self-satisfied smirk. 'I thought I might ask Bob along. You remember my mate Bob? You met him at the King's Head.'

'Oh, yeah. I like him. Yeah, ask him along.'

The train doors opened. Just before he stepped out onto the platform, Mason tapped the boy on the shoulder.

'A word to the wise, mate,' he said. 'Don't let Bob within a mile of her.'

Having skipped the ticket barrier at the top of the escalator, he emerged onto the Charing Cross Road, turned east towards St Martin's Lane, and then cut down Garrick Street.

The whole area was booby-trapped. He passed the restaurant where he and Chris had celebrated her twenty-ninth birthday the year before last. He went by the hire shop where he'd rented clothes for Bart's posh summer party. He cast his eyes down so as to avoid a wine bar in which the three of them had drunk eight bottles of champagne in an attempt to flush some bad speed out of their systems.

Maybe I'll move to Wigan, he thought. I've never been there.

A voice from the other side of the street called Mason's name. It was Elvis.

'Hi.' Mason nodded unenthusiastically.

Elvis trotted across. He was wearing a black tailcoat, drainpipes and reflector shades. He looked like a trendy insect. 'Wotcher, Mason, me old cock-sparrer,' he said. 'Ow's yer arse'ole fer crackin' walnuts?'

'What a charming expression,' Mason replied. 'I need a drink. Let's go.'

They continued down the street towards the Orange Pub.

'So have you made any progress on the Trickster?' Elvis asked.

'No. I've given up on it. I got bored,' Mason lied.

Elvis frowned. 'Hey, what's up?' he asked, putting his hand on Mason's shoulder, and stopping him walking. He tipped his head to one side, pulled his shades down his nose, and met Mason's eyes with his ice-green gaze. He was still smiling, but kindly rather than amusedly. 'Tell your Uncle Elvis.'

Mason humphed and looked away up the street. 'I really want a drink. Several.'

Elvis tutted. 'Come on, Mr Sulky,' he said, taking Mason's elbow and leading him across the road. 'I want to show you something. I was saving this little treat for later, but I think you need it right away.'

Mason wrenched his arm free. 'I just want a beer, okay?' he snapped.

Ignoring the outburst, Elvis set off briskly down an alley. Mason grimaced and followed him, humphing. Elvis turned left into a cul-de-sac, stopped outside a plain black door and rang the bell.

'*El-vis.*' Mason was almost pleading by now. 'I really am not up for anything but a few beers. Now can we *please* just go to the fucking boozer and get some down our necks?'

At that moment the door was opened by a small, slight, middle-aged man wearing a dark suit, a grey waistcoat and a *pince-nez*. He looked like a pre-war solicitor.

'Sure, it's Mr Sirhan,' he said, addressing Elvis. 'An' howarya, me fine fella?' His smooth Dublin accent was thick as Irish butter; his voice deep and dark as Galway Bay.

'Never better, Fionn,' Elvis said, shaking the man's hand. 'I'd like you to meet my friend Mason. Mason, Fionn Cahill.'

'Hi,' Mason intoned, dully.

'Nice t'meetcha. Come in, the two of yis.'

He led them down a linoleumed corridor into a large kitchen-diner. All the surfaces were spotless, the cupboards gleamed and the sink looked like an advertisement for domestic detergents. There was a large smoked-glass table with chrome legs, and Fionn motioned them to sit at it.

'Hope y'don't mind settin' in the parlour,' he said. 'And y'must excuse the state o' the place. As me oul' ma used to say, a quarter after twelve, an' not a babby in th' house is washed. Can I offer youse some tea?'

'Sure, dat'd be grand,' Elvis said, in imitation of Fionn's brogue.

'Not bad,' Fionn grinned, as he filled the kettle, 'but you still sound like an Irish cop from a Jimmy Cagney movie, sure.'

'And you don't?'

'Anyways,' Fionn asked, joining them at the table, 'what can I do fer yer?'

'I'd like you to throw one for Mason here,' Elvis said, 'if you've got the time.'

Fionn looked at Mason, sitting there in his kitchen scowling like an eight-year-old.

'Surely. It'd be a pleasure.'

'Hang on a minute,' Mason interjected, 'what's going on? Throw one what?'

'Fionn is a Tarot-reader, Mason,' Elvis explained. 'And a good one, too.'

'Ah,' Mason nodded. 'Well, thanks and all that, but I think I'll give it a miss. I really don't go for that stuff.'

'D'ye think it's nonsense, then?' Fionn asked pleasantly.

Actually, that was not the problem. Mason just didn't want to play. But he was happy simply to be obnoxious. 'Yes,' he muttered.

Fionn was unperturbed. 'So, if you think it's all claptrap, Mason my man, what harm will it do ye t'pass a few minutes indulging me in me primitive superstitions?'

Mason jutted his bottom lip. 'What are you planning to do? Tell my future? Because I really don't want to know.'

Fionn gazed at him thoughtfully. 'Would you describe y'self as a rationalist, Mason?' he asked. 'D'ye like things to be explicable in terms of known and observable phenomena?'

Mason nodded, sullenly.

'Then try lookin' at it this way . . .' As he was speaking, Fionn got up and set about making a pot of tea. 'Have y'ever been in the position where y've got a choice of a coupla things to do? Fr'instance, let's say that this evening ye can either go fer a beer with y'girl, or pass a few hours playin' cards with the lads. Would y'recognise such a dilemma?'

'Spose so,' Mason admitted dubiously.

'An' yer really not sure which it is ye want to do, let's say? Would y'not decide that ye'll settle it on the toss of a coin, now?'

'Might do.' Even Mason was getting bored with himself by now.

'So, we'll say heads for the drink with a young one, and tails the poker game. Would y'toss a coin, please, Sirhan?' Fionn instructed Elvis, as he took three mugs from a cupboard.

Elvis flipped a penny, and smacked it to the table. 'Tails,' he announced.

'The poker game,' Fionn nodded, bringing a laden tea tray to the table. 'There's y'decision, Mason.'

'Can't we make it best-of-three?' Mason asked, realising, now that he was faced with the imaginary prospect of letting some woman down – and the woman he was imagining was Chris – that he didn't want to play cards at all.

Fionn clapped his hands and grinned triumphantly. 'Exactly, young fella! Ye're ways ahead of me. Y'see, this random happenstance of tossing a coin has helped y'see what it is y'really want to do. Y'really want t'go out with y'woman, isn't that the way of it? That's why yer'd have the coin thrown again.' He poured the tea. 'This simple little binary chance has shown yer the future, right enough. A minute ago y'didn't know what yer were going to do, and now you do. Help y'self t'milk.' He pushed a steaming mug across the table.

'Now, if y'like,' he continued, 'y'can see the Tarot as a highly subtle flick of the coin. It provides images and symbols in an infinite variety of combinations, and they spark off all sorts of recognitions in y'head, that y'didn't even know were there.'

'Yeah, okay,' Mason said. 'I can see that.'

'So I'm not going to be sayin' to yer, "Beware a woman carrying a suitcase and wearing green", or any such crap. But I might say, "Ye're in conflict with someone close to you", and you must decide what that means in yer own life.'

It did seem to make a sort of sense, put like that. 'And you're saying that's all there is to it?' Mason asked.

Fionn laughed. 'Jaysus, no. But it's the part y'can attach nice, safe, twentieth-century words to, like "archetype", "cognition" and "unconscious symbology".' He leaned across the table. 'Now, doesn't that make y'feel safer, Mason? If I throw in a little seasoning of Jungian psychology, do you not feel protected from the witches and ghoulies I'm about to conjure?'

Mason regarded Fionn suspiciously. 'Are you making fun of me?' he said, smiling slightly for the first time.

'Oh, no, son,' Fionn replied with a wry twinkle. 'Not hardly at all.'

Mason expected to be taken to a room hung with embroidered runic devices and lit by guttering candles, but Fionn simply pushed the tea tray to one side, and took a deck of cards from a drawer behind him.

'Er, shouldn't we be burning incense or aligning ourselves with the rising sun or something?' Mason asked.

'Is it incense you want now?' Fionn said. 'Well, not in this house, y'don't. It gets into the curtains and hangs around fer days. But y'right enough. There is a little ritual to go through.' He handed Mason the pack. 'Would y'shuffle the deck, please, and then flick through the cards and blow into 'em.'

Mason did so, clumsily, dropping cards all over the place. He straightened them up, and blew as he riffled them.

'Grand,' Fionn said, taking the pack. 'Now, this spread is called the Celtic Cross . . .'

He laid out ten cards in a vaguely cruciform pattern, and surveyed them in silence for a few seconds. Mason tried to take in the pictures, and the names of the cards which were printed in a Gothic typeface. One card, The Lovers, carried the image of a couple embracing. Another, The Five of Rods, showed medieval types fighting with long wooden staffs. The Hanged Man, which lay in the centre of the table, depicted a man suspended from a gibbet by a rope tied to his foot.

'Y're in a period of transition at the moment,' Fionn said. 'Y're not sure where y'going.'

'This is too fucking true,' Mason was about to reply, but then decided that that would be giving Fionn clues. He bit his lip.

'And this transition is made the more difficult because you don't know where y'*want* to go.' Fionn touched and tapped the cards as he spoke, resting his fingers in one place for a moment, and then shifting to another, as if he were playing a musical instrument. 'You see, y've no clear idea of what it is you hope to achieve. Whatever it may be though, it'll have to be something profound. Y'won't settle for anything superficial or second-best. In fact, I'd advise yer to avoid any frivolous involvement that might divert y'from a more important goal.'

That'll be Tess, Mason thought. Oops.

'At sometime in the past, y've made a rash decision that still has repercussions in the present. It's resulted in frustration and created obstacles – but you intended it to do the very opposite . . .'

I should never have split up with Chris, Mason thought immediately. Then he grinned. He was really getting drawn in.

'In truth, you do have this tendency to burn bridges behind y'self, when there's really no need at all.' Fionn paused and took a drink of tea. 'Are y'recognising any of this, Mason?' he asked.

'Uh . . . yeah, I think so,' Mason nodded. 'Go on.' He leaned forward with his elbows on the table, his eyes flicking between Fionn's face and the spread of cards. Elvis was sitting back, his expression serious, sipping his tea and watching Fionn as he spoke.

'Go on,' Mason said again. 'Please.'

'Certainly,' Fionn said, and turned his attention back to the cards. 'Folk are very fond of you – ye're very easy to like. But ye're wary – yer want to trust people, but y'never quite sure. Ye're on the look-out fer betrayal.'

Bloody right. If *your* best friend was screwing the woman you loved, you'd be on the look-out for betrayal too.

'But whatever it is that's hurting you at the moment is of yer own making.'

Mason tutted. That was just unfair. Like he forced them together or something. Like it was his fault.

'Now, here,' Fionn said, tapping a card.

'Er, yeah, I was hoping we might skip that one,' Mason ventured.

The card showed a skeleton with a scythe, reaping a field of skulls. Mason didn't need the Gothic caption to tell him that the card was Death.

'Sure, it's not as bad as it looks,' Fionn said. 'It simply shows that y've got to cut away the dead wood. There are attitudes and ideas that don't work any more, and y've got to get shot of them. But ye're frightened to do it. You want to cling on.'

Mason tutted again. He could see that Fionn was saying he had to give up on Chris. Mason already knew that. Or at least, he knew that he probably knew that. But he'd never heard it said inside his head until that moment.

'And if you do get rid of these old ways,' Fionn said, indicating The Lovers, 'then it's a real Hollywood ending for yer. Y'll be able to achieve that profound and satisfying goal that I told yer about before.'

Ah – of course! Mason thought, grinning and relieved. I get it! Until I stop obsessing about Chris, I'll never get her! Obvious! Why haven't I seen that before?

He suddenly felt very cheered up.

'It all comes out right!' he exclaimed, excitedly. 'You mean I Get the Girl, don't you?'

'Why, Mason,' Fionn smiled, sitting back, 'y'wouldn't be asking me to tell yer the future, now, would yer?'

CHAPTER TWENTY-TWO

Zerkah ran down the corridor towards the lifts, and saw the doors closing. She sprinted forward and dived for the gap, shoving her foot into it. The doors buzzed indignantly and opened again.

'Sir,' she said breathlessly to David Jennings, who was standing inside mulling over his choice of takeaway pizza, 'we've got one! Someone's been sent a card!'

Jennings smiled broadly. 'Get in,' he said. 'We'll pick up a Big Mac on the way.'

Back at her hotel, Suzette Winkworth had found the envelope in her jacket pocket. She'd opened it, and frowned.

'What's this supposed to mean?' she asked Madelaine, who was holding her own jacket up to the light of the window and brushing footprints off it, wittering disconsolately.

Madelaine was a publicist. It was her job to read newspapers. She made the connection immediately. She squealed and dropped her jacket.

'Put it down! Phone 999!' she yelped. Whimpering, she hurriedly pulled the curtains shut and rushed across to lock the door.

By the time Jennings and Zerkah arrived, Suzette had calmed Madelaine down sufficiently to get the story out of her.

'To tell you the truth, I don't buy this bullshit,' she told Jennings, as they sat in the hotel lobby. Zerkah took the card from her, holding it by the edges, and slipped it into a plastic envelope.

'I really think perhaps you should,' Jennings told her. 'What's your schedule while you're in Britain?'

'Coupla signings. Breakfast TV appearance Monday.' Suzette shrugged. 'Not a whole lot.'

'That's when you're vulnerable.' Jennings nodded.

'Vulnerable!' moaned Madelaine, her g'n't glass chattering against her teeth. She was having a very trying day.

'We'll accompany you whenever you make public appearances,' Jennings went on. 'We'll be very unobtrusive, I promise.'

'Whatever,' Suzette pouted. 'But it's a waste of time. I mean, this guy's targeting freaks.'

'Better safe than sorry, Ms Winkworth,' Zerkah suggested, zipping up her handbag.

Back in the car, as they rounded Parliament Square, Jennings looked at Zerkah and grinned. 'Not unequivocally taken with that lady, are you?' he suggested.

Zerkah checked her rearview and changed lanes. 'I'm a good copper, sir. I don't have opinions,' she said, blankly.

Jennings nodded. 'Then I must be a bad copper, because I have very strong opinions. I just keep them out of the job.'

They stopped at traffic lights and Zerkah stared ahead. She tapped her fingers on the steering wheel, and revved the engine.

'If you did have an opinion,' Jennings persisted, 'which you don't, what would it be?'

Zerkah restlessly put the car in and out of first, and crept the lights. 'Come on, come on,' she muttered.

'Really. I'm interested,' Jennings said, still looking at her.

'Well,' Zerkah began, tautly, 'she wants it both ways, doesn't she? She wants to be gorgeous and at the same time say that being gorgeous is irrelevant. I mean, cake and eat it, or what?'

Jennings nodded. 'But . . .'

'Can you imagine what she spends on make-up?' Zerkah continued. 'On her hair? On her clothes? And then she swans around telling other women not to bother. She's a hypocrite. And it gets on my tits.'

She glanced swiftly at Jennings. 'Sir,' she added.

Jennings raised an eyebrow. 'She's harmless enough though, isn't she – if misguided?'

'You're very charitable, sir,' Zerkah said, pulling away from the lights. 'You have to be.'

'Why do I have to be?' Jennings asked. 'And slow down a bit. This is a built-up area.'

'"If I have the faith to move mountains,"' Zerkah said, bringing her foot up off the gas, '"but I lack charity, I am nothing."' She glanced at him again. 'That's what the Bible says, isn't it?'

'Yes,' Jennings admitted. 'Doesn't the Koran say the same sort of thing?'

Zerkah pulled the car into the forecourt of Scotland Yard, and swung into a space. She switched off the engine, and undid her seatbelt.

'More or less.' She nodded. 'But it also says I should have married a man in Rawalpindi who I've never met. So I'm not that convinced about its authority, frankly.'

Jennings pinched his nose thoughtfully. The conversation was moving into an area that he felt was not his business. But he knew so little about Zerkah – her background, her beliefs, her ambitions – and he was curious.

'I take it you're not a practising Muslim, then?' he ventured.

Zerkah chuckled. 'I try not to be,' she said, opening the car door. 'I won't be happy I've made it until I get a craving for pork pie.'

In the Orange Pub, Mason sat at a table mulling over the Tarot reading, while Elvis went to the bar for drinks. He tried to analyze to what extent Fionn's patter had been so generalised that it would have seemed relevant to any old punter off the street – which was exactly what he was, after all. Whatever the mechanics or para-mechanics of the Tarot, he had to admit that it had prompted him to marshal his thoughts. He *was* clinging to outmoded attitudes regarding Chris. He *did* tend to seek out betrayal. An affair with Tess *would* be a superficial diversion.

He reached out and took his beer from Elvis. 'Cheers.'

'Here's to the boys in the band,' Elvis suggested, downing half his pint.

'So, do you believe in Tarot and all that stuff, then?' he asked.

'Do you believe in walnuts?' Elvis replied.

'Oh, don't be cryptic, Presley. I mean, do you believe that they have mystic powers?'

'I know they can be useful. It's more a question of the model you use to explain what's happening.'

'No, it's not. Some things are *provable*. I mean, that's what science is, for God's sake.'

'Science, whatever that means, is just another system of faith, my child.'

'Oh, crap, Elvis,' Mason said scornfully. 'It's a collection of proven hypotheses. Jesus, you're just trying to wind me up.'

'Ah, but how can we be sure?' Elvis said, in a sing-song, pseudo-mystical voice. 'Grasp the hem of my garment, mortal, and I will take you back, back, baa-ack, through the mists of Time itself.' His hands wove a serpentine dance in front of Mason's face. 'And here we are,' he said, 'in downtown Ancient Athens. To your left, the Parthenon, which will be completed any year now, and to your right, a bearded chap inventing mathematics. Now – observe this Ancient Greek walnut.' He produced one from the inside pocket of his tailcoat.

'Why are you carrying a walnut around?' Mason asked.

'For a treat. It doesn't get out much. Watch – if I hold this walnut in the air, like so, and let go of it—' The walnut dropped from Elvis's outstretched hand, bounced on the tabletop and rolled off across the floor. '—it ends up underneath the jukebox, much as expected. But – and this is the reason for our visit to sunny Athens – let's ask a passing Ancient Greek why that happened.' Elvis put on a vaguely Mediterranean accent. 'The walnut, he go to the ground because he is made of earth-elements. He is returning to his natural level.'

Elvis grinned at Mason, spreading his hands. 'A fine theory, I think you'll agree. It covers all the observable facts; it is readily understood; and, so far, no walnuts have shot off into space, so all the empirical back-up is there.

'Now, Mason,' he concluded. 'Would you care to explain to me how gravity works?'

Physics had never been Mason's long suit, but he gave it a shot. 'Uh, well, masses are attracted to each other and, umm, the bigger the mass, the stronger the attraction.'

'Yup. That's a good theory too,' Elvis allowed, magnanimously. 'It begs a couple of questions, of course – like, *why*? – but it's a good theory as far as it goes.'

'But the difference is,' Mason said exasperatedly, 'that gravity's right and the elements thing is wrong. I mean, you can't deny that, surely?'

'Of course, I can't,' Elvis shrugged. 'The gravity-explanation of the travelling walnut is the one I was brought up to believe. I believe it so implicitly, so profoundly, that I think it's an objective truth. That's what faith *is*. We all need some kind of faith – and as far as I can see, it doesn't really matter much which one we choose.'

163

Mason shook his head and frowned. 'No. It's all wrong somewhere,' he murmured.

'Okay,' Elvis said pleasantly. 'Let's not have it spoil our day. Could you reach my walnut out from under the Wurlitzer?'

As they parted at the tube station, three or four pints later, Elvis said, 'I've got something for you.'

'It's not a walnut, is it?' Mason asked, as Elvis reached into his inside pocket.

'No. It's a secret.'

He gave Mason a deck of Tarot cards.

'There's a little booklet in there,' he said. 'Pay particular attention to pages eight to twenty-four, and look at the corresponding cards.'

Mason was touched. He always was by presents. 'Er, well, thanks. Thanks a lot.'

'You're welcome. I put my phone number in there too. Give me a call.'

'Yeah. Of course.'

'Okey-dokey. See you around, *mon Valet des Epées*. And, with those strange words, he disappeared in a puff of blue smoke.'

'You know,' Mason grinned, 'I really wouldn't put it past you.'

CHAPTER TWENTY-THREE

THE PAGE OF SWORDS (le Valet des Epées)

Vigilance. Spying. A discreet individual. A person skilled at uncovering that which is hidden. A perceptive person. A person of insight.

'Well,' Mason told Freda, as he closed the booklet, 'I think I've just been flattered.'

He made some tea and went through to the front room. Freda followed. He'd slipped her an extra meal, and she felt that the least she could do was be friendly.

The answering machine was blinking its message light, but Mason couldn't think of anyone he wanted to hear from, so he ignored it. He turned the TV on with the sound down, so that Freda could watch the afternoon movie, and subsided into the sofa. He took the Tarot cards from the pack and flicked through them.

Page eight of the booklet was headed *The Major Arcana*. Apparently the Tarot pack was comprised of four suits, much like a conventional deck, plus twenty-two powerful cards with heavy symbolic significance: the Major Arcana.

0 (or The Unnumbered Card) THE FOOL (Le Fou)

Thoughtlessness. Folly. Lack of maturity. Enthusiasm. Naivety. Frivolity. Lack of depth.

Mason skimmed the pack for the card. It showed a young man, an adolescent really, walking out of the frame and into the landscape with a Dick Whittington stick-and-bundle arrangement over his shoulder. He was carrying a flower, and a dog was trailing at his heels.

'It's quite interesting, this,' Mason suggested to Freda, who was much too engrossed in Fred Astaire to give a damn.

1 THE MAGICIAN (*Le Bateleur*)

Imagination. Self-reliance. Deception. Flexibility. Sleight of Hand. Application. Guile, or skill used to dishonest ends.

The card pictured a young man at a table on which stood a cup, a sword and a coin. He was holding a wand in the air, and wearing an unflattering broad-brimmed hat.

Taking the occasional swig of tea, and soliciting Freda's unforthcoming comments, he worked his way through the entire Major Arcana.

The High Priestess
The Emperor
The Empress
The Hierophant
The Lovers
The Chariot

He persevered, wanting to read the lot for Elvis's sake, but towards the end he had more than one eye on the afternoon movie. By the time he'd finished, he felt disappointed. He hadn't found any big deal, or happened upon some revelation. It was almost as if Elvis had let him down.

'Here, Freda. Come here.' He fanned the cards. 'Pick a card, any card. Come on. Touch one with your nose. I'll tell you all about yourself. That one? All right, wait a sec. Ten of Cups.' He riffled through the booklet to the appropriate page. 'Uh ... *Home. Abode. Contentment. A happy family life. Domestic security.* Makes sense. Sounds like a very house-cat sort of card.'

He put the book and the cards back in their box and turned the TV up. Fred Astaire's girlfriend suggested that they do the show right here in the barn, or some such tosh. The lunchtime drinking was taking its toll, so he stretched out across the sofa, and Freda, in turn, stretched out across his chest. The TV kept sliding in and out of focus, and soon it wasn't there at all.

Mason was at a party. He was at a table with Bart and Chris and a woman he didn't know. She looked a lot like Chris though. Bart introduced her.

'This is my friend Mason,' he said. 'Mason, I think you already know Chris. Mason's a card . . .'

This isn't right, he thought. She's not Chris. She's someone else.

He didn't want to talk to this woman, so he went upstairs to Chris's room. As he stood outside the door, he could hear noises of love-making. If he looked at the door from the right angle, he could see through it, but all he could see was Chris asleep. Chris opened the door. 'What are you doing out here?' she said accusingly. They went into the room. Someone was hiding under the duvet.

I'm not going to look under there, Mason thought, because this is a dream, so it'll only turn out to be me.

He glanced at Chris. Bart had his hand down her blouse, and was pulling rabbits out of her bra.

'Why don't you stay the fuck out of my dreams?' Mason asked them.

'What a charming expression,' Chris replied, sliding her hand into the front of Mason's jeans.

'Oh, for God's sake,' he groaned, finding himself back on the sofa with Freda asleep on his chest. 'Just when it was getting interesting.'

He lay there for an hour, staring at the ceiling and trying to figure out what to do about Bart and Chris. Almost worse than the anger and jealousy was the sense of foolishness. He had been made to look an idiot; he'd been patronised. He winced as he recalled his ridiculous enthusiasm in telling Chris all about Bart being the Trickster. Christ, no wonder she thought it was funny.

He was so lonely he felt like crying. Whenever he was upset about Chris, he'd called Bart. And on the few occasions he'd fallen out with Bart, he'd spoken to Chris about it. Where was he to go now?

'Oh, fuck it,' he muttered. He lifted the dozing Freda gently onto the arm of the sofa, stood up and left the house.

Barry Wright looked up and grinned as Mason walked into the corner shop. 'Twenty Marlboro Lights?' he asked, chummily.

'Yeah,' Mason sighed.

'Aha! Are you over sixteen?' Barry grinned.

'Just give me the fags,' Mason told him, in a dull monotone.

'Well, it's a big step, mate. Sure you don't want to go away and think about it?'

'Listen,' Mason growled, 'are you going to sell me these fucking cigarettes or not? I mean, I can always go down to the High Street . . .'

'All right, all right. Don't get out of your pram. Jesus, you really need one, dontcha?'

'Cheers,' Mason said, handing over the money. 'I'd buy in extra stock, if I were you.'

Back at the flat, he poured a glass of orange juice, sought out an ashtray, and went back to the front room. He opened the cigarettes, and took one out. He put it in his mouth, flared a match and inhaled.

He inhaled again, held the smoke in his chest for a full half-minute, let it out slowly and then took another deep drag. His head spun. He felt pleasantly giddy.

'I really must get around to giving this up, one day,' he told Freda.

He stubbed out the cigarette and lit another, noticing that the telephone answering machine was still blinking. There were three messages waiting. He hit the button. As the tape rewound, the jabber of speeded-up backwards voices chirruped from the speaker. One of the messages was from Chris. Even in reverse and at high speed, he could recognise her.

BLEEP.

'. . . This is a message for Mr Dixon. Big Screen Video Hire here. You have a video of ours, *Sex Temple Slave Girls*, which is now ten days overdue. You are currently incurring fines of one pound a day. Please return this video immediately. Thank you.'

Oh, very discreet, Mason thought. *What if I'd been some frustrated husband who'd rented the vid to watch when his wife was out?*

BLEEP.

'Hiya, it's Chris . . .'

Fuck off.

'We said we'd arrange something for this weekend, but I'm a bit tied up . . .'

Oh, right. That's what he's into, is it?

'. . . so I was wondering if you were free on Monday or Thursday. We could see a film or a band or something. Anyway, give me a ring. See ya.'

Oh, drop dead . . .

168

BLEEP.

'Mason, *c'est moi* – which, state-educated as you were, you may not realise is French for it's me . . .'

And you can fuck right off an' all, Mason thought, hearing Bart's voice. *It's a little profligate, isn't it, the two of you leaving separate messages? Why didn't you put them both on the one call?*

'. . . You disappeared rather suddenly last night. Am I to assume from this that you and Tess stole away somewhere to compare navel lint? Please ring and fill me in on the sordid details. *Auf Wiedersehen*; which is German for . . . oh, it doesn't matter.'

Through his third and fourth cigarettes, Mason wondered what he was going to do about calling Chris. He certainly couldn't pretend nothing was happening. But then if he acknowledged it, he'd come over as . . . well, what he was. Upset. Heartbroken. Petulant. And the way Chris would argue it, he wouldn't have a leg to stand on. He could practically hear her already.

'Look, we're not going out together any more, right? We haven't been for months. So what am I supposed to do – stay home doing my knitting until you can handle the idea of me having a life? I mean, grow up, Mason. And anyway, I hear you're not exactly steeped in ascetic self-denial yourself . . .'

'Oh, fuck,' he told Freda, 'it's started already. I'm seeing it from her point of view.'

He had to put a stop to that, right away. In the freezer compartment of the fridge he kept an emergency bottle of vodka. He brought it into the front room, glugged a large measure into the orange juice, slammed *Sex Temple Slave Girls* into the VCR and lit yet another cigarette.

Sex Temple Slave Girls was the worst kind of soft-core – not crass enough to be worth a giggle, and not horny enough to be worth a tug. But it was precisely the kind of undemanding dross that complements a wholehearted effort on the part of the viewer to get paralysingly drunk. As nymphomaniac acolytes of the Goddess Clitandra performed the ancient rite of anointing each other with freshly-obtained seminal fluid, Mason sank into a satisfactory emotional morass of belching self-pity and drooling peevishness. By halfway through the movie, when the supply of local kidnappable blacksmiths had dried up and the handmaidens of

169

Lust were forced to consider Sapphic ceremonies to appease the Goddess, Mason had put himself outside most of the vodka.

'I'm going to run out of halcohol,' he observed sadly. 'Run completely out . . .'

'But this is ah-ful,' gasped a minor attendant at the Altar of the Sacred Climax, in a strong Tennessee accent. 'What we gon' do, Vulvata?'

'We gonna hafta locate fresh supplies of Holy Joik-juice, Boobiana,' said the High Priestess, late of Noo Joisey. 'For t'marrow de moon passes troo de house of Clitandra and we gotta get some Blessed Fluid for da ceremony . . .'

'Personally,' Mason hiccuped, 'I'll settle for a beer, if it's all the same to you.'

'Yeah,' the High Priestess continued, shrugging off her vestment and clambering onto the altar, 'when da moon is in da house of da Goddess –' she flung a lithe thigh across Boobiana's chest – 'and da star of Love aloigns wid da Voirgin –' she lowered her face to Boobiana's crotch – 'da temple floor will run wid hot, fresh juices –' she reached back and grabbed Boobiana's nipples – 'in hom-arge to the solstice of sex.'

'It's a neat trick, if you can do it,' Mason pointed out to Freda. 'Simultaneously talking crap astrology and tying yourself in knots. Hic! Oops – pardon.'

He reached out fumblingly for the cigarettes, and tipped sideways onto the floor. On his hands and knees, he belched and lodged a cigarette in his mouth.

'Tell you what,' he continued, 'they should have got Mystic Mel Peters to play the, burp, oh dear, the High Priestess—'

He paused, holding a lit match. Something important had occurred to him.

'Er . . . now, wait a mini-hic, a minute,' he said. 'Ow!'

He dropped the match as the flame reached his fingertips, and it fell onto a newspaper, which smouldered, caught and began to burn. He crouched there, bent over it, woozily watching the little licks of flame as they started to scorch the carpet. For a few moments, he was at a loss as to what to do. Then, in a flash of inspiration, he took the unlit cigarette from the corner of his mouth, groaned, and threw up all over the incipient blaze.

*   *   *

Around lunchtime that day, Chris had hung up after leaving the message on Mason's machine, and frowned slightly. It was most unusual for him not to be in on a Saturday.

She was in what she thought of as a D.H. Lawrence mood – all staring out of the window and awareness of the pulse in the wrist, the landlocked blood, the hormonal cauldron of her femaleness. She resented it; in fact, she'd written articles about how she resented it. She'd railed, in women's magazines, against the way in which those very publications on the one hand conspired in sororial celebration of the menstrual cycle, whilst at the same time blaming it for all the unpredictable vagaries of femininity. Chris had argued that women couldn't go around demanding to be taken seriously as professionals and equals if they were then going to plead inevitable insanity at every full moon. Either women were in control of their lives, or they weren't. Chris was, and said so.

But still, just as her briskly unspecific biology teacher had warned her, she did have *days like these*. Days when she was drawn towards the photo albums in the bedroom wardrobe; or when she wanted to sit in front of the TV, drinking steaming oxtail soup from a mug clasped in both hands; or when she really missed having blazing rows with her mother. She tutted. Ridiculous. She didn't *have* any photos in the wardrobe; outside, it was 75 degrees in the shade, so the soup thing was just daft; and her mother was gone.

And she was thinking about Mason. She was – dammit – she was missing him today. She was thinking about him going away, and she didn't like the idea. She was envisaging him in Paris or San Francisco, meeting some girl in a restaurant and chatting to her, in that self-deprecatingly confident way that he used to have. That he used to have with *her*. She still saw that in him, in flashes, when he forgot to be so supplicant. At those times, she could almost have believed it would work. She had to force herself not to invite him to stay overnight; she had to fight against arranging a weekend away somewhere. Because she couldn't risk that. What if it all went wrong again?

There had been others in between. A week or so here, a month or two there. She'd really liked one or two of them. Liked them a lot. Liked them – actually – a lot more than she'd liked Mason at the time. And as she'd lain in new beds, unfamiliar arms around her, the unexpected contours of a novel body mapped against hers in the dark, she'd seen

Mason walk in, and stop, his face crumpling with disappointment and betrayal. And she'd pushed that vision away, because it wasn't fair on her. It wasn't right that she should feel as if she were being unfaithful. They had split up. They were over. They'd agreed that.

And in the morning, as she found reasons to leave before breakfast, her blouse still damp from last night's dancing, her hair hurriedly pinned up at the back, she imagined bumping into Mason as she walked to the nearest tube, and she had stories prepared of the late-night unavailability of cabs, and the sofas in colleagues' front rooms.

. . . Zif.

Chris knew that none of this made any sense – but she just couldn't find a way through it. However she rationalised, she still couldn't explain her feelings to herself. She hated that.

She was making a salad for lunch when the phone rang. It was Bart.

'Hello, sweet,' he said. 'How's you?'

'I'm great. What's with you?'

'I'm fine. I saw Mason yesterday evening. Without wishing to second-guess events, I think that our problem may be solved.'

He'd introduced Mason to a friend of his, a sharp, bright girl, just his type, and they'd disappeared into the night. Bart had called Mason's place this morning and he was out, so – well, who knows? Maybe the open air-ticket wouldn't be necessary after all.

'Oh, that's good,' Chris nodded. 'Would she treat him right, this woman?'

'Well, she'd treat him. Let's not get picky,' Bart chuckled.

Chris's mobile rang, and she asked Bart to hold on as she answered it. It was David Jennings, saying that he had a lead on the Trickster. They had a card, and this afternoon he and Zerkah were going to a book-signing in Kensington. Would she like to come?

'Yeah – of course. Who's the target?'

'Suzette Winkworth,' Jennings said.

'Ah – the soul-flying woman. Yeah, that makes sense.'

She took down the address of the bookshop and closed the call, before picking up the other phone again.

'Bart, I've got to go. Something just came up. Look, I hope you're right about this piece you've set on Mason. It's not going to help him if he gets turned over, you know.'

'No, no, dearheart,' Bart insisted. 'It doesn't matter *what* happens to Mason right now, as long as *something* does. That may sound callous, but I'd rather he risked a broken leg than sat at the bottom of the ski-slope moping. Incidentally, by "the soul-flying" woman, do you mean Suzy Winkworth?'

'Er, yeah. I'm interviewing her,' Chris lied, instinctively.

'Well, tell her from me she's an idiot,' Bart suggested cheerfully. 'See you, dearheart.'

Thoughtful, and a little disturbed, Chris hung up and walked into the kitchen, where she dumped the half-prepared salad in the bin, and opened a tin of oxtail soup.

CHAPTER TWENTY-FOUR

When Mason awoke the following morning, it was with the notion that he had some peculiarly unpalatable chore to carry out. As he attempted to sit up, a hangover smacked him hard across the back of the head, which served to jog his memory. He had to clear up the vomit in the front room. He'd tried to do it the previous evening, but it had made him gag, so he'd simply closed the door and crawled to bed on his hands and knees.

He peered at the clock. Quarter past ten. He'd slept for nearly sixteen hours. His mouth tasted foul, and his lungs were going yeek-yeek with every breath. He felt unfocussed, as if he'd been over-printed out of register, like a picture in a kid's comic. He was fully dressed, he noticed. He even had his boots on.

'Pitiful,' he croaked. And he dozed off again.

Around noon, he made another attempt to face the day. Rolling out of bed, he tottered unsteadily to the bathroom. As he was having a pee, he noticed a burnt-out cigarette that had scorched a three-inch streak across the low-level cistern.

When did I do that? he wondered, fuzzily. And how many cigarettes did I smoke?

He sat at the kitchen table and drank a cup of tea, steeling himself. In his mind's eye, the front room was simply awash with sick. To his slight shame, he thought briefly about calling his mum and telling her he was terribly, terribly ill, and could she pop round? But then he got up, filled a bucket with hot water, and tottered up the hallway.

When it was all over, and the ashtray had been emptied, and the windows thrown open, and an entire aerosol can of Pinefresh sprayed into the room, he lowered himself gingerly into a very hot bath. He lay there, head spinning, for a few minutes, and then proceeded to scrub himself mercilessly with a scratchy loofah. His skin tingled and glowed, and he practically drew blood, but he couldn't scour away the self-pity and disgust. He swaddled himself in towels, went back to the bedroom and dropped onto the bed, where, at last, he succumbed to the instinct that he'd been fighting since late Friday night. He had a damn good cry.

His thoughts tumbled and spun, like small change in a washing machine. He couldn't switch it off; he couldn't stop the jangle and clatter of images and feelings. Right then, he understood all the sorry gullible wretches grasping out to hold solid, simple beliefs. He'd have done it too, if he'd been offered the chance. A word from a gypsy, succour from the Moonies, the blessing of a spirit guide – anything to stop feeling how he felt. At that moment, if somebody had told him that sacrificing a sheep would make it all right, he would have grabbed a hatchet and headed straight for his nearest inner-city farm. Qualmless, he would have beheaded some innocent fluffy lambkin in front of a daytripping bunch of underprivileged eight-year-olds, and fuck the consequences.

But he just lay there, face pressed into the pillow, fingers clenched in the duvet, wailing. He rolled from one side of the bed to the other, as if he could dodge the misery for a moment or two, but it was like trying to hide from his shadow.

After fifteen minutes, he wiped his nose on the back of his hand, smeared the tears from his cheeks, and got up.

'Silly old sod,' he sniffed, pulling on a T-shirt. 'And don't give me any of that New Man shit, either. That was just out'n'out weeping, that was.'

By the time he'd had another cup of tea, an Alka-Seltzer and some cornflakes, he felt, if not human, certainly mammalian. He and Freda went into the front room to watch some TV. Of a Sunday lunchtime, they particularly enjoyed *The Waltons*. Mason felt another little belching sob bubble in his chest and, without thinking, he reached for the pack of cigarettes. There was only one left, which he'd lit before remembering that he had failed to give up.

One eye on the television, he took the Tarot cards out of the pack and flicked through them idly. He vaguely remembered thinking of something last night, just before flooding the carpet. Something about *Sex Temple Slave Girls* and Melody Peters . . .

The High Priestess . . .

His sluggish synapses coughed and spluttered as he fiddled with the mental ignition. Then, suddenly, the engine of his brain fired and revved.

He leapt up and grabbed a notebook and pen from the TV table. Still sniffing, he thumbed through the Tarot booklet to the section on the Major Arcana, and copied down the names and numbers of the cards on the left-hand side of the page:

0	The Fool
I	The Magician
II	The High Priestess
III	The Empress
IV	The Emperor
V	The Hierophant
VI	The Lovers
VII	The Chariot
VIII	Strength
IX	The Hermit
X	The Wheel of Fortune
XI	Justice
XII	The Hanged Man
XIII	Death
XIV	Temperance
XV	The Devil
XVI	The Tower
XVII	The Star
XVIII	The Moon
XIX	The Sun
XX	Judgement
XXI	The World

Melody Peters – what was it they called her in her publicity? The Pink Priestess?

Beside the words *II The High Priestess*, he wrote *Melody Peters*.

Peter Pinkus, then, was the Magician. Cliff'n'Dawn must be the Lovers. The Reverend Cutforth was obviously the Hierophant.

Who else was there? He cursed himself for having thrown away the hit list. Belinda Bartlett. Where could he fit in Belinda Bartlett? Was there a card called the Airhead?

'Come on, boy,' he encouraged himself aloud. 'Think. *Think.*'

A.G. Sparkes . . .

Ah, yes, A.G. Sparkes was the Hermit, then.

'The Hermit! Elvis *said* that there had to be a recluse,' Mason told Freda. 'Blimey, he picked this up really early on.'

And Al Knox – he of the stopped heart and ghostly grandfather – must represent Death.

Mason was beside himself. 'Who else?' he asked Freda, who was pawing at the top of his pen as he wrote. 'Chuckie Rolls, comedian. The Unnumbered Card – the Fool! That's why Elvis said that Chuckie *wasn't* number one, although he *was* probably the first.'

Mason tapped the pen on Freda's nose, and she clasped her paws around it, and tried to chew it.

'Belinda . . . Belinda . . . Let's think. She played Cleopatra in the sketch so . . . maybe the Empress. Dodgy, though. Umm . . . oh, for Christ's sake, *of course*. What does Belinda do every week? "That's Histowy and Geogwaphy, Bob." She spins the Wheel of Fortune! Very neat. Henry Westlake, the barrister? Justice – has to be. Morris Keen, racing driver and chum to the Martians. Ha! Racing cars! Morris Keen is the Chariot!'

He paused and looked at his list. There was nothing at all from number fourteen, Temperance, to the end. And there were a few gaps: The Emperor, the Empress, Strength and the Hanged Man.

'Can I fit Damon Chiswick in there?' he wondered, pulling the pen away from Freda, and wiping it on his T-shirt. 'Oh, yes. Yes, yes, yes, yes. He played Samson – Strength.'

Mason sat back laughing, and tossed the pen across the carpet, where Freda scurried after it, batting it under the TV.

'*Brilliant!*' he said. 'Really brilliant.'

The Prankster was making a meta-joke. The whole campaign was hung on a mystic hook – the Tarot. It was very sly, very inventive. Mason nodded, grinning. It was very *Bart*, actually.

He turned to the back of the Tarot booklet, where Elvis's number was written, and dialled.

'Hello?' said a female voice.

'Oh, hi,' Mason said, 'is . . . er . . .'

He couldn't bring himself to say, 'Is Elvis Presley home?'

'Does, umm, a tall bald bloke with appalling taste in clothes live there?' he said.

The woman at the other end chuckled. 'Hang on, I'll give him a shout. YAY! PHONE!'

After a brief pause, there was the sound of the telephone being picked up.

'Alexander Graham Bell,' said Elvis's voice.

'Elvis, it's Mason.'

'Well, lansakes! If it ain't the Dixon boy!'

'I got it. I worked it out.'

'Ah, I knew you would,' Elvis chuckled. 'Clever, isn't it?'

'But there's a few I can't fill in. I mean, I figure we're up to number thirteen, Death – but there are a couple of gaps.'

'Well, they haven't been coming strictly in order,' Elvis said, 'but you're right. Something appears to have gone wrong in the low numbers.'

'But, it's just not *like* the Trickster, is it?' Mason insisted. 'To have got it wrong? Maybe we've missed something.' He looked down at his list again. 'The question is what *good* is it, having worked it out? What help is it?'

'Satisfaction? Also, you can have a lot of fun trying to guess who's next.'

'Uh?'

'Well, they're happening in approximately the right order, okay? So the next one is likely to be the Hanged Man, because it appears to have been skipped, or Temperance, or maybe even the Devil.'

'You mean you've been predicting victims?' Mason gaped. 'So who do you reckon's next? Have you got any idea?'

'Sure, yer wouldn't be wanting me to tell yer the future now, would yer, Mason?' Elvis brogued.

'You bloody *have* got some idea, haven't you? Come on.'

'I'll give you a clue concerning someone who I think may well get hit in the next couple of days, all right?'

There was a silence.

'That's it,' said Elvis. 'Unfortunately for you it was a visual clue.'

'Oh, come on, man. Give me a proper clue.'

'Sorry; only one clue per customer. I'll tell you what the visual clue was though, if you like. The clue was – a wink.'

'A what?'

'A wink. I winked, Mason.'

CHAPTER TWENTY-FIVE

Suzy Winkworth sat in Make-Up, watching her item being trailed on the screen above the mirror.

'And after the eight-thirty headlines,' beamed Sally Fairfax, the pert-lipped soapsud who fronted the show, 'Suzy Winkworth will be joining me in the Daybreak Kitchen for our regular Monday feature, "A Bag in the Life of". And we'll be finding out just what a glamorous jetset model like Suzy carries around in her handbag. I can't wait!' She clapped her little hands together.

Suzette winced. But this stuff was necessary to promote the book – and to promote the book, she'd even discuss the contents of her purse with an animated meringue like Sally Fairfax. Not, of course, that it would be her own purse, or 'handbag' as the Brits called it. There was a special 'Bag in the Life' purse in which would be dumped a whole bunch of mutually-agreed impersonal effects – car keys, drywipes, sunglasses, airline-ticket stub, subway coupon. Suzy and the Fairfax bimbo would sit at some mock-up of a breakfast bar with a cup of caffeine-free, pulling this stuff out of the bag item by item and stringing together a lifestyle interview. Suzette could do that kind of shit-chat standing on her head. In fact, on one occasion during her yoga-promoting days, she had.

A girl with a clipboard came up beside her chair. 'They need you on set in five minutes, Ms Winkworth, so as soon as Jenny's finished your make-up, if you'd like to come with me . . .'

She was led to the mocked-up kitchen, where Sally Fairfax was having her nose powdered.

'It's so exciting to meet you!' squeaked Sally. 'I hope you've got some interesting things for us to chat about.'

'Just the stuff that's on the list I agreed with your producer,' said Suzette, sliding graciously onto a barstool.

'Oh, yes, I'm sure. But I haven't seen the list. We always do it like that. It's so exciting, and it makes much better television.' Sally really did look excited; she kept pressing her thighs together and hunching her shoulders, like an eight-year-old playing pass-the-parcel. 'You see,' she explained enthusiastically, 'that way I don't know what's in the bag, and it's a real surprise to me. It's high-risk broadcasting – anything could happen!'

Yeah, right, thought Suzette. If it were to turn out that I chew an unusual flavour of gum, it would be like JFK and the moon landing all rolled up in one.

Actually, the selection of purse items was pretty tame. The only argument had been about the book. The producer thought it *a teeny bit pushy* to have her own book in the bag. Suzette had won the argument by adopting a spurious feminist stance regarding the inclusion of panty shields. After five minutes' impassioned argument on both sides, Suzette suggested a compromise whereby she'd back down on the panty shields if she could keep the book. The producer had rolled over and waggled his paws in the air.

Suzette checked the positions of the cameras, and turned a little on her stool.

'Twenty seconds, please,' announced the floor manager. 'Where's the handbag, for God's sake? Come on, it *is* just a little bit vital. Suzy, love, could you move in a tad? Perfect. How nice to work with a professional. All right. Five, four, three, two, and—'

'Welcome back. Well, today in our regular "A Bag in the Life of" feature, I'm talking to our special guest Suzy Winkworth about the little secrets and necessary items that she carries in her handbag, as she jetsets around the world. Is a handbag a vital accessory to your life, Suzy?'

'Well, of course, a *purse*, as we Yanks call it, is pretty central to any woman's life, I guess. I had a purse stolen one time, and I felt like my entire life had been taken from me.'

'Oh, I know. That's a terrible feeling isn't it? Well, let's see what you do carry in your *purse*, Suzy.' Sally reached into the large and chunkily-chic soft-leather handbag and pulled out a small key. 'Oh, it's a key,' she said, holding it out in her flat hand for the close-range camera. 'A very little one.'

'Yeah, that's the security key to my portable word-processor,' explained

Sally. It wasn't, of course – Daybreak had supplied one. 'I bought the processor when I set off on this promotional trip.'

'So do you write when you're in your hotel room and so on?'

'Oh, sure. Hotel rooms, airplanes, TV studios. Sure.'

'And I wonder what else we have in here. Ah, it's a book. In fact, it's *your* book. Is this your bedtime reading?'

At last, thought Suzy. Here I go.

'I still read it, yeah. The soul-flying technique that I explain in the book is one you can go on improving and understanding your whole life. It feels like nothing else in the world. It feels like freedom.'

'Well, let's see what's next out of the bag. And it's . . . a lipstick.'

'Morning Sky, to be precise.' Suzy said.

This time it really was hers. You couldn't get that colour in Europe, so she had contributed her spare one. She'd supplied a Hershey bar too, because the backward Brits hadn't discovered real chocolate candy yet.

'So, although you don't think that your body matters, you still like to keep it looking nice?'

'Sure. It doesn't *matter* whether your car is clean or dirty, but it doesn't stop you wanting to keep it looking good.'

'Is it right you have to give up sex to do this soul-flying, too?' Sally enquired, and her tone made it clear that it didn't sound like much of a deal to her.

Suzy shook her head. 'The point is, soul-flying is not a *substitute* for sexual gratification – it's better. I just don't need any kind of sexual release any more. You know, I've found that—'

'Oooh! Oh golly!'

Suzy was interrupted by a squeal from Sally Fairfax, who had pulled her hand out of the bag to find that she was holding a small, svelte, black vibrator.

Sally struggled for a suitable question.

'So, umm, I expect you just keep this for old times' sake,' she managed, gamely.

For a horrified second, Suzette just stared at the vibrator. She'd been set up. This was not an item she had put in for the feature. Someone had deliberately included the vibro to embarrass her. She said as much.

'That's not one of the things I put in,' she protested ambiguously. 'I

181

would never put that in there. The only things I put in are my lipstick and, like, a Hershey Bar—'

The viewing audience at home, whilst not able to resist envisaging this, were distracted by hooting female laughter off mike. It was Zerkah Sheikh and Chris Bell, both of whom were cackling with glee, despite Inspector Jennings shushing them.

He frowned, and looked around him at the technicians and celebrities, wondering how on earth someone had managed to tamper with the handbag without any of the three of them noticing.

CHAPTER TWENTY-SIX

Inspector Jennings and Zerkah Sheikh sat in the foyer of the DayBreakTV studios, going through the visitors' book for that morning, while Chris asked around to see if anyone had noticed anything suspicious. Both exercises drew blanks.

As they drove back to the West End, Chris asked, 'What now, then? Just hope another card shows up?'

Jennings nodded, turning to look at her in the back seat. 'How did the Trickster get in without going through security? How did he tamper with the bag so soon before they went on air?'

'Magic?' suggested Zerkah. 'A cloak of invisibility?'

Jennings appeared to consider that theory. 'There's a Father Brown story about an invisible man – invisible because he's so commonplace. He's a postman. The people watching the house simply don't register his presence at all.' He pinched the bridge of his nose. 'Who's invisible in a TV studio?'

'Maybe he wasn't there,' Chris shrugged. 'Maybe he just paid some-one on the inside.' She grinned. 'Anyway, it'll be good fun to write up.'

Zerkah sniggered. Jennings looked at her. She stopped sniggering.

Chris asked to be dropped off at the *Clarion*'s offices, and as she walked to her desk Ray Churchill called her in. He jerked his head towards the TV as she sat down.

'Well, he made Suzy look like a complete twat, didn't he?' He chuckled. 'A word about house style, by the way. "Vibrator" isn't on, but you can get away with "sex-toy."'

'Oh, okay. I thought we just used that to describe the women on page three,' Chris nodded, straightfaced.

'Don't start, Chris,' Ray sighed. 'Anyway – quality story. One of our own accompanies cops to the very scene. "The *Clarion* takes you there" and all that cobblers. Great stuff. You've got yourself well in with this plod, haven't you?'

'Yeah,' Chris said. 'I think we've established a mutually useful working relationship.'

Ray smiled broadly. 'By whatever means necessary, eh? Good girl, good girl.'

'What the fuck does that mean?' Chris asked, colouring.

'Hey – nothing,' Ray said, holding up his hands. 'How you get the stories is your own business, Chris. I don't want to know, all right? We've all got our own special, er, techniques.'

Chris shook her head incredulously. 'Thanks for that. It's nice to know you have such confidence in me.'

'Always have had,' Ray told her, wagging a finger. 'No worries. Look, this Tarot card thing. How long do you plan on keeping that under wraps? Just till the story slows down, yeah? Then we splash it all over.'

Lipping a cigarette, Chris took a deep breath. She was being warned. It had been difficult to convince her editor to let her run with the veiled reference to the cards, but she had managed to assure him it was the best way to keep the story alive. Now he was upping the ante. Keep it lively, or we play the trumps.

'See – I'm thinking that the *Voice* might get this inside track,' Ray continued. 'Who's to say your friend in blue won't feed *them* too? I mean, he's a copper – can't trust the bastards.'

'I do trust him,' Chris said firmly. 'He won't screw us, believe me.'

Ray grinned. 'Well, not *all* of us anyway.' He caught Chris's glare. 'Joke! Just my little joke.'

Chris stood up and made for the door. 'Yeah. I'm aware that you like your little joke,' she said, turning in the doorway.

'Exactly,' Ray nodded. 'Good for morale, isn't it?'

'Oh, it keeps the staff amused,' Chris agreed, smiling. 'The girls in admin have us in stitches talking about your little joke. See you later.'

And she walked out, leaving her editor suddenly puzzled and a little disconcerted.

Sunday had been a pretty blue day for Mason, what with the hangover and the self-pity. He'd spent most of it watching TV and flicking through the Tarot deck, before going to bed early and sleeping like a fossil. He'd seen a DayBreakTV trailer for Suzy the Wink during the afternoon, and got up sufficiently early on Monday to catch her appearance with the bag. As Suzy stormed out of the studio, he called Elvis.

'Yuh?' said a sleepy voice.

'Elvis! Did you see Suzy the Wink on DayBreakTV? You were right – she got hit!'

'This must be the drug squad, right?' Elvis groaned. 'Only the drug squad call this early in the morning.'

'Elvis, get a grip. It's nine o'clock. Look, I'll call you back this afternoon, okay?'

'Weird, though. They don't usually ring for an appointment . . .'

Mason hung up and looked out of the window to the street. He was in a good mood and he wondered why. Part of it was merely relative, of course. It was nine o'clock on a Monday morning, which meant that Chris would be on her way to work. Therefore she was not in bed with Bart – and this was a cheering prospect.

It was a beautiful day. The sun was shining as if it had only recently thought of the idea and was still enthusiastic about it. People on the street were saying good morning for the mere joy of saying it, and with no intention of engaging each other in conversation as a prelude to mugging them. Freda was curled up on top of a dustbin looking cute as all-get-out.

The phone rang, and he ignored it; the machine was set. He couldn't imagine what answering machines were for, if not to allow you to ignore the phone. He popped a small zit on his left shoulder and went to make breakfast. Taking his tea and toast through to the front room, he whacked Junior Walker on the stereo, turned the volume up full blast, and spent the next twenty minutes bouncing around the room singing at the top of his voice, much to the consternation of Freda, who had just come in and was watching warily from behind the sofa. Then, temporarily exhausted but idiotically happy, he pressed the button on the answering machine.

BLEEP.

'Mason. It's Tess. I guess you're still asleep. Listen, I'm doing the evening shift at the restaurant, so I thought you might like some lunch. You could come over to my place if you like, and I'll cook something. Anyway, give me a call before, say, eleven. My home number is . . .'

'Tricky, I think you'll agree,' Mason commented to the cat.

Mason's attitude here was that one bout constitutes a good time, but two bouts starts to look like an affair. And if you're having an affair, you have to begin worrying about the person involved, and being responsible for them, and getting to know which vegetables they won't eat, and hearing about their bloody childhood. All that bonding stuff.

And then, eventually, there would be the difficult conversation . . .

'. . . But I don't understand, Mason. I thought it was going so well. I mean, you've stayed over practically every second night. We went up to the Lakes that weekend. You were acting like it was serious.'

'Well, how would I have acted if I were acting like it wasn't?'

'Maybe I'll go round and explain all this to her,' he mused, reaching for the phone. 'It's the least I can do.'

Tess lived in a top-floor flat beyond the Whittington Hospital, in the buffer zone between grotty Archway and posh Crouch End. Mason pushed the button on the intercom.

'Hello?' crackled Tess's voice.

'It's Mason.'

'Push the door hard. It sticks. I'm right at the top.'

He walked up, grasping a bottle of Frascati, a wine he often bought for lunchtime drinking, on the principle that it was so light it could hardly be considered alcohol at all. Tess was waiting on the top landing, dressed in a white cheesecloth blouse and a long hippydippy skirt.

'Hi,' she said. 'You're looking well.'

'You too.'

'Come on in.'

She led him into the sitting room, which was furnished mainly with cheeseplants and cacti. There was a large poster of James Dean from *Giant* and another of Buster Keaton. The sofa was one of those spongy ones that contrives to slide you gently onto the floor.

'Nice place,' he nodded, scanning the room.

'It's not much, but it's Home Sweet Home.'

Oh, please, Mason cringed. *Don't say things like that – I'm trying to like you.*

'I brought some wine,' he said, unnecessarily.

'Oh, great. Hang on. I'll find an opener and some glasses.'

While Tess clattered about in the kitchen, he flicked through her CDs

– the expected mix of crop-haired pseudo-dyke whingers and retro-sulky Brits with contiguous eyebrows.

'Would you like to put some music on?' Tess asked, handing him a corkscrew.

She owned a Beatles compilation, which was the equivalent of having a book called *Shakespeare: The Edited Highlights* in Mason's opinion, but it would have to do. As the lovable moptops observed ruefully that they should have known better, he opened the wine and poured two glasses.

'Cheers,' Tess said, taking one. 'So. How did you feel on Sunday morning?'

What – you mean, morally? Physically? Is this a trick question?

'Oh, I had a bit of a thick head, y'know. Nothing too dreadful.'

She nodded, as if he'd given the right answer. 'So, anyway . . . I thought I'd do a mushroom omelette and a salad, or something. Is that okay?'

'Perfect, yeah.'

'Well, do you want to come through to the kitchen and chat while I cook? It won't take long. Or do you want to stay in here and listen to some music?'

'I'll come and chat.'

He sat on a rickety chair in the tiny kitchen whilst Tess broke eggs and sliced mushrooms on the formica table. She talked self-deprecatingly about her acting career ('. . . if you can call it a career. Two deodorant commercials and *Juno and the Paycock* in Aberystwyth . . .'), and he contributed anecdotes concerning the many jobs he'd drifted through before becoming an unemployed graphic designer. As she rattled on, he wondered what her bedroom was like. Neatly arranged ranks of creams and oils, he guessed. Bottles marked 'patchouli' and 'camomile'. A book by Anthony Sher on the pine bedside table. A single rag doll slumped paraplegically on the windowsill. That Robert Doisneau poster of the couple kissing in a railway station.

Christ, you're a snide bastard sometimes, he thought. *And, anyway, as you have no intention of getting to see the bedroom, what difference does it make?*

'I hope the omelette's all right,' she said, as they sat down to eat at the little kitchen table. 'There's a knack with omelettes and I don't think I've got it. Are you one of these people who don't think a meal's a meal unless it includes meat?'

'No, not at all. But I generally work on the principle that if it didn't have parents, I won't eat it.'

Tess sniggered. 'Yeah, I used to go out with a guy like that once ...'

Hello. Here we go ...

'I used to think,' she continued, 'that that's why he had such a foul temper – because he ate so much red meat.'

Mason felt he should attempt to turn this opening into a conversation. 'So did you try a controlled experiment? I mean, did you dissuade him from consuming so much cow?'

'Yeah, I tried to, actually. And guess what?'

'He still had a foul temper?'

'Yes!' Tess laughed tinnily. 'He was just as bad!'

She was really nervous. It was like sitting with someone who was waiting for a dentist's appointment.

When they'd finished the omelette, which Mason wolfed enthusiastically, they went back through to the sitting room. Mason sprawled on the sofa and lit a cigarette and Tess sat cross-legged on the floor.

'I thought you'd given up smoking,' she said, passing an ashtray from the bookshelf.

'Yeah, me too.'

They sat in silence for a while. Usually, in such a silence, Mason would be desperate to find something to say, knowing that the other person was thinking, 'God, you're turning out to be a riot, you, aren't you?' But Tess was so tense that he felt relaxed by comparison. She seemed to have taken on the ice-breaking problem, and he was quite happy to let her deal with it. He just smoked his fag and looked at James Dean, thinking.

He thought about Bart's advice that he should move on from Chris. He thought about the Tarot reading, which implied much the same thing. And he glanced at Tess, fiddling with her hair and swaying to the music. He thought about being in bed with her. Thing was, he was over the worst part – the first contact. He was here in her flat. Something could develop. If he gave himself a chance, he might become fond of her, fall in love. Might get happy.

Suddenly, Tess leapt to her feet.

'Do you want coffee? Sorry – I should have offered you some before.'

'No. I'm fine.'

'Or tea? I've got Earl Grey and—'

'No, really. I'm fine. Sit down. Why are you so jumpy?' He put his cigarette in the ashtray and held a hand out to her. 'Come and sit down.'

She sat on the sofa, and he pulled her towards him so that their noses were no more than a hand's width apart.

'Just. Calm. Down,' he told her, interspersing the words with little kisses on her forehead. She looked solemn and apologetic. And very fanciable.

Oh, what the hell, Mason thought. *It's not like I'm promising to marry the girl or anything.*

He kissed her again, open-mouthed.

I mean, she's a grown-up, for God's sake. It's not like I'm seducing some sixteen-year-old.

His palm caressed her breast, and she moaned softly.

And, after all, she started it.

He felt her hand slide up inside his T-shirt and clench hard against his stomach. They slid down so that he was lying half-across her, and he ran one hand under her tie-dyed skirt onto her cool thigh.

Not to mention inviting me round here for . . . mmm . . . lunch. She knows what she's . . . ooh, yes . . . doing.

She had a hand on his Wranglered behind and was pulling him tight against her hip. She gasped as he brushed the ball of his hand across the swell of her knickers.

And I couldn't . . . ahhh . . . stop her now, if I wanted to. It would be . . . ooh . . . crueller to stop than to carry on . . .

'Stop!' panted Tess, turning her face from his. 'I'm sorry. Stop. Please.'

'What?'

Mason unmanned all stations and hitched himself up onto one elbow.

'I'm sorry,' she breathed, closing her eyes and leaning her head back on the sofa.

'What?'

'I can't. I'm sorry. It wouldn't be fair. You're a really nice bloke . . .'

'What?'

'I just can't get involved with anyone right now. I'm sorry. You must think I'm a dreadful pricktease . . .'

Mason tried to find a variation on his current theme, but nothing seemed to cover the situation quite as well as . . .

'. . . What?'

'I mean, I really fancy you and everything – like, obviously, right? But, I just don't want to lead you on or something. You know. Because, well, it wouldn't be fair. I'm still really hung up on this other guy, and—'

'Oh, Jesus,' Mason groaned, slumping back onto the cushions and flinging an arm across his face. 'Spare me the details.'

'Yes, of course. Sorry. You're not furious with me, are you? Really, it's not because of you. Honestly. You're a really sweet man . . .'

Mason got back home in a temper so foul that, sweet man that he was, he almost called Tess to tell her that it was nothing to do with eating red meat – it was just her.

The time was half-past five. He'd spent a couple of hours sublimating his frustration by totalling video-zombies at an arcade in Archway. Back at the flat, Freda came to the front door to say hello, and to suggest that a snack might not be entirely out of the question. Mason told her to sod off and die. Collapsing onto the sofa, he stabbed the button on the answering machine. As it rewound, he recognised Chris's voice.

BLEEP.

'Hi, Mason. It's Chris. You haven't called back. Then again, I've not been around much and my machine's not working, so maybe you *have* called—'

'Well, actually, I bloody haven't – so there,' Mason snapped.

'As it turns out, I can't make tonight anyway. Something's turned up. Work – y'know. So let's make it Thursday night. Call me at the office before then. You won't be able to get me at home this evening. Okay. See you.'

The cow, Mason thought. Standing me up at the last minute! Jesus, I might have arranged my whole week around seeing her tonight. Who the fuck does she think she is?

His next impulse was to phone Bart. It was what he usually did when he was at a loose end. He picked up the phone, stopped, and put it down again. Freda sidled in, looked at him measuredly for a few moments, and then jumped up onto his lap. He stroked her, thinking.

'This is ridiculous,' he told her. 'Why don't I just speak to him and get the whole thing out in the open? Then we can agree, like rational adults, that he's a selfish, treacherous slimeball, and then we never need see each other again.'

This seemed the sensible way forward, and Freda didn't come up with any objections, so Mason dialled Bart's number.

'You are listening to the dulcet tones of Bartholomew Scott,' said Bart's answering machine. 'I regret to say that the young master is not at home at present, but if you would care to state your business, then Mr Scott will endeavour to attend to you at the earliest opportunity—'

'Listen to the pretentious twat,' Mason growled, holding the phone briefly to Freda's ear.

'Oh, and here is a special message for the light of my life,' the tape continued. 'If that's you, dearest sweet, I'm not going to be back until about seven-thirty, so perhaps you'd like to show up, fragrant and wanton, at around eight o'clock. I shall be waiting with something chilled – and, indeed, something piping hot.'

Mason was stunned for a couple of seconds.

'Bastards!' he yelled – and Freda shot out of the room in fright. 'Fucking bastards! Lying cow! Deceitful, happy, lovey-dovey bastards!'

He slammed down the phone, and then stormed into the kitchen. Freda, sensing that this might not be a good moment to enquire about tonight's menu, zipped out through the catflap.

Mason tore from the kitchen pinboard a photo of him and Bart drunk outside a pub in Hampstead. He rolled it into a tube and shoved it into an exquisite green-glass goblet that Chris had brought back from the Far East. Trembling with fury, he put a match to the photo.

The flame caught, and in a very few seconds, it heated up the glass, which shattered with a sudden and satisfying ker-chank.

'Good,' Mason said, and went to the pub.

It was twenty-nine minutes after five, and Mischief was sat in the shade of a tree in Ravenscourt Park. From this vantage point, one could see number 83 Denholm Crescent.

Not that number 83 Denholm Crescent was much to look at. It was a neat and trim West London semi, much like number 81 and number 85. But inside number 83, Mischief knew, was Desmond Makepeace. There were rumours abroad concerning the sexual proclivities of TV wine guru Desmond Makepeace. Such rumours abound in show business circles. Scandal is the engine of social intercourse in studio canteens and scribblers' drinking clubs.

On the strength of one such inside story, Mischief had been researching the target's movements.

As well as being famous for his show *Raise a Glass with Makepeace*, Desmond was a spirit medium. He even incorporated his psychic gift into the television programme, saying, for instance, that this sturdy, composed Rioja, with its uncompromising nose and muscular body, travelled superbly – which was why Don Cortez had taken a dozen cases with him to the New World. Desmond knew this for a fact, having asked the dead explorer himself the previous evening.

Late one Monday afternoon, on the first day that Mischief had been keeping tabs on him, Desmond had left the TV studios after recording that week's show and taken a cab to this anonymous little house in Ravenscourt Park. He had stayed for two hours, during which time Mischief had observed several men scurrying shiftily up the path to the unremarkable front door.

When Desmond left, Mischief stayed right there, sitting on the grass in the darkening park. Eventually a statuesque redhead emerged from the house. Mischief followed her as she took a tube back into the West End and installed herself at the bar of the Plucked Phoenix on Brewer Street. The redhead was one Sandy Westwood; and Sandy Westwood, by her own admission, liked a drop.

She also liked to talk. Over the course of four or five engineered Monday-night meetings, she talked a lot. Mischief, charming, fascinated and flattering, was always there, ready to stand Sandy a port-and-lemon and laugh at her outrageous tales of how the average man's IQ dropped about eighty points at the sight of a thigh-length boot. From Sandy, Mischief learned that Desmond was a creature of habit, turning up at Denholm Crescent every Monday around five 'regular as clockwork'; it also became apparent that Desmond's particular hobby qualified him superbly for a place in the roll-call of the cards.

Five fifty-five. Mischief took a mobile telephone from an inside pocket and dialled.

'Yeah?' said a voice.

'Are you in position? And are you wearing a crash-helmet, as I told you?'

'Yeah. Listen, the money better be where you said, or you're gonna be sorry.'

How are you going to make me sorry? thought Mischief. *You don't know who I am, you idiot.*

'It'll be there. The first instalment was, wasn't it? In exactly one minute, you go in.'

Mischief hit the button and called the local newspaper, whose offices were a few hundred yards away on the High Street. The phone was picked up on the eighth ring.

'*Turnham Guardian,*' said a voice.

'I'd get yourself around to Denholm Crescent, if I were you. It's all happening down there.'

Mischief hit the button again, and dialled the emergency services.

'What service do you require?'

'Fire! Hurry!'

'Fire service,' came an efficient male voice.

'Quick. Eighty-three Denholm Crescent. Fire. There's smoke and everything. Denholm Crescent. Help. Please hurr—'

Mischief cut off the call and checked the time. Twenty seconds to go.

At that moment, a figure in a black and yellow crash-helmet dropped over the back fence of number 83 Denholm Crescent and ran across the lawn to the rear of the house. He was prepared to break windows, but this proved unnecessary. He simply tossed the smoke-bomb into the kitchen, and scooted back over the fence.

Within seconds, the alarm was raised.

Mischief watched as three dishevelled, pinstriped men and one leather-clad woman rushed from the front of the building. The men just kept on rushing, all the way to the cab-rank on the High Street, but the woman caught her five-inch stiletto in a paving stone, and stopped to pull it out. Behind her, the through-draught sucked an impressive plume of smoke into the front garden just as the fire brigade arrived. As grim, burly firemen clattered into the house, two more women emerged, choking and spluttering. Smoke was now belching black from every downstairs window. There was a commotion in the hall. Some large and awkward object was being manoeuvred down the stairs. One fireman emerged, shaking his head and wiping tears from his eyes. He walked over to the tender, and slapped a colleague on the shoulder.

'Oh-dear-oh-fuckin-lor,' he chuckled breathlessly. 'You're not gonna believe this one ...'

From the cloud of smoke that enshrouded the front door, there were shouts of 'Down a bit your side!' and 'Steady, steady'. A fireman backed out of the cloud carrying one end of what appeared to be a goalpost. There was a foot attached to it, held tight by a metal ankle-cuff. Two more firemen staggered from the smoke, supporting the crossbar of the contraption. It was a crucifix, of sorts, in the shape of the Greek letter pi.

And fixed upon it by straps and padlocks at every extremity, and dressed in a studded collar and fifteen-denier white crotchless tights, was Desmond Makepeace.

'We couldn't find the keys to the bastard thing,' the fireman by the tender told his colleague, weeping with laughter. 'And you can't fuck about when the place is going up, can you? So we had to yank it off the wall and bring the whole bleedin' lot out.'

To the accompanying clickety-click of the local hack's camera, the firemen carried Desmond and his A-frame across the street, and gently laid the entire assembly on the grass outside the park gates. A small crowd gathered round, silent and gaping. Someone threw a blanket over the weeping Desmond, who had not opened his eyes since the firemen burst into the upstairs chamber.

'Thank you,' he gulped, and attempted to grab the blanket between his teeth and drag it over his face. Some children giggled and pointed, and were pulled away by their tutting mothers. No one noticed the anonymous figure who strolled out from under a nearby tree, flicked away a cigarette and sauntered towards the park gates.

Mischief glanced contemptuously at the weeping, ruined Desmond Makepeace, strapped and chained by his raw wrists and ankles to the cross. Tears were dripping in silent rivulets into his ears.

'That is not a happy medium,' grinned the Joker, grinned the Wild Card, grinned the Tiger's Smile.

CHAPTER TWENTY-SEVEN

Bart did indeed get back to his flat by seven-thirty, just as his answering machine had promised. Mason saw him arrive.

Mason was standing – was vibrating, actually – in the doorway of a hardware shop across the street. He'd been there for twenty minutes, looking at the ironmongery and sipping a can of extra-strength lager. He was drunk in the clear, alpine fashion of a man who honestly wants to be smashed but can't seem to get fuzzy enough.

He watched Bart step out of the cab grasping a huge bouquet of roses and a bottle of tissue-papered champagne. He saw him bound up the white steps to the street door and insert the key. He clocked the devil-may-care gait, and the poncey little twirl that Bart performed in order to close the door behind him with one foot. He noted the light coming on in the second-floor apartment a few moments later – and the light was cosy and carefree and hateful.

Mason tossed the half-full beer can into the gutter, where it threw up spectacularly. He lit another cigarette and leaned back against the shop door, sucking in a deep drag and closing his eyes.

'Calm, Mason,' he said. 'You have nothing to prove. Let them do the squirming.' He finished the cigarette in three long sucks, and flicked the butt out across the pavement and into the pool of beer. Then he pushed himself forward from the door of the shop, walked across the street and up the steps.

He pressed the button marked 'Scott'.

'You're early, dearheart,' Bart's voice crackled from the speaker. 'This enthusiasm endears you to me.'

The door buzzed and Mason pushed it open.

'Actually,' he said under his breath, 'it's me – Mason.' He trudged up the stairs.

Bart's door was ajar, and from inside he heard, 'Come in, come in. I'm just opening the fizzy stuff.'

He pushed the door aside and walked through the immaculate Regency-decorated hall into the sprawling and elegant main room. Bart was standing at the window with his back to the doorway, throttling a bottle of Moët.

'Er . . . have I come at a bad time?' Mason said, pleasantly. 'Are you expecting someone?'

Bart whirled round. 'Mother of Christ!' he gasped. 'You made me jump.'

'Sorry. Just thought I'd drop in.'

Bart puffed air through his lips. 'No. No, fine. Sorry. Bit of a start, that's all. I was expecting someone else. Er . . .'

Mason dropped into the plush William Morris settee. 'Oh, sorry. Well, I'll only stay a minute. Any chance of a glass of that champagne?'

Bart glanced at the bottle in his hand as if it had just alighted there unexpectedly. 'Yes! Why not? Absolutely,' he said, walking across the vast Persian rug. 'Absolutely. Why not? Yes!'

'Certainly,' he added, handing Mason the glass.

Mason took the champagne flute and held it to the light to see the bubbles. 'How you been?'

'Since . . . ?'

'Saturday,' Mason reminded him.

'Ah, yes. Saturday. Of course. So did you slip the Dixon length to tender Tess?'

'Yup.'

'Glad to hear it,' Bart nodded.

'Thanks for setting me up.'

'Oh, pshaw. What are friends for?'

'Beats me.'

Bart poured himself a glass of champagne. 'So,' he said, perching himself carelessly on the edge of a three-hundred-year-old writing desk, 'to what, if I may invoke a cliché, do I owe the pleasure of this unexpected visit?'

Mason sipped the champagne. 'I was just passing,' he said, gazing around the room.

Bart pursed his lips, and took his cigarette case from a pocket. He tapped a Sobranie on the desk. 'Mason . . .'

'I'll have one of those, if you've got one spare,' Mason told him, nodding at the cigarettes.

'Of course.'

He tossed a smoke across, and they both lit up.

'I was about to say,' Bart continued, with a resigned grimace, 'that given your rather spiky tone and your offhand attitude, you must think I'm stupid if you expect me to believe that this is a visit with no particular purpose.'

'Zat right?'

'But then, I imagine that you feel I've been treating you as if you were stupid, too.'

'I think you think I'm blind and stupid and disposable, yes.'

Bart sighed and ran his fingers through his floppy hair. 'Oh, Christ, Mason. Okay, let's get it over with. I *knew* you'd feel like this. I *said* you would. All I can say is . . . well, we couldn't help it. It just *happened* . . . God, that sounds feeble.'

Mason stood up and paced across to the window, beating his cigarette against the air in frustration. It wasn't that he was lost for words. He had plenty of words. He simply didn't know where to start. He turned back into the room, and looked at Bart, still sitting on the edge of the desk, rolling his cigarette case over in his hands.

'Fifteen fucking years we've known each other, Bart.'

'Nearer seventeen,' Bart sighed, without looking up.

'Jesus, is it? Well, you must have known how much this would hurt me.'

'You might say I had an inkling.'

The doorbell buzzed.

'Wait a minute,' Bart said. 'Allow me to get the door.' He picked up the intercom phone. 'Hello, darling. Yes. Look, Mason's here. Yes, even as we speak. Loath as I am to employ an expression that makes us sound like criminals, I think the game is up. Yes. Well, come in – what else?' He turned back to Mason. 'She's on her way up.'

'So I gathered.'

They sat in silence for a moment, avoiding each other.

'I suppose,' Bart ventured, 'it's out of the question that you might wish us every happiness?'

Mason snorted. 'Not *this* week, Bartholomew. Give me a break.'

The sound of heels clattered in the corridor, and the door swung open.

'Oh, Mason,' she cried, even before she was quite in the room, 'sweetheart, please don't be too hard on us. Are you terribly shocked and disappointed?'

Mason looked at her, radiant as she was with love and worry. As she reached for Bart's hand, he felt utterly beaten.

'Do I feel shocked and disappointed?' he winced, rabbit-punched by his own stupidity. 'No. Neither shocked nor disappointed even *begins* to cover it, Mum.'

CHAPTER TWENTY-EIGHT

A little before seven, Chris called David Jennings on his mobile.

'Have you heard about Desmond Makepeace? I think he's just become card number twelve – the Hanged Man.'

Jennings tracked down the station to which Makepeace had been taken, and at a little after eight, he met Chris there. He talked to the duty officer, and then came back to Chris who was standing by the window, watching her colleagues from the press gather outside.

'They've got him in an interview room. I'm about to go and talk to him – and before you ask, no, you can't come with me.'

Chris frowned. She had suspected he'd say that, and was trying to find some irresistible angle that would persuade him otherwise. As she was casting around for one, a uniformed officer approached them.

'DI Jennings? I'm Bob Wyman. You want to see our celebrity perv?'

Jennings nodded, a slight furrow appearing between his eyebrows. 'If I could, Inspector Wyman, yes.'

'Fair enough. We haven't worked out what we're going to charge him with yet, but I'm sure we'll think of something.' He chuckled. 'Here – we had to dress him. Went to lost property and found something. You'll like it.'

'Why would we want to find something to charge him with?' Jennings asked evenly. 'What's he done?'

Wyman shrugged. 'Well, you tell me. I was thinking of public indecency. You know, flashing his cock in the street or whatever. Don't worry, I'll come up with something that'll stick.'

'He was carried out to the street involuntarily,' Jennings said. 'I can't see that working.'

Chris looked from Jennings to Wyman and back. The local copper was missing the point completely. He couldn't see that Jennings was not arguing the toss about what would stick. He was questioning the ethics of making a charge at all.

'Anyway,' Wyman was saying, 'I'll take you down to the interview room if you're ready.'

Chris touched Jennings's elbow. 'Could I have a word with you first?'

Jennings nodded and asked Wyman to give him a minute, then retreated to the corner to speak to Chris.

'Why have they got problems charging him?' she asked.

Jennings explained that going to a brothel was not an offence, and neither was being tied naked to an A-frame in crotchless tights – even if some police officers thought it should be.

'Not very moral, though, is it, in your own world view?' Chris suggested.

'It's not a criminal offence,' Jennings repeated firmly. 'I'm not a judge. I'm a copper.'

Chris nodded. 'Right – he'll just walk out of here, if you have your way. In that case, when you see him, it's only as a possible lead in the Trickster case. So why should I not be there? Listen, there are about twenty photographers outside. If Makepeace thinks he was crucified this afternoon, he should see what the papers'll do to him tomorrow morning. He could do with a sympathetic hearing. Let me give him that.'

Jennings ruffled his hair, thinking. He glanced out of the window at the slavering Leica pack. Eventually he turned back to Chris and nodded.

'Okay. If he agrees, you can be there.'

Chris smiled. 'Thanks, David.'

They were led down a corridor. Wyman opened the door to the small, bare interview room, and at the table, chaperoned by a uniformed constable, sat Desmond Makepeace. His face was tear-streaked and baggy. He was smoking a cigarette shakily, and he was wearing a sky-blue taffeta ballgown.

Wyman chuckled, and turned to Jennings. 'I think it's very fetching, don't you?' He grinned at Makepeace. 'It's very *you*, Desmond. Honest.'

Chris, standing at Jennings's side, felt him tense. She noticed his fists clench. And he spoke, very quietly, very measuredly, to Wyman.

'Find this man a coat. Yours, if necessary. Just find one.'

Wyman snorted. 'No fucking chance!'

Jennings turned and looked at Wyman. His cheeks were spotted red with fury, and his eyes were bright and pale.

'Find him a coat, Inspector,' he said, almost whispering – but the colourlessness of his tone was like the clarity of simmering oil. You wouldn't want to dip your finger in to test it.

There was a short, gulping silence and then Wyman, looking suddenly a little nervous, scurried off. Jennings dismissed the other copper and introduced Chris to the fidgety and trembling Makepeace, who seemed to accept her presence without registering it particularly. They both sat down, and Jennings asked whether he might ask a few questions. Makepeace nodded, lighting another cigarette from the stub of its predecessor.

'I've brought this on myself,' he gulped tremulously. 'Bound to happen. Bound to.'

Chris almost commented that his choice of verb, given the circumstances, was remarkably apposite, but she managed to bite it back, knowing that Jennings would not appreciate the facetiousness. She had to remind herself, looking at the ridiculous and haggard wine expert, that this was a man who talked regularly to the spirits of departed historical figures. His entire life was a charlatan's trick, either spouting rubbish about a Chardonnay's overtones of autumnal rain and Renoiresque vistas, or revealing that Napoleon had vouchsafed to him a fondness for Belgian truffles as an *amuse-gueule* for post-prandial calvados.

Jennings was assuring Makepeace that he wouldn't be charged, and that every effort would be made to get him out of the station without having to face the photographers. Then he pulled a Tarot card from his pocket. It was the Hanged Man: a figure suspended from a gibbet by one foot, his hands tied behind his back. Jennings held the card up.

'Do you recognise this?'

Makepeace peered at it for a moment through watery eyes. The watery eyes widened.

'Yes!' He'd received just that card in his mail a few days previously, he said. He'd ignored it. What did it mean?

'It means you're number twelve,' Chris told him.

'I saw him, you know,' Makepeace stammered. 'The agent of my ruin. I saw him through the window.'

From his vantage point on the cross in the upstairs room, Makepeace had seen a slim man about six feet tall vault the back fence and sprint up the garden, holding a package to his chest. It must have been the smoke bomb. He was wearing a motorcycle helmet – a black one with a yellow stripe – blue jeans and a leather jacket.

Jennings nodded. 'Well, it's not a lot to go on, but it's a start. Thank you, Mr Makepeace.'

Ten minutes later they were standing in the front office of the station, Makepeace wearing a long black coat over his crotchless tights. He was looking out through the window at the assembled press corps, and his bottom lip was quivering.

'We'll go out through the back,' Jennings told him. He put a hand gently on Makepeace's arm.

'No!' Makepeace insisted, pulling away. 'I . . . I must face them. I deserve it. I must take what's coming to me . . .'

He took a deep breath, pushed open the door of the station, and walked out into the flashes of the cameras. His demeanour managed simultaneously to convey shame and defiance.

Jenning turned to Chris, shaking his head. 'He didn't have to do that,' he said perplexedly, as the door swung shut. 'I don't get it.'

Chris smiled wryly. 'He likes it. He likes humiliation. It's his thing.' She chuckled. 'I think the Trickster has made his day, to be honest.'

The force of his own embarrassment kept Mason at Bart's apartment for a good three-quarters of an hour. Apparently, there were things he was expected to say – and, really, he felt he should say them.

He reassured Bart and Maria that he could handle it. He insisted that he should be the first to congratulate them. He pressed home the bright and original notion that worse things happen at sea. He killed the bottle of champagne and then he split.

Standing on the corner of Kensington Church Street and Notting Hill Gate, he slapped himself across the face. It stung like hell, but it didn't clarify anything. He desperately wanted to see Chris and apologise, or forgive her, or be forgiven, or be blamed, or something. He wanted to hear her voice.

He went into a callbox, and called her flat – knowing she was out – and listened to her answering message. He redialled and listened to it again. Then he phoned Elvis, remembering his number at the third attempt.

'Yo, Mason, my man,' Elvis said. 'Whatcha got thass hot?'

'Do you fancy a drink, right away?' Mason asked, trying to keep the pleading out of his voice.

'To be honest, I was just on my way out of the door, but you can meet me where I'm going, if you like,' he said. 'Are you okay, baby? You sound blue, chile.'

'I'm out of it. I'm all wrong,' Mason said. 'Just fuck off – I'm talking! Sorry, not you, Elvis. There's some woman hassling me for the phone. Where do I have to be?'

'Meet me by Putney Bridge in an hour. North bank, by the spooky church. You know it?'

'Yeah. Thanks. I'll see you soon.' He hung up the phone.

'There's no need to be rude, young man,' fumed the woman, who was fiftyish and frumpy. 'You might show a little civility. It costs nothing, you know.'

Mason considered the logic of this.

'Neither does my dick,' he said. 'I'll show you a little of that if you want.'

It was dark, and the snaggle-toothed churchyard looked very spooky indeed. Despite the lively honk and chug of traffic across the bridge behind him, Mason felt uneasy about the shadows and rustlings from the graves on the other side of the wall. He turned his back on it, and looked out across the road to the river, as it looped east towards Wandsworth.

'BOO!'

'Yah!' Mason screeched, leaping halfway across the pavement.

He turned to see Elvis, grinning like a cadaver, in the graveyard, just beyond the wall.

'You can't beat the old gags, Mason. That's *why* they're the old gags.' He leapfrogged onto the street and they strolled towards Fulham, with Mason scurrying to catch up, clutching his heart. Off the New King's Road, they took a side street that boasted a small parade of shops. One was a restaurant called Pastarotica. Its logo, hung on a sign across the pavement, was a picture of Michelangelo's David with a large fusilli pasta where the Victorians might have put a fig leaf.

'This is us,' Elvis said, pushing open the door.

The restaurant was bubbling. Every table was occupied and the air zizzed with conversation and blue cigarette smoke. The walls were hung with homoerotic line drawings After a few moments, a dark-eyed woman in a rubber dress came over.

'Hello, Judas,' she said to Elvis, wearily. 'Nice of you to come.'

'Hi, Joy. I said I would. Looks like it's going well.'

'First night,' Joy sighed. 'Bound to, really. All one's friends turn up. Place'll be empty tomorrow.'

'Table for two?' Elvis asked, brightly.

Joy scanned the restaurant. 'Hang on.' She yelled across to a booth occupied by two men drinking coffee. 'Oi! Are you two faggots going to sit there all night? Because you're completely screwing up our cash-flow projections.' She turned back to Elvis. 'That table's just asked for the bill. Have a beer on us while you're waiting. Maybe you can drink the profits before I can.'

'That's Joy.' Elvis grinned at Mason, as they took a seat at the bar. 'She co-owns this place with her partner, Sunny. Joy's the frontwoman, because Sunny's not too good with the public – she gives off very negative vibes, if you know what I mean.'

'Sunny must be a gas.'

They got some beers, and slurped them. Then, in Yogi Bear's voice, Elvis said, 'So what's with you, Boo-Boo?'

'For a start, my best friend isn't having it off with the woman I love.'

'Ooh, I hate it when that happens.'

Over the course of a couple of drinks, Mason related his misapprehension concerning Chris and Bart, his ill-advised fling with Tess and his discovery of the truth about Bart and Maria. Elvis didn't say a word. The more Mason tried to expand on the misery and confusion of the last three days, the more ludicrous it seemed. He couldn't believe what he'd put himself through. By the end of the story, he was completely cheered up.

'. . . And then,' he chuckled, 'I toasted the happy couple, told them that I wasn't so much losing a mother as gaining an inheritance, and left to phone you.' He rested his forehead on the bar and shook with laughter. 'Oh, God, what a jerk. What a first-class, copper-bottomed, Olympic-standard schlemiel.'

'Well,' Elvis said solemnly, 'I'm glad we've had this little chat. I'll send the invoice to your office. What does your dad think of all this? You never mention him.'

Mason winced. 'Well, it's a long story, but the upshot is ... Nah, I can't be bothered. I have no dad.'

Elvis pursed his lips. 'What, never?'

'Hardly ever.'

Joy appeared behind them. 'Table's ready. Come on.'

Installed in the booth, Mason scanned the menu, frowning.

'What *is* this place?'

'It's a spaghetti joint, essentially,' Elvis said, 'but it specialises in sexually explicit pasta. Joy realised that you can make pasta in any shape you like, so she designed some rude ones.' He tapped his menu with a finger. 'I think I might have the labia pescatore.'

Mason grimaced, and ran an eye over the specials. 'Do you recommend the genitalia alfredo? I'd have a side salad, but I'm frightened to ask about the dressings.'

Once they'd ordered, Elvis said, 'I fingered Suzy, then.'

'I'm sorry?' Mason asked. He was preoccupied with an etching on the wall beside him and, for a confusing moment, Elvis's comment seemed relevant to it.

'Suzy Winkworth.'

'Oh, with you, yeah. Temperance, right? Card fourteen. Very clever.'

'So – are you back on the case?'

Mason shrugged. 'I dunno. I suppose so, but I've lost my prime suspect.'

In explaining the romantic tangle of his life to Elvis, he'd omitted to mention his original conviction that Bart was the Trickster. It hadn't seemed germane to the melodrama. So now, as he wincingly stabbed his genitalia with a fork, he related the whole thing.

'But, when you analyse it,' he concluded, 'my main evidence is shot away. Bart was at the TV studio, and therefore on the video, because he was collecting my mother after her Telethon appearance. Apart from his being in the area when Belinda and Damon got hit, I had nothing to connect him with the Trickster at all. It was just speculation, really.'

'But he still fits your perpetrator profile,' Elvis pointed out. 'And you haven't proved it's *not* him. Plus, you now have the structure of the cards to work with.'

'True.'

'Which means that we might be able to guess the next victim, and catch the Trickster in the act.'

'We?'

Elvis shrugged. 'Doesn't have to be "we", I suppose. I don't need you anyway. I can do it alone.' He grinned.

'All right, all right,' Mason said. 'Why are you so interested in this?'

Elvis flung his arms wide, slapping a passing waiter on the side of the head. 'Mason – I'm interested in *everything*!' he exclaimed.

Over coffee, they came up with a potential victim who might fulfil the role of the Devil – Y.A. Watt, leading warlock and author of *The Microwave Coven: Witchcraft as Meta-Science*, which he was currently promoting on various chatshows. They could think of no one who might represent either the Empress or the Emperor, both of which were now way back down the order of the cards. Mason was convinced that they'd simply missed a couple of stories in the media, or that two scams had been attempted, but had not come off for some reason.

'No,' Elvis said, 'they're still outstanding. Our boy's just waiting for the right opportunity.'

'Could be,' Mason admitted. 'But maybe we should trawl through some back issues of the newspapers to make sure.'

'Let's give it a week,' Elvis suggested. 'We've already got enough to do.'

'If I'm to keep my editor from headlining the Tarot connection, I'm going to have to give him the suspect,' Chris told Jennings, as he dropped her off near her house. 'They'll knock up an artist's impression – that sort of thing.'

Jennings nodded, not looking at her. He was thinking.

'Yes, all right.' He pressed his palms together, as if comparing the lengths of his fingers, and mused. 'He made two calls: to the local paper and to the emergency services. I'll get Zerkah to track the number.'

'Of course!' Chris exclaimed, halfway out of the car. Then she slumped. 'Unless he used a public phone.'

'No, the timing's wrong,' Jennings said, tapping his fingertips together.

'The smoke-bomb and the calls were practically simultaneous. He must have used a mobile.'

Chris grinned. 'Then we've got him.'

'Possibly.' He frowned and rubbed his nose. 'Do you really think that Desmond Makepeace gets some sort of kick out of being humiliated?'

'For a copper, you're really quite innocent in lots of ways, aren't you?' Chris smiled.

Jennings shrugged. 'I don't get out much.'

When he got home, as he opened the front door, he immediately sensed tension. He listened for a moment, and there was a crash of breaking glass from the kitchen and Sue screamed, 'Bugger!' Jennings strode down the hall, still in his coat, and peered around the kitchen door. Sue was standing, hands clawed to her temples, looking down at a shatter of glass and pooled milk. She turned her head and glared at him.

'Where the hell have you been? You promised you'd be home by eight.' She stepped over the mess and swept past him towards the door. 'I'm late for my class. You can clear that lot up. If you'd been on time it would never have happened.'

'Is Jake in bed?' Jennings asked, shucking his jacket, and hanging it on the stand in the hall.

'I doubt it,' Sue snorted, and slammed the door behind her.

Jennings returned to the kitchen, and opened the cupboard to find a dustpan and brush. As he bent to pick up the larger shards between finger and thumb, he heard Jake's tentative footfall on the stairs.

'Don't come into the kitchen, son,' he called, looking along the hall. 'You'll get hurt.'

CHAPTER TWENTY-NINE

On Tuesday morning Mason was woken by a phone call from Elvis, breaking the news about Desmond Makepeace whose sorry photo was all over the tabloids.

'Poor bastard,' Mason croaked, wiping the sleep from his eyes.

'But this is not the most exciting part,' Elvis said. 'I think I've found our Emperor and Empress.'

'Yeah?' Mason asked, disentangling himself from the duvet and, to his own disgust, lighting a cigarette. 'How do you—' He broke off and coughed phlegmishly. 'Oh, God. That's horrible. Sorry. How do you figure that?'

'It's in *The Times*. Tomorrow, apparently, Their Divine Highnesses Emperor N'Gala Mebila and Empress Sayna of Pamalia are dropping in on Liz and Phil to shoot the breeze.'

'Of *where*?'

'Pamalia – it's four square feet of mineral-rich dust in south-west Africa. Whitey borrowed it for a couple of hundred years and then gave it back to the locals just before anyone discovered that the funny-coloured rocks were worth a few bob. The Pamalians are sitting on the largest single motherlode of platinum in the western hemisphere.'

''Snice for them,' Mason admitted. 'But why should the Trickster care?'

'Their Divine Highnesses, as their title implies, are gods. Back in Pamalia, they're in charge of the weather, earthquakes, crops and, indeed, the platinum, all of which belongs to them personally, on account of their ancestors having created it.' Elvis chuckled. 'I love the way we leave these countries with a political infrastructure cloned from our own popular democracy, don't you?'

Mason drowsily considered the practicalities of being ruled by human gods. 'So the Pamalians are having no weather while the gods are on their holidays, then?'

'They've left the climate on a timer to deter burglars,' Elvis suggested. 'Anyway, I would imagine that the idea of divine rulers swaying the elements with their merest word would get right up the Trickster's nose, hm?'

'Sure. I guess so.' Mason frowned. 'But this is, like, a state visit or something. The security'll be incredibly tight. No one'll be able to get anywhere near Mr and Mrs Divine, surely?'

'Ah,' Elvis said. 'Except that on Thursday they're doing a walkabout at that huge shopping place across the river – the Lambworth Centre. It seems they want to meet ordinary mortals and also see if there's anything worth buying – like a mall, for instance. Anyroad, they're going to be vulnerable. A Chuckie Rolls-type attack might be on the cards.'

'Risky for the Trickster.'

'I can't see how he can resist. I think we should attend. I'll speak to you Thursday morning. Ten four. Over and out.'

Mason got up and went out for the papers and a bottle of milk. He sat at his kitchen table and read the reports. The Desmond Makepeace hit upset him. All the others had been – well – mischievous. Even the hit on Arnie Sparkes, although it made his life uncomfortable, didn't actually *harm* him in any real way. But Desmond was totally destroyed. In the following weeks, he lost his TV show and his newspaper column. His grinning, ruddy face disappeared from the wine section of the supermarkets. Not surprisingly, and perhaps with the faintest merry irony, he took to drink. And all of this because he fancied he could talk to Those who had Gone Before.

Except, of course, that was only the reason he'd been *targeted*. It wasn't the reason he'd been shunned by his profession. He'd been made a pariah because he had a harmless little kink that he could afford to indulge, and that kink had become public. To Mason, the destruction of Desmond's life seemed out of proportion to the original petty idiocy of pushing a glass around a table in a darkened room.

Mason sipped his tea, and lit a cigarette, looking at the picture of Makepeace outside the police station, hunted and huddled in a long black coat, his stockinged feet sticking out beneath it, scurrying towards a cab. He wondered how much the Trickster had known about what went on in the knocking shop in Ravenscourt Park. He tried to imagine that the Trickster hadn't actually planned for Desmond Makepeace to be so totally humiliated. Perhaps the idea had simply been to have him caught slinking out of a brothel – which would have been embarrassing, but not ruinous. But, no. Makepeace represented the Hanged Man, so the Trickster must have known precisely what he got up to in there, and had exploited it.

For the first time, Mason found himself hoping that Bart *wasn't* the Trickster. There was something premeditatedly cruel, or at least uncaring, about the Hanged Man scam, and he didn't like to think that Bart had that in him. Mason had known Bart a long time and had never suspected that he carried the kind of anger needed to fuel such a trick. Mason didn't want to discover that Bart might be that incensed, that dark, that contemptuous.

On top of which, it looked as if his old friend was going to be, in some arrangement, his stepfather. And Mason already had one father who tapped incomprehensible wells of anger.

'Oh, I still haven't heard from him, by the way,' Mason told Freda, as she sprang up onto the table 'Not that I care.'

Ray Churchill loved the Trickster suspect. He bounced around the office gleefully punching the air.

'Fantastic! Are you sure the *Voice* haven't got this? Fanfuckingtastic! Killer! We'll go big on it tomorrow. Artist's mock-up, the lot.'

'We can do a photo,' Chris suggested. 'There's no face, so the legals can't touch us. I'll get a crash helmet, find a model – all that.'

'Yes! Menacing shot of him coming at the camera. Brilliant!'

'We know quite a lot when you think about it. Height, build, clothes. He's obviously fit enough to scale a six-foot fence, so that gives us a youngish bloke. We could make him quite mysterious and sexy.'

'Mondo!' Ray Churchill beamed. 'Shove a banana down his Wranglers. Something for the girls!'

Chris organised a photo session in Kentish Town for that afternoon, and then, realising that she would end up in North London at the end of the day, she went home to change. On her way to the studio, she stopped off in Camden Town to buy the crash helmet, jeans, jacket and various items of greengrocery. The male model turned out to be quite cute. She flirted with him offhandedly, and noted that purchasing zucchini had been an unnecessary precaution. She told the photographer to get the shots to the art department by eight at the latest, and then she left. It was five o'clock, and she was only a few minutes' walk from Mason's. She headed for Muscovy Street.

'Blimey – hello,' Mason said, opening the door.

She kissed his cheek and walked through into the front room, dumping the crash helmet and clothes on the armchair.

'Where have you been recently, you elusive person?' she asked, collapsing onto the sofa. 'I thought we were going out on the razz.'

Mason looked sheepish. 'Er, yeah. Sorry. Been a bit busy. But I'm free tonight.'

At Chris's suggestion, they went west, to a pub that had been important to them once.

'Lager?' she asked, leaning on the bar and waving a tenner at the barman.

'Yeah, thanks,' Mason nodded. 'Why are you all dolled-up?'

She was wearing a black embroidered blouse, long flowered skirt and, unusually for her, pale lipstick and dark eyeliner. Her earrings were a complex jangle of silver and pearls, like icicles on mistletoe. Mason suspected that he'd bought them for her a few Christmases back, though he tended not really to remember these things.

Chris shrugged. 'I just felt girlie today. Shall we sit in the garden?'

They found a wooden table by a trellis of clematis. The evening was still warm, and Mason put on his shades against the sinking sun. He was slightly surprised that he hadn't got around to calling her during the day, despite having no reason not to. He gave his feelings the once-over, and was even more surprised to find that he was pleased with his own forgetfulness. To have her slip his mind gave him a thrill. It was as if the very processes of jealousy and anger, although inappropriate, had distanced him from her. He felt, if not freed, then at least paroled.

'So what you been doing to make you so hard-to-get?' Chris asked.

Well, I went into a major sulk because I thought you were having it off with Bart; I had an ill-advised fling with a waitress; I had my Tarot thrown by an Irishman dressed as an undertaker; I figured out the Trickster's puzzle; I discovered that it's in fact my mum who's having it off with Bart; I ate penis-shaped pasta . . .

'Nothing much,' he shrugged.

'Have you proved that Bart's the Joker?'

'No – but I haven't proved he's not either. However, he may not have the time to be the Joker, on account of being a bit preoccupied by an affair with my mother.'

Chris gaped. 'You're kidding!'

'Nope. He's all over her like a damp duvet.'

'Wow. How do you feel about that?'

'Er . . . well . . .'

Actually, Mason thought, it's a good question. How *do* I feel about that?

And he didn't really know. He was so relieved that it wasn't Chris, and he felt so foolish for thinking it might have been, that he hadn't considered it directly. But now she came to mention it – it was quite stunning. His best friend was *having sex* with his mother.

'I suppose it's a bit weird, really,' he told Chris. 'But – you know . . .' He shrugged.

'How old's your mother again?'

'Forty-four. She was barely seventeen when she had me. And Bart's, what, thirty-three. It's within the bounds of acceptable behaviour, I guess.'

Chris shook her head, smiling. 'I can't believe you're so blasé about it,' she said. 'Give them both my love, if you see them before me.' She looked around the garden. 'Do you remember the last time we were in this pub? Must be close on five years ago.'

'Yeah. We saw some retropunk band and I nearly got beaten up.'

'Ha! There was *no* chance of you getting beaten up,' Chris laughed. 'As soon as the fight broke out, you were through the door at a straight run, dragging me by my safety-pin earrings.'

Mason protested. 'Oh, come on – I'm getting better. I nearly picked a fight with a four-eyed little shrimp at a party the other day. But, you're right, it was a bit wet of me. Must be because I was brought up without a father-figure. Maybe I should see a shrink.'

'God, you don't want to do that. See someone who charges forty quid to tell you that you need to spend another forty quid?'

'I don't think it happens quite like that.'

'Of course it does. They can't even prove that it *works*. And at those kind of prices, they should be issuing guarantees. I mean, can you imagine going into a garage with your car and them saying, That'll be forty quid an hour labour. And you go, Well, how many hours will it take? Dunno, they say. Well, when will you know? When it's fixed. But you're sure you can fix it? Not necessarily. But what if you make it worse? Tough.'

Mason laughed. 'Ah, the power of a well-chosen analogy,' he said.

'No, *seriously*,' Chris insisted, with a flash of real anger. 'That's how these people work. It's completely bloody criminal.'

Mason could see the conversation getting out of hand. He changed the subject. 'Getting back to the Trickster, my mate Elvis and I have figured out the pattern of the Trickster's campaign. Do you know anything about Tarot?'

Chris's eyes widened. 'Bloody hell! You've figured it out. It's the Major Arcana, isn't it?'

'Fuck,' Mason gaped. 'I thought I was going to surprise you. I thought Elvis and I were the only ones who'd got it.'

'Outside of the cops, I think you are,' Chris smiled, touching his hand. 'And *they* had something else to go on.'

'Hm,' Mason tutted disappointedly. 'Are they trying to predict victims too? That's our plan.'

'So, who's next, then?' Chris asked, grinning.

'Well . . .' Mason said, brightening – and then he stopped. 'Have you got your journalist's head on? Because I'm assuming you're not going to use this. If I wake up tomorrow to find this all over the *Clarion* I shall be pissed-off in the worst way.'

Chris leaned across the table and took a cigarette. Blowing smoke out in a jet, she said, 'I won't use it. But if you get the Trickster bang to rights, or you set it up so you think you might, will you give me a call?'

'What if it's Bart?' Mason asked. 'I don't want him splattered across the front page of your rag. It's like you said to me – he's a friend.'

'*If* it's Bart, and *if* it's not going to break anyway, I won't use it. But, then again, if it *is* Bart and it *is* going to break, it would help to have a sympathetic hack on it.'

'A characteristically nice moral get-out, Bell.' He sipped his beer.

'So, back to my original question, who's next?'

Mason leaned across and took one of Chris's cigarettes. He didn't want to give her a lead on the Emperor and Empress – he still hoped to surprise her.

'No idea,' he lied. 'It might be someone we've never heard of, like the Reverend Cutforth. Someone inoffensive like that.'

Chris snorted. 'Inoffensive? Bollocks he was. The guy was flogging the idea that terminal cancer could be cured by flash Yanks in Armani suits. And I don't mean the AMA.'

'That's a bit harsh,' Mason said.

'Not as harsh as terminal cancer. Anyway – you'll keep me informed, okay?'

'Yes, I will,' Mason replied, a little uncomfortably.

From inside the pub came the sound of electric guitars being tuned.

'Shall we go in and watch the band?' Mason suggested, getting quickly to his feet.

'Yeah,' Chris agreed brightly. 'Let's boogie and shake our funky stuff and all that. I can't remember the last time I bopped around with a bit-of-all-right. Can you?'

Mason could, but he decided against saying so.

They danced for an hour, giving the second-rate r'n'b combo a lot more enthusiasm than they deserved. By the time they called it quits, Chris's blouse was plastered to her body with sweat. It looked good to Mason, but only in a general sort of way – not specifically because it was Chris. They went through to the saloon bar and had a cooling drink, both out of breath.

'Phew,' Chris gulped, pushing a dripping strand of copper hair from her face. 'Am I getting too old for this kind of thing? I mean, would it be more graceful if I just subsided into my thirties with a resigned sigh?'

'Speaking as a mere stripling,' Mason said, 'I really wouldn't know. But, well, by your time of life, the bones become brittle, the breath shorter, the joints less willing to jive and twist—'

'Oh, shut up.' She grinned, draining her pint. 'Do you fancy fish'n'chips and a walk along the river? We could sit on a bench by Chelsea Bridge and pretend we're the poster for *Manhattan*.'

They bought cod and chips at an overpriced chippie on the King's Road, and then headed towards Chelsea Embankment and the river. They had a furious mock argument about whether it was better to put the vinegar on before the salt or vice versa. They stopped for a minute or two whilst Mason made repeated attempts to toe-punt the balled-up chip-paper into a litter bin across the street, and then they turned east along the Thames.

There was a breeze lifting off the water, and Chris, who had brought no coat, asked Mason to put an arm round her. He wasn't sure that was wise, so he gave her his jacket. They strolled along in silence for a while, peering across at the Peace Pagoda in Battersea Park, or just watching their feet keep step.

Mason felt odd.

'Tell me about this Elvis character,' Chris suggested.

'Ah. Yes. Well. He's pretty difficult to describe,' Mason said – but he had go at it. Chris accused him of exaggerating, but he insisted that, if anything, he was understating Elvis's peculiarities.

'I'd like to meet this guy,' Chris laughed. 'Invite me out for a drink with him sometime.'

'Sure,' Mason shrugged, but he found that he didn't really like the idea. It wasn't that he was possessive about Elvis; it was just that he'd come to value those parts of his life that didn't involve Chris. He liked to have somewhere to go where she wasn't an issue.

They sat on the wall facing out across the river, looking towards the power station. Mason nodded towards it.

'Shall we have our brilliant-architecture-or-dreadful-eyesore argument?' he asked.

'No, love. We've done that one to death over the years,' Chris said, smiling faintly. She seemed subdued all of a sudden.

'Okay,' Mason shrugged.

Chris had her hands deep in the pockets of the jacket, the collar turned up around her chin. She raised both her feet so that her legs were straight out above the water, and stared at her shoes.

'Mase,' she said quietly. 'Are you seeing somebody?'

Mason cocked his head on one side.

'Would you want me to tell you?' he said, after a few seconds.

She let her feet drop back against the wall. 'I don't know. I've thought about it. I suppose I'd want you to *tell* me, but I wouldn't want to *know*.' She turned and looked at him. 'It's just that you've kind of disappeared from view recently. The other time you did that was last spring, before our summer fling. And it turned out you were seeing that singer with the green hair.'

'Ruth. Yeah, God, she was a mistake . . .'

'I mean, it's none of my business, I know. We haven't been going out together for months so, y'know, there's no reason you should tell me what's going on in your life.'

'Though, by the same argument,' he pointed out, 'there's no reason I shouldn't.' He felt strangely in control, and it had been a long time since he'd felt that around Chris. He didn't really know what to do with it. He lit a cigarette.

'Oh, shit. Sorry,' Chris said briskly. 'I shouldn't have brought it up. Some of that stuff just lingers – you know. Let's talk about something else.'

Mason wasn't about to let it go that easily. 'If you're asking me if I still love you,' he said, smiling, 'then I guess I do – inasmuch as it's possible to stay madly in love with someone you only see once a fortnight.'

Chris turned to him, with a look that, on a less cynical face, could only have been described as soppy. 'Yeah, me too,' she sighed. 'But I'm sure we'll get over it.'

They hailed a cab and it took them across the river and downstream towards Chris's flat at the Oval. As they turned past the cricket ground, Mason said, 'I'll get out at the corner by the tube.'

'You can come back for a bottle of wine if you like,' Chris suggested.

'No, better not. I'll miss the last train.'

'That's okay. You can get a minicab from mine later.'

'No, I think I'll get the tube. I'm knackered.' He leaned forward to the driver. 'Can you stop opposite the station, mate? Thanks.' The cab drew up by the lights, and he opened the door. 'It's been a really nice evening. Thanks. I'll call you, all right?'

'You do that,' Chris said. 'Aren't you going to give me a kiss?'

He bent towards her, and she put an arm around his neck and pulled him close. Her mouth opened as they kissed, so he opened his too. It lasted about four times as long as simple courtesy demanded.

'I'm illegally parked 'ere, y'know,' the cab driver pointed out irascibly.

Mason backed out of the cab. 'See you,' he said and slammed the door. The cab turned right towards Stockwell, and he jogged between the cars to the station.

What was that all about then? Mason wondered, surreptitiously rearranging the front of his jeans as he rode down the escalator. Does that mean she thinks I'm seeing someone, or she thinks I'm not? Was that some kind of turning point in the relationship?

As if any one single event could be a turning point, he thought.

As if, after all this time, one fleeting snog would spin everything around.

Zif . . .

CHAPTER THIRTY

'I'm glad you decided to wear something inconspicuous,' Mason remarked, when he and Elvis met in the Lambworth McDonald's at midday on Thursday.

Elvis was wearing a Prohibition-era baggy suit with lapels so broad you could have landed a seaplane on them. This sartorial museum piece was complemented by a snappy hat, white spats and a kipper tie that might have been designed by a premenstrual parrot.

'We don't, after all, want to attract attention to ourselves,' Mason pointed out, ketchupping his cheeseburger.

Elvis sighed. 'No sense of style, the younger generation. Here's the plan: we trail around after Mr and Mrs Divine at a discreet distance, keeping a look-out for any suspicious characters.'

He apparently saw no humour in this at all. Mason shook his head, and chomped.

'At the first sign of something going down, we do not stand aghast like the other gawkers; we watch for anyone making a getaway.'

There were plenty of policemen scattered conspicuously around the mall, and Mason assumed there must be plain-clothes fuzz all over the place too. An area of pavement by the entrance was roped off and a large banner over the glass doors read, LAMBWORTH COUNCIL WELCOMES THE EMPEROR AND EMPRESS.

Mason sat on a bench just inside the mall, from which he'd be able to see the Pamalian limo draw up, and watch the royal couple walk towards him into the Centre. Elvis went up to the first-floor promenade, and mingled anonymously.

The joint was not exactly jumping. There were a few kids standing around holding limp yellow-and-blue Pamalian flags, and the only adults who seemed to be taking an interest were the staff of the Housing Department, who had been instructed by the mayor to take a day off from evicting tenants in order to turn up and swell numbers.

Mason took the Tarot pack out of his pocket, and flicked through it, thinking. He'd got to know the Major Arcana by heart, and was fascinated now by their intricate symbology. It was a story, beginning with the Fool – naïve and hopeful – and unfolding through wonder – the Magician – mysticism, romance, disillusionment, change – the Hierophant, the Lovers, the Hermit, Death – to success and eventual understanding – the Sun, the World. It was the story of growing up.

At least, that's how the story seemed to Mason. He smiled wryly, riffling the pack. Fionn was right, of course. The symbols were so universal – so vague, really – that they could be interpreted in any way that suited the interpreter.

Like a man opening the Gideon Bible at a random page, hoping for some message, Mason cut the cards and turned up ... of course. The Hanged Man. He chuckled. The card of hesitation, stasis, indecision.

Mason shuffled the pack again.

'Best of three, eh?' he murmured.

'Sir?' said Zerkah Sheikh. 'You know what you said about things that are out of place being interesting?'

She and David Jennings were standing on the upper walkway, surveying the shoppers below. It had been Zerkah who had made the connection between Pamalian royalty and the Trickster's campaign. Jennings had been delighted with her, and had been saying so all the way over in the car. Zerkah had half-wished he'd leave it be. She'd blushed and covered her discomfort by driving too fast. She had no mechanisms for handling direct praise.

'What I said about what?' Jennings asked, distractedly. He was punching a number into his mobile, and listening to the ring. He held his hand up to Zerkah, asking her to wait a second. 'Er ... it's Inspector Jennings again,' he said, evidently to a messaging service. 'Just in case you didn't get my other message, er, we're at the Lambworth Centre, following up a lead. Er ... I left a message at your office, too. Umm ... anyway, you've got my number. Well, in case you haven't, I'll give it to you again ...'

He was leaving a message for Chris Bell, agitated that he couldn't find her. Zerkah pursed her lips.

'So, anyway, hope you get this before it's too late. Umm . . . right. Bye then.' Jennings cut the call and turned to Zerkah. 'She must be working,' he suggested. 'I'd hate her to miss a scoop.'

Zerkah nodded. 'Yes. She's a busy woman.'

'Quite.' He pocketed the phone. 'What were you saying?'

'About things out of place,' Zerkah said. She nodded towards the mall below. 'I was just thinking – how often do you see a man studying the Tarot in a shopping centre?'

At twenty to one, there was a little flurry of activity. A policeman told Mason to put out his cigarette. A long black limousine ghosted up to the kerb, flanked by police bikes, and Mason stood up to get a better view. The kids waved their flags, the Housing Department staff cheered convincingly and the Emperor and Empress of Pamalia got out of the car. And continued getting out of it. Between them, they must have been more than thirteen feet tall. The Emperor was wearing a dazzlingly white suit, and the Empress was wrapped in an ankle-length arrangement of yellow and orange silk, her beaded dreadlocks clicking softly against her bare shoulders.

'Wow', Mason murmured. And so did the copper standing beside him. 'Wow,' they said in unison, and both sat down on the bench, awed.

Their Divine Highnesses surveyed the scene calmly and smiled at the gaping onlookers, who were frozen in mid-cheer, impressed as anything. The Mayor stepped forward to gabble his speech. There was a lot of hands-across-the-water nonsense, to which the royal guests listened with grave disinterest. The Mayor paused for breath at the bottom of page two and the Housing Department, rather spitefully, burst into terminal applause. The Emperor thanked the Mayor in a sentence of his native tongue, and then, trailing the goggle-eyed crowd in a train behind them, Mr and Mrs Divine progressed into the mall. As they passed by the bench, Empress Sayna offered a regal little smile in Mason's direction. It was all Mason could do not to stand and bow. His eyes followed the couple as they continued along past the health food shop, and then he glanced up towards Elvis on the balcony.

'Did you see that?' he mouthed.

Elvis, setting off along the walkway, gestured impatiently that Mason should concentrate on the job in hand, and Mason trotted off to catch up with the crowd.

The Emperor and Empress went to What She Wants ('You're going to be disappointed, love,' Mason thought), Marks and Spencer, Ernest Jones and W.H. Smith. Mason found himself wanting to apologise for the tackiness of it all. Every so often he'd catch sight of Elvis, skimming along a gallery or disappearing behind a pillar, and he'd try to focus his attention on the real task of the day. Not that it helped. Of the Trickster – in the shape of Bart or anyone else – he saw nothing.

Elvis materialised at his shoulder, as the Emperor paused to bestow a crop-ripening smile on the woman from the AA stall.

'Anything?'

'Not a sausage.'

'I don't get it.' Elvis frowned, scanning the area. 'They're leaving in a minute. When's our boy going to make his move? He's never going to get a better chance to fill the Emperor and Empress slots than this.'

Mason nodded towards the milling crowd. 'Come on,' he said. 'We're losing them. They've still got to make it all the way back to their car.'

The Divines took their time wending to the limo. Children kept sidling forward to give them flowers, and the Empress seemed happy to stop and accept every bunch. By the time they reached the entrance of the mall, her arms were full of roses, lilies and a small yucca plant. As the door of the limousine was opened by a uniformed chauffeur, Elvis and Mason pushed through the press of shoppers, anxiously waiting for the high-power hose or the exploding bouquet or whatever it would be. Elvis was standing on tiptoe and trying to look in every direction at once. Mason was silently praying that Mr and Mrs Divine would get away unharmed. Ignoring the Mayor, who was hoping they might stop to hear the rest of his speech, Emperor N'Gala Mebila and Empress Sayna telescoped themselves smoothly into the limo, waved to the delighted onlookers and were borne away through the traffic of the South Circular.

Elvis stood on the kerb, profound perplexity in his bright green eyes. 'I don't get it,' he murmured, watching the limo accelerate away in the slipstream of the police bikes.

'Let's have a beer,' Mason said, taking his friend's arm and dragging him towards the Lamb and Trifle.

'We've missed something,' Elvis pondered aloud, as they made their way across the High Street. 'You were right – we've definitely missed something. It was just so *perfect*. Why didn't the Trickster go for it?'

Mason pushed open the door of the pub. It was nearly empty, and very dim after the bright sunshine of the street. A television was babbling away on a shelf above the bar.

'Yes, gents?' asked the barman, turning away from the TV. He seemed to be unusually cheerful for a South London barman. He was grinning all over his face.

'Two lagers, please, mate,' Mason said.

Elvis tossed his wide-brimmed hat onto the bar, and ran a hand across his marble skull.

'We haven't missed a *hit*, I'm sure of that. We've missed some information. We've made some wrong assumption.'

'Three ninety, mate,' said the barman. He was still sniggering.

Mason handed him a fiver.

'We just need to think it through again,' he said. 'We just need to get inside the Trickster's mind.'

'You'd have to be a complete fucking *weirdo* to get inside *that* bastard's mind,' offered the barman, chuckling as he made change. 'Yeah, you'd need to be a nutter to suss that bastard.'

Elvis sat up, immediately interested. 'What?'

'Well, that's what yer talkin about, innit? This Joker feller doing his thing on the telly just now? On *Midday South East*. Wiv that witch bloke.'

Elvis was appalled. 'What? Which witch? Y.A. Watt?' he screeched, unhelpfully.

'Yeah, that's the geezer. 'E was talkin' about spells an' all that bollocks, sayin' you could make it rain if you knew the right words an' evryfin. 'E's sayin' the spell to make it rain, an all that, right? An' suddenly, hurhurhurhur . . .'

'Suddenly what? Suddenly what?'

'Suddenly, oh dear, hahahaha, all these *frogs* fall on 'im! Dozens of 'em! Hahahaha! Fuckin' *frogs* all over the place. All jumpin' about and croakin'. One of the little bleeders just sits there on 'is *'ead*, right? What a berk! Fuckin' frogs *all over* 'im. Hahahaha . . .'

Elvis closed his eyes and took a deep breath. Then he looked at Mason, calm and singleminded.

'Nyah, you realise,' he drawled nasally, 'dat dis means war ...'

'Follow him,' Jennings had said. 'Can't pull someone in just for owning a Tarot pack – and, anyway, where would it get us? Follow him.'

So Zerkah followed him – which was not as easy as it sounded. She had taken an orange juice in the pub where the suspect had spent an hour with a skeletal, bald type in gangster clothes. She played the quiz machine in the corner, feeling very obvious and female and Asian. She was one question away from winning eight pounds fifty when the suspect drained his beer and left the pub.

A teenager was at her shoulder, watching her play. 'Prospero's in *The Tempest*,' she told him, hoiking her handbag over her shoulder and heading for the door. As she slipped out onto the street, she heard the chink-chink-chink of the prize money in the hopper.

He walked fast, the suspect. Zerkah had to scurry to keep a considered twenty yards behind him. He stopped at a newsagent, and Zerkah hung around outside, pretending to read the handwritten ads for childcare and massage. She watched the suspect flick through top-shelf magazines. Eventually, when the shop was empty, he plumped for a publication called *Thigh Highs*.

He descended into the tube, and Zerkah panicked as she scurried down the steps. She didn't want to stand right behind him in the queue for the ticket machine, but then again she didn't want him getting down to the platform and hopping on a train while she was still looking for change. And, actually, she didn't know where she wanted a ticket to. And – damn – she'd put all her change in the quiz machine.

As she hung back watching the suspect feed coins into the slot, Zerkah realised she was breathing shallowly and fast. She was flushed and excited. She was doing *proper coppering*. She remembered her father, tugging his beard and wailing when she announced that she was going to be a policewoman; her mother, tight-lipped, asking whether she was doing this deliberately – trying to kill daddy, what with his heart and all. But look – *look* – a copper, now. Little Zerkah – little Trouble, little Grief – a police officer, trailing a criminal.

The suspect negotiated the automatic barrier, and Zerkah strode up to the station attendant and flashed her warrant card. 'Police,' she muttered – and the attendant pulled back the gate and let her through.

She was relaxed by the time she got to the station platform. The suspect was right there in the crosshairs, and he was going nowhere without her. When the train arrived, she boarded the same carriage, and didn't even look at him between stations. She strap-hung, and read the advertisements, knowing she had him taped. She was wondering if he had a mobile phone in the pocket of that tatty denim jacket. She'd traced the number from which calls had been made before the Makepeace hit, and it had led only to an anonymous pay-as-you-go phone. No help at all.

He got off at Camden, and she kept him in sight, up the escalator, out to the street, along past the market. As she followed, she took out her own phone and dialled the number that she'd spent the previous morning tracing. She was disappointed, as she listened to it ring, that the suspect didn't stop and dig in his pocket to answer it. She stayed back as he doglegged into a sideroad, and she dawdled when he turned into the gate of a Victorian maisonette. As he opened the door, Zerkah strolled forward, making sure she passed him as he went in. She watched him, through the window, walk into the front room. She doubled back, to see him leave the room, disappear into the rear of the flat.

She slipped in through the gate, and peered through the window. And there, on the sofa, was a leather jacket and a black crash helmet with a yellow stripe.

She nearly shrieked.

Got him.

CHAPTER THIRTY-ONE

Were you to pull on a pair of stout walking shoes in Paris, and stride out due east with the notion that you would not stop for lunch until you passed someone wealthier than Yashimo Naganitaki, you would eventually fetch up on the shores of the North Pacific feeling more than averagely peckish.

Yashimo Naganitaki was the essence of prosperous modern Japan decanted into gila-skin loafers. His personal fortune humiliated his pocket calculator. His platinum Amex really was. Yashimo, in short, could afford to buy his round. *Everybody* knew that ...

'Who is this Yashimo guy again?' Mason groaned, as he took a seat in a coffee shop on the Strand.

It was a quarter to eight in the morning, and he'd been up for an hour. He'd even been awake for some of it. Elvis had phoned at six-thirty, babbling in a terrible cod-Oriental accent about Yashi-something. He'd commanded Mason to be at the Parma Grill Café by half-past seven. Mason had dressed and left the house without opening his eyes. It was so early that Freda couldn't even be bothered to hassle him for breakfast.

Mason had been amazed to discover that they ran tube trains at that time of day. Having got off at Charing Cross, he staggered along the Strand, unshaven and puffy, and a passing wino had asked him where he managed to get hold of the stuff so early.

He tottered into the Parma Grill Café and spotted Elvis at a window seat, wearing a T-shirt that bore the legend 'I heart-symbol Pearl Harbour'. He was engaged in the repulsive process of internalising a fish-finger sandwich.

'It lives! It lives!' Elvis lugosied, as Mason slumped onto the banquette. 'My creation lives! Coffee?'

'Thanks. I repeat – who is this Yashimo guy?'

'Have you had breakfast?'

'Be serious. I left my stomach in my other suit.'

'Well, eat something. It could be a long day. Hey, Mario!' Elvis called to the woman at the counter. 'Two eggs lookin' atcha, tomato, mushrooms, three rashers and a fried slice, please.'

'Oh, Jesus,' Mason croaked, and rested his forehead on the table. When breakfast arrived, he simply stared at it in horror.

'Now you eat that all up like a good boy,' Elvis soothed. He leaned across the table and forked a mushroom. 'Open wide—'

'All right, all right,' Mason grumbled. 'I suppose I'm going to have to get back on solids sometime.'

As he ate, Elvis explained about Yashimo Naganitaki and his mind-boggling wealth.

'He's here in Britain today to attend the opening ceremony of the futuristic feat of corporate architecture that bears his name – the Naganitaki Tower.'

'The Tower,' Mason mumbled, through a mouthful of eggs. 'Aha. Is that the pyramid-shaped thing in Docklands?'

'That's the one. It boasts the world's most sophisticated computer-controlled working environment. The air-conditioning, lighting, security, even the coffee machines are run by a central computer. And not only is the physical environment tuned to perfection, the psychic ambience is tiptop, too. Thanks to the ancient Oriental science of feng shui, the life-energies of the building, the décor, the furniture and the workers harmonise into an unbroken harmony of harmonious harmony.'

'Actually, this rings a bell,' Mason said through a mouthful of bacon. 'A harmonious one, naturally.'

Elvis leaned over and dipped a piece of toast in egg yolk, and then gestured towards the window with it.

'The man and his entourage are currently occupying floors five and six of the Savoy – which is that impressive building across the street.' He popped the toast into his mouth. 'And we are going to follow Mr Naganitaki all day and all night so that when the Trickster hits, we'll be on the spot.'

'And what if I've got plans for today?' Mason asked, wiping his mouth with a napkin.

'You haven't,' Elvis said firmly. He pulled some earmuffs and a bed-mask out of his pocket, donned them, and stretched out on the plastic-upholstered seat. 'Right, I'm going to have a nap. You take the first watch, Chooch,' he said.

'Okay, TC,' Mason muttered.

The front page of the previous day's *Clarion* was pinned to the wall of the operations room. It carried the picture that Chris had set up, of a sinister crash-helmeted figure scaling a fence. Underneath, the caption read, *The Faceless Menace.*

Zerkah sipped her coffee and gazed at the image. For her, now, the menace was not faceless. She knew what he looked like. He had pale grey eyes, a full, childish mouth, a weak chin, a straight, thin nose. His hair was dark brown and straggly, falling over his collar. He looked very ordinary, in his faded jeans and his even more faded denim jacket. He was just a bloke in a pub. And he was the Trickster. The whole country carried that image of him that Chris Bell had conjured – but only Zerkah knew what he looked like. He belonged to her alone.

She could hear laughing in the corridor, snatches of conversation between the coppers who had derided her through Police College, patronised her, mocked her for her colour, her culture, her gender – for herself, really. All those cropped, spotty, white, male trainees who'd called her 'Paki'. All the bull-necked, sneering, dismissive skippers. 'Ethnic bloody diversity? Tell me that when you've been in a ruck with twenty football thugs, Fatima. Gender equality? Try again when you've chased a villain down Tottenham Court Road, love.'

The door opened, and Inspector Jennings walked in. He folded himself into his chair and put his feet up on the desk.

'How did it go, sir?' Zerkah asked.

Jennings pinched his nose between his index fingers. 'Well, I told DCI Jagger that we had a suspect, and that we needed a team to stake him out twenty-four hours a day. I explained that we were constrained on resource and that I required a commitment of manpower to leverage our potential for a successful conclusion.'

'And?' Zerjak said, hopefully.

'And he told me to piss off,' Jennings sighed.

Zerkah squealed and clapped her hands. 'Yes!'

'I apologise for the expletive,' Jennings said, reaching forward to pick up a pen and lodge it in the corner of his mouth, 'but I felt you should be aware of exactly the attitude that leaves us entirely on our own in pursuit of a resolution of this case.' He tapped the pen against his teeth. 'It's a terrible problem, this understaffing issue in the law and order arena,' he grinned.

By ten-fifteen, Mason's bum was numb from sitting in one place too long and every time he shifted his weight from one buttock to the other, a gallon of cappuccino sloshed about in his stomach. He'd developed a little nervous tic of glancing towards the Savoy at ten-second intervals, and he was putting off going for a pee in case the Oriental billionaire left while he was splashing his boots.

And he got to thinking. Certainly Bart was still in the frame, but he wasn't that convincing a suspect. The chances were that the Trickster would turn out to be some complete stranger; no one with whom Mason had any connection at all. Life was like that. But, then, snoring on the banquette opposite, there was Elvis.

Mason ordered another coffee and applied the profile he'd developed of the Joker. Money: well, Elvis never seemed to be short of a few bob. Time: he didn't seem to have a regular job. Sense of humour: well, yes, if a slightly weird one. Scathing attitude to the other-worldly: no. But what he did have was a sense of mischief for its own sake.

Mason had to admit that it looked a pretty good fit. For a start, Elvis had twigged the Tarot thing so early in the game that it was almost uncanny. Also, he'd foreseen the hit on Suzy Winkworth, and generally seemed to be all over the Trickster's modus. Okay, he got the Emperor and Empress wrong – but then if he were laying a false trail, that's exactly what he *would* do, isn't it?

Mason thanked the woman who delivered the coffee to the table, and tapped out a thoughtful cigarette. There was still some unexplained motivation here. Elvis had gone out of his way to become involved with a Trickster sleuth; he'd taken the project on wholeheartedly after that chance meeting in Soho. So, if he was the culprit, what was in it for him?

There was something going on – Mason knew it. There was something going on and he was missing the point.

He lit his cigarette and winced.

Christ. It was becoming a habit.

A little after eleven o'clock, a group of immaculately dressed Orientals emerged from the hotel. They were followed by an equally svelte Japanese child of about ten. An enormous stretch-Cadillac drew up on the Strand – it was too long to turn down the little approach road to the Savoy itself – and sat there purring.

'Elvis! Elvis, wake up,' Mason hissed, kicking out under the table.

'Action?' Elvis asked, tearing off his mask and earmuffs, instantly awake.

The little boy had climbed into the limo and the men were following him. Elvis glanced across at them.

'Thar she blows,' Elvis cried. 'Let's go.' He rushed out into the street and Mason hobbled after him; his leg had gone to sleep. The Caddy was pulling away towards Charing Cross. Mason glanced up and down the street – there was no sign of a taxi.

'Shit, we're going to lose them, Elvis,' he said, turning. '. . . Elvis?' Elvis had disappeared. 'God, I *hate* it when he does that,' Mason said, crossly. He stamped his foot; not out of petulance, but in an attempt to get rid of the pins-and-needles.

Suddenly Elvis shot out of a sideroad and screeched to a halt at the kerb by Mason's side. He was wearing a leather flying hat and goggles. And he had provided transport.

'Climb aboard, Skip,' he yelled. 'It's chocks-away time.'

Mason stared aghast at the pursuit vehicle.

'Isn't she a fine old girl?' Elvis grinned proudly. 'Look, I've brought you your own helmet. Got to wear it, Skip – in-flight safety regulations.'

He handed over headgear identical to his own and a set of goggles. Mason took them mechanically, and they hung loosely in his hand.

'Come on then,' Elvis chivvied. He cupped a hand over his mouth. 'Hound Dog One to Control Tower, Hound Dog One to Control Tower, are we cleared for take-off?'

'Fucking hell,' Mason murmured. He climbed aboard Hound Dog One, and Elvis pushed off into the oncoming traffic.

Riding a tandem bicycle is a skill. It requires almost telepathic coordination between the pedallers, and a certain amount of mutual trust.

By the time they had tailed the Cadillac to Knightsbridge, Mason had discovered that tandem riding was not one of his foremost talents.

Keeping pace with the stretch was easy in London traffic. Throughout the ride, Elvis provided in-flight patter, switching characters between bomber ace, barnstormer, jumbo pilot and stewardess. Mason kept his head down and pedalled. He couldn't tell whether he was terrified or embarrassed. As Elvis chained Hound Dog One to a parking meter outside Harrods, Mason watched the group of Orientals file into the store.

'Who's the kid?' he panted, as they trotted across them.

'That's no kid; that's our man,' Elvis said.

'He's a midget?' Mason squealed, following Elvis through the glass doors.

'He is *vertically challenged*, yes. They reckon that he's personally worth about twenty million dollars per inch, under normal atmospheric pressure.'

They skipped onto an escalator, several yards behind the Japanese. Elvis had been right; it was the beginning of a very long day. They trailed Naganitaki and company all around Harrods and then dogged him to the King's Road. They hung around outside while he took a late lunch in a wincingly pricey restaurant in Fulham. They tracked him to Mayfair and watched him buy old maps in Shepherd Market; and then they pedalled furiously to keep up with him all the way back to the Savoy.

It was five to five.

'*Now* can I go for a piss?' Mason asked, as they resumed their look-out in the Parma Grill Café.

When he got back to the table, Elvis was staring up at the hotel, deep in thought.

'Bugger me sideways if the Trickster's not going to hit at the opening ceremony of the Tower itself,' he murmured, admiringly. 'We'll eat here and then set off for the Docklands on Hound Dog One.'

Mason lowered himself gingerly onto the seat.

'No,' he groaned. 'Sorry and all that, but absolutely not. I'm not cycling another inch. I'm not used to this lark. I've got an arse like a baboon.'

At eight-thirty, the stretch-Cadillac left for the docks – and Mason got to say something he never thought he would get to say.

'Follow that car,' he told the cabby.

'You know this offends my sensibilities, don't you?' Elvis asked, stretching his legs in the back of the taxi.

'When it comes to a choice between your sensibilities and my perineum,' Mason told him, 'there's only one queue, as far as I'm concerned. Oh, can I use your phone to call Chris?'

As the cab journeyed east, Elvis enthused about the Naganitaki Tower.

'Essentially, it's just a huge gadget. This is what YenCo, Yashimo's company, do best. They're just incredible at making gadgets.

'For instance, they were the people who came up with the idea of a digital watch that *ticked*. Brilliant, eh? I mean, a digital watch doesn't *need* to tick, but people just like it. If there's one thing that Naganitaki knows about it's the power of advertising. The Tower itself *runs adverts*. Because all the lighting is controlled by computer, they have huge great slogans zipping across the face of the building all night. The computer just makes the right office windows light up in sequence. It's amazing.'

The cab turned a corner and there, at the end of a long boulevard, was the Naganitaki Tower. In the gathering dark, it was immensely impressive. The windows were lit up in such a way that the building read,

YENCO
CORPS

The letters were a hundred feet high. Green and red spotlights played over the face of the building, and bounced off into the night. The pyramid was made entirely of glass, and those windows that weren't illuminated were filled with the image of the pink and grey sky to the west.

As the cab got closer, the words YENCO CORPS slid away round the edge of the building and were replaced with

ONE
WORLD

'Can you just stop here, please?' Elvis told the driver.

'Wow, it's pretty impressive, isn't it?' Mason admitted, gazing towards the building and the large crowd in front of it. 'You can see why they wanted to do this ceremony at night.'

They walked up the broad approach to the Naganitaki Tower.

ONE
VISION

it informed them.

They passed a couple of camera crews, framing the entire structure in shot. They were still two hundred yards away from the forecourt, in which brightly lit fountains splashed over oriental sculptures. The world's press and scores of onlookers were milling about amongst the fountains, and in front of the smoked-glass doors of the main entrance, a raised platform had been constructed. A knot of sharp-suited Orientals were gathered at its base.

ONE
FUTURE

the building suggested.

Elvis and Mason positioned themselves on either side of the road, away from the throng.

Suddenly, an Eastern-influenced fanfare blasted out from the public address system, and flashlights started zapping from the press snappers. The music thrummed to a climax, and a white spot lit up the platform as Yashimo appeared, flanked by two of the suits. Yashimo's subordinates stayed well back on the platform, Mason noticed, and must have been standing on a lower level than their boss, because the Big Man didn't look unusually little.

WELCOME
!!!

offered the Tower, cheerfully.

'Good evening,' said Yashimo Naganitaki, leaning towards the mike. His English was perfect mid-Atlantic, his manner formal but relaxed.

'First of all,' he said, 'allow me to thank you all for attending this evening. And, of course –' he gestured to the vast sign behind him – 'welcome. The Naganitaki Tower represents the culmination of an ambition I have had for many years . . .'

It was a standard corporate speech, boosting the technological perfection of the Naganitaki Tower in particular, and YenCo in general. It touched on the ancient Oriental science of feng shui and how it had been applied to the design and layout of the building.

'And so,' Yashimo concluded, 'I will now set free the symbolic butterflies, and declare the Naganitaki Tower – open!'

He threw a switch in front of him and, from somewhere behind the podium, hundreds of butterflies were released into the air. At the same moment, a gigantic animated butterfly flapped across the face of the pyramid, and red and white fireworks exploded in the sky above the Tower.

The spectators gasped and clapped, as the butterflies fluttered suicidally against the plate glass in blind insect panic.

'Pretty impressive, huh?' said a voice in Mason's ear.

It was Chris.

'Hiya,' Mason shouted, above the racket of the fireworks. 'I think I might have got you down here for nothing.'

ONE
WORLD

the building remarked.

'Well, the Tower fits. It looks too good an opportunity for the Trickster to miss, really,' Chris yelled back.

ONE
VISION

the Tower pointed out, brightly.

'Yeah, that's what we thought,' Mason bellowed. 'Or at least, Elvis did. That's him, over there.'

He pointed towards Elvis, who was staring fixedly at Yashimo.

ONE
FUTURE

came the inevitable illuminated punchline.

The skyrockets were still star-bursting in the night air at the pyramid's apex and the onlookers were oohing and aahing and picking dead butterflies out of their hair. Chris and Mason surveyed the scene, waiting for the Trickster to strike. Yashimo and his court were climbing into their long black car.

'I don't think it's going to happen,' Mason shouted, turning to Chris, as the stretch-Cadillac pulled away.

The last firework exploded in the night sky, and its retort echoed back from the far side of the river. Everything seemed quiet and finished.

'I said,' Mason repeated, as Yashimo's car accelerated down the boulevard, 'I don't think anything's going to happen.'

Chris squinted over his shoulder towards the Tower. 'Oh, I don't know,' she smiled.

Mason turned and looked up at the great glass pyramid.

FUCK

OFF

it suggested, simply.

And, after a moment's thought, it added,

SHORT

ARSE

CHAPTER THIRTY-TWO

'Bart called me as I was on my way to meet you,' Chris said casually, starting the car. Elvis was in the passenger seat, and Mason in the back. 'He's invited us out to dinner in Covent Garden. Shall we go?'

'Sure,' Mason said. 'Fancy that, Elvis?'

Elvis was not taking part. He was too busy muttering. 'The Trickster didn't even have to *be* there. The sonofabitch didn't even have to *be* there. He just bunged someone a wedge, and split. If he gave some computer boffin enough money, he'll be untraceable.'

'Your mum's going to be there too,' Chris said, wheeling west. She glanced at Elvis. 'I think you'd like Mason's mum.'

'When's the Trickster going to do something *personal*?' Elvis asked. 'When's he going to do something he has to *be there* for?'

Mason was completely knackered. He'd been up a long time, and he'd done some serious pedalling. He ached all over. On top of that, Elvis was not making much of an impression on Chris, and Mason felt responsible. He'd done a big sell on what a fascinating type Elvis was, and now the type was being tedious. He hadn't even done a funny voice.

Chris pulled the car round a juggernaut and gunned it through the City. 'You can't expect the Trickster to knock your socks off every time, Elvis,' she said. 'I guess if you're setting up this kind of scam on a regular basis, you have to take them where you can.'

'Humph,' Elvis humphed, and withdrew into silence for the rest of the journey.

They parked the car on Kingsway, and trailed through into Covent Garden. As they crossed the piazza a voice cried, 'Mason, darling! And Chrissie!'

It was Maria.

'Oh, hi,' Mason said, as she swept towards them.

'Hello, Maria,' Chris smiled. 'How are you?'

'Topping,' Maria replied, in an echo of Bart. 'Never better.'

'Oh, er, this is Elvis,' Mason said. 'Elvis – my mum, Maria.'

'What a dame! What a dame!' Elvis cried, back to his usual self.

'How nice to meet you, Elvis. Mason has told me absolutely nothing about you, I'm afraid. But then he tells me so little.'

La Tour was a standard French eaterie with ideas above its station – its station being Covent Garden tube. When they arrived, Mum scolded the maître-d' for not being sufficiently precognitive to realise that when she had booked for four she'd meant five. The maître-d' apologised for this unforgivable lapse and found a table, as Mason gave the place a quick once-over to make sure that it wasn't the kind of restaurant where they folded the napkins into tiny Sydney Opera Houses. It was a close shout, but he reckoned he could manage to force a little something down. Bart turned up just as they were ordering aperitifs. He slalomed nimbly between the outstretched tongues of panting women at the other tables, and drifted gracefully to a halt next to Maria like a fey hang-glider.

Glancing at Mason, he bent down towards her. 'At the risk of offending your offspring – although the child is going to have to get used to it – give us a kiss,' he said. They kissed, and Bart turned to the rest of the table as he took his seat.

'Chrissie,' he hammed, 'what a terrible disappointment to see you here. For years I have carried around the notion that you are the most exquisitely beautiful woman ever to lower a toilet seat – but now I come across you in Maria's company, I find that you are, and can only ever be, a valiant runner-up. Still, number two in the entire human race is not bad, surely?'

Chris grinned. 'I may never recover from this terrible blow to my ego,' she confessed.

'Bear up, old girl, bear up. How are you, Mason?'

'Had a couple already, have we?' Mason asked.

'I did allow myself a snort on the way here, yes. Would you say me nay?'

'Not at all, mate,' Mason told him. 'I'd like you to meet Elvis. Elvis, this is Bart. Bart and I go back a very long way. So far, in fact, that I even managed to have a two-way conversation with him once.'

As they ordered, Mason realised that he felt slightly nervous. The situation reminded him of a party he'd once been to, where he noticed three women he'd slept with all talking together in the kitchen. There was much sniggering and whispering of confidences. He doubted they were trading make-up tips. He went out into the garden and banged his head repeatedly against a greenhouse. Now, as he looked around the table at his mother, his best friend, his ex and his . . . what was Elvis? . . . his new friend, he had the oddest sensation of watching four channels at once.

Elvis was being subdued and polite, talking to Maria about her work. Chris and Bart were gossiping about mutual chums from ten years back, and how they'd all lost touch. Mason couldn't think of anything sensible to say, though he felt he should contribute. Being well brought up, he usually tried to avoid speaking with his mouth full – so he decided to keep it full of wine. An attentive waiter made it very easy for him.

'. . . We were just coming back from the Docklands,' Elvis was saying. 'We went to catch the Trickster's latest production.'

'Oh, and what was that?' Maria asked.

Elvis related the tale of their day – objectively and without gags, but still managed to build the tension. When he reached the punchline, Maria howled with laughter, and Bart spluttered through his gazpacho.

'But how did you *know*?' Maria said. 'How did you know that this Yashimo person would be the next victim?'

'It was on the cards,' Elvis told her cryptically. 'Mason?'

Mason took up the story. As he spoke, he watched Elvis making as if to listen, but actually staring at Bart. Mason couldn't bring himself to look in Bart's direction, so he addressed himself exclusively to his mother.

'. . . And so, because the Trickster's got to number sixteen, it had to be the Tower. And Elvis figured that the Naganitaki Tower was the one.'

Maria shook her head in admiration. 'It's brilliant. Aren't you clever? Bart, isn't it brilliant?'

'It's exceptional,' Bart agreed, lighting a cigarette. 'Extraordinary.'

'And have the three of you been working on this since the beginning?' Maria asked.

'Oh, no. Not me,' Chris said. 'I was only let in on it a few days ago.'

'Amazing,' Maria laughed. 'So what's next? Who's next?'

'The Star,' Elvis said. 'If the Trickster sticks strictly to the sequence – and he doesn't necessarily – it'll be the Star.'

'Except that one of them's been missed out,' Chris put in. 'So the whole scam might jump back down the order.'

Mason nodded. 'Yeah. Two, in fact, have been missed out. Elvis and I disagree about this. I think maybe we just didn't see them.'

Elvis leaned back in his chair, and gazed around the table, his eyes coming to rest on Bart. 'No,' he said. 'I still think the Trickster's got this taped. If anything's been missed out, it's been missed out for a reason.'

Bart tapped his cigarette. 'Well, don't look at me, old thing. I haven't an idea in my head. But I've said it before and I'll say it again – I think the Trickster is a good egg.' He raised his glass. 'Shame and humiliation to charlatans everywhere, and more strength to the Trickster's sense of humour.'

'Whoever he is,' Maria agreed, knocking back her champagne.

A little later, as Mason was coming back from the loo, Bart got up from the table and gestured him towards the bar.

'I have something for you,' he said, pulling an envelope from his inside pocket.

Mason blinked and took the envelope. 'What is it?'

'Twenty thousand free air-miles. I've been clocking them up for years. They cost me nothing, so this is not some patronising loan. It's a gift.'

'Bart, look, thanks, but—'

Bart held up a slim hand. 'I've transferred them to your name. You can use them, or sell them or whatever you like. But . . .' He swept his hair back. 'Use them, please. I shall miss you terribly, but I want you to get out of . . . I want you to be happy. You're not happy here, my old friend.'

Mason glanced towards the table, and caught Chris's eye. She was looking towards him, solemn and concerned, but she immediately looked away, scratching her forehead and sucking on her cigarette. Maria spoke to her and she broke into a smile, replied, carried on seamlessly.

'Does Chris know about this?' Mason asked; but he could tell from her demeanour that she did.

'It doesn't matter,' Bart said, firmly. 'It doesn't matter what she knows or what she thinks. This is for *you*, Mason – be selfish about it.'

Mason flicked the envelope against his chin thoughtfully. Twenty thousand miles. He could go and see Harry in Algiers. Work in his bar. He could fly to Delhi and get on the first train to anywhere. He could take up Maggie's offer of a few months' bed and board in the Appalachians.

He looked up at Bart, and grinned. 'Would you see to my frail old mother while I was away?'

Bart chuckled. 'Nightly,' he promised.

By the time the main course was over, Mason had reached that happy stage of drunkenness in which a profound affection for one's dearest cries out to be expressed. Mason was expressing it to Bart.

'No, really, man, I'm dead happy for you. *And* me mum. Dead happy.'

Maria was shifting her gaze between her son and her lover, smiling indulgently and fondly in turn. Mason felt that this was worthy of comment too.

'Look, Mum, I know you think I'm drunk – well, I am, a bit – but that's not the point. I mean, in vino thingie, right? I mean I'm really, really happy for you. Okay?'

'Absolutely, darling,' she said.

Mason was slumped forward on his elbows, and Chris and Elvis were leaning around the back of him, talking about the Tarot and associated methods of divination. The conversation was heated, but not unfriendly. Elvis was letting Chris do most of the running. Mason glugged an entire glass of claret and leaned back, so that his face was between them. He didn't want them to feel left out.

'Don't get her angry,' he told Elvis. 'You wouldn't like her when she's ang, hic, angry.'

Chris pushed him gently back to the table, and carried on pointing out the absurdity of tealeaf reading to Elvis. Mason looked at the tip of his cigarette for a few seconds. It was fascinating. Then he got to his feet, and swayed a little.

'Look, people,' he announced, 'it occurs to me that I'm getting very pissed here. I think it's because I'm completely fucking shagged-out. So, before I really offend someone, I think I'd better go home. Thanks for the meal, Bart. Er, goodbye, everyone.'

'Here,' Chris said, standing up, 'I'll come down to the Strand with you and put you in a cab. Bart, will you order me a sorbet? I'll be back in a minute.'

Amongst bye-byes and give-me-a-calls, Chris steered Mason out of the restaurant, and down to the main drag. She hailed a cab and gave him a twenty-pound note.

'No – it's okay . . .' he began.

'Shut your trap, Dixon, and accept with good grace for once in your life. You going to be okay?'

'Sure. I'm just really, really tired. Look – about Bart's air-miles—'

'We'll talk about it later. Get in the cab.' She kissed him quickly as she held the door open. 'Call me, sweetheart. Tomorrow.'

'Yuh.'

She shut the door, and leaned through the front window to give the driver the address. The cab nosed out into the traffic, and Mason was asleep before the indicator had clicked off.

Zerkah Sheikh was sitting in an unmarked police car twenty yards down the road from Mason's apartment. She was eating a bar of chocolate very slowly – one chunk every half hour. She was also listening to the radio, and had heard news of the hit at the Naganitaki Tower, though one had to read between the lines of the BBC report to appreciate exactly what the building had said.

'Oh, balls,' she muttered to herself. 'The Tower. Damn.'

She looked up as a cab stopped outside the suspect's apartment. The suspect had a name now. The electoral roll had given her that. *Dixon, Mason James.* Further investigation had revealed that he was born on 21st March 1972, the child of an unmarried teenage mother – now a minor celeb – and one Marty Puxley, occupation Artist – now very famous in America. Zerkah could see how the illegitimacy and the subsequent desertion by the dad could have warped Dixon, filled him with vengeful resentment. In constructing the Trickster's campaign, he was obviously hitting back at the bohemian culture that had failed him as a child.

'Don't get too excited,' Jennings had said. 'We don't know it's him yet.'

'Sir, he was looking at the Tarot just before the Emperor and Empress turned up!' Zerkah had insisted.

'Yes – but nothing happened to them.'

'Okay, what about the black crash helmet with the yellow stripe?'

Jennings admitted that the helmet was a strong circumstantial factor. 'But it's not proof. The possession of any mass-produced item is a very shaky basis for a theory.'

Zerkah beamed and played her trump. 'I've checked with the DVLA. He hasn't got a motorcycle licence.'

'Oh, very good. Very good indeed,' Jennings had said, nodding. 'Go on then, stake him out. But be careful.'

Zerkah watched as Dixon stumbled out of the cab and up to the front door. He stood back as he put the key in, keeping his shadow from obscuring his view of the lock. He was pretty drunk.

'Been out celebrating, Mason?' Zerkah murmured. She watched him stagger into the hall and slam the door behind him.

It was time to call it a night. He wasn't going anywhere. Zerkah popped the last square of chocolate into her mouth and turned the key in the ignition.

At that moment, her mobile phone chirruped. She picked it off the passenger seat and held it to her ear. 'WPC Sheikh,' she said, automatically.

There was a short silence, and then the call was cut. Zerkah looked at the LCD and frowned. Then, recognising the number, she slapped her hand to her mouth.

Of course. *Of course.* He had her number, because she'd called him the previous day. He was sitting there in the flat, drunk on his bed, and he'd wondered who had phoned him on that anonymous pay-as-you-go mobile. He'd hit call-back – and she'd casually let him know that the police were onto him.

'Stupid, stupid, *stupid* Zerkah,' she muttered, banging her forehead against the steering wheel.

She had, she knew, a lot to learn.

'WPC Sheikh, indeed.'

Standing on the bridge, Mischief tossed the phone from hand to hand, conjuring possibilities, following lines of thought, anticipating threats.

The river was silent, still, painted with the images of the buildings on the south bank. A pleasure cruiser was approaching from the Westminster side, all bass beat and laughing conversation carried across the water.

Mischief held the phone above the syrupy murk, ready to drop it in, so that it could bleat forlorn and forgotten until it drowned. But – no – there were three hours left on the card. Bought time. Seemed a pity to waste it.

As the pleasure boat chugged beneath the bridge, Mischief's hand opened, and the phone fell towards the deck. Maybe it would smash. Maybe it would survive. Maybe someone would pick it up, curious and then delighted. Three hours' free calls. Why not, eh?

And those calls would be confusion and noise. Create enough confusion and noise, and you were safe. The charlatans knew that, as if it were the alphabet. Mischief thought about the picture on the front page of the *Clarion*. The whole country was looking for a sinister figure in a crash helmet. Confusion. Assumption. Passive acceptance.

Why, for God's sake, didn't they think it through? The truth was as plausible, as likely, as *obvious* as the misapprehensions and dead-ends. When this all came out, as it must eventually, would they all throw up their hands and puff and say, 'Well, who'd've thought it?' Why were people surprised by the truth?

Mischief looked up and down the bridge, and it was empty. The moon was both hung above the Shell building and immersed in the river, swaying duplicitously. London's eyes were closed, and its ears were deaf to the bubba-dum-bubba-dum from the sound systems of the pleasure boats, oblivious to the drunken karaoke renditions of three-minute lies.

There on the bridge, Mischief breathed in deeply, arms spread wide, and yelled up towards the self-obsessed City.

'It's me, isn't it? It's obviously *me*!'

CHAPTER THIRTY-THREE

The note must have been there when he got home, but Mason was too out of it to notice. The following afternoon though, when he woke up, he found it on the mat. It was scribbled on a page torn from a notebook:

Dropped by, but you were out. I'll try again another time. Martin.

Mason stood there in the hall, staring at the scrap of paper, holding his cup of tea and chewing a forgotten slice of ham he'd excavated from the fridge.

Martin? He didn't know anyone called Martin. He guessed it must be for next door. They had people turning up at all hours, on account of them being low-rent dope pushers. He dropped the note on the floor so he'd remember to deliver it later, and made his way back to the kitchen, in the hope of digging out more ham.

Mason was a great fan of Tom and Jerry cartoons. He loved them. He could tell whether it was a classic Fred Quimby just from the recording quality of the theme tune. One of his favourite recurrent gags was the reaction shot in which Tom has seen something, not registered it and then, having sauntered another five paces, suddenly screeches, his fur spiking out all over his body, limbs stiffening in the air and his jaw hitting the floor like a roller-blind. Strolling back into the kitchen, Mason suddenly performed a perfect and involuntary imitation of that gag.

Martin.

Martin was his dad.

He rushed back up the hall, and grabbed the note from the mat. He turned it over, scrutinising it, as if there might be something he'd missed. He analysed it minutely, every which way. He slid down the wall to the floor, holding it in both hands, gazing at it.

Dropped by, but you were out. I'll try again another time. Martin.

Dropped by . . . So, what did that mean? Walked up the road? Came in a cab, especially? Happened to be passing? Certainly he must have made some kind of effort to get the address – from Maria presumably. So 'dropped by' meant 'made active attempt to meet you'. Okay.

. . . *but you were out.* Yes, Mason nodded. I was out. Because I have a life. Because I wasn't hanging about indoors waiting for you to call.

I'll try again another time. What – today? When it suits you? In another fifteen years? What?

Martin. Oh, that hurt. *Martin.* Not 'Dad'. Not even 'Your father'. Martin.

Mason sat on the floor in the hall, looking at the note for an hour. He couldn't name what he felt, because he felt everything from icy rage to terrible loneliness. Somewhere around the twenty-minute mark, he even had a fit of giggling.

Dropped by, but you were out. I'll try again another time. Martin.

Mason shook his head and closed his eyes.

'Jesus,' he sighed. 'I mean, *Jesus* . . .'

David Jennings froze the frame of the video, and sat back in the chair. He crunched his teeth hard on the biro that was sticking out of his mouth, and it fractured with a crack. His eyes still fixed on the screen, he picked fragments of plastic off his tongue, and flicked them away with his fingers.

'What is going on here?' he asked himself aloud.

He was in the video room on the third floor of the Yard, watching closed-circuit TV recordings of the previous evening in Docklands. He'd fast-forwarded through three tapes before recognising Dixon on the fourth. He'd been surprised to see him there at all. Despite Zerkah's conviction that they'd got their man, his instincts told him that they hadn't. And yet, there he was, fuzzy but recognisable in the infra-red shot, getting out of a cab with a tall, gaunt friend, and loping towards the Naganitaki Tower.

Jennings let the tape roll, watching the young man leaning against a bollard, lighting a cigarette, obviously watching proceedings intently. The first flashes of the fireworks illuminated Dixon's face, the thud of the explosion following on the soundtrack a second out of sync. And then Jennings saw a woman walk up behind the suspect, tap him on the shoulder, turn towards the camera as another bright flash sharpened every feature of her profile. It was then, startled, that Jennings hit Pause, and edged back a frame or two. The woman was unmistakeably Chris Bell.

Those feelings suppressed and denied in anticipated situations can leap upward and demand attention when summoned by some unforeseen stimulus. Seeing Chris's face, bright-lit, smiling, sudden, Jennings's immediate reaction was tender delight. He couldn't pretend otherwise – he was too honest. His heart zipped out in a flutter like a budgerigar from a cage and, although he netted it immediately and shoved it back onto its perch, he had to admit that even the speed of his reaction was a dead giveaway. He was shocked at himself. And confused as well. It was as if some sober box in the middle of the table had gone off like a party-bomb in his face, all tickertape and trinkets and indoor fireworks.

He closed his eyes, breathless, picking over the debris as the smoke cleared. He fingered pink streamers of affection, feeling the texture of them, like something remembered from childhood. He smelled the bitter cordite of jealousy, hanging there in shifting, ungraspable clouds around the lightbulb. He felt guilt, scattered on his head like artificial snow, powdering his shoulders. Desire hung in strands like crazy-string across his lap, too sticky to be brushed away.

'What is going on here?' he asked himself again.

He thought of Jake, and Jake's mother, and all that that meant. He thought of the long drop of wallpaper in the well of the stairs, and how, when they had decorated the hall, they had constructed a platform over the upstairs banister – rickety as it was, but effective – and he'd lowered the long strip of flowered paper down to Sue, unrolling it fold by fold with gluey fingers as she'd slid it into place, pressing it against the lining paper with her pregnant stomach, and laughing at herself.

'Let's call him William Morris Jennings,' she'd suggested, and he'd nearly toppled off the platform, giggling.

The wallpaper on the stairs was scuffed and grimy now. Jammy-fingered and gouged. It was time to redecorate, or move house.

The door of the video room opened, and Jennings hit eject on the remote control, swift and guilty-looking. Three coppers came in, the first holding a video-tape, and they grinned as they saw Jennings there, reaching for the cassette that popped from the VCR.

'Any good?' one of the coppers asked him. He indicated their tape. 'Just in from the Vice Squad. You'll like this.' He glanced at his colleagues, smirking. 'Got nuns in it, apparently.'

Mason folded the note from his father and slid it behind the clock on the mantelpiece.

He thought of his mum's test of love – 'When something important happens, who do you call?' He could have called her, actually, because she must have known how to get in touch with his dad. But Mason wasn't sure yet that he *wanted* to get in touch with him. He could have called Bart or Chris. He could even have called Elvis. But he didn't. He didn't call anyone. In fact, he went out.

Even that took some doing, but he was determined not to allow himself to sit inside, waiting, jumping every time the phone didn't ring, finding excuses to stand at the window and look along the road.

He went to Camden Lock market and wandered about with his Walkman on, listening to an old soul compilation. He marvelled at the tat that people were prepared to buy from the ramshackle stalls. As a kid, he'd thought the market was a unique, special place, with its Indian wall-hangings and tie-dye T-shirts and love-beads. He imagined that all these nose-ringed punks and fading hippies that sat boredly behind the stalls were the sales-end of some sort of raggle-taggle, ill-advised marketing operation. They had a mate in Goa who bought the stuff up from chummy local artisans and they shipped it out in tea-chests to squats in Kentish Town, where the stall-holders and their long-haired, ten-year-old children – Cobain and Fern – unpacked them with excited glee, cooing over the groovy new line in mock-jade tongue-studs or soapwood joss-stick holders.

Then, when he travelled a bit in his early twenties, he found that Amsterdam had a market just like Camden's. As did Paris. As did Barcelona. As did *Winchester*, for Christ's sake. He was appalled. This was a huge global operation. It wasn't run by little commune-style eco-entrepreneurs who owned the cutely inefficient lines of supply. It was underwritten and organised and driven by some faceless corporation.

If it was a cottage industry, the cottage had a thatched-lead roof and a security-grille on the rose-bowered door.

But people believe the image, he was thinking as he sat on the lip of the Lock eating a falafel. We're all suckers, one way or another.

In the headset, Junior Walker was proclaiming himself to be a road-runner, baby. Mason put his hand in the pocket of his jacket for his cigarettes, and pulled out the envelope that Bart had given him the previous evening. He thought about what he would be leaving behind, were he to get on a plane, just go. The Trickster mystery, of course. Elvis would probably be pissed off, but he'd get over it. His mum and Bart – but they were obviously okay with it, having given him the out. And Chris. He'd be leaving Chris. He'd be out of her sight. He wondered if that would work, whether it would make her realise that . . . and he shook his head, tutting at himself. Even thinking of leaving, he considered it in terms of its effect on her. That wouldn't be leaving; that would be staying. It would be backing off merely in order to throw a longer shadow.

He fingered the envelope, and tapped it on his knee. Belize, he thought. Always fancied Belize.

At which moment, 'Papa Was A Rollin' Stone' kicked in on the Walkman.

Mason groaned resignedly and crammed the envelope back in his pocket. There was that too, of course. All his life, he'd tried to understand why his dad had run away, and now, when it seemed that the old sod was coming back, he was thinking of legging it himself. No. One way or another, he'd have to sort that out, get it straight, before he skipped. He was damned if he was going to be like his dad, and bugger off just because things got complicated. Mason had no idea what he intended to do, or how it would turn out, but he knew had to do something. Something practical.

He stood up and strolled back towards the High Street; past the woman throwing Tarot for wide-eyed Spanish tourists, past the herbal-remedy shop, past the place that flogs mystic Gaelic earrings and past the trestle table crowded with candles that can calm your shattered nerves and cure your migraine. He went to the earth-food van and bought five veggie-burgers, and then he walked up towards the station handing them out to the sorry-looking bastards crouched in their mad overcoats in shop doorways.

And then he went home.

Jennings and Chris had fallen into the habit of holding briefing meetings in the pizza place every four or five days. As he waited for her half-an-hour after seeing her on the CCTV video, Jennings gulped back, like heartburn, his terrible and unexpected personal feelings, and attempted to focus on the professional issue.

He had made an agreement to keep Chris informed about suspects. But if she *knew* the suspect, she might be implicated in the Trickster's campaign – and that, he realised with a start, would be why she had made the bargain in the first place.

He tried to lay out all the possible combinations of possibilities that fitted the facts. Dixon was the Trickster, but Chris didn't know it. He was, and she did. He wasn't, but she'd told him about the Tarot. The crash helmet was irrelevant.

That was the tough one. He couldn't see any plausible explanation for Dixon having the crash helmet that didn't imply some kind of involvement. It was too neat to be coincidence. And if he accepted that involvement, he couldn't keep Chris out of it without swallowing the even more far-fetched coincidence that the *Clarion*'s Trickster correspondent just happened, amazingly, to be a friend of the Trickster.

He rubbed his eyes with his fingertips. If it was Dixon, it was Chris. It had to be.

And as he massaged his closed eyes, watching the black explosions on his eyelids, he found himself wondering how he could prove that it *wasn't* Dixon, and therefore not Chris. He'd have to turn the suspect's life over, find out who his associates were, his beliefs, his obsessions. See if there was anything at all that might suggest he had reason and opportunity to conduct the Trickster campaign.

Jennings swallowed dyspeptically. For the first time in his career, he was hoping that the path through the woods to the truth would take him in a certain direction – through this copse, not that ditch, to this clearing, rather than that brook. He was considering routes, rather than following spoor.

'You all right?'

Jennings dropped his hands and looked up at Chris, who pulled out a chair and sat down opposite him.

'Yes, I'm fine, thanks,' he said. 'Bit of a headache, that's all.'

'I've probably got a paracetamol in my bag,' she suggested, opening it, and rummaging. 'So – anything new on the Trickster?'

Jennings accepted the pill she offered and poured a glass of water.

'Not from me,' he shrugged. 'Have you got anything?'

CHAPTER THIRTY-FOUR

When Mason got in, he found that all the people he hadn't rung had rung him.

BLEEP.

'Greetings, pop-pickers. Elvis at the mike! Have I got an idea, or what? Not 'arf. Call me tonight. Right? Right! All right . . .'

BLEEP.

'A brief call, *mon brave*, concerning your Elvis character. Did I unwittingly offend? He seemed to be viewing me with a critical eye, though for what reason I can't imagine. Was I impolite, in some obscure way? Pass on my apologies if this is the case. Toodle-oo.'

BLEEP.

'Mason, it's Mum. Your friend Elvis – I'm sure I know him from somewhere. A long time ago, but there was something very familiar about him. It's been gnawing at me all night. I think he had hair when I knew him, and I'm certain he wasn't called Elvis. Do you know anything about his background? Give me a call if you can shed any light.'

BLEEP.

'Hi, it's Chris. This might amuse you. A story just came in over the wire from Connecticut. Some guy shoots his father stone dead. The police take him down to the precinct and call up the District Attorney. The District Attorney is appraised of the details, and then goes through to the Assistant DA's office. "Can you take this one, Bob?" says the DA. "I can't do it. I don't think I could prosecute my own son." Discuss. See you soon.'

BLEEP.

'It's Elvis again. It's twenty-past three. If you get home in the next hour or so, could you go round to my place? Tell Ellen to give you the beans and then bring them down to Kennington Police Station. I've tried calling her direct, but she's got the phone off the hook, which probably means she's on her head in a corner going "Om". Thanks. Oh, wait a minute – do you know my address? It's 2 Eldritch Place – basement flat.'

Mason called Elvis's number. It was engaged. He grabbed the *A-to-Z* and sprinted to the tube station. He'd planned to spend the rest of the day trying to work out what to do about his dad, but it sounded as though Elvis was in schtuck, and Mason figured he could just as easily mope and ponder on the train as he could at the flat.

Ellen, he assumed, was the woman who had answered the phone the first time he'd ever called Elvis's place. He supposed she was his wife or girlfriend. He didn't much relish the prospect of telling her, a complete stranger, that her other half had been nicked.

Eldritch Place was a shabby Georgian square between Borough and the Elephant. The basement flat of number two was down some stone steps at the front of the building. The door was peeling purple, and a crystal windchime hung in the dusty front window. There was a very old, fat, black cat asleep in the windowbox. Mason knocked on the door, apprehensively. It was opened, after a short delay, by a tall, slender woman of about his own age.

Mason was dumbstruck. Paper-white skin and waist-length hair, black and thick as despair. She looked like something Dante Gabriel Rossetti might have dreamed up on a particularly spectacular laudanum jag.

Her green eyes scanned him up and down. 'What can I do for you?' she asked, expressionlessly.

Mason had several ideas on this subject, but even if he'd had the guts to trot one out, he'd have been discouraged by her T-shirt, which read *Noli Me Tangere*.

'Uh, I'm looking for Ellen. Elvis sent me,' he ventured.

'You've found her,' said the vision. 'What's he done now?'

'He said to ask you for the beans, whatever that means. I've got to take them to Kennington nick. Oh, I'm Mason, by the way.'

'Hi, Mason. He's been arrested again, huh?'

'I guess . . .'

Ellen sighed. 'All right. Hang on there. I'll be right back.' She turned back into the house, and Mason saw the back of her T-shirt, which read *Noli Etiam In Re Cogitare*.

'Blimey,' he muttered, and walked back up the steps to the street.

After a few minutes, she strode up the stairs two at a time, stuffing a wad of cash into the back pocket of her faded jeans. 'We'd better get a cab,' she said. 'Come on.' She set off purposefully towards the main drag, and Mason started after her, wondering how to broach the question which was uppermost in his one-track mind – to wit, what exactly was her relationship with Elvis?

'So, er, does he get arrested a lot then?' he asked, keeping it general.

'Yeah. All the time,' Ellen replied. 'But he rarely gets charged. They can't figure out what he's done wrong. Hardly surprising he gets dragged in though – I mean, look at him. If I was a policeman, I'd pull him out of sheer curiosity.'

'Yeah,' Mason laughed weakly, in a pathetic attempt to be likeable. 'Yeah, know what you mean.'

Ellen glanced at him sidelong. 'So you're the one who phones up at the crack of dawn,' she observed.

'Oh, yeah. Yeah, sorry. Did I wake you that time?'

'No. I'd been up for hours. I was just bringing him breakfast in bed, the pampered old fart.'

They'd reached Borough High Street, and Ellen was looking up and down the road for a cab. 'This is hopeless,' she tutted. 'We might as well walk it.'

'No, there's one,' Mason pointed out excitedly. 'TAXI!'

The cab swerved across the traffic and stopped beside them. They climbed in, and Ellen gave the destination. It was a journey of only a few minutes, and they passed it in silence. Mason was trying to figure out how an oldish geezer like Elvis managed to pull a heart-stopping woman like Ellen. It was almost disgusting. In his opinion, she really ought to be going out with someone her own age.

As they approached the police station, Mason started rummaging in his pockets for the fare.

'It's okay. I'll get it,' Ellen said, as the cab stopped. 'He's my dad, after all.'

She passed a delicate fistful of change through to the driver, glancing at Mason out of the corner of her eye. 'Put your tonsils away,' she instructed him, with a faint smile.

As they were getting out of the taxi, Elvis Presley himself appeared at the door of the police station. He waved and bounded across. 'Get back in the cab,' he said. 'Hi, Mason. Hello, Ugly. They decided not to charge me.'

'I interrupted a thesis for this,' Ellen remarked.

As the taxi took them back the way they had come, and as Elvis apologised profusely to Ellen for jeopardising her academic career, Mason sat in silence and studied them both.

The eyes should have given him a clue. Those bright green eyes. Though, on Elvis, they made him look mad. On Ellen, they made everyone else look mad.

They filed into the extraordinary front room of the basement flat in Eldritch Place. A fishing net was looped across the width of the ceiling; it was heavy with rubber lizards, their stubby stiff limbs poking through the holes. The walls were lined with shelves, on which were crowded shoals of multi-coloured glass fish. The television, suspended on stout ropes, hovered above an undisciplined yucca, as if about to nest amongst the fanning leaves. The carpet was woven into a picture of Big Bird from Sesame Street.

'Nice room,' Mason said.

'Please don't congratulate him,' Ellen grimaced. 'He's a sick man. Do you want a drink? Vodka's all we've got.'

'Vodka's just what I fancy,' he assured her, ingratiatingly.

'Just as well.'

She looked over at Elvis, who was ringing up half-a-crown on an old-fashioned till. The till tinged two-and-six on little labels the shape of shields in its display window, and the drawer shot open.

'Dad,' Ellen said, 'I'm going to get Mason a drink, and then I'm going to my room to sort out some charts. But if you roll a joint, bring me some through.'

Elvis produced a cellophane envelope full of grass from a compartment of the till drawer. 'Hey, listen – y'got it!' he Yanked. 'Y'wanna fix me a dustbowl martini, no rocks?'

'Nope,' she said, as she went out towards the hall.

'She's a treasure – loves me really.'

'Mason,' Ellen called from the kitchen, followed by something he couldn't make out. He wandered through.

'Sorry?' he asked.

'Do you want orange or tonic?' She was taking a can of baked beans out of a cupboard.

'Er, juice, please.'

Ellen twisted the baked bean tin, and it came apart it the middle. She took the wad of cash out of her back pocket, and put it in the can, which she fitted back together.

'Clever,' Mason nodded.

'He doesn't like banks,' she said, replacing the tin in the cupboard. 'Our larder's worth a fortune.'

Mason took the drinks through to the living room and plonked them on a coffee table – which took the form of a woman in her underwear on all fours – and then he sat on the sofa.

'So what did the police pull you in for?'

'I made a fuss in a cinema,' Elvis shrugged, lighting a joint. 'And the manager, fascist running-dog lackey that he was, called the bobbies.'

'What kind of fuss?'

'Well, I just got a bit overexcited and started demanding that they rewind the film. I was watching *Moonquest I: The Star Pirates*.'

'The Cliff and Dawn thing?'

'Ah, now, no. There you are, you see. It's a *Cliff* thing, but it's not a *Dawn* thing. She's not *in* the first one. That's half the point. In fact, that's *precisely* half the point.'

'What are you on about?' Mason asked, accepting the spliff.

'Listen – how long have Cliff and Dawn been walking out together?'

'I don't know. Couple of years?' Mason suggested, sitting down on an ancient balding couch.

'Yes. But what if I were to tell you that they would not have suited the Joker's purpose until two or three months ago?'

Mason took a long suck on the joint. Elvis was suggesting that Cliff and Dawn were picked because of their work on *Moonquest II: The Legend of Grendor*, rather than because they were a couple. So, what was there about the movie that made them candidates?

And then, simultaneously with the dope, it hit him.

'Oh, Jesus,' he grinned ruefully, exhaling a long jet of smoke. 'We went to the Lambworth Centre for nothing, didn't we? We were chasing the wrong bloody card.'

* * *

In the executive suite of the Naganitaki Tower, the head honcho of YenCo was pacing the floor and venting in Japanese.

'I don't give a *fui-chi*'s toss how much it costs. Post the reward advertisement in all the papers – just make sure that the Corporation stays anonymous. I want this son-of-a-*lo'tai* nailed to the wall—'

'Certainly, Yashimo-san,' nodded Loo Sing, his second-in-command. 'Incidentally, we've reached a dead end with the computer boffin. He admits he was bribed, but all the negotiations were carried out across a modem. He never met the organiser.'

'That two-timing *ho'na*sucker,' Yashimo spat, clambering up on to his chair, and kicking his tiny feet venomously against the desk.

'We have however traced the modem calls back to a bureau in Holborn. We have a description of someone who was hiring time on the days in question.'

'That's more like it! Good work,' grimaced Yashimo. 'I swear I'm going to have this bastard's *mai-fui*s for breakfast.'

'That'll be neat,' Loo Sing remarked. He produced a sheet of paper. 'Look.' He passed the piece of paper across. 'The policeman is outside. Shall we give him this information?'

Yashimo pondered. 'No. We keep it to ourselves. We're only calling the police in to let the British Home Office know I'm pissed off. We'll deal with this Trickster *pah'ti* in our own way. If the copper gets there before we do, we'll have to come to some arrangement with the government.' He put the sheet of paper face down on the desk. 'Wheel him in.'

Loo Sing went to the door and ushered David Jennings into the room. Yashimo surveyed him as he walked across the carpet, hand outstretched. His tie was askew and his trousers were baggy and creased. His shirt was untucked, and one couldn't help noticing the intermittent flash of a hairy white stomach.

'Thank you for giving us your valuable time,' Yashimo said in English, as Jennings introduced himself. And then, in Japanese to Loo Sing, he remarked, 'Look at the state of this clown. Forget that bit about having to come to some arrangement with the government.'

At about the time Yashimo Naganitaki was pacing the floor of the executive suite, Elvis was doing much the same thing in the front room of 2 Eldritch Place.

'What I'm suggesting is that we set up a target that the Trickster can't resist. At the moment, we're running around like something with its head cut off, trying to second-guess our quarry. What we need is bait, so that the quarry comes to us.'

'Sorry. I'm not with you,' Mason admitted. The joint was taking its toll. 'Do you think you could not jump about so much? I'm having trouble with my binocular vision.'

'We can't think of anyone who might be the Star, right? And we're getting pretty good at figuring them. If we can't find a starry candidate, the chances are that the Joker can't either. So we supply one.'

'We supply one?'

'Stella Sky, author of *Cheating Death*. It's a book that tells you that the inevitable aging process, and the inevitable conclusion of that process, is in fact completely evitable.'

'Never heard of her.'

'I just made her up. All we do is prepare a press release, and announce a personal appearance by Stella at a mall or something. We flood the media with the PR pack -- then we turn up for the personal appearance and wait for the Joker to strike.'

'Ubub,' Mason mumbled. The vodka was doing nothing to take away the strong aftertaste of the grass. 'And who do we get to play Stella?'

'Well, I thought we could find you a wig and a nice frock—'

'*Oh* no. No, no, no. Fuck right off. Maybe Chris could do it.'

'Don't be stupid. What if the Trickster's Bart? He'll recognise her.'

'Oh, right. Sorry. Could I have a cup of coffee?'

'But Ellen could do it,' Elvis said. 'She's a natural. Anyway, your task this evening is to go home and throw together a book jacket and a layout for the press release. You're supposed to be a graphic designer, after all. I'll give you a photo of Ellen to incorporate in it.'

'And what makes you think the papers will run with our scam?'

Elvis reached for the joint. 'Wait till you see what I put in the press release.'

CHAPTER THIRTY-FIVE

The following lunchtime, sitting on a bench in Brent Cross Shopping Centre, Mischief scanned the papers again, while waiting for Anna Kanistrova to show up. All the dailies were carrying full-page advertisements to the effect that the reward on the Joker's head had been raised 'by an anonymous party' to half a million quid. Catching the perpetrator had become big business.

The Trickster threw *The Times* and the *Clarion* to one side and groaned. It was all very worrying – but then this was what you got for telling the world's richest dwarf to fuck off. What was worse, the hits were harder and harder to arrange. Nobody who had the slightest connection with mumbo-jumbo was prepared to do live TV any more. Most of them would think twice about making any public appearance at all.

Mischief grinned, got up from the bench and walked into the bookshop where Anna Kanistrova was about to launch her latest work.

In 1976, Anna Kanistrova had been made a Heroine of Socialism, in recognition of the committedly Marxist fashion in which she had squatted in a high-tech milk churn and been fired into space. As her tiny craft hurtled towards the big dead rock in the sky, Anna had concentrated the full force of her collectivist ideals on the task of peeing into a zero-g bottle. And as she'd emerged from behind the moon's impassive pock-marked face, she had brought a tear of pride to the eye of Soviets everywhere by declaring the moon a part of the USSR. She'd had the presence of mind to claim the rest of the solar system for Communism, too.

In truth, despite her propagandist broadcasts, Anna had not been impressed by the moon. It looked a barren and funless place to her. Even as she whizzed through the cosmos in her silver shuttlecock, she had longed for the fresh winds and sparkling surf of home. On her return to Earth, she headed straight for the Aral Sea, where she had been brought up. Due to the time-consuming pressures of becoming a heroine, she had not been back to see her parents and her native countryside for nearly six years. She was shocked by what she found.

As part of the drive towards greater production, the rivers that fed the Aral had been diverted to irrigate the vast cotton fields to the north. What had once been an enormous inland sea, alive with fish and fishermen, was shrinking to a small polluted puddle. The sea was receding like thin hair.

Deeply affected by the desecration of her childhood home, Anna had become a closet environmentalist. She got hold of books and articles from the West, and began a lonely, covert crusade to save the planet from mankind's ungovernable appetites. When she emigrated to Paris in the nineties, Western publishers bust a gut in the race to sign her up. From a publishing point of view, she had everything: she was a recanting heroine of discredited socialism; she was green as an unleaded lettuce; and, to top it all, she didn't have an agent.

Anna had originally been attracted to the idea of the Earth as a goddess – Gaia, the Great Mother. This notion was at first symbolic, but by the time she came to write her book, Anna Kanistrova was convinced of the reality of her vision. The Earth was a caring, self-aware organism, and this benign Mother was being raped by her children. It was Anna's contention that Gaia felt actual *pain* as oil-drills were driven deep into her gut; that she writhed in mute agony as her arteries were blocked by hydroelectric dams; that she was racked and choked as her forest-lungs were butchered and burned.

Anna's book, *Mother Nature's Murdering Sons*, was about to receive serious coverage. The marketing people had really gone to town. From the ceiling of the shop there hung several six-foot polystyrene globes, copies of the book's logo – the planet Earth bleeding from a dagger wound in the Urals. There were posters and cardboard cut-outs of Anna on every wall and in every aisle. Despite the environmentally friendly message of the tome in question, the cardboard images represented a significant drain on the world's wood-pulp resources. It took a lot of cardboard to make an Anna. Perhaps in an act of unconscious homage, Anna Kanistrova had bloated to resemble the planet she was campaigning to save. What with her dress of swirling blues and greens, and her close-cut cap of white hair, it was all one could do not to colonise her.

A knot of journalists were gathering in the current affairs section of the shop, glugging warm Liebfraumilch. Various green activists and idle passers-by were forming a semi-circle around Anna's desk. Their murmuring faded as the manageress of the shop introduced the author. Mischief stepped back from the rail of the gallery that overlooked the shopfloor and turned towards Sociology/Psychology, as Anna stood to address her public.

'I am very happy to be here today, and to see so many new friends,' Anna Kanistrova began. 'It is not necessary for me to say how terrible is the health of Mother Earth . . .'

A polystyrene planet was suspended from a thin plastic wire which fed through a ring in the ceiling, then stretched across the gallery and was tied off to a small hook between Gardening and Black Issues. Mischief untied the wire from the hook, being careful to maintain the tension so that the globe did not move.

'The spirit of Gaia is sick, both for herself, and for the sins of her children. Yes, we are her children, and we are behaving so badly to our mother.'

Mischief wrapped the end of the plastic wire around two fingers, and edged casually along the gallery, keeping it taut.

'And yet, as it is with all good mothers, Gaia cares for us still. However we will abuse her by poisoning her lifebloods and scarring her beautiful face, she weeps for her children and wishes for them only a happy life.'

Every gaze was turned on Anna Kanistrova, whose bright evangelist's eyes were incandescent with passion and worship.

'You see, my friends,' she cried, clutching her fists to her breast, 'if we abuse Mother Gaia, as now we do, we will perish – like a new baby who is deserted in the forest.' She gazed around at her little audience, and spread her arms as if to hug them all to her enfolding bosom. 'So, I beg you,' she begged them, 'be good to Mother Gaia – because she will reward you with a rich life of healthiness and good things; she will cherish and protect you with her deepest love.'

There was a breathless pause, whilst Anna surveyed the audience with a beatific smile.

'Thank you,' she concluded – and the world dropped on her head.

Her cranium broke through the flimsy polystyrene, and the entire lightweight assembly sat unsteadily on her shoulders for a moment, before Anna pitched forward across the table. As she fumblingly clasped her arms around the Earth and made jerky attempts to thrust it away, the scene resembled nothing so much as two grown-up planets endeavouring to make a baby planet.

Mischief slipped unnoticed from the shop as the hacks' cameras recorded the event for tomorrow's rags.

'So much for the cow that jumped over the moon,' thought Mischief, lighting a cigarette and melting into the milling press of lunchtime shoppers.

CHAPTER THIRTY-SIX

Mason looked up from the printed sheet.

'Former blue-movie star Stella, 26, discovered the secret from a randy Tibetan monk?' he quoted, incredulous.

Elvis twitched his eyebrows and grinned. 'Told you it would be good.'

They were in Eldritch Place again. Mason was reading through the press release that was to support the fictitious Stella Sky's immortality manual. It had been two days since Anna Kanistrova's world fell in on her. Elvis and Mason, though irritated at not having foreseen the hit, were immensely relieved that it had been the Moon, rather than the Star, that the Trickster had dealt.

The front door opened and Ellen walked in. For reasons he couldn't quite fathom, Mason leapt to his feet.

'Hello, Mason,' Ellen said, tossing a sports bag into the corner of the room.

'Hi. Hello. Good. How are you? I'm fine,' he blubbered.

'Fine. Is that the press release?'

'Oh, yeah. This is it, yeah. Here.' He handed it to her, and she sat on the arm of the sofa and began reading. He watched her anxiously while Elvis studied his mocked-up bookcover. It showed a woman playing cards with a hooded skeleton. The woman had a pile of money in front of her and looked smug; the skeleton was holding his skull in his bony hands, in an attitude of despair.

'A graveyard?' asked Ellen, raising an eyebrow.

'Yes, it's perfect,' Elvis said, looking up from the artwork. 'We're going to launch the book in a graveyard. It's what the punters want.'

Ellen read a little more. 'Doves?'

'Certainly,' Elvis smiled. 'There has to be some gimmick, in order to give the Trickster something to mess up. I got the idea from Yashimo

Naganitaki's butterflies. Stella will release a flock of symbolic doves from a crate.'

Ellen shook her head, smiling.

'Are you sure you want to do this, Ellen?' Mason asked.

She looked at him, and chuckled. 'You bet. It's going to be a hoot.' She turned to Elvis. 'I talked to Dave and Rob. They'll do the set-up for us. It'll cost you two ounces apiece and a bottle of Jack Daniels.'

'Very reasonable,' Elvis said.

'Hang on,' Mason interrupted. 'Who are Dave and Rob?'

'We need someone to set the props up,' Elvis explained. 'It can't be us, because with any luck the Joker will be watching at a safe distance waiting for a chance to mess things up. If it turned out to be your pal, it'd a bit of a giveaway for us to be seen setting it up, wouldn't it?'

'I thought we'd given up on that idea?' Mason frowned. 'I thought we decided we had no evidence to go on?'

Elvis reached for his skins and started to fix up a joint. 'You haven't been paying attention. We have all the evidence we could want. Now it's just a question of setting the trap.'

Mason wondered why he felt so anti the whole thing. Maybe it was because he thought of the pursuit of the Trickster as his own little project – and now it seemed like it was being taken away from him.

He tried to brighten up. 'Well, I'll get this stuff over to Chris, then, so she can puff it in the paper.'

Elvis shook his head. 'Nope. We'll just send it to the *Clarion* in the same way we send it to everyone else.' He licked along the edge of the Rizla. 'If Stella gets bigged-up by the main inky pursuer, the Trickster might smell a hippo.'

'That's "smell a rat", surely?' Mason said.

Elvis and Ellen grinned. 'The hell with *rats*,' they chanted, in gleeful unison. 'Have you ever smelled a *hippo*?'

Mason smiled weakly. Having made himself the sucker in what was obviously a family joke, he felt more excluded than ever.

Zerkah Sheikh had been tailing Mason for the best part of a week, and she was beginning to find it dull. In fact, the only person she knew who had a life duller than hers was Mason himself.

She'd got to know his routine. Although she turned up in the car outside his flat at eight sharp, he never emerged into the front room much before eleven. He'd watch the TV, drinking tea and eating toast. He'd chat to the cat. He'd pop out to the corner shop around lunchtime for cigarettes and a few provisions. He'd watch more TV and then disappear mid-afternoon, reappearing twenty minutes later with damp hair and scraps of toilet paper stuck to his face, turning red. He'd let the cat in at teatime, and chat to her again, sitting on the sofa. Sometimes he'd go over to his friend's house in Borough, and Zerkah would have to follow him on the tube, and kill time on a bench in the square, reading her book until he came out and took the Northern Line back to Camden. Most evenings, he lay on the sofa and smoked, not even looking at the TV, but gazing into space. He seemed to be thinking. He did an awful lot of thinking.

In the late afternoon of the fifth day, Zerkah called David Jennings.

'Am I wasting my time here, sir?' she asked. 'I mean, perhaps I was wrong.'

'No!' Jennings said, quickly. 'Not a bit. Stick with it. What's he up to?'

Zerkah glanced over at the window of the front room. 'Nothing,' she said wearily. 'He bought some drawing paper two days ago. That was exciting.'

There was a silence on the line, then Jennings said, 'I've just had DCI Jagger down here. We're high profile, all of a sudden. Naganitaki has been talking to the high-ups, and Jagger's under pressure. Reading between the lines, we're only still on the case because he can't think of anyone he'd rather see fail.'

Zerkah winced.

'Listen,' Jennings said, 'has he done anything – *anything* – to make you think he might still be our man?'

'No, sir,' Zerkah admitted, defeatedly.

She heard Jennings exhale, and the tap-tap-tap of a biro against his teeth. She could picture him gazing at the photo of Jake as he pondered.

'All right; get back here. There's a publicity item in the papers that we ought to follow up. We're off to Putney.'

As Zerkah was driving away down the street, and Mason was getting ready to meet Elvis for the Stella Sky hit, the phone in the front room rang.

'Hello, dearheart, it's Bart. Or if you prefer, hello, son, it's your common-law stepfather.'

'Hi, Bart. How's you?'

'In the pink and far from blue, old pal o'mine. This is true of you also, I hope?'

'I'm okay, yeah. How's me mum? Is it all going all right?'

'That's what I rang about. Maria and I are engaged in a small dispute. And this dispute, I'm afraid to say, centres upon your mother's one-and-only.'

'You?'

'No, *you*, you nincompoop. Maria insists that you'd rather be best man, while it's my contention that you'd prefer to give the bride away.'

'Ah.'

'So we find ourselves in a cleft stick. And only you can help us out.'

'Umm, congratulations. It's good to know that your intentions towards my mother are honourable.'

'That is a slur, and I vigorously deny it. Listen – do give the problem some thought. We want to join ourselves in holy thingie as soon as clerically possible.'

'Jesus, you haven't got her up the duff, have you?'

'Umm . . .'

'Christ, you *have*!'

'It was semi-intentional. And anyway, we're not sure yet. But the possibility brought the decision into sharp focus. We'd like to get married before we know for sure. Just so the little so-and-so doesn't feel responsible. You're speechless, I can tell. Speak to me, Uncle Mason, speak to me.'

'It won't be Uncle Mason. It'll be Brother Mason. What's she want to get married for, all of a sudden? She never thought it necessary when she was having me.'

'Now don't be bitter, Brother Mason.'

'You've only been going out together a few weeks.'

'Actually, old love, it's been a few months. We may have misled you on that score. But we've known each other for years. Nearly as long as you and I. Listen, Mason – give her a call. She's terrified that you're going to be angry with her.'

'Is it okay for her to be having babies at her age?'

'Take my word, Mase, that if she is indeed in that happy state, I'll make sure that everything is eff'n'dee. That's *fine'n'dandy*. Call her straight away and call me tomorrow.'

'Yeah. Bye.'

'Toodle-pip. Stay calm. So long.'

'Hi, Mum. It's me.'

'Hello, dear.'

'Well then . . .'

'You spoke to Bart?'

'Yeah. I'm, er, amazed.'

'Yes, of course. But we don't know for sure yet. We really do want to get married anyway. It's not just because there might be a baby. What do you think, Mason?'

'I don't know.'

'Well, just say the first thing that comes into your head.'

'Oh, come on. Don't treat me like a first-time caller on some poxy phone-in.'

'I'm sorry.'

'Actually, if you want to know, I'm fucking pissed-off that I heard it from Bart. You should have called me. I mean, don't you trust me or something?'

'God, you sound like your father sometimes.'

'How would *I* know? I guess I'm just a triumph of nature over nurture. Do you deep-down think you're pregnant?'

'Yes, I think so.'

'And you're happy about it? And you're happy about getting married?'

'Very.'

'Okay, if you're happy, that's all that matters. Jesus, this is weird. I sound like your dad rather than your kid. I'm all worried and pleased for you at the same time. Is this what it's like to be a parent? How the fuck have you managed this for the last twenty-seven years?'

'It's been a joy, darling. I've loved every minute.'

'Yeah, well . . . Listen, I'm a bit confused and that, but, y'know, congratulations.'

'Thank you. You'll always be my boy, you know.'

'Yeah. I'm afraid you're stuck with that.'

'Jesus Christ,' Mason said to Freda, as he dialled Elvis's number, 'I'm turning into a Walton – I really am.'

'Elvis, call it off.'

'Come again?'

'Call it off. I don't want to do it.'

'Don't be daft, Mason. In four hours' time, we'll have trapped the Trickster.'

'I don't *want* to trap him. Look, even *you* think it's Bart. But things have changed. I can't tell you what, but I don't want to do it any more. It would fuck too many people over. Let's just let him get away with it. Please.'

'Mason, why do you think—'

'Don't ask me why. I can't tell you why. Come on, you're supposed to be Mr Big-Vibey-Sensitive. Just listen to me. I want it left be.'

'Change of subject. You seen your dad yet?'

'No. The old git still hasn't— Did I tell you about my dad?'

'No. He did.'

Mason dropped the phone.

CHAPTER THIRTY-SEVEN

When Mason called back, Elvis spilled the whole thing.

'Early nineteen seventies, St Martin's School of Art,' he explained. 'I was editing some satirical paper with a circulation of about three, and your dad contributed drawings. We did the whole hippy bit together. Went to India, saw Hendrix at the Isle of Wight, booked Genesis for the Student Union before they were big. Y'know . . .'

Mason listened, shaking his head, sucking hard at a cigarette, as the story unravelled.

After college, Elvis said, Marty Puxley started to make a name as a cartoonist, became a bit famous, but they remained mates. They even shared a flat in Cricklewood and, as Mason had to admit, you can't get much matier than that. But the two of them fell out, in the end.

'Why?' Mason asked. 'What happened?'

Elvis paused. 'Actually – what happened was you.'

The way he told it, Elvis's role in Marty Puxley's life was that of the friend who is kept apart from the general run of things. He was the curtained-off chum with whom Mason's father spent his lost weekends. The one who got the brimmed-over monologues of dissatisfaction, who shared the late-night laddish hilarity, who provided the sofas on which Marty fucked loose women without Maria knowing.

'I met your mum a couple of times, but only in passing,' Elvis said. 'I met you too, quite often, when you were little. After your mum and dad split up, and Marty had you in Camden on weekends, I used to meet you and him for lunch at greasy spoons on Haverstock Hill.'

Mason sniffed and shifted the phone to the other ear. 'Go on.'

The crunch came, Elvis said, when Marty moved, as if by capillary action, to the States. Elvis told him he was abnegating his responsibilities by leaving his kid. 'Life,' he told Mason's dad, 'gives you things to deal with. You more than most, Mart. You're talented and funny, and that'll open up all sorts of possibilities. Still – life has also given you the boy. And you have to deal with those possibilities as well.'

'Your old man and I had a big bust-up about it, to be honest,' Elvis said.

'But Dad fucked off anyway,' Mason muttered.

'Yeah. And we just drifted apart.' Elvis took a deep breath. He continued a little sheepishly. 'So, early this year, your dad's back in England, and he's thinking about getting in touch with you. He contacted me and asked me to find you – just to see what you were like, to figure whether you were the sort of person he'd want to meet. He picked up from your mum that you were going to be at Raphael's, and he passed it on to me. I trailed you to Soho and . . . er . . . introduced myself.'

Mason closed his eyes and furrowed his brow. 'So it was a set-up,' he murmured. 'The whole fucking thing was a set-up.'

'Yeah,' Elvis admitted. 'Yeah. It was. I'm sorry.'

'Why are you telling me this now, Elvis?' Mason asked, tightly.

'Mase, don't push me. I've just done something I thought I would never do. I've broken a promise to a friend.'

Sitting on the floor in the living room, Mason looked at himself in the mirror, phone pressed to his ear. A cigarette was hanging from the fingers of one hand, and on a plate in front of him there was a chicken-roll sandwich that he'd been about to eat when the first phone call came. He was wearing combat trousers and a black T-shirt, ready to go and pull off the Stella Sky scam. He looked ridiculous, he realised. Ridiculous and lost.

'No – why now?' he insisted. He took a long, deep drag on the Marlboro Light, and watched himself blow out the smoke through his nose, like a grown-up.

Elvis sighed. 'I think . . .'

There was a long silence, and Mason waited it out, thinking about his father; a father who would get a friend to check out whether his son was someone he'd like to meet; a father who'd consider all those angles, make all those arrangements. Fuck – what was he afraid of?

'What about the note through the door?' Mason demanded, suddenly. 'So, did I pass? Was the feedback acceptable?'

'I think . . .' Elvis said again.

'What did you tell him about me?'

'Mason . . .'

'Elvis – what the fuck did you say about me?'

'I told him you were a nice kid. And I also told him . . .'

Mason stubbed out the cigarette and immediately lodged another in the corner of his mouth. In the mirror, he was flushed, all head-scratching and fidgety. He shook the matchbox, and it was empty. He flicked it with his middle finger towards the wastepaper bin and it dropped in, with a soft clatter.

'What? What did you tell him?' he said, leaning sideways to grab a lighter from the bookshelf, and firing it up.

'I told him that I like you a lot more than I like him.'

CHAPTER THIRTY-EIGHT

Mason didn't feel he could refuse to go through with the Stella Sky thing after that. He owed Elvis something for his honesty and his declaration of affection. But he did extract a promise that if it *was* Bart, they'd simply shake him by the hand and go out for a curry – and that'd be an end to it.

So, a couple of hours later, they were crouched behind a wall on the park-side of the church, peering across the spooky Putney cemetery at the bait. Under a pair of arc lights borrowed from Ellen's college theatre, there was a table with a candlestick, and a crate rigged up with a spring lid, in which there were a dozen doves. A backdrop had been hung up, bearing a line drawing of Ellen's face. Mason had taken inordinate care sketching it out and inking it in over the preceding couple of days, and he was rather proud of it. As planned, Dave and Rob had set all the gear up and left for the pub. The table, the crate and the backdrop were unprotected.

Elvis adjusted his balaclava, and took a stick of chewing gum out of the pocket of his camouflage jacket. Mason slid down to a crouch, his back to the wall, and lit a fag. It was past dusk, and the graveyard was giving him the willies.

'Do I look like my dad, do you think?' he asked.

Elvis turned and studied him, his head tipped to one side. 'You've got his eyes. And there's something of him about the mouth. But you lack his sneer.'

'Sneers a lot, does he?'

'It's built in.'

Mason tried sneering. He curled his lip and tried to look cynical. 'How's that?'

Elvis grinned. 'Sneer, like groove, is in the heart,' he said.

Mason shrugged, and studied the end of his cigarette. He blew on it, framing the next question. It was a question to which he wasn't sure he wanted to know the answer, and he was trying to find a way of saying it that would prompt a response he didn't mind hearing. He picked at a bit of moss on a stone beside him, and took a long drag.

'So,' he muttered, and decided to go way over the top, in the hope of being pulled back with a platitude, 'why did he despise me so much?'

Elvis was looking out across the cemetery, and he seemed not to have heard. He just kept chewing his gum, eyes fixed on the set-up. He didn't acknowledge the question at all. Mason let it hang there for a good minute, still picking at his bit of moss, and he was rather relieved to be ignored. He'd asked, and that was enough. He was about to move the whole thing on by changing the subject, when Elvis spoke.

'When you were about a year old,' he said, still staring into the middle distance, 'Marty came round to mine one night, and we got ourselves outside a bottle of Glenfiddich.' He turned and slid down the wall beside Mason who stubbed out his cigarette on the mossy stone, and looked up-river, as if he were barely paying attention.

'We talked about magazines and music, women and families. My girlfriend was expecting Ellen, at the time, and the conversation turned to kids. Me, I was very on for the fatherhood thing. Couldn't wait.' Elvis hitched up one shoulder to delve his hand into his pocket, and pulled out a little package, which he unwrapped. He nudged Mason. 'Tuna mayonnaise on granary?'

Mason shook his head, and lipped a fag.

Elvis took a bite of his sandwich, and carried on talking. 'Marty told me I was wasting my time. "Thing with babies, mate," he said, "is they don't need dads at all. Once you've supplied the spunk, your part of the process is over." I can see him now, swigging more scotch, as I slouched on the sofa, listening. He was off on one, and he was always entertaining when he got up a good speed. "Like, I've tried to get involved," he said. "I'm forever changing nappies and spooning slop into the kid's mouth. But, fuck, anyone could do that. She could *employ* someone to do that, just to give herself a break. Doesn't have to be me. Maria's got everything that Mason needs. And she's good at it, too. I'm just some sort of . . . home-help . . ."'

Mason bit his lips. He was looking far up river now, so that Elvis couldn't see his eyes.

'Thing with your dad,' Elvis went on, 'is that he needs to feel that he's important, that he's having an effect. When he went to the States, the real attraction was the circulation of the magazines he could work for out there. He used to say, "A million fucking readers, baby! A *million*! That's a lot of people laughing, you know?" That notion that he's making a difference is very important to your dad.' He took another bite of his sandwich.

There were many things Mason might have said then. The rush of questions clogged his throat. He could have asked why his dad felt that making a difference to his kid was so much less a thing than entertaining a million anonymous Yanks. Or why he couldn't find any joy in simply being a father – as if that ordinary delight was too mundane. Or, actually, why his mother had fallen in love with such a self-regarding wanker. But what he said, swallowing hard, was, 'Yeah. I understand that.'

Elvis put his arm around Mason's shoulders, for which Mason was very grateful just then, and said, 'Look, mate, if I could give you an out here, I would. I wish I had one. But I don't. You're a nice, likeable, together bloke, and you *will* sort this. Just keep breathing – that's my advice.'

There was a moment's hiatus, and then Elvis withdrew his arm, and produced the sandwiches again. 'So! Eat already!' he Jewish-mothered. 'What – you're gonna starve worrying? Eat something yet!'

Mason grinned and took a tuna on granary. He wolfed it, deciding heartburn was preferable to heartbreak.

I mean, fuck him, really, he thought. *Fuck him.*

Elvis turned and peered over the wall again, as Mason flicked crumbs from the corner of his mouth, and then looped the cellophane off a fresh pack of cigs.

'Mason,' Elvis said, surveying the graveyard, 'you know this reward of half-a-million that's been offered on the Joker – who do you think offered it?'

'Well, it was pretty obviously Yashimo Naganitaki, wasn't it? Who else has got that kind of money?'

'Hmm. Look over towards the bridge. There are two men there, and they've been standing around watching our little tableau for nearly twenty minutes. They are, you may notice, of an Oriental persuasion.'

Mason scrambled up and peered in the direction that Elvis nodded. 'Jesus – do you think they're Yashimo's people?'

'Could well be. The interesting question, of course, is how did they know to be here?' He checked his watch. 'Couple of hours. Let's hope we pull a crowd.'

Half an hour passed. The darkness settled deeper, like bad snow, and bats were whishing overhead amongst the trees. Mason had cramp in his left leg, and turned to sit down behind the wall again.

'Hey,' he said, glancing up at Elvis's boot-blackened face. 'We're figuring that the Joker's going to mess with the crate of doves, yeah?'

'Uhuh,' Elvis agreed, not taking his eyes from the bait.

'Well, when he opens the crate, surely all the doves will fly away?'

'Not a chance. I borrowed them from a friend who needs them back tomorrow, so I sprinkled their seed with marijuana. They're not going anywhere.'

'Well, that's not going to be very impressive when Ellen opens the box, is it?' Mason scoffed, massaging his calf. 'A dozen whacked-out doves lying flat on their backs and going "Coo. Wow. Amazing."'

Elvis was still staring fixedly out at the graveyard. 'It won't get that far,' he said. 'A highly suspicious character has just climbed over the far wall carrying a very large bag.'

Mason pulled himself up to the level of the wall. 'Where?'

'Shush . . .'

A young man in a leather jacket wove light-footedly between the headstones towards the bait. He was glancing from side to side, and hunching himself up. He scurried over to the crate and gingerly lifted the lid a crack. He peered inside, grinned at what he saw – twelve doves a-dozing – and pushed the lid all the way back. He reached into his sack two-handedly and pulled out a box that was seven or eight inches shorter than the crate. He carefully lowered it in. Then he took from the sack what appeared to be a white melon, from which dangled some kind of flexible tube. He reached into the crate, and seemed to attach the contraption to the box. With one hand holding the melon, he lowered the lid of the crate again, only withdrawing his arm when the lid was so low that he would have been trapped by it. He picked up the sack, and turned to go.

'Scramble,' Elvis said, vaulting over the wall.

The man, running stealthily away, might well have heard his pursuers sprinting across the churchyard towards him – but in the event, it didn't matter. As he reached the perimeter wall, he was intercepted by the two Orientals, who popped up and grabbed his arms.

'Oy, fuck off!' he exclaimed, attempting to yank himself free.

'You will come with us, thank you,' said one of the Japanese, firmly.

'No I fuckin' well won't,' the man replied, still struggling. 'You're breakin' my fuckin' arm!'

Elvis and Mason clattered to a halt beside the grappling trio, who stopped tussling and looked up into Elvis's bright green eyes framed by the scruffy balaclava. Not for the first time, Mason was surprised by his bald friend, who smiled and then said something in Japanese that sounded very nasty indeed. It certainly got through to the Naganitaki people. They glanced at each other uncertainly, and gulped. There was a muttered exchange in their native tongue, and then they released the young man's arms. They took a few steps backwards, turned, and scurried away across the bridge.

'Thanks, mate,' the young man nodded, shrugging his leather jacket up onto his shoulders. 'They was well out of fuckin' order.'

Mason studied the lad for a moment or two. 'This isn't the Joker,' he said.

'Certainly isn't,' Elvis agreed. 'What did you do to our crate, Sonny Jim?'

The young man glanced from Elvis to Mason and back again, realising that he wasn't yet in the clear. 'Nuffin,' he said, without much conviction.

'More important, who got you to do it?' Mason asked.

The young man flipped a cigarette, and fumbled for a light. Elvis produced a lighter, and snapped it for him. The young man looked at Elvis across the flame, his face spooky-lit and undefined. Behind him, on the bridge, the traffic roared past, and a couple arm-in-arm glanced their way, apprehensive, as if they were plotting something. Mason was holding his breath.

'Makes no odds if I tell yer,' shrugged the bloke, inhaling. 'Some geezer give me 'undred nicker to put that fing in the box. Easy dosh.'

'Sah, wossis bloke like, en?' Elvis said, in perfect Sarf-London, as he pocketed the lighter.

'Just a bloke. I dunno. Bit posh talkin'. 'Snot against the law, so fuck off.'

Elvis beamed at the young man maniacally. 'Fuck off yourself,' he advised him.

The lad gazed at Elvis, weighing up the odds, and decided to take the advice. He turned on his heel and strode away.

As they ambled back towards the bait, Mason said, 'What about Yashimo's guys, though, eh? This is getting serious.'

'I'm more worried about what they said to each other,' Elvis pondered, tutting. 'They decided not to fight us for the leather boy because, quote, *this is not the one in the picture*. Apparently they know who they're looking for.'

He leaned forward to the crate.

'Let's see what the Trickster planned for Stella, shall we?' He flipped the lid.

'Jesus!' Mason exclaimed, and they both jumped backwards in surprise as out popped a horribly lifelike plastic skull. It bobbed drunkenly from side to side on its spring, grinning and nodding at them.

'Nice,' chuckled Elvis, reaching out to catch it. 'Very cute. A Death-in-the-Box.'

Ellen insisted on going through with the Stella Sky show.

'I haven't got myself all tarted up like this just to be sent home,' she said. 'And, anyway, what about my public?'

As Elvis had promised, his daughter turned out to be a natural. She had certainly inherited her father's gift for parody. In her long white robe and her high-cheeked make-up, her black hair gelled into an explosive shock, Stella Sky was every inch the fanatical weirdo. Elvis and Mason stood amongst the onlookers as she explained in a faraway, breathy voice about 'prolonged physicality' and 'natural life juices', conveying the impression that achieving dominion over Death involved an awful lot of spine-softening sex. Stella came over as a lubricious cross between Marilyn Monroe and Morticia Addams. There wasn't a man in the audience who wouldn't have traded life-everlasting for fifteen minutes in a coffin with her.

When the moment came to open the crate, Stella grasped the lid, and with the words 'Fly free, you souls, and escape this place of bones and decay!' she flung it back. The Death's head boinged out. Stella screamed a fey little scream and fainted clean away. As she lay across a gravestone and moaned, the slavering photographers hunched over her, their zooms extended to the limit.

'Well,' said David Jennings to Zerkah Sheikh, as they watched from the edge of the graveyard, 'Mr Dixon would appear not to be the hunted, but the hunter.'

Zerkah nodded glumly. 'Which explains the connection with Chris Bell. He must be working for her.'

Jennings wished now that he'd called Chris and asked her along. He'd have liked to have seen her face when he told her they knew about Dixon, and this trap they'd set.

'Shall we talk to him, sir?' Zerkah asked.

'No,' Jennings said, as they turned and headed towards the car. 'But I think I'll have a little chat with Ms Bell tomorrow.'

While Dave and Rob packed up the gear, and the last of the crowd drifted away, Mason congratulated Ellen on her performance. Then he went over to Elvis, who was leaning on a stone angel and looking out across the river.

'I'm heading home,' he said. 'Nice try, tonight, eh?'

'Yeah. We're getting close.' He looked at Mason sidelong. 'You still in, then?'

Mason shrugged. 'Yeah. Can't give up now, can I?'

Elvis looked at him and chuckled. 'No, you really shouldn't. Believe me. Did you get my clue?'

'Your what?'

'I sent you a postcard with a clue on it. All the best mysteries have clues. Watch your letterbox.'

'You really think you know who it is, don't you?' Mason asked, grinning. He wasn't going to push it. He'd got used to his friend's little teases, and had started to enjoy them.

'I'm absolutely certain I know who it is,' Elvis said, and then he pinched Mason's cheek between finger and thumb, and wobbled it, smiling. 'And so do you, if you think about it, you dimwit.'

Mason pushed the hand away, mock-scowling, said goodbye, and then he wandered up towards the street, to head for the tube station.

'Hiya,' came a voice, as he clambered over the church wall. It was

Chris, standing on the bridge with her arms crossed. She was wearing a long black coat and a frown. Mason was taken aback.

'Oh, hi. What are you doing here? You guessed this one too, huh?' he asked, a little guiltily.

'Well, *you* certainly didn't tell me about it,' she grudgingly pointed out. 'You want a lift home?'

He looked at her askance. 'It's bloody miles out of your way.'

'Doesn't matter. Come on.'

They walked thirty or forty yards north into Fulham, where Chris's car was parked. Pulling on his seatbelt, Mason looked across at her. 'You seem a bit subdued. You okay?'

'No, I'm bloody not. You set that one up, didn't you, you bastard? And you didn't tell me about it.'

Mason winced, embarrassed. He was uncomfortable that he'd allowed her to be dropped from the scam. It seemed a kind of infidelity, somehow.

'Uh ... yeah. Sorry. Elvis wanted the whole thing done straight. Er ...'

'Evidently. I thought I was *in* on this now. I thought I was *included.*' She pulled the car out into the street, and gunned it toward Hammersmith.

'Yeah,' he sighed. 'I'm sorry.' He had never been very good at dealing with her anger, though he loved the way she could rage and sulk so openly. He was constantly impressed by her ability to present her passions, as if to say, *You caused it. What are you going to do about it?*

'But, really,' he ventured, after a tense silence, 'if it had come to anything, I'd've called you up right away. You'd still have got the story—'

'Get in lane, you tosser!' she yelled. They were pulling on to the Hammersmith roundabout. 'Jesus. It's got bugger all to do with the story, Mason. It's to do with you breaking a promise.'

He looked glumly out of the window. He *had* promised, he supposed.

'Still,' Chris continued, 'I guess that's just a measure of how much we've grown apart. Promises don't count for so much between Just Good Friends.'

Mason turned to her. '*Chris,*' he pleaded.

She fell into a concentrated silence, her eyes fixed on the road. Mason sighed and leant his head back on the seat, watching the streets whisk by. They reached Camden without another word, although he spent the entire journey trying to find the next sentence. As they pulled up outside his flat, he said, 'I'm really sorry if I acted badly. The idea wasn't to exclude you or anything.'

Her expression had softened. She turned towards him. 'No,' she said, with a damaged little smile. 'I know. That's not what I'm angry about, really.'

'Well,' Mason said, relieved. 'As long as you understand.'

She reached for a pack of cigarettes on the dashboard. It was empty, and she tossed it over her shoulder onto the back seat, and stared at the steering wheel. 'It's just . . . I don't know what I'm doing, half the time, Mase. I mean, I feel like I'm losing you – like you're drifting away from me. You've got this whole different life I'm not involved in and . . . To be honest, I don't like to think of you being happy without me.' She banged the steering wheel hard with the ball of her hand. 'So why the fuck don't I *do* something about it?' she demanded angrily.

There were tears in her eyes. Mason attempted to lean over and hug her, but the inertia seatbelt jerked him to a halt halfway across.

'Oof! Er, hang on a sec,' he said, fumbling with the release. '. . . There.' He put his arm around her and pulled her into his shoulder. She squeezed him rather more tightly than was comfortable, and dug her hands into the skin of his back. He suspected she was crying now, but he couldn't think of anything he could usefully do about it.

'It's all so complicated,' she gulped, muffled against his denim jacket. 'I can't tell what to do any more.'

'Oh, sweetheart,' he soothed, 'it'll all turn out all right, you'll see.'

'And you can take that fucking patronising tone out of your voice too,' she added, sniffing.

'Sorry,' Mason said. 'I momentarily forgot how difficult you are to be nice to.'

CHAPTER THIRTY-NINE

'So, you're not going to work then?' Mason asked.

He was making scrambled eggs, and Chris was sitting cross-legged on a kitchen chair dressed only in one of his shirts. He liked that. It made him feel like a nineteen-sixties movie. In all those Michael Caine films, the women always wandered around in the morning wearing one of the hero's shirts.

'No. The hell with it,' Chris said, screwing up one eye against the plume of smoke that curled around her cheek. 'I deserve a day off.'

'Won't your editor be pissed off?'

'Undoubtedly. But the hell with him, too. I'll ring and tell them I'm working on something. They can like it or lump it.'

Mason shared the eggs on to two plates, sprang the toast from the toaster and put the lot on the kitchen table.

'What were you planning on doing today?' Chris asked, forking food into her mouth.

'Oh, I dunno. Wash some clothes. Put my videos back in their boxes. It's a packed and busy life, I can tell you.'

'Did you put salt in these eggs?'

'Can't remember.'

'They scramble better if you use a copper bowl, did you know that? It's something to do with oxidisation.'

'Amazing. Remind me to buy shares in copper before this news hits the markets.'

It's just like real life, this, Mason thought, as they ate. *Chatting over breakfast. Using both slots in the toaster. Making tea in a pot. If I'm not careful, I might get very, very happy.*

'Oh, I'd better call Elvis,' he said, laying down his knife and fork. 'See if we can work out what to do next.'

He scraped the rest of his scrambled egg into Freda's bowl, and dumped the plate in the sink.

'Call him from Brighton,' Chris suggested.

Mason stopped and looked at her. 'What?'

She blew out a long jet of smoke. It travelled the length of her bare legs as she stretched them on to a spare chair. 'Well, I've got nothing in particular to do today. You don't do anything in particular *any* day. The weather's nice. So – let's go to Brighton.'

Sitting back down at the table, Mason frowned and then shrugged. 'Well, I s'pose we could.'

'Yeah. Good,' Chris said. 'I'll go and get dressed.' She stood up and kissed him on the forehead. 'Don't look so dubious. We'll get the train down there. It'll be fun. It'll be like old times.'

'Oh, God. Is that a good idea?'

Chris was right on both counts. Brighton was fun, and it was just like old times. There were waves of laughter and an undertow of tension. Mason was nervous of being pulled in again. As soon as he felt a wash of tenderness breaking over him, he'd hold his breath and wait for his sense of perspective to buoy him to the surface. Every instant was tangy with emotion and import. They went to the pier and played video games. They had lunch in a rather nice French restaurant. They walked along the front – not actually hand-in-hand, but certainly giving the impression to passers-by that hand-holding was an imminent possibility.

In the afternoon, Chris said she fancied going shopping in the Lanes, and Mason, to his own surprise, summoned the self-control and confidence to say that he'd leave her to it, if that was okay with her. And it *was* okay with her. It was an adult and reasonable agreement. As he wandered down towards the funfair at Black Rock, Mason congratulated himself on not having meekly agreed to the shopping, and then trailed around after her trying not to look bored.

He bought an ice cream and looked out at the sea as he strolled. The sun was high and the sky was the unsubtle shade of blue that five-year-olds paint it. The tatty old funfair was just as it had been when he'd first gone there ten years before with a bunch of mates celebrating the end of their exams. In fact, they were still playing 'Wake Me Up Before You Go-Go' over the tannoy by the dodgems.

It was about three o'clock, and the place was overrun with little kids. The hormone-driven teenagers and whelk-scoffing tourists wouldn't be there till dusk. Mason watched the Whiplash ride finish, and then climbed into an empty car, first checking the seat for loose change. As the shouter entreated passers-by to roll up for the next ride, he gazed along the beach to the pier.

Much as he was enjoying himself, he couldn't quite work out what was happening.

If he'd spent a morning like that with any other woman, he would have had to conclude that he was at the start of an important relationship. He'd have been flirting like a peacock on a day-pass. He'd have been anticipating a night of relaxed conversation and consolidating sex. But with Chris . . .

'To be honest,' he said out loud, without thinking, 'I haven't the first fucking idea *what* I'm doing.'

'Pardon?' asked the grubby young man who had just arrived to collect the money.

'Uh, sorry. Nothing,' Mason flustered, looking up and taking out his wallet.

'You want my advice, mate, tell 'er you love 'er,' the grease-smeared bloke said. 'Fifty pee.'

'What?' Mason asked, handing over a five-pound note. 'What are you – psychic?'

The bloke rummaged in his money-pouch for change. 'Fella on his own goin' to the fair in the arternoon – bound to be finkin about a bird. *Bound* to be. You 'aven't got anything smaller than a fiver, 'ave yer?'

'Er . . . maybe. Hang on,' Mason said, lifting his bum to reach into the pocket of his jeans. 'It's that obvious, is it?'

'Obvious? It's a cinematic soddin' cliché, innit? I mean, it's nonna my business – but go for it, is my advice. Tell the woman you love 'er. 'Ere, look – y've got three twenties there.'

'Yeah, well,' Mason said, handing over the coins and taking back the fiver. 'It's not as easy as that.'

'Never is, sunshine, when yer inside it. But that's what it'll come down to in the end. Ten pee change.'

'Thanks. And, umm, thanks for the advice.'

'No need t'fank me. I've got this compulsion t'play a patriarchal role in order t'validate me own beyayvyer. Enjoy the ride.'

CHAPTER FORTY

Vince Pegg, editor of the *Daily Voice* ('Britain's Choice'), was having a shitty day.

At nine o'clock he'd been summoned to the sanctum of the paper's proprietor where it had been suggested to him that in a circulation war, just like in a real war, you got no prizes for coming second. And second, the proprietor pointed out, was where the *Voice* was currently coming.

'You're a good editor, Vince,' the boss had said. 'But then, Rommel was a good general, and look what happened to him.'

Vince had no idea what had happened to Rommel, and said so.

'He committed suicide, Vince,' the boss told him. 'Having fucked up the Desert Campaign, he topped himself. Bear it in mind.'

'Thanks,' Vince said, and went back to his office.

A little before ten, just after setting fire to his wastepaper basket with a badly-snuffed match, he got a call from his mole at the *Clarion*. There were whispers that Ray Churchill, Vince's opposite number on Britain's leading tabloid, had made a some kind of deal with the YenCo Corporation, who had supplied an identikit of the Trickster. The *Clarion* planned to run with it tomorrow. Vince groaned. He popped a bicarb, lit another cigarette and slid down into his generous leather chair. He didn't like all this stuff about Rommel committing suicide, but he had to admit the effectiveness of the analogy. What he needed were some big guns to hit the *Clarion* where it hurt.

Oh, please God, give me artillery, he prayed.

There was a knock on the door.

'Come,' Vince belched.

The door opened and in walked Clive Hare, staff photographer; a round young man with no nose to speak of and a roll-up. He looked like a degenerate eight-year-old.

'Morning, Clive. For you I can do what?'

'Hi. Got something for you. Might be fun,' said Clive in his charac-teristic staccato style.

'Fun. That'd be a fucking first today, son. What is it?'

Clive sat in the guest chair, and took a couple of ten-by-eights out of a folder under his arm. 'I was going through these. Stella Sky's thing. Last night.' He handed Vince a shot taken in the Putney graveyard. 'And I remembered this. From the Naganitaki Tower. A previous Joker thing, right?' He pushed another print across the desk. 'Look,' he said leaning across and pointing at the Naganitaki shot. 'See this figure here? Now. Look at this one from the Stella Sky picture. See? Same person.'

Vince peered from shot to shot. The kid was right. It was the same person.

'I've been back through the other Joker shots. Right back to Chuckie Rolls. Not just mine. Mike's and Alex's too. But I can't find any more. So. Maybe it's nothing.'

Vince looked up, grinning broadly. 'Son,' he said, 'that's why I'm the editor and you're up to your elbows in chemicals and lenses. To you, it's maybe nothing. To me, it's a fucking Panzer Division . . .'

David Jennings checked the messages on his mobile for the third time that afternoon, but there was nothing from Chris Bell. It was unusual. He'd left her a voicemail first thing this morning, and she always got back to him within an hour.

'Sir,' Zerkah said, looking up from her computer, 'would it be okay if I knocked off at a reasonable hour today? I mean, nothing much seems to be happening.'

'Yes, of course,' Jennings nodded. 'Got something planned for tonight?'

'Just going round to my sister's to watch a film and have dinner. Not very exciting.'

Jennings glanced at his watch. It was twenty-past three. An early day looked like a good idea. He shut down his computer.

'So what sort of films do you like, Zerkah?' he asked, as the computer played its little closing-down chime.

'Oh, all sorts. We're hiring an Asian blockbuster tonight. Bollywood – you know?'

'Er, no, not really,' Jennings admitted. He felt on the back foot. 'This would be a traditional Indian sort of adventure, then?'

Zerkah was tidying the papers on her desk into neat piles. 'Oh, God no; they've got into making Asian versions of Western films now. Schwarzenegger's a big favourite.' She shot a quick look at Jennings, who was nodding interestedly. 'Tonight, we're going to get *Turbanator II*.'

'Really?' Jennings nodded. 'Isn't it fascinating how these cross-cultural phenomena—'

'Sir,' she interrupted, 'that was a joke. You're supposed to laugh.'

Jennings frowned perplexedly, and then grinned. 'The sad part is, I'll fall for that sort of thing again and again, won't I?'

'Sorry,' Zerkah giggled. 'So what will you do with your evening?'

Jennings shrugged. 'I'll cook, I think. I enjoy that. And then help Jake with his homework. He's doing a project on Native Americans.'

'Indians,' Zerkah suggested, mischievously.

'Don't start. It's about pantheistic belief, really. You know, gods in nature and all that.'

'Do you mind him learning about those ideas?'

Jennings stood up and took his jacket from the wire clothes hanger that was looped into the top drawer of the filing cabinet. 'No, not at all. He should learn all there is to learn about faith, if he's going to make any intelligent decisions.' He paused and smiled. 'He told me the other day about the Cherokee belief that the wind is caused by the rustling of leaves on a tree. He said it made sense to him, so what was the problem?'

'What did you tell him?'

'I explained about the confusion of cause and effect, and how easy it is to get them the wrong way round. I pointed out the—'

Jennings stopped, one arm in his jacket, the other reaching behind to catch the empty sleeve. He was staring at the pinboard on which Zerkah had stuck the accumulating evidence in the case. There were the Major Arcana, all twenty-two of them, arranged around the board, and in the centre, the two cards that had been obtained from actual victims. There was a video-capture of Dixon, and of his bald, gaunt friend, to whom they still needed to put a name. There were photos of the ex-suspect's famous parents – Maria Dixon, agony aunt, and Marty Puxley, the satirical cartoonist. There was a black-and-white of Bartholomew Scott, the socialite, who was close not only to the Dixons but also to Chris Bell. And there were cuttings from the *Clarion* – the picture of the crash-helmeted man, and various other front pages carrying stories of the Trickster's hits.

Jennings put his hand to his mouth and sat down heavily in his chair.

'Oh, my goodness,' he breathed, looking at Zerkah. 'You were right. We *all* should have known better . . .'

Mason had once had a little fling with a vegetarian hippychick pseudo-mystic flowerchild called Rain. Not his usual speed, he had to admit, but she had some terrific Oriental techniques. Rain had espoused the philosophy that one should treat every human being with whom one came in contact as if they were the Buddha. A bit over the top, Mason felt, but he saw the point. So he didn't dismiss out of hand the unsolicited insight of the bloke on the Whiplash. In fact, he was still considering it as he and Chris took their seats on the train back to London.

She was reading some glossy 'make-friends-with-your-aureola' maga-zine, and he was just gazing out of the window, watching Sussex roll by, and, all casual, he muttered, 'It'd be really nice if you stayed over at my place again tonight.'

He winced a little as he said it, realising it was neither a declaration of undying love, nor a cool acceptance of whatever fate might hold in store. But it was the best he could manage at the time.

Chris looked up at him from *Is Leonardo the World's Sexiest Hunk?* and wrinkled her nose. 'I don't think it'd be a very good idea if I stayed, do you? I mean, two nights running?'

Mason contrived to nod and shake his head simultaneously. 'You're right. It'd be a *terrible* idea,' he conceded hurriedly. 'Stupid, stupid idea. Out of the question.'

'Though God knows what difference it would make,' she mused, looking past him at the fields zipping past, and smiling slightly.

He shifted tack, gauging her tone. 'None at all in the long run, really,' he hazarded. 'As if it could. Ha! A preposterous notion.'

'Well . . .' Chris hesitated. 'Okay – it'd be nice to stay. But only on one strict condition . . .'

'Yes?'

'Only if you give me a damn good seeing-to.'

Mason grinned, delighted.

'Oh, well,' he said, shrugging, 'if you're going to start imposing ridiculous conditions, forget it . . .'

285

*　　*　　*

They stopped off for dinner in the West End, and got back to Mason's flat a little before midnight. There was an envelope and a cat on the doormat. Mason picked up the former and Chris scooped Freda into her arms, tickling her behind the ears.

Mason tore open the envelope as they went into the kitchen, and Chris opened the fridge to get Freda's food out.

'Who's it from?' she asked offhandedly. 'And if it's a girl, lie to me.'

Mason sighed and passed her the letter, taking the tin of catfood from her, and picking up Freda's bowl.

'Missed you again, mate,' she read aloud. 'Can you make lunch tomorrow? I'm at the CGH, of course. About noon? Martin.'

She looked across at Mason as he forked disgusting mackerel and salmon mush into the blue plastic bowl.

'Your dad?'

Mason nodded, and put the food on the floor for Freda.

'Well?' she persisted.

He straightened up, leaned against the wall, and watched the cat gulping down her late dinner. 'I wonder what percentage of that muck is actually salmon or mackerel,' he frowned. He reached his cigarettes from the pocket of his jacket, and lipped one. 'Precious little, I imagine.'

Chris walked over to him, took the cigarette from his mouth before he could light it, and put her arms around his waist. He was still looking sideways, at Freda.

'Well?' she asked again.

He turned to her, rubbing his mouth with his palm. 'I really don't know,' he said. 'Fuck.'

'What's the CGH?'

Mason sighed. 'Covent Garden Hotel. When he was first in America, but still coming back, that's where he used to stay – and where I stayed with him, from time to time. Always the same room. 202. Amazing I remember, actually.'

'But he knew you would,' she pointed out.

'Yeah. Arrogant bastard.'

She squeezed him, and then turned to fill up the kettle. 'Tea?'

Mason nodded.

'You can't *not* go, can you? In the end?' she said.

'I don't know. I'll think about it in the morning.' He lipped the cigarette again. 'Listen – actually, I don't really want tea.'

Chris grinned, and flipped the off-switch on the kettle. She pushed her hair back, and glided over to him, eyes on his, unbuttoning her blouse.

'No,' she whispered, putting her arms around his neck. 'I know what you want, Mase.'

Four o'clock in the morning, and Mischief lay awake in the dark, staring at the ceiling.

This place again. This room. Those same curtains. The same lampshade, quilt cover, wardrobe. The same smells, the same noises outside, the same maddening click of the radiator cooling.

And all the same feelings. The panic of finding yourself here, as if no progress had been made at all over the years. The pull towards people and places you know, and the goosefleshy impulse to run away – like before. The desire to scream and fight and baulk at the ordinariness of what's on offer: the mundane happinesses that everyone else seems to embrace. Like zombies.

But not *everyone* is stupid. There are brilliant, insightful, sharp people – one's friends, even – who seem able to take on these tenets, these workaday principles, and live by them. So it must be something else that makes one shy away, spitting. Some glitch in one's own personality.

And yet, you have to be honest. If you rage inside against all the dumb beliefs and the myopic philosophies, then you must express it, surely? Because the alternative is to go along with them, betraying your own heart and becoming more and more twisted inside.

Whatever else I may have done, thought Mischief, I have always been honest. Oh, sure, there have been petty deceptions – you can't avoid that. But on the big stuff, I've been straight with people, and true to myself.

And, of course, if you are unquenchably, burningly honest, then people get hurt sometimes. Particularly those who are closest to you, within scorching distance of that flame. But, for God's sake, better that than to lie, to say you can manage what you know you can't manage, to make promises you fail to fulfil.

Mischief slid out of bed, and lit a cigarette, standing by the window and looking out at the empty street, thinking back over the last few months.

There was something here to be finished – and it *would* be finished. And then . . . well, who knows? It was as if the completion of the Trickster game would somehow shift perceptions, and allow new possibilities to take shape. Mischief didn't know yet what those new potentials were, but they were there, just out of sight, beyond the end of the street, and they were waiting to be found.

And in the meantime, there was the boy – as, one way or another, it seemed there had always been the boy. In the back of the mind, ever-present, despite career and lovers and money and distance – always Mason. Perhaps something could be rebuilt with him. Perhaps that, at least, was a possibility that already had a shape.

Mischief sighed, and stubbed out the cigarette in the familiar old ashtray. Whatever they were, these formless possibilities, they were a bit frightening. Honestly.

CHAPTER FORTY-ONE

Mason woke up to the sound of tea being made in the kitchen. He rolled over and buried his nose in the perfumed pillow beside him. After a bit, giggling happily, he sat up and looked around the bedroom, smiling at the discarded knickers on the floor and the earrings on the bedside table. He got out of bed and pulled on a bathrobe, beaming like an idiot, and walked through to the kitchen like he owned the place. He *did* own the place, of course, but it felt much more like his when Chris was there.

She was sitting at the kitchen table, wearing one of his T-shirts, reading her magazine.

'Morning, beautiful,' he said. 'Call it an uncanny deduction, but I suspect you've got nothing on under those jeans. And I like that in a woman.'

She tutted goodnaturedly. 'There's tea in the pot.'

'Great.' He sat down and poured himself a cup.

Chris closed her magazine, and looked at him. 'What are you going to do, Mase?'

He beamed at her. 'Beautiful morning, isn't it? I wouldn't be surprised if it got up into the eighties today. We should go to the seaside. Oops – no. We did that yesterday.'

She shook her head, still smiling, and stood up. 'Do you fancy a bacon sandwich?'

'Thank you, that'd be lovely.'

As she opened the fridge, she said, 'Oh, there's a postcard for you, from Elvis.' She took it from the cup-shelf and handed it to him. It was a tourist card, bought in Philadelphia of all places, with a picture of the Liberty Bell, and the inscription 'The Symbol of American Freedom'. On the back, there was a message.

> Lovebirds in the air
>   seemed a suited pair,
> But only the Joker knew
>   that a suited pair was two.

It was signed, 'The King of Rock'n'Roll'.

'What's it mean?' Chris asked, laying rashers out on the grill.

Mason slurped his tea. 'It's something to do with Cliff Benching and Dawn Mabbut. We thought they represented the Lovers, but Elvis figured out that they were actually the Emperor and the Empress respectively, because of the parts they played in the Moonquest movies.' He frowned. 'I don't get this "only the Joker knew" bit, though. I mean, it was Elvis who figured it out.'

'Perhaps it *is* Elvis,' she said, sitting down again. 'I wouldn't put it past him.'

'The thought had occurred to me,' he admitted. 'But it doesn't seem likely, since the Stella Sky thing. If it were Elvis, that entire set-up would have been a huge and pointless effort, just to throw me off track.'

'The whole *thing* requires huge effort,' Chris suggested. 'That wouldn't deter the Trickster at all.'

Mason went for a shower whilst the bacon was sizzling, and thought about whether he was going to go and meet his dad. He didn't need to think much. He *knew* he was going. Chris had been right – how could he not?

'I'm going to meet my dad,' he said, coming through to the kitchen, towelling his hair. 'Will you be here when I get back?'

She handed him a bacon sandwich and kissed him on the lips. 'If you want me to be, yeah.'

He smiled and hugged her, and, given it was a good half-hour before he had to leave, he put the bacon sandwich down on the dresser and coaxed her back over the kitchen table, as she unknotted the cord of his bathrobe.

A little after eleven, Mason set out to meet his estranged father with a spring in his step and, in his heart, the happy knowledge that whatever weirdness awaited him, he had someone to go home to, at last.

Mason read a lot of newspapers, and he had noticed that every so often one or other of the Sunday supplements would run a har-de-har piece called something like 'The New Etiquette'. Where to sit your son's new wife's first husband at the wedding reception. How to introduce your child's schoolchum's lesbian parents at dinner parties. That sort of thing. But he'd never seen anyone address the knotty problem of what to wear when going to meet your dad for the first time in fifteen years.

Had he been asked for advice by someone facing that dilemma, he would have said 'go casual'. There is no necessity, he would have suggested, to prove that you're a grown-up, or that you are living above the poverty-line, or that you are aware of the gravity of the encounter – so your one and only suit is totally unnecessary. Mason had thought this through. In fact, he thought it through on the tube, gazing at his reflection in the opposite window, wearing his one and only suit.

And this was the least of his anxieties. Dozens more were screaming for a share of his apparently unlimited supply of angst.

He thought about how he should address Marty Puxley. 'Dad'? 'Father'? 'Martin'? Should he shake his hand, hug him, nod politely? What if I weep, he wondered, or lose the power of speech, or just faint clean away? What if *he* does?

He checked for cigarettes as he left Covent Garden tube station. He had decided he was going to smoke, whether the old man liked it or not. And drink too, given the chance.

He didn't even know if he'd recognise him. In Mason's mind's eye, his father was in his mid-thirties. His hair was collar-length and curly, darkest brown with a few grey strands. He was thin as a nun's smile, and all adam's apple and knuckles. He might be totally grey now, and fatter. Having lived on the West Coast, he might have a ponytail, despite being a bit bald on top. Might even have a Yank accent.

But Mason was willing to bet that he still carried a sketchpad with him at all times, and had a pocket full of pencils somewhere. And he would still let his eyes dart around incessantly, even as he was speaking to you, looking at people, and breaking off mid-sentence to doodle the outline of a profile he'd just seen, or the particular way a person arranged their body on a chair.

Mason was approaching the Covent Garden Hotel by this time, and his mouth was dry. He had to focus on the simple act of walking, which had suddenly become less than instinctive. He felt very detached from himself, and not really in control of his limbs. He reached the door and looked at it. He tried to concentrate.

Door, he thought. I can manage doors. You push them, on the sticky-out bit.

He pushed, and walked carefully into the lobby. The bar was to his right. When he used to come to this hotel as a kid, the bar had seemed a very grown-up place, where he never ventured.

As he stood there, fists clenched, the memories slipped and tumbled like books from a collapsing shelf. The lift tinged and opened. Mason recalled that sometimes, after putting him to bed upstairs, the old man would slip away here for a drink and to meet friends. Mason would wake up, and wander to the lift in his pyjamas. He'd come down to the lobby, and hover by the door of the bar, peering in. He might even have been dragging a teddy bear. His father would notice him eventually, and hustle him back to the room.

Stranded there again by the door to the bar, Mason remembered the beer on his father's breath and the way his hands smelled. Elegant, thin hands – smelling of nicotine. Smelling, in fact, of Old Holborn roll-ups. Mason was sure of that because he used to be sent across the road to the tobacconist's sometimes. 'Half an ounce of Old Holborn, please, and a packet of Rizla Green.' One of those sacred litanies from childhood that's never forgotten. He'd say it over and over as he left the hotel and trotted along the pavement. 'Half an ounce of Old Holborn, please, and a packet of Rizla Green.'

He remembered the picture on the Old Holborn pack – a row of Victorian houses. He remembered clutching it tight in his little fist with the change ('Don't forget the change') as he scurried out of the shop; obediently looking both ways as he came back across the street; scampering up the stairs. (Why, he wondered, did he never take the lift, going up?) He remembered watching the intricate dexterity with which his dad made a cigarette out of a scrap of paper and tendrils of dark tobacco. He realised, suddenly, that he'd started smoking as a teenager simply because it made his hands smell like his dad's.

And here he was again, in the lobby, looking into the bar, trying to find him.

Mason gulped and opened the door and stood there, in everybody's way, feeling like a great gangly scruffy idiot in an out-of-date suit, lost and useless. He scanned the tables, not seeing his dad – but not seeing anyone, really. Just moving his eyes about desperately, and hoping he'd be rescued.

A waiter pushed past him, and Mason apologised for existing. 'Sorry, sorry, my fault. I'm in the way. Sorry.' He walked to the bar, slowly, waiting to be noticed. He sat on a barstool. No one called, 'Mason – over here!' No one touched him gently on the elbow to attract his attention.

'A drink, sir?' the barman asked.

'Yes.' Mason told him, and gazed from side to side along the bar.

The barman waited. 'What can I get you?' he prompted.

'Er . . . A white wine. No, a beer. No – hang on. Umm . . . A white wine – yes.'

'House?'

'Lovely.'

He spun on the stool, and couldn't see his father, but he knew he was a bit early. Three minutes early, in fact, according to the clock on the wall, which the barman, even when repeatedly pressed, insisted was accurate. He got through the wine, and another, and several cigarettes – each with not much more than one long hard suck.

It was twenty minutes past twelve, and Mason was beginning to wish he'd brought the note with him, because he was no longer sure it had specified noon. His dad's handwriting was a bit squiggly. It might have said 'one'.

By half past, he was convinced that it had said 'one', and he thought he'd better slow down on the Australian Chardonnay. Apart from anything else, he'd checked the wine list and discovered he couldn't pay for it. He was just lighting another cigarette and wondering if his credit card would bounce, when a voice behind him said, 'Mason?'

He swivelled to see that his mum was standing there, and Bart a little further back.

He blinked and gulped, and Maria hugged him, all sudden and tight. Mason was looking over her shoulder at Bart, who was smiling a serious sort of smile. Only one person could possibly have told them he'd be there.

'Oh, fuck,' Mason croaked, his bottom lip quivering. 'He's not coming, is he?'

CHAPTER FORTY-TWO

Maria and Bart sat Mason down at a table, cooing condolences and patting various bits of him, as if he were a five-year-old who'd just seen his puppy steamrollered. He knew he must look pretty awful, because Bart made him drink scotch while his mother wittered on about getting a phone call and rushing up here and how Dad always was a bastard and always would be and it didn't matter because she loved Mason to bits . . .

Mason wasn't really listening. He just wanted to get out, before he cried. He let them fuss over him for a while and then he said that he'd better be going – he practically had to bite his mother's hand before she'd let go of his arm – and he walked out into the street in a daze. He wandered up towards Soho, for no good reason at all.

The imagination flips like a coin when you're in shock. For a while, Mason tried to convince himself that he'd somehow screwed up the take, and that he should go back and try it again – and this time his father would be there. And then he got angry, and had visions of hunting the old man down and stabbing him to death in an alley or bar. No jury on earth would convict, he felt.

He was on the Charing Cross Road now, and he stopped by a newspaper stand, and looked up and down the street, with no particular place to go. People were strolling past in the sunshine, all with very particular places to go. People with proper lives involving proper dads. That, Mason felt, is what happens if you have a proper dad. You have places to go and things to do, and you go there and you do them, because half your fucking mind isn't constantly occupied with figuring out what it is about you that makes you unworthy of a father.

But surely, he thought, rubbing his forehead, surely it wasn't my fault that Dad pissed off and left me?

He looked back, searching for some reason for it. He pleaded with himself to make sense of it.

I mean, I was just a little boy. I don't think I was especially naughty, or difficult. I don't think I was unlovable. My mum loved me. And other people seem to care for me, even now. They turn up when they say they're going to, and spend time in my company, and appear to enjoy being around me. Mum and Bart. And Elvis. And Chris, of course. They don't mess with my mind and tell me lies and just leave me sitting in bars. So – for Christ's sake – it wasn't my fault, was it?

A man in a pricey suit pushed past him, to get to the newspaper vendor.

'Sorry,' Mason said, instinctively.

Then he thought, 'No. I'm *not* fucking sorry. *He* pushed *me*.' And, in that moment, he decided he was going to stop being sorry, and gullible, and pushed. Why should he be?

He rounded on the bloke as he paid for his paper and turned back towards the road. He put up an admonishing hand, about to give the guy a piece of his new-found mind, and ask him what sort of ignorable, stupid, no-account half-wit he thought he was buffeting the fuck around. And then he saw the front cover of the *Daily Voice*, which the man was holding up and about to open.

The headline read, 'The Face of the Joker!' And beneath it was a photo of Elvis, with the Naganitaki Tower behind him.

Everything went soggy inside Mason, like spinach.

'Oh, shit,' he breathed. 'You moron.'

The bloke gave a look of perplexed contempt and shoved Mason backwards. His spine slammed into a lamp-post, and he stood there, defeated and brainless, completely unamazed at his own stupidity.

He slid down the lamp-post to his haunches, and put his face in his hands. By Leicester Square station, he sat down and wept.

One can crouch, sobbing, on a major London thoroughfare for quite some time without anyone asking what's wrong; so Mason was surprised to feel a tap on his elbow after only a minute or so. He didn't look up – he knew what he must look like. A man of twenty-seven in a second-hand suit, weeping and snotty and curled up by the kerb in the middle of a summer's day in the city. He didn't want to acknowledge any witnesses to that.

The photo from the front page of the *Voice* shimmered in front of his closed eyes. It *was* Elvis, then. Mason huddled there, trying to shake the image, contemplating how wilfully dumb he must have been not to have seen what Elvis had been doing to him. God, he must have had a laugh. He must have been chortling like a butcher, on the quiet. And Mason suspected Ellen was in on it too. Christ – Elvis might even have told Marty Puxley. In which case, Mason didn't blame the old git for not showing up. Difficult to keep a straight face, one would imagine.

Again, there was a tap on Mason's arm.

'I'm fine,' Mason choked, his face buried in wrapped elbows. 'Leave me alone.'

'What's troublin' you, friend?' said a soft, concerned American voice.

Mason looked up to see a smiling, blond man in a dark suit, clasping pamphlets and leaning towards him, his hand outstretched.

'Oh, Christ,' he groaned.

The stranger smiled even wider. 'Yes, friend. You may have hit upon the answer to your problem right there. Christ the Redeemer is waitin' t'soothe your anguished soul.'

Sighing, Mason struggled to his feet, brushing his bum with both hands, and sniffing. He turned to walk into the station and the evangelist strolled alongside him, taking a Bible out of his inside pocket.

'Tell me, friend, d'you want Jesus to come inna your heart?' he asked.

Mason looked at him, as they descended the stairs together. 'If he gets me out of this mess, mate, he can come in my mouth,' he promised.

Walking down the street towards his flat, Mason was looking forward to nothing more than collapsing on the sofa and having Chris be nice to him – so it was a bit of a shock to find she wasn't there. Elvis, however, was. He was sitting in the kitchen, reading the papers and eating bourbons.

'Hello, Mase,' he said cheerfully, as Mason came in. 'Chris has gone to the pub for fags. Cuppa?'

Mason stood there, silent for a moment, as Elvis reached a mug down from the shelf. He was considering punching him.

'You've made me look a right prat, haven't you?' he said, swallowing. 'I'm sure it's been a hoot. Now kindly fuck off out of my house, and stay fucked off.'

Elvis gestured towards the *Voice*, smiling, as he poured tea from the pot. 'What – that? You don't believe *that*, do you?' He topped up the mug with milk. 'It's not true, Mase. I'm not the Joker.'

Mason looked at him, narrow-eyed, as the tea was pushed across the table. He took it, and licked his lips, still searching Elvis's face.

'Honest,' Elvis shrugged. 'It's not me.'

There was a short unblinking silence.

'Oh,' Mason sniffed, eventually. 'That's all right then.' And he sat down at the table.

In truth, Mason didn't want to believe it was Elvis, because then he'd have had to throw him out. And he didn't want him to go. He didn't want to be on his own. He put his elbows on the table and massaged his eyes with his fingertips.

'I take it your dad didn't turn up?' Elvis said, sipping his tea.

'No,' Mason muttered, with the little shivery intake of breath that follows tears.

Elvis nodded, and said that he had talked to Marty the previous evening and had been told about the plan to meet. 'I knew he wouldn't show,' he said. 'I could hear it in his voice – and I've know him too long. I'm afraid he's a total coward, your father.'

'Must be where I get it,' Mason suggested, reaching for a newspaper from Elvis's pile.

'Drink your tea,' Elvis said, putting his hand on the newspapers, and nodding towards the mug.

Mason shrugged, and slouched, and drank his tea. He was too empty to do anything other than what he was told. He was mechanical.

'He's still important, your dad, you know,' Elvis said, offering a biscuit. 'He always will be.'

'Whatever.'

'You'll see. Did I ever tell you about *my* father?'

Mason considered for a moment. 'No, I don't think so.'

'He was a German prisoner-of-war. A flier. He was held in some camp in Buckinghamshire. He was made to work on the land, where he met my mother, fell in love and got her pregnant. He'd been awarded the Iron Cross for valour in the invasion of France, despite being passionately anti-Nazi. He was only on the bombing run during which he got shot down because the Luftwaffe knew that the mission was suicidal, and they hoped he'd be killed. They suspected him of being part of a plot to overthrow Hitler, but they had no proof. He was from an old and noble family – an honourable, compassionate man who had actually helped Jews over the border into Switzerland during the rise of the Brownshirts. In 1944, when my mother was carrying me, he was sent back to Germany as part of a trade for captured British spies. The Gestapo collected him at some border-meet with the British. He was tortured and eventually shot – but he never betrayed his comrades in the anti-Nazi underground.'

'Blimey,' Mason breathed. 'I'm sorry.'

'Don't be,' Elvis smiled. 'I made it all up. He was a prisoner-of-war, but that's all I know. But he was so important to me as a kid that I invented him, and now that's the image I have of him. You can't help your dad being a big deal, Mase.'

He grinned and took a large yellow silk handkerchief out of his tweed jacket pocket, and leaned across the table. He pinched the hanky around Mason's nose.

'Blow,' he said.

Mason blew, disgustingly, and managed a watery grin. 'I'll be all right,' he told Elvis, but it was as much query as statement.

'You'll be wonderful,' Elvis said. 'Er, keep the handkerchief.' He leaned back and swivelled in the chair to open the door of the fridge, from the milk-shelf of which he took a bottle of champagne, and three condensation-misted glasses. 'Now – next item on the agenda . . .' He lined up the glasses on the table.

Mason frowned, quizzically. 'There's more?'

'Yeah.' The cork popped. Elvis poured champagne in to two of the glasses, and handed Mason one. 'To the Joker,' he said.

Mason sipped. 'Why?'

Elvis smacked his lips. 'Good Lord, that's fine stuff.' He tipped the bottle and studied the label. 'Those clever old Albanians.' Putting down his glass, he linked his fingers, rested his chin on them, staring across at Mason with his goblet-green eyes. 'Things have become simultaneously complex and simple, my friend,' he said.

'Have they?'

'They have.'

'Right then.'

Elvis picked up the top newspaper on the pile, and displayed the front page. There was his picture, with the Naganitaki Tower illuminated in the background. 'There are two remarkable things about this newspaper, Mase,' he observed. 'And the first is, vampires don't usually show up on photos.'

Mason chuckled. 'If that were true, it'd have completely fucked Christopher Lee's movie career, wouldn't it?' He knew it wasn't a great gag, but he was doing his best to keep above the surface.

Elvis ignored it. 'But you can see their point, can't you? I was there. And –' He turned to page three, which had a picture of him at the Stella Sky hit – 'I was there too. Moreover, I do seem to fit your perpetrator profile, don't I?'

'Yes,' Mason admitted, warily.

'But so does someone else. Run that profile past me one more time, Mase.'

Mason couldn't see where this was going. He reached for his fags again, and the matches. With an unlit cigarette between his fingers, he started counting off the profile points on his fingertips. The matches castanetted as he pushed each digit back.

'Money. Have you got money?'

Elvis grimaced in frustration. 'No, not me. It's not me. Who else has money?'

'Well, Bart.'

Elvis shrugged, lips pursed. 'Yes, okay. Bart. No one else?'

Mason furrowed his brow. Who else? Well, everyone but himself, really.

'Time,' he said, counting off another finger. 'Spare time.'

Elvis nodded, hunched forward over his champagne glass, staring at him. 'Who?'

Mason frowned. Bart, again, obviously. And . . . who else?

Elvis was rocking to and fro, egging him on to see it, but Mason wasn't up to his intellectual best.

'Yeah, I'm thinking. I'm thinking,' he protested. 'I mean, it's not that I'm stupid, but I've had a very trying day, what with the tension and the expectation and the disappointment and—'

He stopped.

Oh, bloody hell. No. Oh, no.

'Money. Time,' Elvis coaxed. 'What else?'

'Sense of humour,' Mason muttered, sitting back, and lodging the cigarette in the corner of his mouth.

Mason heard his own voice saying what he always said when the subject came up.

He was a funny man, my dad. Really – very, very funny. My mother has told me a million times how funny he was . . .

'Who?' Elvis said again.

Mason's head was lowered, and he was kneading his scalp with all ten fingers. He looked up at Elvis, from under his fringe. 'It's not, is it?' he asked, in a whisper.

'Keep going,' Elvis said. 'What else?'

'Contempt for fuzzy, ill-thought-through opinions.'

Those scathing, derisive drawings, Mason thought, his skin tingling, the hairs on his forearms standing up. The gleeful, mocking lines of the caricatures that the Yanks were willing to pay so much money for. So much money that he left me behind, and went to be flattered and fêted in the brilliant sunshine of California.

But now he was back, of course, in his home town. Wealthy and bored and with fifteen years behind him of tolerating the West Coast idiocies of colour-therapy and Alexander Techniques and seaweed diets. And he finds that his countrymen have taken them on too. It's not just the foreigners any more who subscribe to this desperate crap – it's his own. Mason could see how that must have pissed him off, and amused him, and fired up that instinct in him that needed to make a difference.

The logic of it beaded on Mason's forehead, trickled down his face, stuck to him like damp cotton.

And Elvis, Marty's old friend, would have known, of course. Marty would have shared that secret with him, as he shared with him the secret of Mason himself. So Elvis wasn't some kind of funky, in-touch genius – he simply had the inside track on the thing from the start.

Mason slumped forward and laid his head on the table. 'Oh, Christ,' he groaned. 'What a fucking idiot I am.'

'Access to the media,' Elvis prompted, gently.

'Yeah, yeah, I got it,' Mason mumbled into the pine. Obviously his dad had access to the media. He'd spent his life in print. He was celebrated and pursued by all the ink'n'schedule shakers who wanted him to do cartoons for their studio-set backdrops and their Reviews of the Year.

Mason thumped his forehead repeatedly on the table. 'Oh, for God's sake.'

'So – what are you going to do about it?' Elvis asked. 'The Joker is more than a little interested in how you're going to react to this.'

Mason banged his head on the table a couple more times, and it hurt.

'Oh, fuck,' he offered.

All he wanted was for it all to go away. The horrible neatness of it – Dad the lost father and Dad the discovered Joker – was too much for him. He just wanted to curl up in bed with Chris, and nuzzle into her shoulder and deal with ordinary concerns, like sex and snoring and who would get up to make breakfast. It didn't seem fair that he should have his life so folded over and made into something he hadn't planned, like some kind of sadistic origami.

The front door bell rang.

'I'll get it,' Elvis said, pushing back his chair.

Mason humphed.

'So will I,' he muttered. 'Eventually.'

CHAPTER FORTY-THREE

Mischief had an excellent memory for faces. It went with the job. And there in the saloon bar of the pub around the corner from Mason's apartment, was a face that Mischief knew from somewhere.

From a photograph. Several photographs. The shoulder-length hair, the sulky mouth, the somewhat forbidding, cynical expression. Where was it from?

And then it clicked. That face featured in Maria's photograph albums, the ones she'd trotted out with maternal pride after dinner, when the conversation had turned to Mason. It was the face that had caused so much grief in Mason's life. It was the face of his miserable obsession.

Mischief thought of walking over there, tapping the table, saying, 'What the hell do you think you're doing, messing with the boy like this?' Perhaps, in some tiny way, it might help.

But – no. No one had the right to interfere. It was Mason's to sort out, as it always had been. Whatever Mischief might feel for Mason or want to feel for him, this was separate. No one's business but Mason's alone.

And, on top of that, Mischief couldn't be sure, deep down, that to speak to this stranger in a bar would be any more than a remote indulgence; an attempt to get something right for Mason in penance for having got so much wrong.

'Same again?' said the barman, taking the empty beer glass.

'Yeah,' Mischief admitted. 'Same again and again and again . . .'

Mason sat there in the kitchen, watching the bubbles rise in his champagne glass. He felt as if his dad had made a fool of him twice over – and all in the same day.

Oh, Jesus.

He leaned back, looking at the ceiling, and groaned with embarrassment. He pressed the heels of his hands into his eyeballs and, wincing, he thought through the last couple of months. He wondered how the situation would have gone if he and Elvis *had* caught his dad pulling off a Joker stunt. That would have been some scene, huh? As father and son reunions go, it would be right up there with *A Boy Named Sue*, and Oedipus's little contretemps with his old man.

Chris came in, followed by Elvis, and they both sat down at the table. Elvis poured her some champagne, and she put her hand over Mason's.

'Sorry your dad let you down, Mase,' she said.

'Yeah,' he muttered, and turned his hand over to squeeze hers.

She looked at Elvis. 'And you've told him the rest?'

Elvis shrugged. 'I was just finishing up the details.'

'Are you okay? Mase. Is everything okay?' Chris asked.

He sighed, and smiled at her weakly. 'Doesn't really matter, in the end, does it – the whole Joker thing? There are more important things in life.'

He leaned forward and hugged her, and she hugged him back. In all of this, he realised, she was the only one who hadn't lied to him at some point. Maria and Bart had their little secret. Elvis had kept schtum about knowing his dad. And Marty himself had fucked about from start to finish. Only Chris had been straight – even, Mason suspected, when it would have been easier on her to have protected him from the truth.

Right then it seemed to Mason that it was even more important than love, the truth.

He squeezed Chris hard and then sat back. 'Well,' he said, 'the Joker game is over, then. No point in going on with it, really.'

Chris paused in the middle of lighting a cigarette. 'Oh, God, no. It's got to be finished. We can't stop now.'

Mason glanced at Elvis, who held up a hand. 'Wait. I'm not sure we're all speaking the same language here. Mase, what did you make of the clue I sent you?'

Mason shrugged, and reached the card down from the pinboard on the wall beside the table. He read the little rhyme out loud.

> 'Lovebirds in the air
>   seemed a suited pair,
> But only the Joker knew
>   that a suited pair was two.'

He handed the card to Chris. 'Well, it's Dawn and Cliff, isn't it? We thought that they were the Lovers but they turned out to be the Emperor and the Empress.'

'Yes,' Elvis nodded. 'But before we worked that out, the Joker said, "One's been missed lower down the order." One. Not two. The Joker knew, of course – and let it slip.'

'So you did talk to Dad about the campaign!' Mason exclaimed.

Elvis waved the interjection aside. 'I told you earlier that there were two remarkable things about this newspaper.' He tapped the *Voice*, lying on the table in front of him. 'The second is that both the *Voice* and the *Clarion* are running the same headline today – "The Face of the Joker!" – but, oddly, with different stories.'

Mason wrinkled his nose perplexedly. He looked from Elvis to Chris and back again, unsure of what he was supposed to say.

'Show him,' Chris murmured.

From the bottom of the pile of newspapers, Elvis pulled a copy of the *Clarion*. It was folded in half, and Mason could see the headline – 'The Face of the Joker!' Elvis held the paper up, and unfolded it.

There, beneath the excited block letters, was a photo, obviously taken from a work-ID or passport.

Mason stared at it, blinking, for several seconds, as Elvis and Chris watched him. The clock ticked on the kitchen wall, and Mason could hear bubbles bursting in the champagne glass in front of him. He closed his eyes, and then opened them again. The photo was still there. And it made sense.

'Oh ... my ... God,' he breathed eventually. 'Oh, my God.'

It was Chris.

CHAPTER FORTY-FOUR

The previous evening, when David Jennings had had his flash of insight, he'd refused to share it with Zerkah.

'I need to think this through,' he'd told her. 'We'll talk about it tomorrow.'

Zerkah had not slept a wink.

At seven-thirty the following morning, she was waiting outside the doors of Scotland Yard when Jennings arrived. He grinned.

'Yeah, okay. Let's go for a coffee and a chat,' he nodded, before she could speak.

They walked to a café across the street, and Zerkah nearly screamed with frustration as Jennings took his leisurely time at the counter deciding between an apple danish and a chocolate croissant.

'What, then, sir?' she demanded, when they finally settled into a booth.

Jennings sucked the froth from his cappuccino, and swallowed. 'You remember when we got the forensic report back from the lab, and I explained that Chris Bell must have touched the card in the pizza place? You said that she should have known better. I think she did.' He tore an edge off his danish. 'Cause and effect, you see. We assumed that her prints were on the card because she handled it in the restaurant. But what if she handled it in the restaurant because her prints were on the card?'

Zerkah clapped her hand to her mouth, wide-eyed.

'Oh, wow!' she exclaimed, muffledly.

Jennings chuckled. '"Wow"?'

'Oh, wow, sir,' Zerkah amended.

'Last night, I thought a lot about that lunch with Ms Bell,' Jennings continued. 'A few things occurred to me. For a start, she was more interested in the nature of the lead than in the story. Second, she was very careful to make sure that the Hierophant was the only card we had.'

He munched contemplatively. 'And she also did her level best to get me away from the table. She kept topping up my wine. She tried to knock my glass over, and to drop a pizza in my lap. She wanted a moment alone with the card.'

Zerkah clucked her tongue, amazed. 'We'll need more than that, sir,' she pointed out, although she was profoundly impressed.

'Yes, of course. But the incidents build. Who is invisible in a TV studio – or anywhere, come to that? Those whom you expect to be there. The one person we weren't watching on the morning that Suzy Winkworth got tricked was Ms Bell – because she was with *us*.' He sipped his coffee. 'Then there's the only occasion she didn't come to a stake-out – the possible hit on the Emperor and Empress of Pamalia. She didn't answer her phone, made no effort to make contact. And at that time she was dropping frogs on the unfortunate Y.A. Watt.'

Zerkah thought about the *Clarion*'s frontpage of the man in the crash helmet; about how convincing and compelling it had been and how it had become everybody's image of the Trickster. It had certainly fooled *her*. And Chris Bell had engineered it, of course.

She shook her head, astonished.

'So – are we going to tell her we're on to her?' she asked Jennings.

He pinched his nose between steepled fingertips, and stared out of the window for a few seconds. Then he pushed his chair back, and stood up.

'That,' he told Zerkah, 'is what we sleuths call a two-danish question.'

He turned towards the café counter, and then stopped mid-stride, as he noticed, lying on the next table, a copy of the *Clarion* with Chris's face on the front page.

He tutted and looked over his shoulder at Zerkah.

'Well, that's that one answered,' he sighed. 'Come up with another two-danish question. I'm desperate.'

Chris leaned forward with her elbows on the kitchen table.

'I wanted to tell you, Mase – but I couldn't. And anyway, you were having such fun working it out.' She grinned at him, and poured some more champagne. 'It was a challenge, wasn't it?'

Mason was finding it hard to breathe. 'Oh, my God,' he whispered, looking at her.

Elvis chuckled. 'I figured it out when the three of us had dinner with your mum and Bart, after the Naganitaki Tower. Chris told me more than she meant to. About her parents –' He glanced at Chris who nodded an okay – 'which provided motive. And about the money she had inherited when she reached thirty last year. And, of course, she made the reference to one card having been missed early on.'

Mason shook his head. 'God,' he muttered again. Elvis and Chris both seemed to think all this was highly amusing.

'The other night, at the Stella Sky set-up,' Chris continued, all gleeful now, 'it all came to a head. Acting on a remarkably helpful press release, I drove down to Putney with a skull on a spring and a backseat crammed with various-size boxes. I sat in the car and watched the set-up for a little while, and I noticed two Japanese, just standing there on the bridge – which made me a bit wary. So I went along to the pub and paid some bloke a hundred quid to pay *another* bloke a hundred quid to install the pop-up death's-head. I watched proceedings from a safe distance and – whaddya know? – the hired help got nabbed by the Japs. And then, along came the cavalry in the shape of my ex-boyfriend and his loony alien buddy.'

She winked at Elvis. 'So I mobiled my moronic editor, who was about the only person who knew where I was supposed to be at that time. Turns out he'd just had a top-secret meeting with the men from the Naganitaki organisation.'

'Oh, my God,' Mason offered once more. Elvis handed him a champagne glass, and he sipped at it, still staring at Chris.

'It seems that they'd worked up an identikit of the Joker – of me, in fact. They'd traced the Tower hit to an internet café in Holborn, and they got a description and made a sketch. Then they noticed that it looked not unlike the picture of me that's headed up all the Trickster stories – so they came looking. My editor must have been creaming at the thought of getting an exclusive on this. I would imagine he made a deal with them for the coverage.'

'And he told them Chris was in a graveyard in Putney,' Elvis put in, 'covering the Stella Sky story.'

'Exactly,' Chris nodded. 'Anyway, I got most of this out of him on the phone, then I headed for home.' Chris laced her fingers together and looked down at the end of her cigarette. 'When I got to my place, I found two more Oriental types hanging about outside. Scared the shit out of me.

I was absolutely *furious*, naturally, but I was also very frightened. I didn't know where to turn. So . . . well, I did what I always do when I'm angry or scared. I ran to you.'

She lifted her head, and looked across at Mason, smiling, almost bashfully.

'You did what?' he said quietly, reddening.

'What's up?' Chris asked. 'That's *good*, isn't it?'

At last, Mason found his voice. 'So all that stuff about being afraid of losing me – that was all crap, was it?' he demanded. 'Good old Mase, the port in a shitstorm! This offer includes bed, breakfast and bunk-up, and all at a fraction of hotel prices! Jesus!'

'Mason, hang on—' Elvis began.

Mason stood up suddenly, the chair clattering to the floor.

'You calculating cunt!' he spat.

'No – that's not what I meant,' Chris protested. 'It's just I realised—'

'Christ, you never cease to amaze me, you really don't. Fuck – how stupid do you think I am?'

He pulled his arm back with the champagne flute in his hand, as if to fling it against the wall – but he couldn't do it. With a sob of frustration, he slammed it on to the table. Then he turned and strode down the hall, and left the flat, slamming the door behind him. He heard glass breaking – the front-door pane – but he didn't look back. He just ran blindly away.

'Hm, well. That could have gone better,' Elvis observed, as he walked out of the kitchen and along the hall to check the damage.

Chris sighed and slumped in the chair. She reached for her cigarettes and tapped one out wearily. She lit it, and exhaled.

Mason didn't understand. He just didn't get it. He inhabited a binary world in which all questions had light-switch answers. You love someone or you don't. You want out or you want in. You hold or you let go.

But life wasn't like that. That was the sort of childish life that the charlatans peddled. Easy, uncomplicated. Buy into this faith and the world becomes simple.

Lies, all lies.

Chris watched the bubbles rising in her champagne glass, as it stood on the pine table. She remembered another glass of champagne on another pine table – the kitchen table at home. It was her seventeenth birthday, and she had just received the offer of a place from Sussex University. The open envelope was lying beside the glass. Beyond that was a tub of taramasalata, and a plate of pitta bread, stiff and cold. Jess Bell, her mother, was sitting opposite. She was tanned, having just returned from Durban, and she was maniacally cheerful.

'Oh, darling, I wish I'd known about the uni place when I talked to Daddy,' she was saying. 'He would have been thrilled.'

The teenager looked down at her hands in her lap. Her nails were painted purple. She was wearing faded jeans and a T-shirt that read 'World Party – Ship of Fools'. She didn't want to argue, but she had to say what had to be said.

'I don't think I should go, Mum. I'm not sure that university is what I want.'

Jess nodded, still smiling. 'Well, ask Daddy. He'll know what's best.'

And the angry confusion rose in Chris's chest, fizzy and brimming. She wanted to grab her mother by the front of her sweater and scream that Dad was dead, that this was Chris talking, that she wanted help, advice. But her mother was happy now, having been duped by some Afrikaans con-artist; she was smiling and content, and Chris couldn't bring herself to puncture that. And she missed her dad. Her mother was right – he would know what to say, were he here. But he wasn't and ... but ... and ... but ...

Complex. Very, very complex. Very contradictory. Life just is. You have to deal with it.

Elvis came back in to Mason's kitchen. 'Does he have a toolkit, do you know?' he asked.

Chris jerked her head towards the dresser. 'Spanners and stuff in the left-hand drawer.'

Elvis opened the drawer, and rummaged. 'He didn't give you time to put your proposition, did he?' he remarked.

Chris nodded. 'He needs to go and rage. But he'll be back.'

Elvis turned, and leaned against the dresser, tapping a hammer in the palm of his hand. 'You *do* come over as calculating, you know,' he said, looking straight at her.

'Do I?' Chris shrugged. 'I know he'll be back. So do you. Should I pretend there's some doubt, to make myself look *nicer*?' She stubbed out her cigarette. 'It's just the truth.'

'You're very keen on the truth, aren't you?' Elvis observed. He wrinkled his nose. 'But how can you tell whether what you think is the truth is objectively—'

Chris held up a hand. 'If you think you're going to pull me into some Cartesian doublebind and make me look inconsistent, forget it. I know what I know and I act on it. That's all there is to it.'

Elvis nodded. 'Must be nice to have such strong faith,' he suggested. 'How you doing on hope and charity?'

CHAPTER FORTY-FIVE

In the movies, when someone storms out, it's just a fade to black and cut to the next scene. In real life, as Mason suddenly realised, you find yourself marooned on the High Street, having forgotten your cigarettes, and with no idea of what you intend to do next.

He checked his wallet. He had enough for a couple of pints and a pack of fags, so he wandered in to the Three Muses, which passed, through sheer lack of competition, as his local. It was a self-consciously bookish pub, with photos of famous literary drunks on the walls, and a shelf bearing tatty copies of *Under Milk Wood* and *Lucky Jim.*

Mason ordered a pint of Guinness and allowed himself to be robbed blind by the cigarette machine, and then he took a seat at a table overlooked by the raddled black-and-white image of Charles Bukowski.

After a couple of mouthfuls of stout and a contemplative smoke, his tempestuous mood had died down to a half-hearted drizzle. He was still angry, but most of all he was weary. He was tired of being jerked around and surprised. He was fed up with being the last to know. He was exhausted by the apparently endless supply of twists that seemed to be his lot.

But, really, he thought, she could have told me. I mean, not just because I was trying to find out, but because we're . . . I dunno. Lovers. An item. That's what lovers do – they tell each other stuff.

He knew he'd been a bit melodramatic, accusing Chris of sleeping with him just to avoid the Naganitaki people – but it did confuse the issue. He wondered whether she would have come back to him – if that's what she had done, actually – even without that excuse. Maybe it didn't matter what the prompt was. He remembered that when he was pining for her after they first broke up, he seriously considered walking in front of a bus, getting himself quite badly injured, just to supply the hook for a tearful reconciliation. So what did it matter *why* she had come back – as long as she had?

He was a bit panicky about shouting at her now. Not a great move, three days into a rekindled affair, despite any justification of unusual mental cruelty. And halfway down a glass of Guinness, he was starting to think his justification looked a bit weak.

He could see that the Joker campaign must have been a huge project for her. All that organisation and covert planning. And it was important too. A massive symbolic fuck-you to all the cranks and charlatans and spooks who had exploited her mother, and destroyed her childhood. It was an intensely personal quest. She had something to do that involved no one but herself.

He lit another cigarette and thought about his mum and Bart. Why should they have told him about their relationship? None of his business. And his dad, too, in the end. Mason could see that he wasn't a real part of Marty Puxley's life, his career, his America. There was no reason for him to go out of his way to include his son.

Everyone had something to do. And they got on and did it, privately, like grown-ups. He, on the other hand, had absolutely nothing to do at all. If he had – if he'd some direction, some goal – then maybe he wouldn't be so overly interested in the lives of those around him, and wouldn't feel so excluded when he wasn't kept informed minute by minute.

He shook his head, and grimaced into his beer.

His trouble, it seemed to him, was that he never had anything planned for tomorrow. All his tomorrows were devoid of any real point at all. He just wished – he almost wished out loud, there in the pub – that there was something for him to do, to be involved in, to be driven by.

He winced as he looked back on his obsession with catching the Joker. It was pathetic, really. Thinking it up, getting it done, making the world take notice – *that* was worthwhile. But splashing around in its wake and feeding off it – that was the act of a very unimaginative and undirected individual. Not unlike, when he came to think of it, an individual who might dream and sob for years after the end of an affair, still thinking it would all come right.

Yeah, Chris was fond of him, and they were close, and she even fancied him. But she didn't love him. She hadn't done anything to make him think so. If he were the love of her life, she would have included him on the Joker thing – but she hadn't. She had, in fact, been honest.

Damn, Mason thought, I probably should have seen that earlier.

He gulped down the rest of his pint. On the bedroom floor back at the flat, there lay a denim jacket. In the pocket of the denim jacket was an envelope. And in the envelope was a ticket to anywhere in the world.

It was time to use it.

David Jennings and Zerkah Sheikh had driven down to the Oval to see Chris Bell, but she wasn't in. Her place was staked out by a couple of Japanese, though.

'I find it difficult to think of them as being on our side,' Zerkah remarked, as she steered the car around the square and back towards the main drag.

'Hm?' Jennings murmured.

Zerkah glanced at her guvnor. He was in a strange mood. He hadn't said a word all the way from Westminster. No bright little historical anecdotes concerning the buildings they passed. No breezy chatter about her life. It was twenty-past twelve, and he hadn't even mused aloud on the theme of possible lunch venues.

'Where to now, sir?' Zerkah asked, as they reached the junction.

'Take a right,' Jennings muttered, with a tilt of his head. 'To Clapham.'

'Yes, Inspector-sahib,' Zerkah said cheerfully, but the attempt to raise a smile, or even to provoke an embarrassed protestation of implicit equality, failed. Jennings merely stared out of the side window, gnawing at the cuticle of his ring-finger.

'Left here,' he said when they got to Clapham High Street, 'and next right. Stop opposite the school.'

The children were in the playground, rushing around, shouting, chattering. Jennings asked Zerkah to wind her window down, and he didn't even say please.

Zerkah scanned all the identically blue-sweatered kids, and tried to recognise Jake from the photograph in the office. She shifted slightly to look at Jennings behind her. He spotted his son at the moment she turned, and his face softened, his eyes liquefied.

Zerkah moved her gaze back towards the playground.

'Point him out to me, sir,' she asked.

'There, picking up the red ball. See?'

'Oh, yes. I've got him. He really looks like you, doesn't he?'

Zerkah watched Jake run back to the football game with the ball, and kick it up the pitch. He was the goalie. He stood and shouted at his team, jigging from foot to foot as the action all happened at the other end of the tarmacadamed field. The opposing team gained possession – though Zerkah wondered how they could tell, as both sides were dressed in blue – and the pack of small boys rushed down towards Jake's goal, all in a cluster, like midges.

'Come out, come out. Meet the attack,' Jennings was muttering. But Jake bounced up and down on his goal line, let the attackers come almost to him and then dived ineffectually as the ball zipped past between the goalpost cones. He got up and shrugged, apparently unconcerned, Turning, grinning, he jogged back towards the fence to retrieve the ball.

'Do you plan to have children, Zerkah?' Jennings asked, his eyes still on Jake.

'Not so much a plan as an assumption, really, sir,' she said. 'But not quite yet.'

'It changes everything. Everything. It's impossible, before you have children, to understand how anything could be as important in your life. Everything else becomes just fluff. Only the child matters.'

Zerkah had learned a lot from Jennings; he'd taught her that the things people omit to say are informative, and worth pushing.

'I suppose that Jake and your wife are more important to you than even the job, then, sir,' she suggested, offhandedly, turning to look at him.

His eyes shifted to hers, and he pursed his lips. 'Those three, in that order,' he said. He paused. His hand came up to his mouth, and he gnawed at the nail of his ring-finger again. 'Definitely.'

In the playground, a teacher rang a handbell to signal that lunch had come to an end. The children all scampered into lines, immediate and efficient.

Zerkah grinned. 'God, she's got them well trained, hasn't she?'

'Looks like it,' Jennings admitted.

'Every school has a teacher who you know you don't mess about,' Zerkah said. 'And that one there is this school's example.'

Jennings nodded.

'Meet the wife,' he said.

Zerkah blinked and looked again at the teacher, who was gesturing the first file of children through the school door. She was very good-looking in a thin-lipped way – dark-complexioned and straight-backed, and she had a gorgeous figure. And she was married to David Jennings. Zerkah felt suddenly disorientated and hot, as if she had stumbled upon her parents snogging. She ran her eye over the lines of kids, trying to see Jake, but he had disappeared, become just one blue sweater in the ranks of obedient little children whose playtime was over.

Jennings leaned back in his seat, and ran a hand through his thin hair. 'She's a superb teacher, you know. She has a talent for it.' He tapped out a little tattoo on his thighs with his palms. 'Anyway – now let's go and find Ms Bell, shall we?'

Elvis was nailing a board over the broken front-door pane, and he raised an eyebrow as a somewhat sheepish-looking Mason walked up the path. He took a nail from the corner of his mouth.

'Feeling better now, missy?' he asked.

'Yeah. Sorry. Is Chris still here?'

Mason had sat in the pub for another pint, working out how to apologise to Chris, and say that he understood that she didn't feel about him like he felt about her, and he saw now what a wet, heavy, joyless drag he must have been for the last couple of years. He rehearsed the entire speech, which was to finish with the announcement that he was going abroad.

He walked in to the kitchen, opened his mouth, and was about to launch into his nakedly contrite monologue, when she looked up and said:

'I've got to finish it, Mase. I have to.'

He paused for a second, looking at her, then he ditched the script and replied. 'Okay. Oh, sorry, by the way.'

She nodded and pushed her hair back. 'It's okay. Look, this is very important to me. They're bastards, those people. They're smug, manipulative bastards. I have to finish it. And . . .'

She hesitated.

'What?' he asked.

'I'm going to need some help.'

Elvis came in behind, and put his arm around Mason's shoulder. 'They're onto her, you see. The advantage of being a journalist – having an excuse to be anywhere – is now a positive drawback. They know her face. The other hacks at any venue would see her a mile off.'

Mason nodded. 'Yeah. Tricky.'

'I have a hit set up for tomorrow, to represent the Sun,' Chris continued. 'And I was going to ask Elvis to do it . . .'

'But I'm all over the papers too,' Elvis pointed out. 'Pity. I'd've enjoyed it.' He squeezed Mason's shoulder.

'So,' Chris said, raising an eyebrow.

'So,' Elvis repeated.

Mason glanced between them, warily. 'Uh-oh,' he said.

'Have you got anything planned for tomorrow, at all?' Chris asked, innocently.

Mason looked at Elvis, and then back at Chris, both of whom were smiling encouraging, conspiratorial smiles.

'Actually, I have, yeah. I'm going to Belize,' he said, offhand but decisive. And saying it, he felt a little rush of power, control. He had something to do and he was going to do it.

Chris frowned. 'Not *tomorrow*. I mean—'

The front-door bell rang.

'Yep, tomorrow,' Mason said, as he turned to walk down the hall. 'Just going to go to Heathrow and go.'

He grinned as he walked to the front door. The look of surprise and disappointment on Chris's face was thrilling. He was ahead of her for once.

He opened the door to be faced with a slightly tubby, dishevelled, middle-aged man and, hanging back a little, an Asian woman in neatly-pressed jeans.

'I'm a Satanist,' Mason said immediately, assuming they were Jehovah's Witnesses.

The man smiled and held up a windowed wallet, which contained a warrant card with his photo on it.

'Detective Inspector David Jennings,' he said. 'And this is WPC Zerkah Sheikh. Could we take a minute of your time?'

'Er . . . what have I done?' Mason asked.

Jennings shrugged and chuckled. 'Who knows? What do Satanists do?'

He folded his wallet and put it away. 'We were just wondering if you'd seen Chris Bell recently. To be honest, we'd like a chat with her, but she's not home and she's not answering her calls.'

Mason took a pack of cigarettes from the inside pocket of his suit jacket, and lipped one. 'Why do you want to see her?' he asked, lighting it.

'Ah, now, I can't tell you that,' Jennings replied. 'Protocol – you know. Have you read the newspapers today?'

Mason exhaled. 'No. Haven't been out.'

The chink of glasses could be heard from down the hallway.

'Sorry, you have company,' Jennings said. 'We won't keep you. But, if you do see Ms Bell, could you ask her to get in touch with David Jennings?'

'Sure,' Mason nodded. 'Sure. I'll let her know.'

'Nice suit, Mr Dixon,' Zerkah said, as they turned to go.

'What do you think?' Jennings asked Zerkah, as they returned to the car.

'Well,' Zerkah said, strapping herself in. 'He's wearing a suit – which means he's going out or he's been out. The tie was loose, so he's obviously been wearing it a while – so I'd say he lied about having been home all day. He had a full packet of fags – and I know his routine, he doesn't keep cigarettes in the house. He must have bought them this morning, which clinches the lie. He denied having seen the papers, but didn't ask why you asked. So I reckon he *has* seen them. On top of which, he showed little sustained interest in why we wanted to see Chris – which means he already knew.'

Jennings smiled. 'Very good. But try this. He's wearing the suit because someone he wanted to impress was coming round. That person also brought the cigarettes. The visitor's a woman – one he's hoping to seduce – so the last thing he wants is for her to overhear him talking about another woman. For the same reason, he wanted to get rid of us in a hurry, which explains his lack of curiosity about the newspapers.'

'You don't believe that, do you?' Zerkah asked.

'Actually, no,' Jennings admitted. 'But it's just as plausible. And if there's one thing we should have learned over the last few weeks, it's to look for alternative plausibilities.' He looked back at the front door of Mason's flat. 'Do you think Chris is in there?'

Zerkah shrugged. 'Shall we wait and find out?'

'No,' Jennings said, ruffling his hair. 'She'll want to finish the game. She has to. And we have to catch her doing it. Our speculations aren't enough. There are three cards still to go—'

'The Sun, Judgement and the World,' Zerkah nodded.

'Plus, of course, the one she's missed – the Lovers,' Jenning said. He frowned. 'You know, I'd love to know why she skipped that one.'

'Please,' Chris said. 'I have to finish it. Please help, Mase.'

Mason had no mechanisms for saying no. Although he realised that she didn't love him, that hadn't stopped him loving her. And – oh, God, this might be the thing that turned it around. He hated himself for thinking that, but he thought it. She was asking him for something, for the first time in three years, and if he delivered, then perhaps . . . Perhaps this could just be the spark that re-ignited the pilot light in her heart.

Last attempt, then. That was all. One more go at it, and then – well, he'd at least be able to get on the plane having given it a shot.

He smiled, and put his hand out to touch her face. 'You bloody *know* I will, don't you?'

She grinned, and lifted her hand to stroke his. 'No – I really wasn't sure you would.'

Elvis popped a champagne cork and let the froth glug out into the empty glasses, as Freda hopped up onto the table, mewing.

'Weren't you?' he said, scratching the cat between the ears. 'The *rest* of us were.'

CHAPTER FORTY-SIX

The following morning at six o'clock, Mason found himself on Tower Bridge. It had been closed to traffic, and he was mingling unconvincingly with a film crew, rehearsing excuses for standing in for the expected make-up artist, whom Chris had cancelled.

He consulted the call-sheet Chris had given him, listing everyone involved in the shoot.

'Er, excuse me, Mr Kilroy,' he said, approaching the director. 'I'm Jack Wright, Make-Up . . .'

'Pete. Call me Pete,' said Pete Kilroy, distractedly. 'Set your stuff up in that trailer over there, the one that says Make-Up and Costume on the door. It's going to be a bit cramped, but the budget, frankly, is shit.'

The shoot was a commercial for Sol-Block, a sunscreen preparation, and it was to star Darryl Matlock, the bronzed and hunky star of *McLintock Quay*, an Australian soap that went out every afternoon on Channel 6. As well as exercising his thespian talents as the dimpled Mickey McLintock – a part he played with all the depth and sensitivity of a whole-rye crispbread – Darryl Matlock also took the lead in the Sol-Block Sun Oil campaign. 'Remember, mate,' he'd confide chummily to camera, 'the sun's a bit like a big breaking wave out on the Reef. It's bonza fun to go up against it – but yer gotta show some respect. That's why I use Sol-Block Sun Oil. So don't boil y'self – oil y'self. With Sol-Block.'

Mason despised the grinning, talentless berk; he was the male equivalent of a cheesecake bimbo. And Chris wasn't keen on him, either. He'd done an in-depth lifestyle interview designed to show the real man behind the hype and glamour. He'd been asked whether he tired of being seen as a bronzed and muscular sex symbol.

'Well, there's more to Darryl Matlock than that,' the bronzed and muscular sex symbol confided. 'Fr'instance – it's not something I talk about much, but I was born with this ability to see people as they really are.'

He could detect auras.

'Take you, for a case,' he told the interviewer. 'I look at you and you give off different colours, right? Like, I can tell you're quite an uppy sorta person – but something's eating you at the present time. All your colours are muddied, sorta thing. Also, if I can be blunt with you, I'd guess you were prone to constipation.'

Chris had worked out a hit that tied in neatly with Darryl's supernatural sensitivity. She'd supplied Mason with a chilled bottle of a colourless liquid that reacted to body heat, putting on a little psychedelic show of blue-to-red shift. All Mason had to do was cover Darryl in the stuff.

Leaving Pete Kilroy to shriek at the crew, Mason walked over to the trailer indicated. Twenty yards beyond it, at the southern end of the bridge, the road was taped off, and a large crowd of fans and hacks were waiting for something interesting to happen. Mason climbed the steps of the trailer and opened the door. A young woman bending over a suitcase looked past her shoulder at him.

'Hi,' she said. 'Who are you?'

'I'm Jack Wright,' Mason said. 'Make-up. Maureen couldn't come because—'

'I'm Lindy.' She waved her arm around the trailer. 'Isn't this a complete *hole*?'

'Er, terrible,' Mason agreed. 'Uh, where should I set up?'

'Take the table with the good light,' she suggested. 'Heaven knows, *I* don't need it. The entire wardrobe consists of a choice of ten pairs of swimming trunks. I'm looking forward to an easy day.'

Mason went across to the table and got out all his gear. He laid it out with the kind of precision he hoped a professional would employ. He moved the chair back, glanced at the bulbs around the mirror and moved the chair forward again. He caught his reflection, as he unpacked the bag.

You're a highly paid professional, he insisted.

'Well,' Lindy said. 'I'm going down to the set, and see what's happening – which'll be nothing at all, of course.'

'Right, yeah,' Mason agreed, dismissively. 'Nothing'll be happening all right. Sure. Why not?'

Arranged in the middle of the road a third of the way along the bridge was a beach hut, some palm trees and a sun-lounger. The whole shebang was surrounded by huge, hot, bright lights.

As Lindy and Mason watched, a helicopter swooped across the river behind them, and lifted away again with a deafening flukka-flukka-flukka.

'Jesus!' Mason gasped. 'What's that in aid of?'

'It's so they can get a shot. You know – Darryl says, "Sol-Block. Because there's nowhere that the sun don't shine," and then they cut away to the chopper shot and you can see that he's sitting on a set on Tower Bridge. Didn't you get a copy of the script?'

'Umm, no. Does that matter?'

'No, not a bit.' Lindy said. 'You're quite new to this business, aren't you?'

'Uh, pretty new, yeah,' Mason admitted.

'Well, don't worry,' Lindy reassured him, laying a hand on his arm. 'We all had to start somewhere. Just do your job – you'll be fine.'

Oh, please, he thought. Don't be nice to me. I can't bear it. If only you knew what I was here to do.

He attempted to smile. Taking a deep breath, he looked around.

'Tell me,' he asked Lindy. 'Those two Japanese guys over there – what's *their* job?'

It was two hours before Mason had to do anything. Pete Kilroy insisted on run-through after run-through to get his tracking shot correct. Darryl Matlock stood beside the sun-lounger, and as the camera was wheeled towards him, he sat down and picked up a bottle of Sol-Block. Then Pete would talk to the cameraman, Darryl would stand up, the camera would be pulled back to its starting position and they'd do it all again. Before each rehearsal, the assistant floor manager had to plead with the teenies to quit yelling at Darryl. Mason divided his time between surreptitiously watching the Japanese gentlemen on the other side of the lot, and openly staring at the constantly cheerful Matlock.

God, he thought, he's loathsome. All tanned muscle and perfect teeth. All chummy g'days and facile charm. What a plasticised prick.

Eventually, the floor manager yelled, 'All right. Kill the lights. Darryl to Make-Up, please. Everyone else take ten for a cuppa.'

Darryl wandered off the set and stood behind the camera, waving to the fans who were bawling his name. Mason screwed up his courage and walked over.

'Darryl,' he said. 'Would you like to . . . er . . .'

Darryl turned. 'G'day, mate. You Make-Up?' he smiled. 'You going to make me look presentable?'

'Uh, yeah. If you'd like to come this way . . .'

They climbed into the trailer, where Lindy was laying out various pairs of trunks.

'G'day,' Darryl said with a full-beam smile. 'What's today's cozzie?'

'Pete wants the psychedelic ones,' Lindy said. 'Very snazz, y'know?'

Mason hovered, trying to shepherd the star into the chair, convinced he was going to screw up the whole charade. Darryl pulled his T-shirt over his head, kicked away his gym shoes and peeled off his Levi's. He sat down in his shorts and faced the mirror. Mason flexed his fingers, trying to look as though he was making informed and professional decisions.

'I guess you're going to have to soak me, mate,' Darryl said helpfully. 'I'm supposed to just've got out of the ocean.'

'Yeah. Right. Uh, the problem here,' Mason bluffed, 'is what we call *shine* . . .'

'I can see how it would be,' Darryl nodded, encouragingly

'Well, er, I think we'll start with just the teeniest bit of eye-liner,' Mason suggested.

'Reckon I'll need me whole eyeballs painted,' Darryl grinned. 'Had a bit of a razz last night.'

Mason cluttered around in his case and found a pencil. He felt quite confident about this bit. He'd done Elvis's eyes eight times the previous day. He was surprised at how steady his hand was.

'Look up,' he murmured, leaning in to Darryl's face.

'So – there aren't many bloke make-up artists about, mate, are there?' Darryl said, as Mason traced his lower eyelid.

'Uh, no. Other eye.'

'So what got you into the business?'

'Oh, you know. Just sort of drifted in,' Mason said.

'Know what you mean, blue. Same here. Reckon I'd still be working for the Melbourne Parks Department if it hadn't been for dumb luck. And I was a bloody great gardener too. Pity I'm such a shit actor. Tell you a funny thing I realised last night?' Darryl said, as Mason rummaged around in his box for something to do. 'I was looking at a bottle of Sol-Block, 'cause they send me cases full of the shit gratis, and I worked out that Sol-Block is an anagram of bollocks!'

He laughed delightedly – and Mason snorted a giggle too, before he remembered what a twat Darryl was.

'Bollocks! I love it!' Darryl went on. 'Wouldn't that be great, if they mistyped the script? Imagine it. I'm up there on me lounger, flashing the pearly-whites and dying for a beer, and I say, "When you're having fun at the beach, don't forget to rub on y'bollocks." Hahaha! Killer!'

Mason wished Darryl would shut up. Or at least be a little less likeable.

'What's that stuff, mate?' Darryl asked, as Mason took a small bottle from a chillbag and tipped some of the colourless liquid onto a piece of cotton wool.

'It's new, glycerine-based,' he said, as rehearsed. 'We rub it on, then spray you, and it makes the water droplets more photogenic. It's really good.'

'Oh, right. Whack it on. Wow – that's cold! You been storing it in the Esky?'

'Yeah.'

Keep the fluid cold, Chris had said. Don't let it start changing colour before he gets on the set. Mason smeared the stuff all over Darryl's chest and neck. Replenishing the cotton wool at intervals, he did his back and legs. Finally, he blotted it on to Darryl's friendly, trusting face.

The floor manager stuck his head into the trailer. 'Can we have the artist on set, please? We're ready to go.'

Mason doused Darryl with water from a spray-bottle, and ran a comb through his damp hair. Lindy handed him a pair of swimming trunks which he changed into, totally unabashed, right there in front of them.

'Well, thanks, mate,' Darryl said, shrugging on a bathrobe. 'Now let's go and sell over-priced shit to the masses.'

'What a nice fella,' Lindy smiled, as the door closed and the shrieking started up again. 'Really genuine, you know?'

'Yeah. I'm afraid so,' Mason sighed. 'You're dribbling, by the way.'

Lindy laughed. 'We'd better get out there. I'd bring your water-spray, if I were you, in case he needs re-damping.'

The assistant floor manager was pleading with the fans for silence as Darryl sauntered onto the set. He handed his bathrobe to a gopher, and took his position in front of the sun-lounger.

'Lights, please,' Kilroy shouted, and the set was flooded with tropical summer. 'All right, let's try to get this first time. And . . . action!'

Even from twenty feet back, Mason could feel the heat of the lights. As the camera rolled in, attended by its little gaggle of technicians, Darryl sat back on the sun-lounger, and picked up the bottle of over-priced shit.

'It's beaut to be out on a day like this,' he recited, laying the accent on thick, 'but the sun can do damage to unprotected skin, mate. So, I use Sol-Block Oil. It helps you get a full-on tan, and at the same time protects you from harmful UVs . . .'

The director, who had been watching with his arms crossed, dropped his hands to his sides and gaped. The camera operator peered out from behind the lens to look at Darryl with the naked eye. Little squawks of concern could be heard from way back along the bridge. Darryl was beginning to look very odd indeed.

'So, if you're going for a healthy skin-tone, rub on Sol-Block,' Darryl told the camera, with an affable grin, 'because there's nowhere that the sun don't shine!'

Sorry, mate, Mason thought.

Darryl was a fluorescent bruise of cerise and turquoise. He was lit up like a tourist trap. Put a bouncer in front of him, and he could have passed for a Las Vegas stripjoint.

'CUT!' screamed the floor manager. 'What the fuck is going on?'

It was time to go. Mason turned and strode quickly towards the end of the bridge. Ahead of him, two hundred teenage girls were bleating in dismay. In a wave of tears and hormones, they broke through the tape and galloped towards him, heading singlemindedly for the object of their concern. Working against the flow, Mason was buffeted from side to side by stampeding girlies and puffing hacks, but eventually he made it to the foot of the bridge. He didn't dare look back in case he saw Darryl's technicolour body being ripped to souvenirs.

Chris's red Sierra was parked a hundred yards away. Its brake lights flashed and the engine turned over. The lights flashed again, frantically, and Elvis's head appeared through the sun-roof.

'Mason, run!' he hollered, pointing.

Mason glanced behind to see the two Japanese suits pounding along the pavement in his direction.

'Oh, fuck,' he muttered.

He began to sprint as the Sierra pulled out into the road. He could hear running feet gaining on him, but he was almost level with the car as it rolled forward in second, the back door flung open. He dived onto the rear seat, as a hand closed around his ankle. The car took off. Mason jerked his leg in panic and felt his plimsoll come loose. Elvis leaned back to slam the door, and they careered away along the street.

One of the Japanese flung Mason's plimsoll at the car in disgust as the Sierra rocked left towards the City. Slumped in the back, Mason blew out his breath and stared wide-eyed at Elvis, who grinned at him from the passenger seat.

Mason was trembling. It was a nightmare – literally, it was a nightmare. His recurring one, in which he was pursued by undissuadable sociopaths who intended to do him terrible harm. He put his hand on his chest, which felt tight and breathless.

Easing the car back down to a legal speed, Chris glanced at Mason in the rear-view.

'You okay?' she said. 'In one piece?'

He shook his head, bewildered. 'I lost my shoe,' he gasped, at last.

'But apart from that, Cinders,' Elvis said, 'did you have a ball?'

CHAPTER FORTY-SEVEN

Everyone has a nightmare – the gasping, sweaty one that makes the dreamer fumble panickily for the light. The one that leaves you too scared to go back to sleep but also too rigidly immobile to potter downstairs for a glass of milk. Being chased was Mason's primary shrieking duvet-soaker. He was profoundly upset by having to sprint from the Naganitaki people. It stripped the adulthood off him like cheap paint, and brought out the textured grain of childish terror.

When they got to Camden, Elvis and Chris steered him from the car to the flat. Carrying his remaining plimsoll, he walked blankly up the steps and unlocked the door like a clockwork creature.

'Well, me hearties,' Elvis said, as Mason collapsed onto the sofa, 'I think we should splice the mainbrace. I'll just nip down to the offy and get one. Won't be a tick.'

He slammed the front door behind him, and the flat was silent. Freda strolled in and leapt onto Mason's lap. He started to stroke her absently.

'You okay, Mase?' Chris asked.

'They wanted to *hurt* me, those Japanese guys,' he murmured, perplexedly. 'They wanted to *beat me up* or something.' He was staring across the room at his CD collection, but he was seeing vengeful Orientals. 'Did they have big cleavers?' he asked. 'I'm sure they had great big cleavers.'

'No. They were just running after you,' Chris told him, gently.

'Yeah? Really? I was sure they had great big cleavers . . .'

'Mason, get a grip, love,' Chris said. 'It was only a little sprint.'

'It's just so fucking mad,' he continued, still gazing at the records. 'Why did I put myself in that position? I mean, it's not like I even *care*. It's not *my* fight. It's all right for *you* – you're the Joker. But me – I was only doing it because you *told* me to. It's completely fucking pathetic.'

'Mason, nobody *made* you do it,' Chris said. She lit a cigarette and blew smoke out.

'No. No, you're right,' he agreed, shaking his head. 'That's what's so pathetic.' He turned to her. 'You know, he's a perfectly likeable bloke, Darryl Matlock. A bit brash, maybe – but I can't say I would mind having a drink with him.'

'He peddles crap,' Chris said, irritated. 'Just because he's a third-division actor in a second-rate soap, he has half the Western world hanging on his every utterance – and then he makes out like he's the master of mysterious forces. Auras! Fuck him!'

Mason lifted Freda on to the floor, got to his feet, and walked over to the music rack. 'No. *You* fuck him if you want to,' he said. 'I'm not playing any more.'

Chris looked at him incredulously. '*You're not playing any more*? Christ, you sound like a little kid!'

'Well, I guess you'd know,' he said, not looking at her, as he flicked through the CDs. 'But at least *I* only act like a kid when I'm pissed off. I don't make an expensive hobby of it.'

She leapt up, bright with anger, salt rage in her eyes.

'Listen – they're all bastards!' she insisted. 'All of them! Charlatans and con-artists. They feed like parasites on people's fear and misery; they get fat on the gullible and lost. And all the while, even as they're sucking the blood from your neck, they whisper sugary lies and sooth-ing fairy stories in your ear, so you don't even notice you're being leeched dry.'

Mason slid the disc onto the tray, and pushed it in with one finger. He looked over his shoulder at her. 'Sounds like a pretty accurate definition of a tabloid journalist to me,' he said, shrugging.

Chris stiffened, blanched. She was staring at him, gulping back her fury. '*Just fuck off, Mason!*' she screeched, and strode out to the kitchen, smacking the door with her hand as she went.

'Oh, wait,' he called after her. 'You'll like this. It's "Knock on Wood".' He waited a beat, but she didn't bite.

'Well, Freda, *we* like it, don't we?' he picked the cat up and danced her around in the air as he sang along.

Freda struggled free, and retreated behind the TV. Mason whacked the volume up on the stereo, lay down on the sofa and closed his eyes.

Concentrating on Eddie Floyd's hymn to superstition, he didn't notice Freda leaving. Or Chris, either.

Five hours later, Elvis and Mason were sitting on the floor, surrounded by the debris of an afternoon's dedicated drinking. Four dead wine bottles were ranked along the windowsill, the current bottle of port was down to its last half-inch and Freda was curled up asleep in an empty pizza box.

'Where'd I put my fags?' Mason asked, woozily.

Sighing, Elvis lay back, flat out on the carpet, his arms flung wide.

'C'mon, Elvis, what'd I do with, hic, my cigarettes? Help me look, you lazy bastard.'

'Okay,' said Elvis, staring straight up, 'I tell you what we'll do, okay? We'll divide the room in half, and you search one half and I'll search the other half. All right?'

Mason frowned at him unsteadily, blinking.

'Well,' Elvis announced after a few seconds, eyes still fixed on the ceiling, 'they're not in the *top* half . . .'

There was a moment's pause, and then they both curled up in fits of drunken giggles.

'Sall right,' Mason said, when he stopped sniggering, 'here they are. I was sitting on them.'

'Where do you think Chris has gone?' Elvis asked.

'Who cares?'

'I think we should try and find her. She's still going to need help with the remaining hits.'

'You do what you like. I'm out.'

'Where do you think she'll go?'

'To hell, with any luck.'

There was a long silence, interrupted by a little belching fit from Mason.

'Right, I'm off home then,' Elvis said, hauling himself to his feet. 'I'll call you if I find her.'

'Whatever. Thanks for the booze,' Mason nodded, also attempting to get up.

'S'okay – stay sat sitting there. I'll see myself out. So long, y'all. Don't be a stranger, now, y'hear?'

Mason slumped back to the floor. 'Bye.'

After the front door closed, he remained cross-legged on the carpet, tipping the fag-ash into an empty glass. Eventually he realised how drunk he was and he crawled to the bedroom, cigarette drooping from his lip, port bottle clasped in his fist. He climbed onto the bed and lay there, hiccupping, stretched out on his back, an arm across his eyes.

'Oh, God,' he whispered, as the dead cigarette dropped from his hand onto the pillow. He was two breaths away from sleep.

'Now what have I done?'

CHAPTER FORTY-EIGHT

On the small stage of the Parson's Green Spiritualist Meeting House stood Iris Potts, an iced doughnut of a woman in her pastel cotton frock and her pink-wool cardigan.

Walking to the lip of the platform, she smiled at her at audience, which overwhelmingly consisted of other women in their confectionery years: brittle crystallized-violet women, powdered turkish-delight women, women moist and spongy as sherry trifle, and sticky baked-alaska women, melting in the afternoon heat.

'Does anybody have an object they would like me to read?' Iris asked, in a reassuring, motherly tone. 'Any little knick-knack or possession of a loved one, who might be with us in this world or gone over?'

Many demerara-speckled hands were raised, and Iris scanned the volunteers. 'Yes, dear,' she said pointing. 'Yes, dear, you. The lady in the beige blouse.'

A thin and tired-looking woman, like yesterday's brandy-snap, came to the front, clutching some small treasure to her chest. Iris Potts's husband, Dennis, got up from his front-row seat and gallantly helped her negotiate the two small steps to the stage.

'What's your name, dear?' Iris inquired – softly it seemed, though she could be heard right at the back of the hall.

'Patsie,' came the nervous reply.

'Patsie,' Iris repeated. 'And are you one of our new friends, or have you been with us at a meeting before, dear?'

'I've seen you before,' Patsie admitted, shakily.

'Ah, isn't that nice? Now, do you have something you would like me to try and read, Patsie?' Iris asked, holding out her hand.

Patsie gave Iris the trinket she had been holding to her bosom, seeming at once eager to show it and reluctant to let it go. Iris regarded it solemnly.

'It's a penknife, isn't it?' she asked Patsie.

Patsie nodded, confirming that a penknife was indisputably what it was.

Iris held it up. It was a sturdy instrument, made to last. Over many years, the silver plating had been worn away in a thumbprint above the folding blade, and the clasp that might link to a keyring was twisted from innumerable bendings in and out. There was no sign of rust, and one could imagine that each of the various blades and gadgets would spring out easily at the merest tug.

Iris enclosed the penknife in her hands, as if she was preparing to pray. She closed her eyes, and raised her chin a little.

There was a fragile hush in the hall.

'Yes . . .' Iris breathed. 'Yes. I'm feeling a very . . . a very *masculine* force. A very *manly* vibration.' She opened her eyes, and looked at the quivering Patsie, who was biting her bottom lip and and nodding slightly. 'There's *love* here,' Iris continued. 'A strong love. And . . .' She closed her eyes again. 'And . . . a sense of loss. Oh, dear. Oh, dear me . . .'

She opened her eyes. 'Yes, a *terrible* loss. And suffering . . .' She sighed, shaking her head sorrowfully.

'Yes,' Patsie gulped. 'Yes.'

'Yes. It's very strong now. The love and the suffering all mixed up together. I'm getting the image of a down-to-earth sort of man. A no-nonsense man.'

'Yes,' Patsie agreed, the hint of a smile shining through the tears that were gathering in her pale eyes.

Iris chuckled. 'But with a sense of humour. A big-hearted fellow, who likes a laugh from time to time.'

Patsie was definitely smiling now, though the tears were teetering on her lashes. Almost imperceptibly, her lips were opening and shutting, as if she were miming the word 'pie'.

'And . . . a name. Oh, it's not very clear . . .' Iris opened her hands and gazed at the penknife cupped in them. She turned her face back towards Patsie. 'A name. Is it – does it begin with a P, perhaps? Or an M?'

Patsie gazed back, willing Iris to pick up the vibration of the name from the precious penknife.

'Or . . . No, it's not clear,' Iris sighed. 'It's . . . I'm getting a B . . .'

Patsie's eyes widened momentarily, and her little fists clenched at her sides.

'Yes,' Iris nodded. 'Yes, I do think it's B.'

Patsie nodded back at her. She could contain her excitement no longer.

'*Bill!*' she cried; but her voice was drowned out by Iris, also crying *Bill!* just a split second before her – or perhaps after. It was difficult to tell.

'Bill. Yes, Bill,' Iris said, smiling at Patsie. 'That's right, isn't it, dear? And I get the feeling of a *big* man. Is that right, dear? A *big* man?'

'Well,' Patsie said doubtfully, raising her hand to indicate Bill's height. 'About so big.'

Apparently Bill clocked in around five-eight.

'No, no, dear,' Iris interrupted. 'I don't mean *tall*. I mean, *well built*. Solid. You know.'

'Oh, yes,' agreed the bird-like Patsie, happily. 'Big-boned.'

'Yes, you're right. Big-boned,' Iris told her.

She clasped the penknife tight in her hands again, and closed her eyes. The whispering and chattering that had started to susurrate around the hall died down. Patsie maintained her expression of apprehensive expectation.

'Now,' Iris murmured. 'What else?'

She gazed straight ahead, and slightly downwards. She appeared almost to be in a trance, her unseeing eyes fixed, as it happened, on her husband Dennis, sitting slap in the middle of the front row. She seemed to have forgotten about Patsie, and about everyone else in the room, though they were all staring at her with faces full of tingling suspense. Iris was breathing heavily, and shuddering a little.

'Now . . . ah . . . I feel . . . that Bill is no longer . . . ah . . . with the ones he loves,' she intoned between breaths.

Patsie nodded slightly, though Iris could not have seen it. In fact, to see it at all, you would have had to have been sitting, for instance, slap in the middle of the front row.

'He's . . . has he? Ah, he's gone over to the other side.'

An expression of panic and dismay flashed across Patsie's features. The entire room was transfixed – with the exception of Dennis who, accustomed to this kind of thing, was fiddling idly with his fingers as they lay clasped in his lap.

'No. No,' Iris corrected herself. 'No. He hasn't gone over. But . . . ah . . . he can't be with his loved ones at the moment. That's right.'

Patsie's shoulders dropped a little, in relief.

'I get a . . . ah . . . a sense of illness here. Ah . . .'

Patsie chewed her lower lip, leaning forward for the next word.

'Hospitals, perhaps,' Iris breathed, still gazing fixedly ahead. 'Yes. Ah, medicine. It's a worrying time. Ah . . . so much suffering . . . But such a love of life! Such fight and spirit.'

Iris's bosom was rising and falling with each tremulous breath.

'A good man. A good, strong, honest man. Fighting . . . fighting hard against so much suffering. And still, yes, still this strong, *strong* feeling of love. *A love that conquers all!*'

With a final, long exhalation of breath, like someone setting down a great burden, Iris let her head and shoulders slump, and she was still.

There were a few moments' frozen silence, and then Iris lifted her head, and turned to Patsie.

'Here you are, dear,' she sighed, handing back the penknife. 'I hope that I've been of some help or comfort to you. Did you get anything from that? Did it make any sense to you at all?'

'Oh, yes!' Patsie beamed, tears running in droplets down her cheeks. 'Thank you so much. Thank you so much.'

'There's no need to thank me, dear,' Iris assured her, patting her arm. 'We all do what we can, don't we?'

CHAPTER FORTY-NINE

'Bart, it's Chris.'

'Good morrow, sweet thing. How are you?'

'Fine. Listen, I need a favour. Do you still know that woman who works on Channel 6's *About Faith*?'

'Phillippa? Yes. A saucy strumpet, once her guard, amongst other things, was down. What of her?'

'Well, they're doing a live transmission from one of Iris Potts's meetings on Thursday, and I want you to find out the format for me.'

'Do you, sweetie? Why would you want me to do that?'

'You just get the gen – discreetly, mind you. I don't want her to realise you've got it, if possible – and then I'll tell you what I want it for.'

'This wouldn't have anything to do with a portrait that has been adorning the front page of a certain tabloid, would it?'

'You're a terrible smartass, Bart, aren't you? Look, do you think you could do it in the next twenty-four hours, and call me? My mobile's about to give out and I haven't got my charger with me, so you can get me at the Holiday Inn Marble Arch. I'm registered in the name of Alice de Crowley.'

'Haha! And then you have the nerve to call *me* a smartass! Listen, come round to the flat this afternoon, and I'll give you whatever I can get.'

She hung up, smiling. That was one of the things she liked about Bart – he was totally unjudgemental. You asked, he gave. No agonising, no weighing of ramifications. He just did it because you were a friend and he trusted your needs.

Whereas Mason was all questions, doubt, prevarication. Even when he acquiesced, he did it with existential spin. '*You bloody know I will, don't you?*' As if he had no choice in the matter. As if he was scripted.

When they'd first met, she'd been fascinated by that. She was younger and less sure. She'd loved the way he had of conjuring every angle, second-guessing every response. Bart had engineered a dinner-party meeting at the flat the two of them shared, and Chris had fancied Mason immediately – the louche slump on one elbow with the cigarette, the unironed shirt, the darting, appraising eyes. She watched him watching Bart, who was holding forth with his accustomed languid articulacy – and though Bart was moisteningly funny, Mason was dry as powdered gin. His intermittent comments were slivers of dark, bitter chocolate on Bart's rich soufflé.

At the close of the evening, when only the three of them were left, he said to her, 'We're fucked now, aren't we? I'm too shy to ask you to stay, and you're too hard to allow yourself to ask to. Tell you what – I'll get Bart to suggest it, which'll let us both off.'

Chris had been both shocked and impressed. God – he *understood.* And he *said* that he understood. All the bouncing rays of possibility and self-consciousness and potential rejection were focussed into the beam of a sentence. She'd laughed and stayed.

Now, though, all this time later, that ploy looked like a trick with mirrors, a way of illuminating the sleight of hand, rather than showing the light. Now, faced with that conjuror's scam, she'd say, 'Just ask. Be honest. *Ask.*' But he never asked – not straight out. He was still performing the same clever defensive trick.

And yet – God – that comment he'd made today about tabloid journalists. The boy still had it. That was what she had loved in him. So fucking smart and quick when he was riled. Was she infuriated? Christ, she was. He could still get to her like that. No one else could get to her quite like that.

Chris opened the minibar and took out a beer, and schlipped it open. She thought again about Mason going away. She gave a little gulping chuckle. No – he'd never go. Never.

But God knows what she'd do if she thought he might.

The mobile phone trilled, and she picked it up. The display told her it was her messaging service calling. She'd been ignoring it for two days, but now she checked in. There were fifteen calls from her treacherous editor, all of which she skipped through, but they were interspersed with halting communiqués from David Jennings.

'Chris – it's David Jennings. Could you call me back?'
BLEEP.

'Chris. You've seen the papers, of course. I really think we ought to talk.'

BLEEP.

'It's David. Look, this is completely resolvable. Please do call me. I think you'll agree you owe me as much.'

BLEEP.

'Chris. This is obviously very difficult for both of us, I'm aware of that. We both have to do what we have to do. But . . . look, just call me. Please. That's all I ask.'

BLEEP.

'David again. Chris – please try to understand – I have to do my job. What's going to happen is—'

BIP-BIP-BIP

Chris's phone died.

'. . . Thing is,' Mason sniffed tipsily, as his companion dozed beside him, 'I miss her even more when we've had a row. I can go a whole week without seeing her when we've had a good day together. But if we've argued, I just want to phone her all the time.'

His bedmate stirred in her sleep, black hair ruffled against the pillow, oblivious to what was, Mason had to admit, a litany of self-pity.

'It seems like I'm always messing it up – but it can't *all* be my fault, can it?' He reached for his cigarettes and lit one, then slumped back and gazed at the ceiling. 'She might need my help. And what have I done? Thrown a petulant little fit and deserted her when she needs me.'

Beside him, the green eyes opened, and gazed at him impassively.

'She'll probably never speak to me again,' Mason sighed, reaching the bottle of port from the bedside table. It was empty. He dropped it onto the carpet, with a belching tut. 'Jesus, I'm so dumb. Just when it was going so well, too. I can't believe I've fucked it all up again.'

With a languorous stretch, and an expression of supreme indifference, Freda got to her feet and leapt down from the bed. There were many things she was prepared to do for left-over pizza, but listen to this kind of drivel wasn't one of them.

It was seven-thirty in the evening, and Mason had just woken up, hungover, still drunk and sahara-thirsty. He tipped himself onto the floor, which seemed to have become very uneven and soft, and stumbled to the kitchen, feeling his way along the wall, one hand on the dado rail for support. He discovered, to his bleary delight, that he'd had the foresight to stash a fresh bottle of vodka in the freezer. It glooped syrupily into a Garfield mug, and he knocked a mouthful back, standing by the window, and looking out onto the little patch of weeds that he referred to as the garden. He swayed and steadied himself against the kitchen door, swallowing hard as he tried to keep the vodka down. It whooshed straight into his system, reactivating several bottles of Muscadet and a lot of port. The fence at the back of the yard tipped to and fro. He gulped back another mouthful.

Bart had once coined the expression 'patchwork guilt', which he'd defined as the feeling that, although you're basically a reasonable and acceptable person, there's a whole bunch of little things in your past of which you're not particularly proud. That warm summer evening Mason added another square of calico inexcusability to the ever-increasing acreage of his personal discomforter.

It started with one of those inebriate notions that seem irresistible at the time. Mason gazed at the dandelions and bindweed in the garden, and decided that something should be done. He wandered out there with his mug of vodka and waded into the overgrowth, tutting and saying aloud, 'It's a disgrace. Total disgrace. Was lovely, this garden, when I moved in. Shouldn't have let it get out of control like this.'

He put the mug down on a rock, and dropped to his knees. He started yanking out handfuls of bindweed, lodging the ripped-up tendrils under one armpit and muttering, 'Awful, awful stuff. Runs riot. Got to go.'

He followed the thick roots across the garden, tugging them up above the soil, hand over hand, following them to their source. 'Stubborn fucking bastards,' he growled, reaching back to pick up the vodka and swig it.

He realised that he needed a tool of some kind. At the second attempt, he got to his feet and staggered back into the kitchen, where he found a breadknife. It also occurred to him that he needed a radio. Because that's what people do when they work in the garden, he told himself fuzzily – they listen to the radio.

Having ricocheted from wall to wall down the hallway, he took the alarm-radio from the bedroom, and eventually managed to plug the lead into a power point in the kitchen. He stood the radio in the doorway to the garden, and then he sloped outside again and sank to the ground. He started hacking at bindweed roots with the breadknife, pausing occasionally to slurp from the mug of vodka. He sawed away, clumsy but diligent, at the woody roots, watching the green insides fracture and fray. He could hear himself breathing hard, as if it was someone else. It was several minutes before he realised that he had forgotten to turn the radio on.

'Silly sod,' he scolded. With the knife still in his hand, he crawled on all fours back to the doorway, warning himself, 'Careful, careful. Dangerous things, knives.'

He hit the button on the radio, and his mother said, '. . . My best advice is to consult your doctor, Alan – will you do that?'

Mason burped with sudden tearful surprise, as the presenter announced that Maria Dixon would be right back after this travel bulletin.

'Mum!' he howled, immobile there on the back porch on his hands and knees.

He picked up the radio in both hands, the knife still in his fist, the point of it wavering beside his eyeball.

'It's me,' he told it, his voice catching. 'It's Mason.'

An eighty-percent-proof tear rolled down his cheek.

'It's *me*!' he whispered.

The station ident played, Maria was reintroduced, and the call-in number announced.

Mason pulled himself to his feet, one hand on the doorframe, and lurched through the flat to the front room, where he collapsed onto the sofa next to the phone. Very, very carefully, he dialled the number, whispering, 'Come on, come on . . .'

'LondonWave. Good evening,' said a man's voice.

'I'm so unhappy,' Mason whined. 'I am so, so unhappy. I need to talk to Maria.'

'Brilliant,' said the man, gleefully. 'Don't hang up.'

'And who do we have on line three?' Maria asked.

'I'm a first-time caller,' Mason said, throatily.

'And what's your name, dear?'

Mason sniffed a couple of times, and then burst into tears. 'Mum,' he wept, 'it's Mason. I'm so unhappy. Help me. I'm so fucking unhappy. Please—'

They cut him off immediately, of course.

*   *   *

Half an hour later, Maria rang the front-door bell. Mason staggered to open it, a bread knife in one hand, a bottle of vodka in the other, his jeans and T-shirt smeared with garden dirt and the green stains of hacked weeds. His face was streaked with grimy tears.

'Hello,' he said, miserably. 'I think I'm going to be sick.'

In the circumstances, Maria was surprisingly reasonable about the entire thing. She simply made her son wash his face and go to bed.

She was still there in the morning when he woke up, making breakfast in the pristine and gleaming kitchen.

'Good morning, dear,' she said as he padded in and slumped into a chair.

'Sorry,' he groaned. 'I was completely out of it last night.'

'Drink your orange juice,' she told him.

She didn't speak again until he'd eaten some cornflakes and got through a couple of cups of tea. She just bustled about putting laundry in the machine and changing the bed linen.

Eventually, she came back to the kitchen and stood there looking at her son.

'Come here,' she said, spreading her arms. He got up and hugged her.

'Does this make me pathetic?' he asked, holding her tight. 'I mean, am I the only twenty-seven-year-old on the planet – outside of Yank soaps – who needs a hug from their mum every now and then?'

'I seriously doubt it,' Maria assured him.

They both sat down at the table, and Maria poured herself a cup of tea. 'Is this about Chris?' she asked.

Mason sighed. 'Leave it be, Mum. Really. It'll do what it does.'

'I know. But someone's got to give you two a boot up the backside. You're obviously not going to do it yourselves.'

'Well, actually, we had a bit of a barney yesterday morning, so I think we're not speaking at the moment.'

'So I gather. She came round for tea with us in the afternoon.'

'Oh, yeah? And you told her she was making a big mistake in letting me slip away, did you?'

'Certainly not. Don't flatter yourself, dear. You were not the central topic of conversation. But I did ask if she'd seen you recently, and I sensed a little anger amidst the affection with which she spoke of you.'

Mason snorted. 'Other way round, I would have thought.'

'The trouble with both of you,' Maria said, 'is that you expect it to be wine and roses all the way. Neither of you is prepared to put in any effort. At the first sign of trouble, one or other of you is off.'

'I blame the parents,' he told her. 'So did she tell you anything else, umm, exciting? Unusual?'

'Oh, this Trickster thing, you mean. Yes. She wanted Bart's help in her next little escapade, apparently.'

'Bart's? What for?'

'Er, for Judgement? Is that the next card? I wasn't really paying attention at that point. I was in and out to the kitchen, trying to keep a Victoria sponge enthusiastic. Anyway, they seemed very excited about it.'

Mason recognised that old frisson of jealousy again. He figured he'd be stuck with it the rest of his life. It would be a recurring twinge that was almost welcome, like rheumatism in a bone broken long ago.

'So who are they going to hit?' he asked, attempting to sound as if he could care more.

'Iris Potts? That psychic woman? She's doing some sort of appearance at a spooky-loonies dinner, where some of the objects, unbeknownst to her, are going to belong to famous people. Apparently the television company consider they've got a bit of a scoop because they're going to give her Prince Charles's pullover, or something. Bart talked this out of some ex-floozie he knows.'

'But what's *Chris* going to do?'

'I don't know, dear,' she said, reaching for a slice of toast and the butter. 'Why don't you phone Bart and ask him?'

'No. No, it's okay. Forget it. It really doesn't matter.' He poured some more juice. 'Umm . . . Have you heard from Dad?'

Maria looked at him, and sighed. 'No, darling. I'm sorry.' She frowned as Mason lit a cigarette, but he was pretty sure that she wouldn't pick this moment to start in on him about it. 'I do think he cares for you, you know. But he just can't cope with some things. He has a lot on his mind, I think.'

She'd always done this, all Mason's life. Tried to give the impression that his father was perfect in every way, except for the small matter of a rather lovable absentmindedness when it came to his son. It wasn't, Mason suspected, that she wanted to protect him, but to make him think that he hadn't sprung from the loins of an irresponsible bastard.

He tutted. 'I'm okay with it now. And he does have some sense of propriety. At least he didn't leave me entirely in the lurch at the hotel.'

Maria looked up from buttering her toast. 'Didn't he? What did he do to make that better?'

'Well, you know,' Mason said, reaching for a croissant. 'He phoned you and Bart to tell you to come and look after me, because he wasn't going to show.'

She put down the butterknife, and sat back, apparently astonished. 'No, Mason. Daddy didn't call us.'

'Huh?'

'Chris did. She told us you were going to the hotel, and that she was worried how you'd react if your father reneged, as he always has.' She leaned across and stroked her son's cheek. 'Chris really does care for you, you know.'

Mason knew that was true. She did. But it was the *way* in which she cared for him that he found perplexing. It could have been anything from real romantic love, albeit obstructed by history and circumstance, to companionable matiness, confused by the same things. He still wasn't really sure where she lay on that scale. And it didn't matter what grimly optimistic resolves he made to stop worrying about it, the quandary still exercised his heart. He could see that it was impossible, despite any intellectual, forensic analysis, to truly believe that someone you loved didn't love you back.

He stared out at the mugged garden for a few moments. He'd really made a mess of it, to be honest. He sighed and tore a lump off a croissant and stuffed it in his mouth. He was buggered if he knew what to think.

'What do you believe in, Mum?' he asked, chomping.

Without a second's hesitation, Maria said, 'Kindness and honesty.' Then she smiled. 'That sounds terribly wishy-washy, doesn't it?'

Mason shrugged, and swallowed.

'Sounds bloody difficult to me.'

* * *

That afternoon, the telephone rang in Iris and Dennis Potts's fussy North London semi. Dennis answered.

'Potts,' he said.

'Hello,' said a female voice. 'Could I speak to Iris Potts, please?'

'I'm afraid she's resting at the moment,' Dennis replied, peering around the living-room door to where his wife was watching *The High Chaparral* with a can of light ale in her hand. 'Perhaps I can help?' As was his habit, he picked up a pencil and prepared to scribble notes on the pad that was kept by the phone. Beside the pad was a card that had arrived in the post that morning. It meant nothing to Dennis.

'Well, I thought *I* might be able to help *you*,' said the woman. 'I'm a great admirer of your wife's work, and I'd hate to see her, you know, ridiculed by people who don't know any better.'

Dennis frowned. 'What do you mean, dear?'

'Well, I work for Channel 6 on the *About Faith* programme and . . . Well, you know this show that your wife's appearing in tomorrow at the *About Faith* dinner?'

'Yes,' said Dennis, calmly. He was quite used to allowing callers as long as they needed to get to the point. You often picked up a lot of useful information along the way.

'Well, you know this Trickster person that's been doing all these terrible things to people who practise the esoteric arts?'

'Ye-es. I know.'

'Well, they've tracked him down. And one of my colleagues on the production team – you know what that is, a production team?'

'Yes!' said Dennis, rather more curtly than he'd intended.

'Well, they're going to give Iris his jersey – this Trickster person's. You know, to see if she can tell. Because, well, he must be a very bad man. And some people on the show think that, you know, she'll say nice things because, well, she usually *is* so nice about people.'

'Well, it's very kind of you to tell us this, er, what did you say your name was?'

'Philippa. Oh! Oh, no! I didn't mean to tell you that!'

Dennis wrote down *Is there a Philippa on production team? Check!*

'Well, don't worry, Philippa. Your secret is safe with us.'

'The thing is,' the woman carried on, 'I don't suppose Iris needs me to tell her these things. You know, what with being psychic. I mean, as if she'd be fooled by a horrid trick like that!'

'No, of course she wouldn't, Philippa,' Dennis reassured her.

'Well, that's what I said to my husband,' the woman explained. 'Iris wouldn't be taken in by a horrid trick like that, I said. Zif!'

CHAPTER FIFTY

Months after the Trickster's campaign became no more than a twenty-second item on TV retrospectives of the year 2000, Mason would still catch sight of himself in mirrors and be surprised.

He expected to see this straight, actually quite-noble nose, like his dad's. But he was confronted with a hawkish beak, bent in a bump at the top and a bit crooked. He didn't mind it – in fact, he thought it lent him a rather rakish charm – but it was a bit like looking at a portrait of himself. He'd find himself thinking, 'Well, not a bad likeness, but there's something not quite right about the shnozz.'

It was Elvis, of course, who convinced him to go. They'd met in the Orange Pub, and Mason told him offhandedly what his mother had let slip about Iris Potts. Elvis had become extremely animated.

'After all this, Mason old love, how can we duck out?' He grabbed Mason's lapels and pulled him across the table, causing beer to slop onto the polished wood. 'What are you? A quitter? Da Boss ain't gonna like dat, Joey. Dis is family – *capisce*?'

He reached into his inside pocket – he was wearing a dappled-grey denim floor-length coat, like something out of a spaghetti western – and produced the list.

0	The Fool	Chuckie Rolls
I	The Magician	Peter Pinkus
II	The High Priestess	Melody Peters
III	The Empress	Dawn Mabbut
IV	The Emperor	Cliff Benching
V	The Hierophant	Reverend Cutforth
VI	The Lovers	
VII	The Chariot	Morris Keen
VIII	Strength	Damon Chiswick

'Look – three to go. She hasn't done the Lovers – we know that now. And Iris Potts must be Judgement.' He sat back, grinned, and sipped his pint, watching Mason stare at the list.

'Elvis,' Mason said at last, 'it's a question of principle. I promised myself that if anyone so much as mentioned further involvement in this Trickster thing, I'd say no.'

Elvis nodded and put his glass down. 'Okay. As you wish.' He leaned across and took the list. There was a brief pause as they both gazed around the pub.

'Hey, Mason,' Elvis said brightly, 'do you think we should remain uninvolved in the final stages of the Trickster thing?'

Mason tutted, and chuckled.

'No,' he said, principledly.

For Zerkah Sheikh, one of the original attractions of being a police officer had been the hours. She loved the idea of the shiftwork rotation – week of earlies, week of lates, week of nights. It meant she wouldn't be available for the desperate ritual of family weekend lunches, or the sororial trips to bloody Lakeside and Allders. But she'd gone and landed herself a plainclothes job, hadn't she? A default nine-to-five, with the departures from that schedule driven by the whim of the Trickster. Might as well work in a bank, for all the help it was in excusing her from tribal custom.

So she lied. This weekend there was a wedding on, and she'd lied big-time. 'Sorry, Ummaji, something's come up. Can't get out of it. Give my love to Nazir and Ausia. Sorry . . . Sorry . . . Bye . . .'

Trouble was, having lied about working, she had to work. She couldn't bring herself to go to the movies, or out with friends. Lying was okay, but cheating was not acceptable. She had to work – and work the full eight hours that covered the wedding. So she went back to following Mason.

It was more difficult now, because he'd met her at the front door and might recognise her. So she adopted a disguise. She smiled at herself as she followed Mason and his bald friend down to the tube. She tutted ironically as she stepped carefully onto the escalator. She almost giggled as the whooshing draught from the oncoming train swept along the platform and she had to put a hand to her thighs to stop her costume blowing up.

She was just an Asian woman in a sari – and she knew that Asian women in saris are indistinguishable to white men.

'I only asked for *five* waiters,' wailed the catering manageress of the Gainsborough Hotel banqueting suite. '*Five*. It's simple enough, surely? I told the agency *specifically*. What am I going to do with seven waiters?'

The two unexpected waiters looked at her sheepishly, and then glanced at the five white-coated individuals arranging glasses and bottles of wine at the linened trestle table at the side of the hall.

'We were told to come,' one of them offered.

'Well, you'll just have to go again. I'm sorry; it's not my problem.' With that, she turned on her heel and strode into her office. The two surplus waiters exchanged disgruntled looks and shuffled back out onto the street.

'Doesn't seem fair, really,' Mason whispered, lining up champagne flutes.

'Life's certainly a bitch,' Elvis agreed, buttoning up his white coat.

'They're probably trying to earn their rent money or something,' Mason observed under his breath.

'I feel dreadful,' Elvis admitted, grinning. 'Really. Honestly. No, I do.'

*   *   *

'Room 306, please.'

'Just putting you through.'

'Hello?'

'Hello, Chris? It's Bart.'

'Hiya, Bart. It should be happening any time now. Don't you wish we were there to see it in the flesh? I've got the TV on.'

'Maybe we *should* be there, dearheart. Maria has just told me that she mentioned it to Mason yesterday.'

'What?'

'Well, at the very least, she mentioned the Potts woman's name – and that's enough, I would have thought.'

'Jesus! They'll swan along there and spoil the whole thing.'

'Well, *will* they? How can they spoil it?'

'Oh, for God's sake, of course they can. Just by attending. The press'll spot Elvis, and the whole impact of Iris picking up the ethereal vibes of the Trickster will be lost. In fact, if she handles the media right, it'll be a triumph for the fraudulent old bat. Listen, I'm going down there. Do you want to meet me on the corner of Blenheim Street? I might need some unrecognisable help.'

'Certainly. I wouldn't miss it for all the—'

'Great. Bye.'

'—uh, cocaine in Kensington.'

Clive Hare, staff photographer of the *Daily Voice*, turned to his scribbler-partner at the press table.

'Rod,' he said. 'See that waiter? With the blond afro wig? That's our boy.'

Rod peered across the room. 'You're not wrong, lad,' he agreed. 'I wonder if anyone else has spotted him.'

'Boss? It's Andy,' said the *Clarion* hack into his mobile. 'That geezer the *Voice* are flogging as the Joker is here. If anything occurs, I'm going to need help. You want to put the Japs on stand-by?'

'Have you seen Chris or Bart?' Mason asked Elvis as they reloaded at the trestle table.

'No. Not a sausage. But I sense their presence on the psychic band.'

'Maybe we've made a mistake. Maybe this has been a wasted trip.'

'What? With all this free champagne about?' Elvis grinned, and downed a glass in one gulp.

Bart had been hanging around at the back of the hotel, peering through the french doors of the banqueting hall. Now he turned away and walked back to Chris's car, which was parked two hundred yards down the street.

He slid into the passenger seat. 'It's an invitation-only do,' he said. 'But I could probably talk my way in, if you like.'

'Did you see Mason or Elvis?'

'I'm afraid so. They're with the caterers, doling out wine and victuals. Elvis is wearing the ugliest wig I've seen in my rich and varied life. He looks like a minor member of the Jackson Five with a nasty case of jaundice.'

'Great. On top of which,' Chris sighed, pointing up the street, 'there are two parked cars on the other side of the road there crammed with Japanese. Do you think you can get in there and pull Holmes and Watson out before the shit hits? I don't want them in the vicinity when Iris does her stuff.'

'I'll certainly give it a try, old darling,' Bart said, getting out of the car. 'Keep the engine running.'

Iris began with a brief discourse concerning her unusual and unasked-for power. It was as much a curse as a blessing, apparently, for life to her was a constant barrage of ethereal impressions and other-worldly broadcasts. Then she invited anyone amongst those present to bring her some trinket belonging to a loved one.

An earring was presented by a middle-aged man. The viewers at home were informed, by a hushed voice-over, that he was the widower of cabaret singer Janet Pelagon, who had died so tragically, only ten months before, in a freak accident involving the propellors of a ship she was launching. The viewers at home probably knew this already, as the bereft husband had been pictured in all the tabloids, staring aghast at the series of small coffins in which his wife had been severally buried. However, neither the TV audience nor the dinner guests could have failed to be impressed by the uncanny accuracy with which Iris conjured Janet's memory with nothing more than an earring to go on.

There were another two similar readings, and then an equine young woman in a pearl-dotted gown came forward with a royal blue sweater.

'This,' the TV presenter whispered over-excitedly, 'is Annabella Bart-Williams, a member of His Majesty Prince Charles's private staff.'

The camera followed Annabella as she wove elegantly between the tables.

'And the garment she is carrying,' the presenter continued, frantically consulting his notes and trying to fit in all the information he'd researched, 'which is knitted in pure Jersey wool from the Channel Islands, just off the coast of the Grand Duchy of Cornwall, which was the only part of the British Isles to be occupied during World War Two, actually belongs to the Prince of Wales, a keen gardener, the future King Charles III himself. Mrs Potts has no idea, of course, to whom this garment belongs.'

As Annabella approached, Iris threw a swift blink at Dennis, who was seated at a table directly in front of her. The knowing nod with which he returned her glance would have been imperceptible to any but the most gifted of sensitives. Iris accepted the jersey from Annabella, thinking it was the Trickster's. A viewing audience of several million knew it belonged to the future monarch, and were fascinated to hear what she made of it. She let the woollie hang across her outstretched forearms, and her eyes clouded with concentration.

There was a long, clenched silence.

In the anteroom, at that moment, Bart was effecting an entrance. The young woman collecting and checking invitations was wearing a badge that read 'Josephine'. Bart approached her with his smile whacked up to full-beam.

'Jo!' he cried, taking her hand and kissing it as she reached out for his invitation card. 'Fancy seeing you here! This is wonderful! You never called, you cruel temptress! You didn't lose my number, did you?'

'Umm –' said the bewildered Josephine.

'To be charitable, let's say you did. Look, what time do you finish here? Let's go for a drink. I'll just pop in and say hello to a few people, and then we'll go for cocktails somewhere. Good idea? Okay. Lovely to see you. I'll be back in half an hour or so.'

And he strode into the hall, leaving Josephine weak at the knees.

'I'm getting,' Iris was intoning, 'I'm getting a vibration of . . . negativity . . . Oh, oh, it's so strong. It's a feeling of . . . yes . . . of anger and hatred. There's power here but . . . it's power used to evil ends . . .'

'Mason! Elvis!' Bart hissed, coming up behind them. 'It is time to take our leave.'

Mason turned, surprised, and began to speak.

'Resist the temptation to enter into debate, old pal,' Bart insisted. 'I am on an errand from Ms Bell.'

Iris was swaying, her eyes turned up to the whites. 'Ohh, the deceit,' she sobbed. 'The betrayal of all that is good and true. It is a dark force. The heat of his anger burns my very flesh!'

The cameras were edging in on the stricken Iris as Bart, Elvis and Mason sidled towards the door. Clive Hare from the *Daily Voice*, who had been keeping an eye on Elvis throughout, nudged his colleague in the ribs.

'They're scarpering. Let's go.'

'No! No!' Iris shrieked, flinging the sweater from her. 'Begone, foul garment!' She fell forward, arms outstretched to the table. Her spirit was psychically drained. Her body was physically exhausted. Her elbow was in a bowl of tiramisu.

The *Clarion* correspondent, seeing his *Voice* counterpart making after Elvis, spoke into the cellphone, on which he was holding an open line to the Naganitaki employees in the cars outside. Several other journalists who had also recognised Elvis began to move towards the door.

The three of them strode swiftly through the anteroom and into the foyer of the hotel. They were jogging as they passed the check-in desk, and up to a fair canter as they skittered down the hotel steps. As they hit the pavement, eight or nine Japanese piled out of two cars opposite. Mason glanced back, and saw the hackpack bundling through the foyer.

'Skates-on time, I think,' Bart announced calmly and burst into an impressive sprint. Elvis accelerated too, and they were both fifteen yards ahead of Mason before he realised they were gone.

'Jesus, not again,' he muttered, and legged it after them, as the Japs shouted and gave chase.

Chris had flung open three doors of the Sierra, and was revving it dangerously. Elvis and Bart were outrunning Mason, who had always considered himself more a middle-distance man. He could hear the pursuers gaining, even through the thumping blood in his ears.

He was no more than fifty feet from the car when he threw a glance over his shoulder – and ran straight into a lamp-post.

'Oh, fuck!' he yelled, as he bounced back onto the pavement. Even before he hit the ground, he could tell that he'd broken his nose.

Bart and Elvis were half in the car. As Mason looked up, he saw Bart getting back out in order to come and help him.

'Doe!' Mason shouted, clasping a hand to his face. 'Ged gowig!'

Bart still had one foot on the kerb as Chris screeched the car into a tight U-turn and gunned it down the street. Elvis's head appeared through the sunroof.

'I'll think of something, bro!' he hollered, encouragingly.

Mason wiped his blood-pouring nose on the sleeve of his waiter's jacket.

'Dat's a comfort,' he groaned, as two Oriental gentlemen hauled him to his feet.

CHAPTER FIFTY-ONE

David Jennings had just got back from dropping Jake off at the leisure centre for a birthday party. As he walked into the living room, Sue was watching Iris Potts's showpiece on TV.

'Jake needs to be picked up at six,' he said. 'Will you get him?'

'Yeah, okay.'

Jennings sat down in the armchair and nodded at the telly.

'Who's she?'

Sue's eyes didn't leave the screen. 'She's the most fabulously gifted clairvoyant. Quite amazing.'

Jennings said nothing. He wondered what Chris would have said. Something articulate and mordant, he was sure. Chris would be a match for Sue.

That sudden image, of his wife and Chris meeting, sent a shudder of guilt through him. He was an instinctive subscriber to the Biblical suggestion that the thought was as damning as the deed. And he had admitted to himself over the last few days that he'd entertained the thought.

He watched Iris Potts as she interpreted vibrations and divined futures. He furrowed his brow, glancing at his wife's rapt expression, and he fought back the unusual urge to make a contentious observation. He drummed his fingers on the arms of the chair, and crossed and uncrossed his legs.

Sue turned her head. 'What?' she demanded.

'I was just thinking,' he said, measuredly, 'that I've seen stage magicians do that, without making any claim at all to other-worldly powers.'

Sue shrugged, which was always dangerous. A flash of the eyes and sudden anger meant she was on the defensive. A shrug meant she was lining up some irrefutable and hurtful riposte.

'I've seen magicians change water into wine,' she said. 'I'm sure they could do wafers into flesh, if they wanted to. What's your point?'

Jennings tightened his grip on the arms of the chair, but his voice remained still and calm.

'Please don't mock my beliefs, Suze,' he murmured.

'Then don't knock mine,' she retorted. 'The difference between you and me –' her eyes *were* flashing now '– is that I'm prepared to accept your convictions. They might be right for all I know. But you – *you* – are *convinced* you're right, and everyone else is wrong. So which of us is intolerant?'

'I *am* tolerant,' Jennings said, aggrieved – and even as he said it, he could see that she'd done it again. She'd got him on the back foot; she'd spun the conversation like a trick table, so that the poisoned glass was in front of him. 'I'm *massively* tolerant.'

'You're not tolerant – you're smug. You graciously allow the rest of us to persist in our wrongheadedness. It's built in to your belief system – the whole exclusive, patronising idea that no one enters the Kingdom of Heaven but through *your* idol. *Christ!*'

The blasphemy was deliberate. It was intended to goad him. Jennings knew that. He took a deep breath.

'I'm sorry you see it that way,' he nodded, swallowing. 'Perhaps you have a point, but—'

'No!' she screamed, slamming her hand down on the coffee table. 'Perhaps I *don't*! Fight me, for God's sake! *Fight!*'

She sprang to her feet and strode out of the room, towards the kitchen. He heard the back door slam, and saw her through the window, almost running up the garden to the bench at the top, where she slumped down and stared at the roses, fists clenched.

He didn't know what to do. His instinct was to go out there, placate, make everything all right – but that, he could see, would be the worst possible move. Then again, he couldn't march up to the rosebed and rage, as she seemed to want him to. He wasn't built that way. He was reflective, analytical. He was a plodder. A plod.

Perhaps he didn't love her enough. Perhaps if he loved her more, he could be what she wanted, or feel things in the way she did. Perhaps he would understand. He must not have been paying enough attention to her, what with his thoughts of adultery and his half-baked fantasies of a different life. Jake, Sue and the job, in that order. That's what he'd told Zerkah. He wondered whether it was true.

He glanced at the TV. The camera swung across the seated audience at their luncheon tables. And Jennings started suddenly. That waiter – it was Dixon.

He leapt up, and grabbed his car keys from the coffee table, heading for the front door. He stopped as his hand reached for the catch. He half-turned.

But, no, Sue needed time, and he needed . . . to do his job. In that order.

'Sir, they've done a runner.'

Zerkah called Jennings on his mobile, and discovered he was on his way to the Gainsborough Hotel. She explained that she'd followed Mason, and had just assumed that he'd found himself a job at last – but now there was a car chase in progress.

'I've called in to Traffic. They're heading for – Oh, wait. I've got a bleep.'

Jennings was trapped in a queue on Chelsea Bridge. He wished to heaven he'd agreed to carry a magnetic flashing light to plonk on top of the car in such situations.

'Sir, I'm back. They've gone to ground in Kensington. Two men and a woman. I'll give you the address. Oh, by the way. Dixon was taken away by the Japanese. God knows where he is by now.'

Jennings was ashamed to find that he wasn't that interested in where Dixon was by now. Two men and a *woman*. In Kensington. Just across the bridge and up the road a little.

'I'll meet you there,' he said tersely as Zerkah gave him the address.

'One of them must have tailed us all the way,' Bart remarked dolefully, turning from the window. 'It's like *Dog Day Afternoon* out there.'

They were in the main room of Bart's apartment, having driven at speed across town, through backroads and longcuts that Elvis had seemed to conjure from thin air, yelling directions into Chris's ear and every so often leaning over from the back seat to turn the wheel himself. But evidently it had done no good; at least one of the pursuers had stayed with them, and now the press, the TV cameras and a sprinkling of Naganitaki men were all lined up outside.

'Shit,' Chris said disgustedly, checking the view from the window herself. 'And only one card from the end, too.' She lit a cigarette and paced around the room.

'The World,' said Elvis, musingly. 'Did you have anything set up for the World?'

Chris accepted a glass of wine from Bart. 'I had a few ideas. I wanted to play a trick on *everyone* – on the whole world. I was thinking maybe some sort of archaeological hoax. Produce a centaur's skeleton. That sort of thing.'

'Lack of ambition has never been your problem, has it?' Bart grinned, turning from the window.

Chris shrugged. 'If this campaign had done any good, I would have made it impossible to spoof the population at large. Gullibility-counts ought to be at an all-time low.' She sipped her wine. 'Bet they aren't though.'

Elvis was sitting at Bart's desk, doodling on the blotter. 'Build,' he muttered. 'A better mousetrap.'

'Could I have a cigarette?' Bart asked Chris. 'I'm out.'

'And the world. Will beat. A path.' Elvis continued, sketching idly.

'And what about Mason?' Chris said. 'Where's he? What's happened to him?'

'He did look pretty terrible,' Bart agreed. 'How do they manage to get so much blood in something as little as a nose?'

'To your door.'

'You don't think they'll hurt him, do you?' Chris said anxiously.

'Not a bit of it, sweetums,' Bart reassured her. 'We've got laws in this country about that sort of thing. Could I press you on this cigarette issue?'

Mason hadn't struggled when Yashimo's people had hauled him off the pavement and slid him into their car. There didn't seem much point, and anyway, his face was agony, and that was all he cared about. He took off his white waiter's jacket and dabbed at his nose, while the two henchman sat on either side of him as if he wasn't there.

'We've got laws in dis country about dis sord of ting,' he told them, sniffing. Neither of them so much as acknowledged his presence. 'I'b beyig held agaidst by will,' he pointed out. 'Dat's kid-dapping, dat is.'

He tried to convince himself that nothing bad could happen. This was

London; it was broad daylight; he had been abducted in full view of the British press; he had friends who knew who had taken him. So what the hell could Naganitaki actually *do* to him?

On the other hand, he had a terrible feeling that, above a certain level of wealth, all laws cease to apply. The rich never get done for anything. They just bung someone a few grand and – abracadabra – the evidence disappears, the witnesses go on holiday and the judge invites the defendant for lunch at his club. Mason suspected that you could get away with anything if you had money.

If I ever get out of this alive, he thought, I swear I'll never again ignore those people who sell *Marxism Today* outside Camden tube.

They had been sitting in the limo for about half an hour in silence, when the carphone rang. The driver answered it, listened and then pulled out into the traffic. It was a nasty moment for Mason. In retrospect, he would see that his imaginings were a bit melodramatic – but right then he saw himself being driven out to the country and being made to dig his own grave before being beheaded with a Samurai sword. And on the strength of that vision he made a dive for the door.

He was immediately disabused of any credence he may have given to the stereotype of the Japanese as slight, weedy people with impeccably meek manners. The admittedly small sample of Orientals with whom he was unexpectedly acquainted turned out to have adopted a direct and muscular approach to the treatment of guests. For the rest of the journey, Mason was pinned back on the seat by the unforgiving hands of the pair of silent thugs whom he began to think of, perhaps rather childishly, as Scyrra and Chalybdis.

He relaxed a little when he realised that the car wasn't heading out of town to a disused mineshaft, but to Kensington. They turned into Bart's street and were confronted by a gaggle of cameras, hacks and sightseers gathered around the familiar front door. The car parked just short of the throng, and suddenly they were surrounded by journalists peering in.

Mason gathered up his blood-soaked jacket and turned to Scyrra. 'Dis is fine,' he said. 'You can dust drop be here. I'll walk de rest ob de way.'

And, at last, Scyrra spoke.

'Shut yer gob, sunshine,' he said.

*　　*　　*

Bart had disconnected the entryphone simply to get some peace and quiet, and was now rummaging through the drawers of his desk for more cigarettes.

'This is insupportable,' he raged. 'If I'm out of smokes, I may have to give myself up.'

'You make it sound like we've done something criminal,' Chris said.

'Well, *I* haven't,' Bart replied, 'But *you* must have, somewhere amongst all these escapades. Have you got another spare coffin-nail?'

Chris tossed him one. 'Not really. Nothing any of the victims would take me to court for. It's not worth it to them.'

Bart lit the cigarette and took a long drag, and perched himself on the windowsill, looking out at the mob. He chuckled.

'Except that you seem to have got right up Mr Naganitaki's nose,' he observed.

Chris pushed herself up out of the armchair and walked over to the desk, at which Elvis was sitting, making a chain of paperclips. She poured herself another glass of wine, and shrugged.

'Well, yeah – but what can he do?'

Bart blew out a long stream of smoke against the windowpane. 'Well,' he said, 'at the very least he has the money and the power to make your life miserable,' he said.

Chris thought about this for a moment.

'No,' she said finally. 'It'll blow over. He'll lose interest. Surely.'

'Only if it's to his advantage,' Elvis suggested, looking up at her.

He hung the chain of paperclips on the outstretched hand of an art deco lady supporting a lamp, and loped to the window. He peered down at the gathered throng of journalists and TV reporters. 'What a mousetrap,' he murmured. 'We've got them.'

He turned to Chris. 'You said you wanted the last hit to be a joke played on the entire world. In that case, you've got to get the world's attention. And what's the best way to do *that*?'

Chris shook her head. 'Don't know.'

'You build a better mousetrap. Well, you've built *twenty-odd* mouse-traps, haven't you? And look out of the window. The world has indeed flocked to your door.'

'What are you on about?'

Outside, someone was yelling for the Trickster to come out, to face the public. Bart tutted, and drew the curtains. The room was suddenly dim, and close.

Elvis went back to the desk and turned on the lamp, his face above it spookily-lit. He grinned, and ran his hand across the smooth dome of his head, staring at Chris and Bart with inspired, bright green eyes.

'Let's sell them one more trap,' he whispered seductively. 'The biggest trap yet. A trap baited with the Grand Fromage ...'

CHAPTER FIFTY-TWO

Ray Churchill, editor of *The Clarion*, picked up the phone.

'Yuh?'

'Ray, I've got Chris Bell on the line. Do you want to speak to her?'

'Chris? Yeah? 'Course! Stick her through!'

'Hello? Ray? It's Chris.'

'Chris, where are you?'

'I'm in a flat in Kensington, surrounded by half your staff and every other bloody hack in the country.'

'So that *was* you driving! Joe said he recognised you. What the fuck is going on?'

'First off, where's Mason?' Chris demanded.

'Is that the bloke with the smashed face? He's right outside your door, with Naganitaki's people.'

'Okay. We'll come back to him. In the meantime, how would you like the Joker's inside story?'

'What? Yeah. 'Course I would! I knew you'd come through for us, love. I always said you were a bright girl.'

'Careful, Roy. You're close to blowing it. Okay, we want two-hundred-and-fifty grand; retained copyright; complete editorial control; and Naganitaki off our backs.'

'Two-hundred-and-fifty grand?' spluttered Roy Churchill. 'Forget it.'

'It's peanuts, Roy. You know it. Now, in order to pacify Naganitaki, you'll have to phone him and tell him that the Joker's confession is going to run in the *Clarion*. Let him know that we are willing to miss out the Tower episode entirely. We'll pretend it never happened, okay? Jesus, you can even pass on the Joker's profound apologies – it doesn't matter. On the other hand, if he won't accept that, tell him that we'll make the Naganitaki scam the central pivot of the whole piece. We'll engrain it so deeply into the minds of the general public that they'll think Yashimo Naganitaki is Japanese for "Fuck off, short-arse" – understood?'

'Uh-huh.'

'Right. Call me back when you've got clearance for the fee and an okay from Naganitaki. Then we're in business. I'll give you the number here. Have you got a pen? Do you remember how to use it?'

'Wait a frigging minute, Chris. What are you doing, negotiating fees with the paper? You're a staff writer, for fuck's sake.'

'Oh, no, Roy. You misunderstand me. Certainly I'll be *writing* the piece, but the fee isn't for me. It's not *my* story. It's the Joker's.'

Three-quarters of an hour later, the carphone rang and the right-hand thug leaned over to answer it. He listened for a few seconds, nodding – almost bowing, in fact – and then replaced the receiver. Then he sat back, opened the door and got out, gesturing for Mason to follow.

'Fuck off,' he said.

Mason studied him suspiciously for a moment, and then scrambled from the car, sharpish. The hacks had lost interest in him, and were all back at Bart's door. Mason stretched and looked around.

'Are you Mason?' a voice said beside him. It was a burly man with a cellphone.

'Dot decessarily,' Mason said, backing away

'Well, you're the only one around here with a broken nose, so I guess you must be. I'm supposed to drive you to hospital.'

Mason frowned. 'Says who?'

The second-floor window of Bart's building opened and Chris leaned out.

'Mase,' she shouted. 'Go with him and get yourself looked at. It's all all right. I'll call you.'

'Wad's gowid on?' he called back.

'Later,' Chris yelled. 'Go to hospital.'

Mason shrugged, sniffed and got in the man's car, holding the bloodied jacket to his nose.

'So how'd you do that to yourself?' the man said, turning the key in the ignition.

'I didden do it to byself,' Mason grumbled. 'By ex-girlfriend did it to be.'

'Jesus,' said the man, shaking his head. 'I remember the days when they just cut the arms off all your shirts.'

Bart was looking out of the window.

'Our car's here,' he announced. 'A beautiful long black Bentley. No less than we deserve, of course. Shall we go?'

'Elvis,' Chris said, 'are you sure you want to do this? You don't have to, you know. You sure you don't mind?'

'Mind?' exclaimed Elvis, donning certain items from Bart's wardrobe. 'I was *born* for this. This entire incarnation has been building up to it.'

As the front door of the mansion block opened, the press and TV reporters surged forward, mikes held out in front of them.

Bart emerged onto the top step and held up his hands for quiet.

'Ladies and gentlemen,' he said, swinging his gaze around the assembled cameras, 'over the last few weeks, some bizarre and outrageous events have caught the interest of the media and the public, not only here in Great Britain, but also around the globe. You gave a name to the genius behind these events – the Joker.

'This was, though you could not have known it, a misnomer. For the extraordinary mind that conceived and executed the incidents that have so preoccupied us all was not engaged in some frivolous game, some empty jest. Yes, it was all very entertaining, but it was more than that, as you will now learn.

'Ladies and gentlemen, may I present, Manicheus the Sorcerer!'

Bart faded back as the door behind him swung open, and into the late afternoon sun stepped Manicheus himself. He was tall, gaunt and utterly bald. His bright green eyes flashed out from the thick black eyeliner that surrounded them. An opera cape was wrapped around his needle-thin frame, and his legs were rooted in immaculate blue suede shoes.

Manicheus surveyed the crowd solemnly, waiting for the clicking of cameras to abate. Then, in a faint East European accent, he said, 'Magic. What iss Magic?

'Is it the cheap party tricks of fake mediums and clairvoyants? Is it conjured by housewifes dancing nakit on ley lines? Is it present in the delusions of pop singers and pin-up girlss?

'No. I know what Magic iss. I haf spent a lifetime studying Magic. It is not science. It is not art. It is not religion. It is a greater power than any of these. It is an alchemy of them all.

'And I, Manicheus the Sorcerer, haf proved this to the world. With the power of Magic, I have humiliated the false prophets and the tawdry charlatans. With Magic, and only with Magic, I have manipulated the liars and the pretenders, as if they were marionettes.

'I haf cast spells so that they stumbled in their tracks; I haf transformed their tools and their instruments; I haf hexed their livelihoods and their lives.

'*That*,' Manicheus the Sorcerer told the scribbling media, '*is Magic.*'

He lowered his head and closed his eyes.

Before any of the reporters could speak, Bart raised his voice and said, 'That's all, ladies and gentlemen. That's all that Manicheus has to say at the present time. Thank you. Thank you.'

He nudged Manicheus the Sorcerer as Chris slipped out of the door onto the steps. The three of them pushed through the crowd and towards the Bentley that was waiting on the other side of the road. Uniformed policemen cleared their way, holding back the throng. As Manicheus ducked through the door of the car, Chris felt a hand on her elbow. She turned and saw David Jennings's serious, rotund face.

'Chris,' he said quietly. 'You're under arrest.'

She bridled, and tugged her arm away. And then she dropped her shoulders and smiled amusedly.

'What's the charge, copper?' she asked, turning to face him.

'Take your pick,' he said. 'Trespass. Bribery. Corruption. Criminal damage.' He paused, and rubbed his mouth with his palm, his teeth clicking on his wedding ring. He looked her in the eyes. 'No. Actually – disturbing the peace.'

Chris chuckled. 'God, I hope so.'

CHAPTER FIFTY-THREE

Mason saw Manicheus the Sorceror on the TV in the waiting area at St Thomas's. He laughed out loud, which is unusual in Casualty, and he was immediately boosted to the top of the queue, on account of being a suspected lunatic. When he emerged from the treatment cubicle, having been told by some spotty twelve-year-old schoolgirl posing as a doctor that it was her considered professional opinion that he had a broken nose, he was met by his mum, who'd been asked to come and get him. She drove him home, and he related the story of his day, through blood-clogged sinuses.

When they got to the flat, Mason found a large envelope propped up in the porch.

As Maria put the kettle on, he sat at the table and looked at the envelope. It was green, magazine-size, and he recognised the handwriting in which his name had been written on the front. It was from his dad.

His mother knew too, of course.

'Aren't you going to open it, love?' she said, sitting down beside him and putting a mug of tea on his one and only coaster.

'Yeah. Eventually. Can't not, can I?'

But he rather resented having to. He'd at last got to a stage where he could dismiss his father – as his father had dismissed him – and he couldn't see why the old man was trying to get to him again.

'This is going to upset me, whatever it is,' he sighed, still staring at the envelope. He looked up at Maria, whose eyes were moist and blinking. 'Do *you* know what it is?' he asked her.

She shook her head, biting her lip. 'He doesn't want to hurt you, Mason, I'm sure. He's ...' She put her hand on Mason's arm. 'He's afraid. He was afraid of you when you were born, and he's still afraid now.'

'Afraid of me?'

She nodded. 'Afraid of what he might feel. He was never good at dealing with feelings.'

Mason nodded, thinking of his father's work – all that scathing glee and the contemptuous mockery of the mundane. He could understand how that cynicism might spring from fear. The fear of sincerely feeling something. Of the vulnerability that accompanies honest emotion. Mason knew that he had more than a bit of that fear himself.

'I know he tried to come and see you,' Maria said. 'He told me. He kept coming here, almost to the door. But he couldn't bring himself to face you. He went to the pub around the corner, and thought about it. And when he did finally get up the courage to do it, you weren't in. But he really did try, sweetheart.'

'Obviously not hard enough,' Mason muttered.

He lodged his finger under the flap of the envelope, and tore it jaggedly open. He slid out an unfolded sheet of drawing paper, and a compliments slip from the Covent Garden Hotel. He turned the sheet over.

It was a tender, careful, considered ink-portrait of a dishevelled and contemplative young man sitting at a pub table. He was staring at his drink, eyes unfocussed, his hands clasped around the glass. A cigarette was curling smoke from the ashtray, wreathing around his face. Above him was a photograph – a raddled black-and-white image of Charles Bukowski.

It was a portrait of Mason.

'My God,' Maria breathed, looking over her son's shoulder. 'It's beautiful, Mason.'

It was. It caught Mason absolutely. And there was no hint of malice or mockery in the execution of it. It was – Mason bit his lip – *loving*.

His mother was murmuring as she leant forward to look at the picture more closely. 'I remember when he used to draw like that. So clean and pure. My God . . .'

Marty Puxley must have been there in the Three Muses when Mason had fled from the flat, the day he'd been stood up at the hotel.

He must have been plucking up the courage to make another run at me, Mason thought. And then, out of the blue, I walked in, bought some fags and a pint and took a seat to think things through. I must have been sitting right next to him, practically. So he did what he does – he drew. Drew this. This portrait of his son.

He picked up the slip of paper that accompanied the drawing, and read its brief message. He felt a tear run down his cheek as he handed it to his mum.

I'm sorry. Love Dad.

Mason was sorry too. He loved the picture. It was his father's language – his best shot.

'If only he'd had the nerve to lean over to me, there in the pub, to touch my arm,' he said to his mother. 'If only he'd just said, "Hello, Mase." That's all he needed to do.'

Maria nodded and squeezed her son's hand.

'But he didn't,' Mason continued. 'He was afraid of me. And you can't carry on like that, can you? You can't spend your life being afraid of what you feel. You have to do something about it. You have to act.'

He looked down at the picture again. 'Anybody knows that. Jesus – even *I* know that.'

'Are you pissed off with me?' Chris Bell asked David Jennings.

They were sitting in the back of the plainclothes car, just down the street from Bart's apartment. Zerkah was across the road, leaning against a parking meter, arms crossed, pretending not to look at them.

'Why would I be?' Jennings said, staring at his hands as he twiddled his thumbs in his lap. 'No. I'm impressed. You were very clever.'

Chris smiled. 'Thanks. Are you going to formally charge me now?'

The policeman shook his head. 'Zerkah picked up a message a few minutes ago. Someone has had a word with someone who's had a word with someone. Apparently you're untouchable – I don't know why.'

'So why did you arrest me?' Chris asked, fumbling in the pocket of her leather jacket.

'I've told Zerkah not to tell me about the message yet. I wanted to talk to you.' He glanced at her. 'Why did you do all this?'

Chris tapped out a cigarette, and hung it in the corner of her mouth as she wound down the window. She lit the fag and inhaled, and then turned her head and blew the smoke out into the warm early evening.

'For the same reason *you* do what you do, I expect. What do you believe in, David?'

Jennings twisted his wedding ring around his finger. 'Specifically?'

Chris shook her head. 'No. It was a rhetorical question. I know what you believe in. Truth, straight dealing, fair play. Same things as me, in other words. And you do your bit to promote those beliefs, just as I do mine. Do you think either of us makes the slightest bloody difference?' She took a deep drag on the cigarette. 'I mean, you tracked me down, fair and square, and now some high-up horse-trading has made that achievement pointless. I tried to raise the general level of credulity, and I've just sold the story of how it was done for a vast sum to an eagerly gullible public. Can't imagine what I think I've proved, to be honest.'

Jennings wrinkled his nose, and rubbed it. 'You *don't* believe in truth, I don't think, Chris. At least, not like I do. You see it as a kind of alchemical possibility, not as a real hard thing that you can hold in your hand. For you, things are missing. For me, they're there.'

'Missing from where?' Chris asked sharply, twisting to look him in the face.

Jennings ruffled his hair and dropped his head, embarrassed. 'It's not really any of my business,' he murmured.

'No, come on,' Chris insisted. 'What do you mean? I want to know.'

There was a pause. Zerkah was walking towards the car. Jennings saw her and held his hand up. She stopped, narrowed her eyes and then retreated to her parking meter, frowning.

'Could I have a cigarette?' Jennings asked, turning back to Chris.

Surprised, she gave him one and struck a match for him. He sucked on the cigarette and then puffed the smoke out in a cloud without having inhaled, like a teenager. He rolled the fag between his thumb and middle finger, contemplating it.

'You think that these noble concepts are unattainable in the world,' he said, watching the smoke rise, 'but . . .' His eyes moved to meet hers '. . . in fact, they're unattainable in *you.*'

Chris flushed. 'Are you saying I'm – what? Dishonest? Ignoble?'

'No,' Jennings said calmly, his eyes still on hers. 'I just think you can't reach the noble, faithful part of yourself.' He shrugged. 'I may be wrong.'

'Look, you sanctimonious—' Chris began, angrily. Then she stopped, and sat back, raising a finger and pointing it at him. 'Oh, no,' she said, shaking her head. 'Take that look off your face. Don't you *dare* pity me, David. Don't you fucking dare.'

He tipped his head to one side. 'You're not content. Isn't that a pity?'

'And you *are*?' she asked tautly.

'Yes,' he said. 'Pretty much.'

'Oh, yeah? Then why are you infatuated with me, and not home with the wife?'

Jennings smiled. 'Well, that's the trouble with contentedness. It gets tried occasionally.' He took another inexpert drag on his cigarette. 'You should try it yourself some time.'

Chris laughed and slumped back. She flicked her cigarette stub out of the window, and reached for the door handle. 'I shall miss you, you know. You give good headspin.'

'I'll miss you too,' he said, as she opened the door. 'Or rather, I shall miss not knowing what I'm missing.'

Chris got out of the car, and then leaned down to look at Jennings. 'Can I use you in the story?' she asked.

'I'd be flattered,' he nodded. 'Make me hopefully hopeless.'

'Or vice versa,' she suggested, grinning. 'See you, copper.'

And she shut the car door and walked away.

Jennings's eyes followed her for a few seconds, and then he glanced down at his watch. The low summer sun glinted on its face, on its metal wristband, on his wedding ring. It was nearly nine o'clock, and Jake would be waiting for his bedtime story. Jennings thought of that walk up the stairs to his son's room – his hand on the banister, the creaky fifth step, the way in which the carpet was pale green at the centre of each tread and darkest sage at the edges. They really ought to organise themselves to redecorate the hall and landing soon. They ought to clear all the junk out of the back bedroom, and make proper use of it.

The driver's door of the car opened and Zerkah got in. She looked at Jennings in the rearview.

'So,' she said brusquely, 'I suppose it's back to the Leper Colony for me, is it?'

Jennings tugged his jacket sleeve down over his watch, and raised his head.

'Good Lord, no,' he smiled. 'You're family now, Zerkah. I'm a great believer in families.'

CHAPTER FIFTY-FOUR

When Maria Dixon appeared on radio shows advising distraught and unhappy people, she talked a lot about 'closure'. As far as Mason could make out, it meant that life's stories should have proper endings; neat little denouements.

Though Mason agreed that that would be satisfying, he didn't think it was the case – not in the real world. In the real world, the echoes of events still reverberate, though increasingly fuzzily, long after the narrative last page. There are flashbacks and backslidings and unresolved niggles to cope with. Like a reformed smoker, you still find yourself coughing stuff up, ages after you ran your last burning dog-end under the kitchen tap.

So, what with the portrait and all the twisty trauma that preceded it, Mason had resigned himself to never really quite sorting out the problem of his father. There wasn't going to be any definitive closure, ever.

But lying in bed for a couple of days with a busted nose, dozing on and off and generally recovering from a very trying couple of weeks, he realised that there was something left for him to do in relation to Marty Puxley. All the communication that there had been between them, scant though it was, had been *at* Mason. His father had dropped him notes, got him to run around, sent him the picture. Mason hadn't had any input at all. Now he wanted his say.

So he wrote his father a letter.

Dear Dad,

Thanks for the drawing. It's beautiful. I appreciate it.

I guess this has been a hard time for you. It certainly has for me. I've been very confused, angry, sad. Maybe you have too.

Except, of course, you've seen me. You know a bit about me. I don't feel I know you at all – and I have to admit, I resent that.

He reached for the orange juice on the bedside table, and read over what he'd written so far. He wasn't sure it was appropriate to say that he resented not knowing the old man. It sounded as if he resented him personally, and that wasn't true any more. Mason couldn't see that it was fair or possible to resent someone just for being who they are.

He screwed up the page and started again.

Dear Dad,

It's impossible for me to know or understand what's going through your head. I don't have any real insight into your motivations or attitudes towards anything, let alone me. So

'So'? So – what?

He bit the end of the pen and wrinkled his nose. He *did* have some insight into Marty's motivations, of course. Both Maria and Elvis had told him. His father was afraid. Mason was just trying to avoid saying that. He was lying, in other words, in order to be kind.

If he told the truth – that he thought his father's cowardice was weak and hurtful – it would be less than kind. Kindness and honesty can be mutually exclusive. As Mason had told his mother, it's a tough gig.

He started a new page.

Dear Dad,

It seems to me that no one can judge another person's decisions, because you can never know what it's like to be someone else. I really don't understand why you couldn't look me in the face, but I have to accept that what you did seemed to you to be right. Which means it was right, in your own terms.

I mean, as long as you are rigorous in your examination of your motives, and as long as the actions that spring from those motives are considered and supportable, then nobody has the right to question you.

Take me and Chris, for instance. I've played all sorts of games – circling her, second-guessing her reactions, acting on those guesses, rather than on what I honestly feel. It's been a long time since I've been straight with her, to be frank. I've always tried to be who I thought she might like. I've never just been myself. Perhaps if I'd acted as I felt – tender, hurt, loving, as opposed to self-conscious, self-protective, self-regarding – then she might have reacted differently to me. Even if she hadn't, at least I'd have known that her reaction was honest, because my presentation was.

You see, you can't go about the place worrying what effect you'll have. You just have to be honest – to yourself, and to everyone else. If you really don't want to face me, then that's okay. On the other hand, if you want to, but you're afraid, then . . . well, I don't think it's good enough.

He took another gulp of orange juice – a little too hurriedly, wincing as the rim of the glass pressed against the swollen bridge of his nose. He scanned the draft, and tutted ruefully. God, he was lecturing his *dad*. He was giving him permission to be himself. Bit bloody presumptuous, really.

He ripped the page up and, sighing, he got out of bed, put on a dressing-gown and wandered through to the living room. In a drawer in the sideboard he kept a little stock of those postcards that they give away free on racks in restaurants. He shuffled through them, and eventually found the one he was looking for. It was a cartoon spoof of Yeames's painting *When Did You Last See Your Father?*, intended to promote some exhibition about childhood memory, or something. The cartoon was by Marty Puxley, of course.

Mason turned it over, and wrote on the back of it,

It's okay.
Look after yourself,
M.

He added his dad's name and the address of the Covent Garden Hotel, and he put the postcard on the mantelpiece, so he'd remember to post it.

He never did send it, of course. He knew, deep down, that it wasn't really intended for his father at all.

ENDPIECE

It had been a gentle, stress-free evening at Chris's. They'd watched some TV, phoned in a curry and drunk some wine. Now they were slumped together on the sofa, shoulder to shoulder, and Mason was wondering whether or not it was the right moment to make his move.

During two days lying in bed with a busted face, he had done a lot of thinking about his feelings for Chris, and he'd decided that his mother was right. He and Chris both gave up on it all too easily. They were both too afraid. He'd resolved to give up being afraid. You have to act on your feelings, he realised. You have to. Whatever the potential outcome, you have to be honest and kind. To yourself.

They hadn't yet spoken of the Joker and the Manicheus scam. Mason had seen Bart, who had given him the inside track on the scene in his Kensington flat, and Chris had phoned in, concerned about the broken nose – but they hadn't talked about the last scene in the Trickster's campaign until now.

'So, did you like the final hit?' she asked, out of the blue.

Mason was gazing at her legs, and thinking what absolutely brilliant legs they were.

'As far as I understand it, yeah. You reckon you've fooled the world?'

'We're in the process of doing it,' she said. 'Elvis and I are writing a totally fictional account of all the hits, chucking in spells and incantations and all sorts of rubbish. It's great fun, and Roy at the *Clarion* just loves it.'

'But will anyone swallow it?' Mason said. He was admiring her hair. It really was the most beautiful, lustrous, strokable hair he'd ever seen.

'Of course they will. Despite all my futile efforts to the contrary, people still believe crap. They always will. I've kind of accepted that.'

'Ain't it the truth. And, incidentally, why aren't I being chased all round town by Samurai-wielding Orientals?' he murmured, not very interestedly.

As Chris recounted the deal she'd made with Yashimo Naganitaki, Mason thought back over all the great times Chris and he had had together. It was all *possible* again – he could *feel* it.

'But that means that you've got no hit for the Tower,' he pointed out when she'd finished.

He *desperately* wanted to sleep with her – in a tender way, not just for lust's sake. He wanted to be close and safe.

'Yeah, well, we've ditched the Tarot angle,' Chris shrugged. 'It makes things too complicated. You have to keep it simple.'

'And anyway,' Mason added, 'you never got a complete set. You never did the Lovers.'

He blinked a couple of times, gazing at her profile. His eyes were misty with tenderness.

'True,' she admitted.

Mason was losing interest in the conversation. He leant back and insinuated an arm around her shoulders. She didn't appear to object.

'So why'd you miss out that card, then?' he asked absently.

'Well,' Chris sighed, 'I had plenty of candidates lined up for the Lovers, but I kept telling myself that they weren't quite right. Eventually I had to admit that I was putting off doing it.'

'Uh-huh,' Mason said, stroking her upper arm.

'And when I thought about *why* I was putting it off, I realised it was because the whole point of the Trickster was to make people look *foolish*, you know?'

She was side-on to him looking more or less in the direction of the TV, and talking to herself really. Just explaining it to herself.

'Sure,' he murmured. He was considering kissing her.

'But people who are in love – I mean, look what they *believe*, look what they *do*. They think that they're going to be happy for ever and ever. They cocoon themselves in their little bubble of mutual admiration. They pine when they're separated.'

Mason paused in the act of leaning towards her, and unpuckered his lips.

'They gaze stupidly into each other's eyes,' Chris continued. 'They hold hands in the park. They babble in an infantile private language. They smooch across the table in crowded restaurants.'

He moved back a little as she turned to look at him. He could hear the rustle of an envelope still crumpled in the pocket of the denim jacket, draped over the arm of the sofa on which he was leaning.

'What it came down to,' Chris said straightforwardly, 'is that I simply couldn't think of any way of making them look more foolish than they do already.'

Mason gazed at her sweet face for a few seconds, and then he retrieved his arm from around her shoulders.

Kind to yourself and honest with yourself. That's what you have to be.

He leaned forward and kissed her cheek, briefly.

'Can you call me a cab?' he said. 'I think it's time I was moving along.'

Something for
the Weekend

Pauline McLynn

When private investigator Leo Street is sent away
to County Kildare to spy on the supposedly cheating
wife of a loathsome client, she's delighted to be
getting away from rainy Dublin and her hopeless,
permanently resting actor boyfriend Barry. The one
catch is that she has to masquerade as a member of a
cookery course and the only piece of culinary equip-
ment Leo can handle is a tin opener – Weekend Entertaining Part One is daunting to say the least.

As she strips away layers of marital infidelity – not to
mention several other scandalous secrets – she battles
with bread-making and brûlée. But where will it all
end – in triumph or tragedy?

'*Something for the Weekend* introduces an amiable anti-
heroine who clearly has a great deal of life in her' *The
Times*

'A fabulously funny novel' *Sunday Independent*

'Packed with cheeky sarcasm and wit' *Company*

'An upbeat, chatty novel' *Daily Mail*

'A novel that demonstrates a sure ear for dialogue'
Marie Claire

'Lively characters . . . satisfying authenticity' *Image*

0 7472 6397 3

headline

Sisteria

Sue Margolis

'A tremendously funny, colourful and gripping read' *Mail on Sunday*

If Beverley Littlestone knew what was good for her, she would steer clear of her sister Naomi, who's just got in touch after a five-year silence. Hasn't Beverley got enough to contend with – like her husband Melvin, invariably engaged in a lunatic scheme with 'failure' written all over it in mile-high neon. Not to mention her daughter Natalie, for whom PMT means Permanent Menstrual Tension.

But Beverley can't say no to her sister – and Naomi's self-serving plans are going to launch Beverley out of suburbia and into a whole new world of drama and desire . . .

0 7472 5774 4

headline

Now you can buy any of these other bestselling Headline books from your bookshop or *direct from the publisher*.

FREE P&P AND UK DELIVERY
(Overseas and Ireland £3.50 per book)

Backpack	Emily Barr	£5.99
Icebox	Mark Bastable	£5.99
Killing Helen	Sarah Challis	£6.99
Broken	Martina Cole	£6.99
Redemption Blues	Tim Griggs	£5.99
Relative Strangers	Val Hopkirk	£5.99
Homegrown	Gareth Joseph	£5.99
Everything is not Enough	Bernardine Kennedy	£5.99
High on a Cliff	Colin Shindler	£5.99
Winning Through	Marcia Willett	£5.99

TO ORDER SIMPLY CALL THIS NUMBER

01235 400 414

or e-mail orders@bookpoint.co.uk

Prices and availability subject to change without notice.